Mary Shelley's Journal

MARY SHELLEY'S Journal

EDITED BY

FREDERICK L. JONES

UNIVERSITY OF OKLAHOMA PRESS
NORMAN MCMXLVII

EDITED BY FREDERICK L. JONES

The Letters of Mary W. Shelley
(NORMAN, 1944)

Mary Shelley's Journal
(NORMAN, 1947)

Publishing Division of the University
Set up and printed at Norman, Oklahoma, U.S.A.
by the University of Oklahoma Press
First edition

To E. S. M. and L. S. J.

Preface

Mary Shelley's journal is the most important single document in Shelley biography. Almost the whole of it has been published piecemeal by Mary Shelley, Lady Jane Shelley, Dowden, Mrs. Marshall, Newman Ivey White, and others. The complete journal is available to the few who have access to the Bodleian Library, the British Museum, the University of Texas Library, the University of California Library, the Yale University Library, the Henry E. Huntington Library, the Library of Congress, or to one of several private libraries. Some scholars have gone to much expense and trouble to make typescripts or microfilms of *Shelley and Mary,* in which it is printed, mainly because they have desired to use the journal. It therefore seems highly desirable that this important document should be made easily accessible to the select but persistent few who have an interest in all facts concerning Shelley. Even though *Shelley and Mary* itself were published and available, it would still be desirable that the journal should be printed separately with adequate editorial equipment. Scattered as it is through the 1,243 pages of *Shelley and Mary,* it has great disadvantages for one who wishes to consult it alone. It is hoped that this edition of the journal will fill a long-felt need in Shelley scholarship.

Because of the general inaccessibility of the journal, there are several misconceptions about it. One is that still hidden away in it is much unpublished information. Every entry in the journal which has any flesh on the dry bones of fact has been published, and a great many of the factual bones in addition. The brief factual entries have virtually all been summarized. The scholar is nevertheless right in insisting upon seeing the journal itself, complete and in order; for he needs to make his own compilations and to draw his own conclusions from the facts.

Another misconception is that the journal is a complete record of Shelley and Mary's life together. Between July 28, 1814, and July 8, 1822, there are 2,903 days. The journal has only 1,724 entries, which means that there are no entries for 1,179 days. Not all of these 1,179 days, however, are entirely lost, for when Mary had neglected her journal for a day, a week, or a month or more, she frequently summarized the main events of the days left blank. Even so, approximately 784 days (or more than two of eight years) appear to be lost forever. Of these 784 days, 49 represent entries in 1814 and 1815 which have been torn out of the MS, doubtless by Mary herself; 432 days represent a lost volume of the journal for May 14, 1815, through July 20, 1816; and 303 days represent days omitted and apparently not summarized. Either by specific daily entry or by summarized entry, approximately 2,119 of Shelley and Mary's 2,903 days are accounted for by the journal.

To the frequent lapses in the daily entries we must add Mary's failure to make even a reasonably complete record of events. The entries, though usually brief, are nevertheless fairly revealing until December 1, 1818, when Mary arrived at Naples. After this date, unrecorded days are frequent until 1820. During 1820 and 1821 Mary made almost regular daily entries, but they are exceedingly brief, often no more than the barest indication of what Mary has read.

In spite of these deficiencies, however, the journal is the richest mine of information about Shelley's daily life: where he lived, where he went, and whom he saw from day to day.

Still another misconception is that the journal may reveal secret, private affairs. These are almost nonexistent, for Mary was from the beginning a very cautious diarist, fully realizing the possibility that her journal might be read by others. One has merely to inspect the journal through certain critical periods in the life of the Shelleys to find out how cautious Mary was. For one thing, there is almost a complete absence of direct information about Claire, and absolutely nothing explicit about Claire and Byron. Mary does not even mention the birth of Allegra at Bath on January 12, 1817. In fact, she even uses a little camouflage by recording several days after the event, "Four days of idleness." The death of Harriet is merely, "A letter from Hookham with the news of the death of Harriet Shelley." The death of Mary's first child is only, "Find my baby dead. . . . A miserable day." The birth of Clara is simply, "I am confined Tuesday, 2nd." The death of her darling William is not recorded at all. A few personal flashes do appear on rare occasions, however; and one may be sure that these have all been quoted and made much of by scholars grateful for something beyond mere fact.

It is this impersonal character of the journal, as well as the abundant evidence in the journal itself, which gives us assurance that the journal (through July 8, 1822) as printed in *Shelley and Mary* is complete. However distrustful one may be of Lady Shelley's judgment about what ought to be omitted, one realizes that Lady Shelley found nothing which needed by any kind of judgment to be omitted. Those few entries in which Mary philosophizes are the least revealing of all. When these passages appear, one begins wishing for a return to bare facts.

That the *Shelley and Mary* text is complete through Shelley's lifetime except for a few unimportant lines, and is also reasonably accurate, is fully proved, I think, by the following facts:

(1) Dowden had access to the MS journal. From it he corrected a few slight errors in the *Shelley and Mary* text, but he did not print a single additional line.

(2) While preparing his *La Jeunesse de Shelley* (Paris, 1910), A. H. Koszul had full access *(plein accès)* to the MS journal and took pains to collate the *Shelley and Mary* text with the MS. He was, of course, especially concerned with the lacunae. But Koszul does nothing to complete the *Shelley and Mary* text except to correct a couple of small errors and to print the entry for March 16, 1814. This entry had been omitted by Lady Shelley because a sheet was missing from the MS journal at that point. Koszul himself found that stray sheet at Boscombe and restored it to the journal book. When Koszul used the MS journal at Boscombe, it was the property of Lord Abinger, who was in no way influenced by Lady Shelley's prejudices.

(3) Miss R. Glynn Grylls, while preparing her *Mary Shelley* (1938), was permitted by Lord Abinger to make unrestricted use of Mary's MS journal and of other MSS. Miss Grylls printed four entries made during Shelley's lifetime directly from the MS. These show only minor differences from the *Shelley and Mary* text. From the MS Miss Grylls printed only one sentence (before July 8, 1822) which is not in *Shelley and Mary* (the last sentence in the last entry for 1819), and this is of no biographical importance. Miss Grylls found a good many unpublished entries after Shelley's death, and from these she printed eleven additional selections. The net result of three scholars (Dowden, Koszul, Grylls) using the MS journal and being free to compare it with the *Shelley and Mary* text is negligible; they found it profitable only to correct a few errors and to print half a dozen lines.

(4) The following fact removes any possibility of doubt concerning the essential completeness and reliability of the *Shelley and Mary* text. In 1938 Professor Newman I. White sent to Miss Grylls a complete list of the missing entries in the *Shelley and Mary* text (to July 8, 1822), requesting her to check them with the MS journal. This check was made, and I have had the use of Professor White's list (which I have checked) and of the MS notes made by Miss Grylls. I discover that Miss Grylls found in the MS journal only nineteen brief entries which are not printed in *Shelley and Mary*. These nineteen out of more than 300 missing entries (i.e., entries never made by Mary) Miss Grylls describes as "innocent and arbitrary" omissions by Lady Shelley. In all likelihood they are accidental (certainly three are such) rather than intentional or "arbi-

trary." From Miss Grylls's notes (and from Koszul) I am able to restore in whole or part six of the missing nineteen; all of the thirteen entries still missing are extremely brief (these thirteen entries are identified in the footnotes). Except for a few unimportant lines and some errors made by Lady Shelley in transcription, we can therefore feel quite confident that we have the journal here complete and reliable in all essentials.

During her lifetime Mary herself published several portions of her journal. In 1817 she published the *History of a Six Weeks' Tour,* which contained a revised version of the journal for July 28–September 13, 1814. In the same volume she included the first half of the long entry for July 21, 1816 (the trip to Chamouni), printed as a part of Shelley's letter of July 22, 1816, to Peacock. In the March, 1824, number of the *London Magazine* (Vol. IX, 253–56), appeared her anonymous essay "On Ghosts," which was made up largely of extracts from her journal. She included (not naming the source) the brief tale of Hogg's apparition (December 22, 1814, entry), the fourth tale related by Monk Lewis and recorded by Shelley on August 18, 1816, and the second of the three tales related by the Chevalier Mengaldo at Venice and recorded by Mary on October 20, 1818. In 1840 she printed in *Essays, Letters from Abroad,* &c., as a complementary part of the *Six Weeks' Tour,* all four of the tales related by Monk Lewis and the entries for August 29–September 5, 1816 (by Shelley), which relate the history of their return to England from Geneva by way of Fontainebleau and Versailles. For the biographical details in her notes to the *Poetical Works* (1839), she unquestionably consulted the journal, and especially for the facts about Shelley's reading from year to year.

T. J. Hogg had in his possession the MS volumes of Mary's journal while he wrote his *Life of Shelley*. He describes the journal inaccurately in his preface (attributing the whole journal to Shelley), and anticipated the use of it, but his narrative stops short of the opening date of the journal. The journal and all other MSS were withdrawn by Sir Percy and Lady Shelley after the publication of the first two volumes of the *Life* in 1858. In 1859 Lady Shelley published her *Shelley Memorials,* which utilizes the facts supplied by the journal, but quotes sparingly from it except for the reflective entries made by Mary after Shelley's death, of which she prints twenty-two pages. Most of the entries printed in *Shelley and Mary* for these later years of Mary's life are included in Lady Shelley's book.

In 1882 Sir Percy and Lady Shelley printed privately all the papers in their large collection which they regarded as possessing biographical significance. The papers thus put into type were entitled *Shelley and Mary* (4 vols.), and twelve copies were printed. The volumes are made up almost entirely of Mary's journal and of letters by Shelley and Mary and their circle, all arranged in a chronological sequence. Lady Shelley herself, according to Sir Percy Florence's introductory note, had arranged and transcribed the MSS. Lady Shelley's purposes were two: (1) to preserve the precious documents; (2) to furnish a suitable biographer (to be selected by her and Sir Percy) with the major portion of their collection in an orderly and easily usable form.

Edward Dowden was elected in 1883, at the suggestion of Sir Henry Taylor, to write the first authentic and fully documented life of Shelley. A copy of *Shelley and Mary* was presented to him. This proved invaluable to him since he could ill afford to neglect his professional duties at the University of Dublin in order to spend prolonged periods of time at Boscombe Manor extracting from the MSS all the information which he needed. Dowden did, however, make several trips to Boscombe, during which he utilized many documents not printed in *Shelley and Mary* and also checked with the original MSS the important papers printed in *Shelley and Mary*. Dowden printed considerable portions of Mary's journal, quoted numerous bits of it, and summarized virtually all the facts. Dowden's *Life of Shelley* (1886) immediately became the standard authority for Shelley biography.

Concurrent with the selection of Dowden to write the authoritative life of Shelley, Mrs. Julian Marshall was chosen to prepare a *Life and Letters of Mary W. Shelley*. Mrs. Marshall drew her materials almost entirely from *Shelley and Mary,* from which she printed a great portion of the journal and many letters. Between them, Dowden and Mrs. Marshall printed in extended, usable form more than half of Mary's journal.

Since 1922, the centenary of Shelley's death, *Shelley and Mary* has become available for use by scholars generally at the Bodleian Library, and at the few other libraries which have since acquired copies of the twelve printed. In 1934 Dowden's copy (then the property of Mr. T. J. Wise) was photostated by the Modern Language Association for deposit in the Library of Congress, where it is available for use through interlibrary loan.

Shelley and Mary has, in consequence, been used a great deal since 1922. Many additional items of the journal have been printed in scattered places. Newman I. White's *Shelley* (1940) very naturally utilizes the journal thoroughly and prints many heretofore unpublished entries. If *Shelley and Mary* and the MS journal were both completely destroyed, the greater part of the journal could be restored by piecing together the portions printed in available books and articles.

The Original MS Journal. The original journal, Godwin's diary, and many other MSS are the property of the present Lord Abinger, who received them by inheritance through Lady Shelley's niece and adopted daughter, Bessie Florence Gibson. Miss Grylls, who was permitted to use these MSS while she was preparing her *Mary Shelley* (1938), has described the five volumes of Mary's journal (pp. 273–75): *VOL. I,* July 28, 1814–May 13, 1815 (pale-green cloth, 7½ x 5 x ½ inches); *VOL. II,* July 21, 1816–June 7, 1819 (brown calf, 7½ x 4¾ x 1 inches; first eight pages contain the lists of books read from 1814 to 1818, "further lists of books" being near the end of the volume, presumably the reading list for 1820); *VOL. III,* August 4, 1819–July 8, 1822 (brownish-red calf, 8 x 4¾ x 1¼ inches; forty-eight pages contain Mary's transcript of Edward Williams's Journal; also "an account of Trelawny's [i.e., Trelawny's account of ?] funeral obsequies for Shelley and Williams"); *VOL. IV,* October 2, 1822–January 30, 1824 (mottled brown cloth, 8 x 6¼ x ½ inches; contains Mary's *The Choice* and other poems); *VOL. V,* September 7, 1826–October 2, 1844 (dull pink leather, 6¾ x 4¼ x ½ inches; last third of the volume is blank).

The Text. The text of this edition of Mary's journal is taken from the Modern Language Association rotograph of Dowden's copy of *Shelley and Mary.* My reasons for believing that this text (except for some entries after Shelley's death) is virtually complete have been stated above. Just as firm is my belief that the text is essentially correct. Unquestionably Lady Shelley misread some words, and it would be surprising if no words were omitted by accident. But there is every reason to believe that Lady Shelley did a reasonably good job of transcribing and of proofreading. I base my opinion upon my experience of comparing with the original MSS the *Shelley and Mary* texts of sixty-six Mary Shelley letters; upon the fact that Dowden makes only trivial corrections in the journal texts quoted by him and sometimes obviously checked with the original MS; and upon my observation of the inconsequential differences between the *Shelley and Mary* text and the text as quoted by Miss Grylls for several entires from the original MS.

There are some discoverable errors in the *Shelley and Mary* text. Some of these are to be detected by comparison with Mary's own printed transcriptions, and by corrections made by Dowden, Koszul, and Miss Grylls, all of whom had access to the original journal. Definitely ascertainable errors are corrected in the text. Those of any significance are noticed in the footnotes; trivial corrections, such as misspelled words, are listed in Appendix I.

It is perfectly clear that Lady Shelley made no attempt to reproduce the punctuation of the original MS. There can also be no doubt that Mary's spelling was improved—though some misspelled words exist in Lady Shelley's text and are preserved in this edition.

It should be understood that I have reproduced the *Shelley and Mary* text exactly except for certain corrections and additions which are properly noticed. I have permitted myself to take only one slight liberty with the text by regularizing the use of quotation marks to indicate titles of literary works. Lady Shelley's practice of using quotation marks to indicate literary titles (a device probably not used by Mary in the original journal) is irregular: some titles are not so indicated, and occasionally an author's name is marked as though it were a title (e.g., "Petronius"). Changes in the use of quotation marks with reference to titles have been made silently. In *Shelley and Mary* the method used to indicate the writer of an entry (Shelley or Mary) is to bracket the name of the writer after the date of an entry; regardless of the number of entries, the name is not repeated (except when intervening letters separate the journal entries) until the writer changes. I have departed from this practice in that I repeat Shelley's name for every entry which is credited to him. (Only fifty-eight entries or part-entries are by Shelley.) Mary's name is used only after one or more entries by Shelley to give emphasis to the fact that the writer has changed. All entries not ascribed to Shelley are by Mary. There is some reason to suspect that Lady Shelley has not given Shelley credit for all the entries or part-entries made by him. In two or three instances I have ventured to suggest that Shelley is the writer. Such errors by Lady Shelley, if they do exist, are by no means serious.

Dates. One should be cautious about using the dates of the journal. This is especially true when one is concerned with an entry which has unrecorded days immediately preceding or following it. After neglecting her journal for a few days, Mary's practice was to summarize the missing days, but she used only the one specific date for the entry, usually (but not always) the date on which she wrote the summarizing entry. In such cases it is hazardous to state that a particular event occurred on the specific date of the entry, or on any particular day, unless Mary has stated a day in the entry itself, as she often does. In order to assist the reader, I have inserted in brackets the additional days which the entry evidently covers. This I have done only when the entry obviously applies to other days than that of the entry date. There can be no doubt that many entries without bracketed dates are also summary entries.

A few examples will help to make this important matter clear. After five unrecorded days, Mary wrote on May 9, 1817: "Read Pliny; transcribe; read 'Clarke's Travels.' Shelley writes, and reads Apuleius and Spenser in the evening." These notations probably apply to the whole period May 4–9, and not specifically to the ninth itself. Again, after three unrecorded days, she wrote on August 29, 1820: "Read Muratori, and Greek; finish Lucretius; walk." She probably read Muratori and

Greek every day during August 26–29; may have finished Lucretius on any of the four days; and probably walked every day. On November 28, 1821, Mary wrote: "Ride with the Guiccioli. Suffer much with rheumatism in my head." Mary probably meant that during November 17–28 she rode several times with the Countess Guiccioli, and suffered with rheumatism every day. Dowden and White were aware of this peculiarity of the journal.

Shelley and Mary's Reading. The journal records Mary's and Shelley's reading more than any other item in their lives. This apparently was the one thing which was to be noticed regardless of what else might be recorded. For Mary's own reading the journal is probably almost complete. For Shelley's, however, it is very incomplete. Through 1820 Mary kept a reasonably good account of Shelley's reading; in 1821 she noted scarcely any at all, and in 1822 none whatsoever. Never, however, did Mary make any attempt to keep an exact record of what Shelley read. In spite of these limitations, the journal is an invaluable source of information concerning what Shelley read and when he read it.

Mary not only made daily entries about what was being read, but kept a separate list of the books read. Her lists for 1814, 1815, 1816, 1817, and 1820 are fairly complete; the list for 1818 is scanty; there are no lists for 1819, 1821, and 1822. These lists are apparently not summaries compiled from the daily entries for the year, but appear to have been made irregularly but concurrent with the daily entries. In no case do they account for all the reading noted in the daily entries. I have printed the lists just as they are in *Shelley and Mary* and have made no attempt to complete them.

This edition will, I believe, add much to the scholar's comfort in his attempt to follow Shelley's development through his reading. Though Mary gave from the journal (in *Poetical Works,* 1839) valuable information about Shelley's reading, and though Dowden and Marshall printed some of the reading lists and White all of them, and though Dowden and White have summarized for the various periods of his life what Shelley read—none of these have attempted to identify the authors of more than a few of the now-obscure books which Shelley read. The scholar has therefore been handicapped at the outset. In this edition the authors of all except a few of the books mentioned have been identified, and in most cases some additional information about the book has been given.

The books read by Shelley have been listed alphabetically according to author in Appendix IV, which also supplies every journal reference to the author or his particular works. Following this is a month by month listing of the authors read by Shelley (in so far as the journal informs us) during any single month. Mary's reading, since it is not of comparable interest to scholars, has not been listed in a similar manner.

In the text or notes I have taken pains to see that the author of a particular work is clearly identified the first time the title appears in the journal. Widely separate references to the same book have the author identification more than once. Some literary works which are universally known have been spared the impertinence of an author identification (such as Shakespeare's plays), but in this respect I have chosen to be generous, even gratuitously so, rather than complimentary.

For the authors whom Shelley read, I have given little or no information in the notes, expecting the curious reader to consult Appendix IV. Since there is no similar list for Mary's reading, it has been necessary to put this information into the notes. When there is no data (beyond the name of the author) in the text or notes about a book being read at the time by Mary alone, this invariably means that later the journal indicates that Shelley also read this book, and therefore the facts about it are to be found listed with Shelley's reading in Appendix IV. In order to keep the reader from making fruitless references to Appendix IV, the editor (when necessary) confesses in the notes his ignorance about a book read by Mary alone. The usual notation is, "Not further identified." In other words, the reader can follow this rule: *All books about which no information is offered in the text or notes were read at some time by Shelley.* For example, the entry for May 9, 1817, states that Mary was reading "Clarke's Travels." The text and notes add nothing to one's knowledge of this book. Since elsewhere in the journal we learn that Shelley read the book, the facts about it (author's name, title, date of publication, and so on) are reserved for Appendix IV, where they can be found under "Clarke."

Shelley's Works. The journal contains remarkably little about Shelley's works. Even the vague notations that "Shelley writes" are relatively few. Mary must, of course, have been perfectly aware of Shelley's preoccupation with his major works. Many of the shorter poems, however, she knew nothing about until she found them among his MSS after his death. All that the journal tells us about Shelley's works has been summarized in Appendix III, which gives an alphabetical list of the works concerned.

The Letters. Mary's habit of noting the letters which she and Shelley wrote and received has proved most helpful to the scholar, whom it has often assisted when a letter needed to be dated or the writer identified. The notes and Appendix II give a complete view of the journal notations about letters written by Shelley and Mary. The notes identify, and give a reference for, all the letters printed. Appendix II lists the letters which are either lost or unprinted. The letters received by Shelley and Mary have not been treated with the same thoroughness, though the record will not fall far short of completeness. They have been identified and supplied with references if they have been printed in *Shelley and Mary,* Dowden's *Life of Shelley, The Correspondence of Leigh Hunt,* or the Halliford edition of Peacock's *Works.*

The journal gives us a far from full record of the letters either written or received by Shelley and Mary. There has been no attempt to notice letters which are known to exist but are not mentioned in the journal.

It will readily be noticed that the dates of the letters which are unquestionably indicated by the journal frequently do not correspond with the dates of the journal entries. This phenomenon is due to various causes. For example, the letter was sometimes incorrectly dated by the writer; or the letter was written on one day and noted in the journal the next day, when it was sent, not written; or the letter was written on one day and completed on the next, or even several days later, though noted in the journal on one day only; or the journal entry is a summary for several days and does not specify the particular days on which letters were written. It will be noticed, too, that at times the journal specifies that a letter was sent, not written.

The Notes. Since the journal is the skeleton of Shelley biography, it is tempting to attach to it voluminous notes which would give it the proportions of a full biography. The purpose of this edition, however, is only to make the journal as usable as possible. The principle followed in preparing the notes has therefore been that of admitting only comments, references, or facts which are necessary if the journal is to be readily intelligible.

Abbreviations Used. In the notes, the following books are referred to frequently. To designate them it is therefore desirable to use the abbreviations below:

Dowden: Edward Dowden, *The Life of P. B. Shelley.* London, Kegan Paul, Trench & Co., 1886. 2 vols.

Grylls: R. Glynn Grylls, *Mary Shelley. A Biography.* London, Oxford University Press, 1938.

Julian edition: Roger Ingpen and Walter E. Peck, eds., *The Complete Works of P. B. Shelley.* London, Published for the Julian Editions by E. Benn, Ltd., 1926–30. 10 vols. (Roger Ingpen, ed., Shelley's Letters, [VII], VIII–X, 1926.)

Letters: Frederick L. Jones, ed., *The Letters of Mary W. Shelley.* Norman, University of Oklahoma Press, 1944. 2 vols.

S&M: *Shelley and Mary.* For Private Circulation Only. [1882] 4 vols. (The Shelley family papers, privately printed for Sir Percy Florence and Lady Jane Shelley.)

White: Newman I. White, *Shelley*. New York, Alfred A. Knopf, 1940. 2 vols.

I wish to thank the Rockefeller Foundation for the Postwar Fellowship in the Humanities which enabled me to complete my editorial task without the distractions of routine academic duties.

FREDERICK L. JONES

Macon, Georgia
April 15, 1947

Contents

Illustrations

Mary Shelley's Journal

Mary Shelley's Journal

1814

ENGLAND

[*Thursday*] JULY 28[1].—[*Shelley*]—The night preceding this morning, all being decided, I ordered a chaise to be ready by 4 o'clock. I watched until the lightning and the stars became pale. At length it was 4. I believed it not possible that we should succeed; still there appeared to lurk some danger even in certainty.

I went; I saw her; she came to me. Yet one quarter of an hour remained. Still some arrangement must be made, and she left me for a short time. How dreadful did this time appear; it seemed that we trifled with life and hope; a few minutes passed, she was in my arms—we were safe; we were on our road to Dover.

Mary was ill as we travelled, yet in that illness what pleasure and security did we not share! The heat made her faint; it was necessary at every stage that she should repose. I was divided between anxiety for her health and terror lest our pursuers should arrive. I reproached myself with not allowing her sufficient time to rest, with conceiving any evil so great that the slightest portion of her comfort might be sacrificed to avoid it.

At Dartford we took four horses, that we might outstrip pursuit. We arrived at Dover before 4 o'clock. Some time was necessarily expended in consideration—in dinner—in bargaining with sailors and custom-house officers. At length we engaged a small boat to convey us to Calais; it was ready by 6 o'clock. The evening was most beautiful; the sands slowly receded; we felt safe; there was little wind, the sails flapped in the flagging breeze. The moon rose, the night came on, and with the night a slow heavy swell and a fresher breeze, which soon became so violent as to toss the boat very much. Mary was much affected by the sea, she could scarcely move. She lay in my arms through the night; the little strength which remained to my own exhausted frame was all expended in keeping her head in rest on my bosom. The wind was violent and contrary. If we could not reach Calais the sailors proposed making for Bou-

[1] The journal for July 28–Sept. 13 was rewritten by Mary and was published in 1817 as a *History of a Six Weeks' Tour*. The *Tour* adds many interesting details and omits others; it was reprinted in *Essays*, &c., 1840.

logne. They promised only two hours' sail from the shore, yet hour after hour past and we were still far distant when the moon sunk in the red and stormy horizon, and the fast-flashing lightning became pale in the breaking day. We were proceeding slowly against the wind, when suddenly a thunder squall struck the sail and the waves rushed into the boat; even the sailors believed that our situation was perilous; the wind had now changed, and we drove before a wind, that came in violent gusts, directly to Calais.

Mary did not know our danger; she was resting between my knees, that were unable to support her; she did not speak or look, but I felt that she was there. I had time in that moment to reflect, and even to reason upon death; it was rather a thing of discomfort and of disappointment than horror to me. We should never be separated, but in death we might not know and feel our union as now. I hope, but my hopes are not unmixed with fear for what will befall this inestimable spirit when we appear to die.

The morning broke, the lightning died away, the violence of the wind abated. We arrived at Calais, whilst Mary still slept; we drove upon the sands. Suddenly the broad sun rose over France.

FRANCE

Friday, JULY 29.—[*Shelley*]—I said, Mary, look, the sun rises over France. We walked over the sands to the inn; we were shown into an apartment that answered the purpose both of a sitting and sleeping room. In the evening Captain Davison came and told us that a fat lady had arrived, who had said that I had run away with her daughter; it was Mrs. Godwin. Jane[2] spent the night with her mother.

Saturday, JULY 30.—[*Shelley*]—Jane informs us that she is unable to withstand the pathos of Mrs. Godwin's appeal. She appealed to the Municipality of Paris—to past slavery and to future freedom. I counselled her to take at least half an hour for consideration. She returned to Mrs. Godwin and informed her that she resolved to continue with us.

Mrs. Godwin departed without answering a word. I met Mrs. Godwin in the street, apparently proceeding to embark for Dover. I walked alone with Mary to the field beyond the gate. At 6 in the evening we left Calais, and arrived at Boulogne at 10. We slept there.

Sunday, JULY 31.—[*Shelley*]—We travelled all day, and arrived at 2 in the morning at Abbeville, where we slept.

Monday, AUG. 1.—[*Shelley*]—We travelled all day and the succeeding night.

[2] Jane Clairmont, Mrs. Godwin's daughter by her first husband. The evolution of Miss Clairmont's name is: Jane or Mary Jane, Clara, Clare, Claire.

Tuesday, Aug. 2.—[*Shelley*]—We arrived at Paris; we engaged lodgings at the Hotel de Vienne. Mary looked over with me the papers contained in her box. They consisted of her own writings, letters from her father and her friends, and my letters.[3] She promised that I should be permitted to read and study these productions of her mind that preceded our intercourse. I shall claim this promise at Uri. In the evening we walked to the gardens of the Tuileries; they are very formal and uninteresting, without any grass. Mary was not well; we returned, and were too happy to sleep.

Wednesday, Aug. 3.—[*Shelley*]—Received a cold and stupid letter from [Thomas] Hookham. He said that Mrs. Boinville's family were reduced to the utmost misery by the distant chance of their being called upon in the course of a year to pay 40*l.* for me. He did not send the money. Wrote to Tavernier.[4] Mary read to me some passages from Lord Byron's poems. I was not before so clearly aware how much of the colouring our own feelings throw upon the liveliest delineations of other minds; our own perceptions are the world to us.

Thursday, Aug. 4.—[*Shelley*]—Mary told me that this was my birthday; I thought it had been the 27th June. Tavernier breakfasted; he is an idiot. I sold my watch, chain, &c., which brought 8 napoleons 5 francs. Tavernier dined; the fool infinitely more insupportable; he walked with us in the evening to the boulevard; he walked with Jane.

Friday, Aug. 5.—[*Shelley*]—Breakfasted with some friends of Tavernier. I committed the mistake of imagining a married woman to be a little baby of nine years' old, and if her child (whom I believed to be her sister) had not possessed a more prepossessing countenance, I should have taken her in my lap and offered her a lump of sugar. The ladies talked of dress and eating. We went with Tavernier to the Police [probably about passports],[5] to the Louvre, and the Church of Notre Dame, the interior of which much disappointed our expectations. At the Louvre we saw one picture, apparently of the Deluge, which was terribly impressive. It was the only remarkable picture which we had time to observe. There was Hell and Heaven also; the Blessed looked too stupid. In the evening we sallied forth in search of H[elen] M[aria] Williams.[6]

[3] This box (or trunk) was left in Paris and was never recovered. See Mary's letter of October 28, [1845] to Hookham in *The Letters of Mary W. Shelley,* ed. by Frederick L. Jones (Norman, University of Oklahoma Press, 1944, 2 vols.; hereafter referred to as *Letters*), and Cyrus Redding's life of Shelley in the Galignani edition of Shelley's Poetical Works (Paris, 1829).

[4] Lawyer or moneylender.

[5] Edward Dowden, *The Life of P. B. Shelley* (London, Kegan Paul, Trench & Co., 1886, 2 vols.; hereafter referred to as Dowden), I, 446.

[6] A friend of Mary Wollstonecraft.

After numerous unavailing inquiries, we met at the Place Vendôme a Frenchman [M. R. de Savi][7] who could speak English; he offered us his services in the necessary inquiries. He took us out of our way for the pleasure of hearing himself talk; he told us that he had assisted in bribing the mob to overthrow the statue of Napoleon; that he was a royalist, and had been in the English army during the reign of Bonaparte; he was the first royalist who had entered Paris. He made us sit down in the garden of the Tuileries, and there, with a smile of abundant and overflowing vanity, confessed that he was an author and a poet. We invited him to breakfast, hoping to derive from his officiousness a relief from our embarrassments.

Saturday, AUG. 6.—[*Shelley*]—M. R. de Savi breakfasted with us; we go with him to M. Peregaux, the banker, who refuses to advance money. I learn from Tavernier the direction of H. M. Williams. Secure that my statement of our history and situation cannot fail to interest, I hasten thither. She is absent in the country; the time of her return is uncertain. On my return to the Hotel we go to Tavernier's office to seek for letters; we hear that Tavernier has letters for us and is gone to our hotel. We return. We had appointed to dine with M. de Savi at 6; we keep the appointment at 8, leaving Jane to wait for Tavernier. M. R. de Savi had relinquished all hope. We return. Tavernier brings a dull and insolent letter from Hookham.

Sunday, AUG. 7.—[*Shelley*]—Tavernier breakfasts. Promises money. The morning passes in delightful converse. We almost forget that we are prisoners in Paris; Mary especially seems insensible to all future evil. She feels as if our love would alone suffice to resist the invasions of calamity. She rested on my bosom and seemed even indifferent to take sufficient food for the sustenance of life.

We went to Tavernier and received a remittance of 60*l*. We talk over our plans, and determined to walk to Uri. We went to sleep early on the sofa.

Monday, AUG. 8.—[*Mary*]—Jane and Shelley go to the ass merchant; we buy an ass. The day spent in preparations for departure. Madame Sa Hôte could not be persuaded that it was secure and delightful to walk in solitude and mountains. We set out to Charenton in the evening, carrying the ass, who was weak and unfit for labour, like the Miller and his Son. We arrived at Charenton late.[8] One horrible spasm.

[7] A. H. Koszul says that R. de Savi "est sans doute le du Rouve-de-Savy de *l'Almanach des Muses,* 1810 ('Epître en vers à M. de . . . qui me pressait d'aller à Paris solliciter un emploi'), et celui de *Trente Odes d'Horace,* traduites en vers (*Moniteur,* 1812, p. 293)."—*La Jeunesse de Shelley* (Paris, Bloud & Cie., 1910), 217 n.

[8] The *Six Weeks' Tour* says "about ten."

Tuesday, Aug. 9.—[*Shelley*]—We sell our ass and purchase a mule, in which we much resemble him who never made a bargain but always lost half. The day is most beautiful. I led Mary on her mule, with the exception of eight miles which Jane rode, to Guignes, a town nine leagues from Charenton. We passed through Gros Bois, Brie, and other villages. We arrive without adventures, though not without feelings of pride and pleasure, at Guignes. Here we heard that the Emperor Napoleon and some of his Guards slept in the same inn.

Wednesday, Aug. 10.—[*Shelley*]—We left Guignes and stopped at Provins. The approach to Provins is most beautiful; a ruined citadel, with extensive walls and towers, stood above the town; the cathedral was beyond; it formed one scene. We slept at a little old woman's whose beds were infinitely detestable.

Thursday, Aug. 11.—[*Mary*]—From Provins we came to Nogent. The town was entirely desolated by the Cossacks; the houses were reduced to heaps of white ruins, and the bridge was destroyed. Proceeding on our way we left the great road and arrived at St. Aubin, a beautiful little village situated among trees. This village was also completely destroyed. The inhabitants told us the Cossacks had not left one cow in the village. Notwithstanding the entreaties of the people, who eagerly desired us to stay all night, we continued our route to Trois Maisons, three long leagues further, on an unfrequented road, and which in many places was hardly perceptible from the surrounding waste. Till now we had not met with one uncultivated field in France, the corn fields, flourishing and rich, seemed innumerable; but now the face of the country was changed, the chalky soil was wholly uncultivated. As night approached our fears increased that we should not be able to distinguish the road, and Mary expressed these fears in a very complaining tone. We arrived at Trois Maisons at 9 o'clock. Jane went up to the first cottage to ask our way, but was only answered by unmeaning laughter. We, however, discovered a kind of an auberge, where, having in some degree satisfied our hunger by milk and sour bread, we retired to a wretched apartment to bed. But first let me observe, that we here discovered that the inhabitants were not in the habit of washing themselves either when they rose or went to bed.

Friday, Aug. 12.—Jane was not able to sleep all night for the rats, who, as she said, put their cold paws upon her face; she, however, rested on our bed, which her four-footed enemies dared not invade, perhaps having overheard the threat that Shelley terrified the man with. We did not set out from here till 11 o'clock, and travelled a long league under the very eye of a burning sun. Shelley, having sprained his leg, was obliged to ride all day. At Echemine we rested. This village is entirely ruined by the Cossacks; but we could hardly pity the people when we saw how very unamiable they were. The cabaret we rested at was not equalled by any description I have heard of an Irish cabin in filth, and certainly the dirtiest Scotch cottage I ever entered was exquisitely clean beside it. We could hardly swallow their food; but went on to Pavillon, a beautiful place, but also desolated by the Cossacks; and, in fact, we did not see a cottage on the road but had been burnt. The account they gave at Pavillon was that they took the cows, sheep, and poultry, and tore down the houses for wood for fires. We left Pavillon a little before 5, and were told that it was three leagues to Troyes, but I have no doubt that it was five regular ones. We met on the road a man whose children had been murdered by the Cossacks. Shelley tells us the story of the Seven Sleepers, to beguile the time. We see vines, the first sign of cultivation for six leagues, but the grapes were not ripe. Much wearied we arrive at Troyes, and get into a dirty apartment of a nasty auberge to sleep. In this walk we have observed one thing, that the French are exceedingly inhospitable, and on this side of Paris very disagreeable. Shelley's sprain determines us to continue our journey in the diligence or some voiture.

Saturday, Aug. 13.—We are disgusted with the excessive dirt of our habitation. Shelley goes to inquire about conveyances. He sells the mule for 40 francs, and the saddle for 16 francs. In all our bargains, for ass, saddle, and mule, we lose more than 15 napoleons. Money we can but little spare now. Jane and Shelley seek for a conveyance to Neufchatel. Two hours of the evening thus spent, Mary is alone, and writes to Mrs. P. They return, having bought a voiture for 5 napoleons, and engaged with an aubergiste to send a mule with the carriage to Neufchatel. Removed to the inn where we hired the mule, and sleep there.

Sunday, Aug. 14.—At 4 in the morning we depart from Troyes and proceed in the new vehicle to Vandeuvres. The village remains still ruined by the war. We rest at Vandeuvres two hours, but walk in a wood belonging to a neighbouring chateau, and sleep under its shade. The moss was so soft, the murmur of the wind in the leaves was sweeter than Æolian music, we forgot that we were in France or in the world for a time.

As we left Vandeuvres the aspect of the country suddenly changed; abrupt hills, covered with vineyards, intermixed with trees, inclosed a narrow valley—the channel of the Aube; green meadows, intermixed with groves of poplars and white willow, and spires of village churches which the Cossacks had still spared, were there.

Many little villages ruined by the war occupied the most romantic situations.

In the evening we arrived at Bar-sur-Aube, a beautiful town, placed at the opening of the vale, where the hills terminate abruptly. We climbed the highest of these hills, but . . .[9]

Monday, Aug. 15.—We rise at 4 and pursue our journey. We left the hills but were delighted to see one at a distance with clouds before it . . .

Tuesday, Aug. 16.—We pursue our journey at 5 in the morning—The country we pass through is full of forests—We have a distant peep at hills—We dine at Champlitte. Adventure with Marguerite Pascal—whom we would have taken with us if her father would have allowed us and certainly I never beheld so lovely a child—Shelley and I walk to the riverside—We sleep at Gray.

Wednesday, Aug. 17.—We rise at 4 and proceed towards Besancon . . . Just as we quitted the fortifications a beautiful scene broke in on us—a castle built high on a rock; hills covered with pine, with a lovely plain in the middle, through which ran a silent river.

The voiturier insists upon our passing the night at the village of Mort. We go out on the rocks, and Shelley and I read part of "Mary, a fiction" [by Mary Wollstonecraft]. We return at dark, and, unable to enter the beds, we pass a few comfortless hours by the kitchen fireside.

Thursday, Aug. 18.—We leave Mort at 4. After some hours of tedious travelling, through a most beautiful country, we arrive at Noè. From the summit of one of the hills we see the whole expanse of the valley filled with a white undulating mist, over which the piny hills pierced like islands. The sun had just risen, and a ray of the red light lay on the waves of this fluctuating vapour. To the west, opposite the sun, it seemed driven by the light against the rock in immense masses of foaming cloud until it becomes lost in the distance, mixing its tints with the fleecy sky. At Noè, whilst our postilion waited, we walked into the forest of pines; it was a scene of enchantment, where every sound and sight contributed to charm.

Our mossy seat in the deepest recesses of the wood was inclosed from the world by an impenetrable veil. On our return the postilion had departed without us; he left word that he expected to meet us on the road. We proceeded thereupon on foot to Maison Neuve, an auberge a league distant. At Maison Neuve he had left a message importing that he should proceed to Pontarlier, six leagues distant, and that unless he found us

[9] After this word ("but"), *Shelley and Mary* (the Shelley family papers, privately printed for Sir Percy Florence and Lady Jane Shelley [1882], 4 vols.; hereafter referred to as S&M) has the bracketed words "[*torn out*]," followed by the sentence under August 17 beginning "Just as we quitted . . . ." This lost sheet of the journal was found at Boscombe Manor by A. H. Koszul, and it is now in its proper place in the MS journal. From the MS notes of Miss Grylls the part-entry for August 15 and the first sentence of the entry for August 17 are restored. From Koszul is derived the entry for August 16 (see Koszul, *La Jeunesse de Shelley,* 428).

there should return. We dispatched a boy on horseback for him; he promised to wait for us at the next village; we walked two leagues in the expectation of finding him there. The evening was most beautiful; the horned moon hung in the light of sunset that threw a glow of unusual depth of redness above the piny mountains and the dark deep valleys which they included. At Savrine we found, according to our expectation, that M. le Voiturier had pursued his journey with the utmost speed. We engaged a voiture for Pontarlier. Jane very unable to walk. The moon becomes yellow and hangs close to the woody horizon. It is dark before we arrive at Pontarlier. The postilion tells many lies.

We sleep, for the first time in France, in a clean bed.

SWITZERLAND

Friday, Aug. 19.—We pursue our journey towards Neufchatel. We pass delightful scenes, being mountains and barren rocks, and scenes of verdure surpassing imagination; here first we see clear mountain streams. We pass the barrier between France and Switzerland, and, after descending nearly a league, between lofty rocks covered with pines and interspersed with green glades, where the grass is short and soft and beautifully verdant, we arrive at St. Sulpice. The mule is very lame; we determine to engage another horse for the remainder of the way. Our voiturier had determined to leave us, and had taken measures to that effect. The mountains after St. Sulpice become loftier and more beautiful. Two leagues from Neufchatel we see the Alps; hill after hill is seen extending its craggy outline before the other, and far behind all, towering above every feature of the scene, the snowy Alps; they are 100 miles distant; they look like those accumulated clouds of dazzling white that arrange themselves on the horizon in summer. This immensity staggers the imagination, and so far surpasses all conception that it requires an effort of the understanding to believe that they are indeed mountains. We arrive at Neufchatel and sleep.

Saturday, Aug. 20.—We consult on our situation. There are no letters at the bureau de poste: there cannot be for a week. Shelley goes to the banker's, who promises an answer in two hours; at the conclusion of the time he sends for Shelley, and, to our astonishment and consolation, Shelley returns staggering under the weight of a large canvas bag full of silver. Shelley alone looks grave on the occasion, for he alone clearly apprehends that francs and écus and louis d'or are like the white and flying cloud of noon, that is gone before one can say "Jack Robinson." Shelley goes to secure a place in the diligence; they are all taken. He meets there with a Swiss who speaks English; this man is imbued with the spirit of true politeness. He endeavours to perform real services, and

MARY SHELLEY

From a portrait by Richard Rothwell, 1841

Courtesy of the National Portrait Gallery

seems to regard the mere ceremonies of the affair as things of very little value. He makes a bargain with a voiturier to take us to Lucerne for 18 écus.

We arrange to depart at 4 the next morning. Our Swiss friend appoints to meet us there.

Sunday, Aug. 21.—Go from Neufchatel at 6; our Swiss accompanies us a little way out of town. There is a mist to-day, so we cannot see the Alps; the drive however is interesting, especially in the latter part of the day. Shelley and Jane talk concerning Jane's character. We arrive before 7 at Soleure. Shelley and Mary go to the much-praised cathedral, and find it very modern and stupid.

Monday, Aug. 22.—Leave Soleure at half-past 5; very cold indeed, but we now again see the magnificent mountains of Le Valais. Mary is not well, and all are tired of wheeled machines. Shelley is in a jocosely horrible mood. We dine at Zoffingen, and sleep there two hours. In our drive after dinner we see the mountains of St. Gothard, &c. Change our plan of going over St. Gothard. Arrive tired to death; find at the room of the inn a horrible spinet and a case of stuffed birds. Sup at table d'hôte.

Tuesday, Aug. 23.—We leave at 4 o'clock and arrive at Lucerne about 10. After breakfast we hire a boat to take us down the lake. Shelley and Mary go out and buy several needful things, and we then embark. It is a most divine day; the farther we advance the more magnificent are the shores of the lake—rock and pine forests covering the feet of the immense mountains. We read part of L'Abbé Barruel's "Histoire de Jacobinism." We land at Bessen; go to the wrong inn, where a most comical scene ensues. We sleep at Brunnen. Before we sleep, however, we look out of window.

Wednesday, Aug. 24.—We consult on our situation. We cannot procure a house; we are in despair; the filth of the apartment is terrible to Mary; she cannot bear it all the winter. We propose to proceed to Flüelen, but the wind comes from Italy, and will not permit. At last we find a lodging in an ugly house they call the Chateau for 1 louis per month, which we take; it consists of two rooms. Mary and Shelley walk to the shore of the lake and read the description of the Siege of Jerusalem in Tacitus.[10] We come home, look out of window, and go to bed.

Thursday, Aug. 25.—We read Abbé Barruel. Shelley and Jane make purchases; we pack up our things and take possession of our house, which we have engaged for six months. Receive a visit from the Médecin and the old Abbé, whom, it must be owned, we do not treat with proper politeness. We arrange our apartment and write part of Shelley's romance ["The Assassins"].

[10] In the *History,* Book V.

Friday, Aug. 26.—Write the romance till 3 o'clock. Propose crossing Mount St. Gothard. Determine at last to return to England; only wait to set off till the washerwoman brings home our linen. The little Frenchman arrives with tubs and plums, and scissors and salt. The linen is not dry; we are compelled to wait until to-morrow. We engage a boat to take us to Lucerne at 6 the following morning.

Saturday, Aug. 27.—We depart at 7; it rains violently till just the end of our voyage. We conjecture the astonishment of the good people of Brunnen. We arrive at Lucerne, dine, then write a part of the romance, and read Shakespeare. Interrupted by Jane's horrors; pack up. We have engaged a boat for Basle.

Sunday, Aug. 28.—Depart at 6 o'clock. The river is exceedingly beautiful; the waves break on the rocks, and the descents are steep and rapid. It rained the whole day. We stopped at Mettingen to dine, and there surveyed at our ease the horrid and slimy faces of our companions in voyage; our only wish was to absolutely annihilate such uncleanly animals, to which we might have addressed the Boatman's speech to Pope— " 'Twere easier for God to make entirely new men than attempt to purify such monsters as these." After a voyage in the rain, rendered disagreeable only by the presence of these loathsome "Creepers," we arrive, Shelley much exhausted, at Dettingen, our resting place for the night.

Monday, Aug. 29.—We set out from Dettingen at 6, alone. We stop at Loffenburgh and engage a boat for Mumpf; the boat is small and frail, it requires much attention to prevent an overset. At Mumpf we cannot procure a boat for Rheinfelden; we proceed in a return voiture; it breaks down a mile from the town. Some kind Swiss convey our little baggage for us, and we walk to Rheinfelden. Unable to procure a boat, we walk on half a league further, where, after being threatened with the evil of sleeping at this nasty village, we get a boat and arrive at Basle at 6, cold and comfortless. Shelley makes a bargain that night, very kindly helped by a stupid bookseller; we get the stove heated and procure supper. Bed very uncomfortable. Mary groans.

GERMANY

Tuesday, Aug. 30.—It is Mary's birthday (17). We do not solemnize this day in comfort. We expect to be, not happier, but more at our ease before the year passes. We leave Basle by the boat[11] that we had engaged; the wind is violently against us, we stop at Thauphane[12] and sleep there.

11 S&M has "in the boat"; Dowden (I, 457), "by the boat."

12 Dowden's note (I, 457): "The name in the journal is either Shauphane or Thauphane. I cannot elsewhere find either name."

The Rhine is violently rapid to-day, and although interrupted by no rocks, is swollen with high waves; it is full of little islands, green and beautiful. Before we arrived at Thauphane the river became suddenly narrow, and the boat dashed with inconceivable rapidity round the base of a rocky hill covered with pines.

A ruined tower, with its desolated windows, stood on the summit of another hill that jutted into the river; beyond, the sunset[13] was illumining the mountains and the clouds, and casting the reflection of its hues on the agitated river. The brilliance and colourings in the circling whirlpools of the stream was an appearance entirely new, and most beautiful.

Wednesday, AUG. 31.—Pursue our voyage in the slight canoe that accompanied our boat. Shelley reads aloud the "Letters from Norway" [by Mary Wollstonecraft]. Arrive at Strasburgh; buy provisions, and proceed. Evening comes on. Shelley finishes "Mary, a Fiction." We sleep at a little village beyond Strasburgh.

Thursday, SEPT. 1.—Pursue our voyage, and, at six leagues from the place where we slept, change our canoe for a large boat. We remain in the boat all night—Schwitz, Schneider, and Hoff.[14]

Friday, SEPT. 2.—We arrive at Manheim early in the morning; breakfast there; the town is clean and good. We proceeded towards Mayence with an unfavourable wind; towards evening the batelier rests just as the wind changes in our favour. Mary and Shelley walk for three hours; they are alone. At 11 we depart. We sleep in the boat.

Saturday, SEPT. 3.—In the morning, when we wake, we find that we have been tied all night to an island in the Rhine; the wind changed against us immediately on our departure the night before. With much difficulty we reach Mayence at 12. Mary and Shelley are alone. Shelley takes a place in the diligence *par eau* to Cologne. We sleep at Mayence.

Sunday, SEPT. 4.—We leave Mayence at 6 o'clock, and proceed in a little boat to reach the diligence. The banks of the Rhine are very fine—rocks and mountains, crowned with lonely castles; but, alas! at their feet are only still towns for ever; yet did the hills half compensate, as in Switzerland the cottages did not pierce into their very recesses, but left something to fancy and solitude.

We read Shakespeare. Our companions in voyage are tolerable. We frightened from us one man who spoke English, and whom we did not

13 S&M has "the river beyond. The sunset . . ."; Dowden (I, 457), "the river; beyond, the sunset . . . ."

14 The *Six Weeks' Tour* amplifies: "three of these [four passengers] were students of the Strasburgh university: Schwitz, a rather handsome, good-tempered young man; Hoff, a kind of shapeless animal, with a heavy, ugly, German face; and Schneider, who was nearly an idiot."

like, by talking of cutting off kings' heads. We arrive late in the evening at our place of rest.

Monday, Sept. 5.—We travel all day by water, provoked by the extreme laziness of the bataliers; we arrive at Bonn at 6 o'clock, and procure a voiture. The sunset this evening is exquisitely beautiful; the hills no longer surround us, but, increased by darkness, the distant ones appear like mountains. After fair and easy travelling of a mile in half an hour, we arrive at Cologne; take places in diligence, and retire to rest.

Tuesday, Sept. 6.—The diligence is the most detestable of things, being five times slower than a snail's walk; that is to say, rather more than a mile an hour. We dine on the road, and see a procession of old women. What a sight such a thing would be in France! The boulevard, two miles long, would not contain one quarter that would be found in a town like that we dined at. We travel all night—three leagues in seven hours. The country is uninteresting.

HOLLAND

Wednesday, Sept. 7.—We arrive at Clêve at 12 o'clock, and travel post the rest of the way. The country it flat, but the hedges are pretty. We are told that we cannot travel all night on account of the robbers. Sleep at Triel.

Thursday, Sept. 8.—We depart at 6 o'clock. Holland is a very flat, uninteresting country, all intersected with canals; and the people have been so stupid as to make a road between two canals so narrow that two voitures cannot, when they meet, pass without spending half an hour in arrangements. We are horribly cheated, and arrive at Rotterdam at 6 o'clock with 20 écus; make arrangements, and talk of many things, past, present, and to come.

Friday, Sept. 9.—We have arranged with a Captain to take us to England—three guineas a-piece; at 3 o'clock we sail, and in the evening arrive at Marsluys, where a bad wind obliges us to stay.

Saturday, Sept. 10.—We remain at Marsluys. Mary begins "Hate," and gives Shelley the greater pleasure. Shelley writes part of his romance. Sleep at Marsluys. Wind contrary.

Sunday, Sept. 11.—The wind becomes favourable. We hear that we are to sail. Mary writes more of her "Hate." We depart; cross the bar; the sea is horribly tempestuous, and Mary nearly sick, nor is Shelley much better. There is an easterly gale in the night, which almost kills us, whilst it carries us nearer our journey's end.

Monday, Sept. 12.—It is calm; we remain on deck nearly the whole day. Mary recovers from her sickness. We dispute with one man upon the slave trade.

ENGLAND

Tuesday, Sept. 13.—We arrive at Gravesend, and with great difficulty prevail on the Captain to trust us. We go by boat to London; take a coach; call on Hookham. T. H. not at home. E[dward Hookham][15] treats us very ill. Call at [Henry] Voisey's. Henry goes to Harriet. Shelley calls on her, whilst poor Mary and Jane are left two whole hours in the coach. Our debt is discharged. Shelley gets clothes for himself. Go to Stratford Hotel;[16] dine and go to bed.

Wednesday, Sept. 14.—Talk and read the newspapers. Shelley calls on Harriet, who is certainly a very odd creature; he writes several letters;[17] calls on Hookham, and brings home Wordsworth's "Excursion," of which we read a part, much disappointed. He is a slave. Shelley engages lodgings,[18] which we remove to in the evening.

Thursday, Sept. 15.[19]—Letter from Maria Smith. Shelley calls on Harriet; meets Hookham; reconciliation. Hookham calls here, and Shelley reads his romance to him; he writes to Voisey; reads the "Ancient Mariner" to us. Mary reads the "Excursion" all day, and reads the "History of Margaret" [by Adam Fergusson] to P. B. S. He reads part of [Godwin's] "Caleb Williams" to us.

Friday, Sept. 16.—Read the "Excursion" and [Southey's] "Madoc." Hookham dines. Mrs. Godwin and Fanny[20] pay a visit to the window, but refuse to speak to Shelley when he goes out to them.

Voisey drinks tea when Hookham is gone; explains Dr. Gall's system. I got to bed; awakened by a noise, and find it to be the arrival of Charles [Clairmont]; talk of many things—the conduct of William [Godwin, Jr.], the convent plan for Jane, and money affairs. He goes at 3 in the morning.

Saturday, Sept. 17.—Read "Madoc" all morning, Shelley out on business. He reads the "Curse of Kehama" [by Southey] to us in the evening.

Sunday, Sept. 18.—Mary receives her first lesson in Greek. She reads the "Curse of Kehama" while Shelley walks out with Peacock, who

15 S&M, "C." Edward Hookham was Thomas Hookham's brother (see Newman I. White, *Shelley* [New York, Alfred A. Knopf, 1940, 2 vols.; hereafter referred to as White], I, 364).

16 In Oxford Street (White, I, 364).

17 Shelley to Harriet, September 15 [*for* 14], 1814 (so misdated by Shelley or by the transcriber) (*The Complete Works of P. B. Shelley,* ed. by Roger Ingpen and Walter E. Peck [London, published for the Julian Editions by E. Benn, Ltd., 1926–30, 10 vols.; hereafter referred to as Julian edition], VII, 295–96). That the fourteenth is correct is proved by the first sentence of the letter: "I have not yet obtained a lodging. I do not know that it will be possible to do so tonight." It was possible, as the journal shows.

18 At No. 56 Margaret Street, Cavendish Square (White, I, 365).

19 For Claire's diary during September 15–25, see White, I, 365–67.

20 Fanny Imlay, usually called Fanny Godwin.

dines. Shelley walks part of the way home with him. Curious account of Harriet. We talk, study a little Greek, and go to bed.

Monday, SEPT. 19.—Shelley goes to [G. B.] Ballachy's;[21] receives notice that the sale is Wednesday. Mary reads Greek and [Dr. Johnson's] "Rasselas." In the evening Hookham calls. Mary reads [Veit Weber's] "The Sorcerer." Shelley writes his romance. Write[s] to Amory.[22]

Tuesday, SEPT. 20.—Shelley writes to Hookham and Tavernier; goes with Hookham to Ballachy's. Mary reads [Godwin's] "Political Justice" all the morning. Study Greek. In the evening Shelley reads [Southey's] "Thalaba" aloud.

Wednesday, SEPT. 21.—Read Greek. Hookham calls, and Shelley goes with him to the sale.[23] Mary reads Greek and "Political Justice." No bidder at the sale. Hookham dines with us. In the evening Shelley reads one canto of "Thalaba," but he is both sleepy and tired; go to bed early.

Thursday, SEPT. 22.—Walk out and buy prints. Mary reads "Political Justice"; Shelley writes Greek. In the evening a mistake happens with regard to Harriet, by receiving a letter which had been written to Bexhill. Shelley goes there [probably to Harriet's home in Chapel Street], and hears that Harriet is gone out of town; receives a letter from H. in a far different style. Shelley draws, and Mary reads [M. G. Lewis's] "The Monk" all evening.

Friday, SEPT. 23.—We call at Hookham's, and at a bookseller's buy a guinea's worth of books. Read "Political Justice." A letter from my Father. Hookham dines with us. Shelley reads "Thalaba" to us in the evening.

Saturday, SEPT. 24.—Shelley and I go to Ballachy's; meet Pike;[24] buy some prints; read Greek. Shelley finishes "Thalaba"; talk; go to bed.

Sunday, SEPT. 25.— [*?Shelley*]—Read two odes of Anacreon before breakfast. Mary draws. [*Mary*]—Read "Political Justice"; walk out with Shelley. Peacock calls; Shelley goes with him to Warry's.

Monday, SEPT. 26.—Shelley goes with Peacock to Ballachy's, and engages lodgings at Pancras. Visit from Mrs. Pringer. Read "Political Justice" and the "Empire of the Nairs" [by J. H. Lawrence].

Tuesday, SEPT. 27.—Read "Political Justice"; finishes the "Nairs"; pack up and go to our lodgings in Somers Town [5 Church Terrace, Pancras].[25]

21 Moneylender.

22 Shelley's solicitor.

23 Claire's diary: "Shelley goes with Hookham to the Sale—Is obliged to buy the Reversion etc.—"—White, I, 367.

24 Moneylender.

25 At Mrs. Page's (White, I, 368).

Wednesday, SEPT. 28.—Peacock calls. Jane goes to Hookham's. Shelley goes with Peacock to Ballachy; go into the Bank; call at Ellis and Pike's and at Finnis'.[26] Read Greek. Peacock spends the evening with us. Hookham calls whilst we are out. Finnis calls.

Thursday, SEPT. 29.—Shelley goes to Westminister [*sic*] Insurance Office. Mary reads "Political Justice"; walks with Shelley to Kentish Town fields. Read "Political Justice" in the evening.

Friday, SEPT. 30.—After breakfast walk to Hampstead Heath. Discuss the possibility of converting and liberating two heiresses;[27] arrange a plan on this subject. On our return find a letter from Mrs. Boinville and from Amory. Peacock calls; talk with him concerning the heiresses and Marian;[28] arrange his marriage.

Saturday, OCT. 1.—Peacock comes. After breakfast we all walk to Hackney. M. H.[29] and Mary call at Mrs. Hugford's [school]; see Eliza, Helen, and Anne. Peacock dines with us; talk in the evening of our running away scheme.

Sunday, OCT. 2.—Peacock comes after breakfast; walk over Primrose Hill; sail little boats; return a little before 4; talk. Read "Political Justice" in the evening; talk.

Monday, OCT. 3.—Read "Political Justice." Hookham calls. Walk with Peacock to the Lake of Naugis and set off little fire-boats. After dinner talk and let off fireworks. Talk of the West of Ireland plan.

Tuesday, OCT. 4.—Shelley is out all day calling on Ballachy, Finnis, and Ellis; business all unsettled. Read [T. J. Hogg's] "Alexy Haimatoff"; study a little Greek. Read "Political Justice." Write to Isabel [Baxter]. Shelley writes to Hogg[30] and Mrs. Boinville.

Wednesday, OCT. 5.—Peacock at breakfast. Walk to the Lake of Naugis and sail fire-boats. Read "Political Justice." Shelley reads the "Ancient Mariner" aloud. Letter from Harriet,[31] very civil—400*l.* for 2,400*l.*

Thursday, OCT. 6.—Peacock breakfasts with us. He goes to Ballachy's. Read "Political Justice." Shelley very unwell; he reads one canto of "Queen Mab" to me. Peacock calls again before dinner. The books arrive

26 Ellis and Finnis were both moneylenders.

27 Shelley's sisters, Elizabeth and Hellen. For the "liberating" scheme, see Dowden, I, 478; and White, I, 372.

28 Marianne de St. Croix. See note to Jan. 2, 1815, entry.

29 Probably an error for M. J. meaning Mary Jane (Claire).

30 Shelley to Hogg, October 3, 1814 (*Harriet and Mary,* ed. by W. S. Scott [London, The Golden Cockerel Press, 1944], 39–41).

31 Shelley replied on the same day (Shelley to Harriet, October 5, 1814, Julian edition, VII, 303–304).

from Hookham; Hookham calls. Read [E. DuBois's] "St. Godwin"; it is ineffably stupid.

Friday, Oct. 7.—[*Shelley*]—Read "Political Justice." Peacock calls. Jane, for some reason, refuses to walk. We traverse the fields towards Hampstead. Under an expansive oak lies a dead calf; the cow, lean from grief, is watching it. (Contemplate subject for poem). The sunset is beautiful. Return at 9. Peacock departs. Mary goes to bed at half-past 8; Shelley sits up with Jane. Talk of oppression and reform, of cutting squares of skin from the soldiers' backs. Jane states her conception of the subterranean[32] community of women. Talk of Hogg, Harriet, Miss Hitchener, &c. At 1 o'clock Shelley observes that it is the witching time of night; he inquires soon after if it is not horrible to feel the silence of night tingling in our ears; in half an hour the question is repeated in a different form; at 2 they retire awe-struck and hardly daring to breathe. Shelley says to Jane "Good night"; his hand is leaning on the table; he is conscious of an expression in his countenance which he cannot repress. Jane hesitates. "Good night" again. She still hesitates.

"Did you ever read the tragedy of 'Orra' [by Joanna Baillie]?" said Shelley. "Yes." "How horribly you look—take your eyes off." "Good night" again, and Jane ran to her room. Shelley, unable to sleep, kissed Mary and prepared to sit beside her and read until morning, when rapid footsteps descended the stairs. Jane was there; her countenance was distorted most unnaturally by horrible dismay—it beamed with a whiteness that seemed almost like light; her lips and cheeks were of one deadly hue; the skin of her face and forehead was drawn into innumerable wrinkles—the lineaments of terror that could not be contained; her hair came prominent and erect; her eyes were wide and staring, drawn almost from the sockets by the convulsion of the muscles; the eyelids were forced in, and the eyeballs, without any relief, seemed as if they had been newly inserted, in ghastly sport, in the sockets of a lifeless head. This frightful spectacle endured but for a few moments—it was displaced by terror and confusion, violent, indeed, and full of dismay, but human. She asked me (Shelley) if I had touched her pillow (her tone was that of dreadful alarm). I said, "No, no! if you come into the room I will tell you." I informed her of Mary's pregnancy; this seemed to check her violence. She told me that a pillow placed upon her bed had been removed, in the moment that she turned her eyes away to a chair at some distance, and evidently by no human power. She was positive as to the fact of her self-possession and calmness. Her manner convinced me that she was not deceived. We continued to sit by the fire, at intervals engaging in awful conversation relative to the nature of these mysteries. I read part of

[32] S&M, "sublime"; corrected by Dowden (I, 480) from the original MS.

"Alexy [Haimatoff"]; I repeated one of my own poems. Our conversation, though intentionally directed to other topics, irresistably recurred to these. Our candles burned low, we feared they would not last until daylight. Just as the dawn was struggling with moonlight, Jane remarked in me that unutterable expression which had affected her with so much horror before; she described it as expressing a mixture of deep sadness and conscious power over her. I covered my face with my hands, and spoke to her in the most studied gentleness. It was ineffectual; her horror and agony increased even to the most dreadful convulsions. She shrieked and writhed on the floor. I ran to Mary; I communicated in few words the state of Jane. I brought her to Mary. The convulsions gradually ceased, and she slept. At daybreak we examined her apartment and found her pillow on the chair.[33]

Saturday, OCT. 8.—[*Mary*]—Read "Political Justice." We walk out; when we return Shelley talks with Jane, and I read [Mary Wollstonecraft's] "Wrongs of Woman." In the evening we talk and read.

Sunday, OCT. 9.—Read the "Wrongs of Woman"; translate some Greek; read "Political Justice." Hookham calls; Peacock calls. Walk to the Withered Tree. In the evening Shelley reads Abbé Barruel to us.

Monday, OCT. 10.—Read "Political Justice." Go with Shelley to Finnis and Oxford Street. Go with Shelley to the churchyard (St. Pancras); receive no intelligence but what we conceive to be false. On our return find a letter from Harriet informing us of what she imagines a dangerous illness. Peacock calls; Shelley goes with him to Dr. [J.] Sims;[34] he is not at home. Read "Posthumous Works."[35] Peacock dines. Read [Shelley's] "Zastrozzi." Shelley writes to H[arriet] S[helley]. We think of calling on her; call on Dr. Sims, and return. Send a porter; he returns with a verbal message from H. S., and a letter from Dr. Sims, with his opinion —not a very favourable one.

Tuesday, OCT. 11.—Read "Political Justice." Shelley goes to the Westminster Insurance Office. Study Greek. Peacock dines. Receive a refusal about the money; its all that conscientious Lawrence's[36] fault. Have a good-humoured letter from Harriet, and a cold and even sarcastic one from Mrs. Boinville. Shelley reads the "History of the Illuminati," out of Bar[r]uel, to us.

Wednesday, OCT. 12.—Read "Political Justice." A letter from [James] Marshall;[37] Jane goes there. When she comes home we go to Cheapside; returning, an occurrence. Deliberation until 7; burn the letter; sleep early.

[33] For Claire's account of this adventure, see Dowden, I, 482.

[34] Harriet's physician, of 67 Guilford Street (Julian edition, VII, 298 n.).

[35] Of Mary Wollstonecraft, ed. by W. Godwin (1798, 4 vols.).

[36] Moneylender.

[37] Friend and assistant of Godwin.

Thursday, Oct. 13.—Communicate the burning of the letter. Much dispute and discussion concerning its probable contents. Alarm. Determine to quit London; send for 5*l.* from Hookham. Change our resolution. Go to the play.[38] The extreme depravity and disgusting nature of the scene; the inefficacy of acting to encourage or maintain the delusion. The loathsome sight of men personating characters which do not and cannot belong to them. Shelley displeased with what he saw of Kean. Return. Alarm. We sleep at the Stratford Hotel.

Friday, Oct. 14.—[*Shelley*]—Jane's insensibility and incapacity for the slightest degree of friendship. The feelings occasioned by this discovery prevent me (Shelley) from maintaining any measure in severity.[39] This highly incorrect; subversion of the first principles of true philosophy; characters, particularly those which are unformed, may change. Beware of weakly giving way to trivial sympathies. Content yourself with one great affection—with a single mighty hope; let the rest of mankind be the subjects of your benevolence, your justice, and, as human beings, of your sensibility; but, as you value many hours of peace, never suffer more than one even to approach the hallowed circle. Nothing should shake the truly great spirit which is not sufficiently mighty to destroy it.

Peacock calls. I take some interest in this man, but no possible conduct of his would disturb my tranquillity. Hear that Eliza and Helen[40] go to Norfolk in three weeks. Converse with Jane; her mind unsettled; her character unformed; occasion of hope from some instances of softness and feeling; she is not entirely insensible to concessions; new proofs that the most exalted philosophy, the truest virtue, consists in an habitual contempt of self; a subduing of all angry feelings; a sacrifice of pride and selfishness. When you attempt benefit to either an individual or a community, abstain from imputing it as an error that they despise or overlook your virtue.

These are incidental reflections which arise only indirectly from the circumstances recorded. Walk with Peacock to the pond; talk of Marian and Greek metre. Peacock dines. In the evening read Cicero and the "Paradoxa." Night comes; Jane walks in her sleep, and groans horribly, listen for two hours; at length bring her to Mary. Begin "Julius," and finish the little volume of Cicero. The next morning the chimney-board in Jane's room is found to have walked leisurely into the middle of the

38 *Hamlet,* with Edmund Kean, at the Drury Lane Theatre.

39 S&M, "security." Corrected by A. H. Koszul from the MS journal (*La Jeunesse de Shelley,* 237, n. 4).

40 Shelley's sisters.

41 S&M, "sat"; corrected by Dowden (I, 483) from the original MS.

room, accompanied by the pillow, who, being very sleepy, tried to get into bed again, but fell[41] down on his back.[42]

Saturday, Oct. 15.—[*Mary*]—After breakfast read "Political Justice." Shelley goes with Peacock to Ballachy's. A disappointment; it is put off till Monday. They then go to Homerton. Finish [Godwin's] "St. Leon." Jane writes to Marshall. A letter from my Father. Talking; Jane and I walk out. Shelley and Peacock return at 6. Shelley advises Jane not to go. Jane's letter to my Father. A refusal. Talk about going away, and, as usual, settle nothing.

Sunday, Oct. 16.—Peacock calls. Talk of various plans. Hookham calls. P. and H. walk out together. When P. returns, Shelley, M. J. C.,[43] and I walk out round by Kentish Town; after dinner, talk.

Monday, Oct. 17.—Go to Peacock's in the morning and stay there all day. Shelley goes to Ballachy's, but does not succeed. Read "Political Justice." In the evening Hookham calls; talk all the evening. Letter from Hogg. Few friendly spirits in the world.

Tuesday, Oct. 18.—Read "Political Justice." Shelley goes with Peacock to the lawyer's, but, as usual, does not succeed. Jane and I go to Pancras; on our return we find that Shelley had returned and gone after us; he returns; he and I talk upstairs by ourselves. In the evening we return to Pancras. I go to bed soon, but Shelley and Jane sit up, and, for a wonder, do not frighten themselves.

Wednesday, Oct. 19.—Finish "Political Justice"; read "Caleb Williams." Shelley goes to the City, and meets with a total failure. Send to Hookham. Shelley reads a part of [Milton's] "Comus" aloud; he goes to sleep early; we go to bed about 11. Get an Italian translation of Plutarch.

Thursday, Oct. 20.—Shelley goes to the City. Finish "Caleb Williams"; read to Jane. Peacock calls; he has called on my Father, who will not speak about Shelley to any one but an attorney. Oh! philosophy!

We hear that Harriet has left her father's house. Hookham calls at breakfast time; that man comes strictly under the appellation of a "prig." In the evening read Memoirs of Voltaire. Shelley goes to sleep early; go to bed about 10.

Friday, Oct. 21.—Read [Voltaire's] "Zadig." Shelley goes to Tahourdin's;[44] returns with Peacock; call on Finnis. Read "Life of Alfieri" [by himself].

Saturday, Oct. 22.—Finish the "Life of Alfieri." Go to the tomb and read the "Essay on Sepulchres" [by Godwin] there. Shelley is out all

42 For Claire's diary for this day, see Dowden, I, 484.

43 S&M, "M.,J.,C." [Mary Jane Clairmont].

44 A lawyer.

the morning at the lawyer's, but nothing is done. Read Voltaire's Tales; take a little walk. Starling[45] calls; he receives a bill for a month. In the evening a letter from Fanny, warning us of the Hookhams.[46] Jane and Shelley go after her; they find her, but Fanny runs away. Read "Louvet's Memoirs." Peacock calls in the morning.

Sunday, OCT. 23.—Go to Skinner Street. Jane receives information from Fanny. Call at Peacock's; breakfast there. Shelley and Peacock go to Hookham's; he is out. Call at Tahourdin's. Jane and I return to Pancras; Shelley returns. He writes to Harriet[47] and Godwin; I write to Isabel. Talk of plans. Peacock dines. Jane goes to Harriet; she returns. We send a porter. At 9 Shelley goes. Answer from Harriet.

Monday, OCT. 24.—Read aloud to Jane. At 11 go out to meet Shelley. Walk up and down Fleet Street; call at Peacock's; return to Fleet Street; call again at Peacock's; return to Pancras; remain an hour or two. People call; I suppose bailiffs. Return to Peacock's. Call at the coffeehouse; see Shelley; he has been to Ballachy's. Good hopes; to be decided Thursday morning. Return to Peacock's; dine there; get money. Return home in a coach; go to bed soon, tired to death.[48]

Tuesday, OCT. 25.—Write to Shelley.[49] Jane goes to Fanny. Read "Elements of Morality."[50] Grow alarmed. Send to Marshall. Hear that Jane is coming home; she returns; they want her to go into a family; learn the account of Fanny in Wales, and that Charles knew of the treachery of the Hookhams, and did not tell Jane when she asked him; this is very bad. Hear of Patrickson killing himself—Flather is the true assassin. This is another of those cold-blooded murders that, like Maria Schooning, we may put down to the world.

Call at Peacock's; go to the hotel; Shelley is not there. Go back to Peacock's. Peacock goes to Shelley. Meet Shelley in Holborn. Walk up and down Bartlett's Buildings. Shelley is much shocked at hearing of Patrickson's death. Come with him to Peacock's; talk with him till 10; return to Pancras without him. Jane in the dumps all evening about going away.

Wednesday, OCT. 26.—A visit from Shelley's old friends [the bailiffs];

[45] A moneylender.

[46] The troubled days of October 22–November 9, during most of which Shelley was separated from Mary because of the danger of arrest on account of debts owing to Chartres, are related in detail by Dowden, I, 490–505; also see White, I, 377–83. The trouble began with Fanny's letter of warning.

[47] Shelley to Harriet, [?August 23, 1814] (Julian edition, VII, 306–307).

[48] Claire's lengthy account of this day is printed by Dowden (I, 492–93 n.).

[49] Mary to Shelley, [October 25, 1814] (*Letters,* I, 3–4).

[50] *Elements of Morality for the Use of Children, translated from the German of C. G. Salzmann* [by Mary Wollstonecraft] (1790, 2 vols.).

they go away much disappointed, and very angry. Go to St. Paul's. Meet Shelley; spend the morning with him. He has written to T. H[ookham] to ask him to be bail. Return to Pancras about 4. Read all the evening.

Thursday, Oct. 27.—Write to Fanny all morning. We had received letters from Skinner Street in the morning. Fanny's very doleful, and C[harles] C[lairmont] contradicts in one line what he had said in the line before. After 2, go to St. Paul's; meet Shelley; go with him in a coach to Hookham's; H. is out; return; leave him and proceed to Pancras. He has not received a definitive answer from Ballachy; meets a money lender, of whom I have some hopes. Read aloud to Jane in the evening; Jane goes to sleep. Write to Shelley.[51] A letter comes inclosing a letter from Hookham consenting to justify bail. Harriet has been to work there against my Father.[52]

Friday, Oct. 28.—Walk out; read; go to Shelley; he has written to Hookham concerning my Father. Letter from Sir J[ohn] Shelley asking particulars. Go home to Pancras about 4. At 6 a letter comes from Mrs. Godwin; she is a woman I shudder to think of. My poor Father! if——but it will not do. Read I don't know what. Write to my love.[53]

Saturday, Oct. 29.—Read; go to Shelley; walk with him for an hour and a half; come home; talk with Jane. Shelley is not well. In the evening sleep from 9 till 12. Shelley comes at half-past 12.

Sunday, Oct. 30.—Rise late; talk with Shelley all day.[54] Hookham calls; advises Shelley not to return to the London Coffee House. This man has repented him of his wicked deeds. In the evening Shelley and I go to an inn [the Cross Keys] in St. John Street to sleep. Those that love cannot separate; Shelley could not have gone away without me again.

Monday, Oct. 31.—After breakfast Shelley goes to Ballachy, who makes a rascally proposition for 300*l.* a year till his father's death for 15,000*l.* of *post obit;* referred for further deliberation. Meet the Farmer; he asks for a settlement. I read Carnot's "Mémoire";[55] he is a commonplace man. Shelley returns; talk with him. At dinner time Jane comes in; she dines with us. I wrote to her in the morning, and Shelley in the afternoon. Shelley writes also to the Sussex man who made a proposal. In the evening very tired; sleep.

Tuesday, Nov. 1.—Learn Greek all morning. Shelley goes to the

[51] Mary to Shelley, [October 27, 1814] (*Letters,* I, 4).

[52] For Harriet's activities against Godwin, mentioned several times in the journal, see White, I, 376.

[53] Mary to Shelley, [October 28, 1814] (*Letters,* I, 4–5).

[54] Shelley remained at home with Mary on Sunday, when bailiffs had no power to arrest him.

[55] S&M, "Memorial"; probably an error for Lazare N. M. Carnot, *Mémoire adressé au Roi en Juillet 1814* (Paris, Plancher, 1814), a widely-read pamphlet.

'Change. Jane calls. People want their money [at the Cross Keys Inn]; won't send up dinner, and we are all very hungry. Jane goes to Hookham. Shelley and I talk about her character. Jane returns without money. Writes to Fanny about coming to see her; she can't come. Writes to Charles. Goes to Peacock to send him to us with some eatables; he is out. Charles promises to see her. She returns to Pancras; he goes there, and tells the dismal state of the Skinner Street affairs. Shelley goes to Peacock's; comes home with cakes. Wait till T. Hookham sends money to pay the bill. Shelley returns to Pancras. Have tea, and go to bed. Shelley goes to Peacock's to sleep.

Wednesday, Nov. 2.—A letter from Shelley.[56] Go to Holborn with Jane; return gloomy. Write a long letter to Shelley. A good night to my love.

Thursday, Nov. 3.—Work; write to Shelley; read Greek grammar. Receive a letter from Mr. [David] Booth;[57] so all my hopes are over there. Ah! Isabel; I did not think you would act thus. Read and work in the evening. Receive a letter from Shelley.[58] Write to him.[59]

Friday, Nov. 4.—Read in the morning and work; read Greek grammar. Go out to meet Shelley; walk with him for an hour. Return to Pancras and work.

Saturday, Nov. 5.—Work all morning; read a little Greek grammar; work in the evening. Call at Peacock's lodgings to see Shelley; he has settled Lambert,[60] and meets Charles Clairmont; he tells him about it. They were going to sell off part of their stock at 41, to meet L.'s demand. Hear of Charles Clairmont's going to the West Indies; this is a very dangerous voyage, for I think it will not agree with his health. Return to Pancras without Shelley; he arrives at half-past 12.

Sunday, Nov. 6.—Talk to Shelley. He writes a great heap of letters. Read part of "St. Leon." Talk with him all evening; this is a day devoted to Love in idleness. Go to sleep early in the evening. Shelley goes away a little before 10.

Monday, Nov. 7.—Work all the morning. Go to Shelley at 3; return at 5. Work and read in the evening; go to bed at 10.

Tuesday, Nov. 8.—Write to Izy [Isabel], and work all morning. Go to Shelley in the evening; it rains, thunders, and lightens; stay with him about two hours; return to Pancras in a coach. Talk with Clara all evening. Go to bed at 10; hushed to sleep by the Blacksmith's little son (who

56 Shelley to Mary, [? November 1, 1814] (Julian edition, IX, 104).

57 Fiancé of Mary's friend Isabel Baxter.

58 Shelley to Mary, [November 2, 1814] (Julian edition, IX, 105).

59 Mary to Shelley, [November 3, 1814] (*Letters*, I, 5–6).

60 Godwin's creditor.

has a party, because it is his birthday) drumming on a tin kettle. Shelley has met [Charles] Clairmont, who gives him news about Hogan.[61] Hogg drank tea at Peacock's the night before; very witty, but, Shelley says, cold.

Wednesday, Nov. 9.—Pack up all morning; leave Pancras about 3; call at Peacock's for Shelley; Charles Clairmont has been there for 8*l.* Go to Nelson Square. Jane gloomy; she is very sullen with Shelley. Well, never mind, my love—we are happy.

Thursday, Nov. 10.—Jane is not well, and does not speak the whole day. We send to Peacock's, but no good news arrives. Lambert has called there, and says he will write. Read a little of Petronius, a most detestable book. Shelley is out all the morning. In the evening read "Louvet's Memoirs." Go to bed early. Shelley and Jane sit up till 12, talking; Shelley talks her into a good humour.

Friday, Nov. 11.—Read "Louvet's Memoirs" all day. Shelley is out all the morning. In the evening a letter comes from Hookham wanting 24*l.* Shelley goes to him. Read "Louvet's Memoirs."

Saturday, Nov. 12.—Finish "Louvet's Memoirs." Shelley writes. Begin the "Life of Louvet," to write it. Write and talk in the evening.

Sunday, Nov. 13.—Write in the morning. Very unwell all day. Fanny sends a letter to Jane to come to Blackfriars Road; Jane cannot go. Fanny comes here; she will not see me; hear everything she says, however. They think my letter cold and *indelicate!* God bless them. Papa tells Fanny if she sees me he will never speak to her again; a blessed degree of liberty this! He has had a very impertinent letter from Christy Baxter. The reason she comes is to ask Jane to Skinner Street to see Mrs. Godwin, who they say is dying. Jane has no clothes. Fanny goes back to Skinner Street to get some. She returns; Jane goes with her. Shelley returns (he had been to Hookham's); he disapproves. Write and read. In the evening talk with my love about a great many things. We receive a letter from Jane saying she is very happy, and she does not know when she will return. [Thomas] Turner[62] has called at Skinner Street, but he says it is too far to come to Nelson Square. Very unwell in the evening.

Monday, Nov. 14.—[*Shelley*]—Mary is unwell. Receive a note from Hogg; cloth from Clara. I wish this girl had a resolute mind. Without firmness, understanding is impotent, and the truest principles unintelligible. Charles calls to confer concerning Lambert; walk with him. Go to 'Change, to Peacock's, to Lambert's; receive 30*l.* In the evening Hogg calls;[63] perhaps he still may be my friend, in spite of the radical differences of sympathy between us; he was pleased with Mary; this was the

[61] Godwin's creditor.

[62] Godwin's friend and husband of Cornelia Boinville (see White, I, 429, 706).

[63] This is Hogg's first appearance in Mary's house.

test by which I had previously determined to judge his character. We converse on many interesting subjects, and Mary's illness disappears for a time.

Thursday, Nov. 15.—[*Shelley*]—Disgusting dreams have occupied the night.

[*Mary*]—Very unwell. Jane calls; converse with her. She goes to Skinner Street; tells Papa that she will not return; comes back to Nelson Square with Shelley; calls at Peacock's. Shelley read[s] aloud to us in the evening out of "Adolphus' Lives."

Wednesday, Nov. 16.—Very ill all day. Shelley and Jane out all day shopping about the town. Shelley reads [C. B. Brown's] "Edgar Huntley" to us. Shelley and Jane go to Hookham's. Hogg comes in the meantime; he stays all the evening. Shelley writes his critique[64] till half-past 3.

Thursday, Nov. 17.—As ill as need be. Shelley writes his critique, and then reads "Edgar Huntley" all day. Go to bed early.

Friday, Nov. 18.—Read "Edgar Huntley" all morning and finish it. Very ill indeed. A great deal of talking, as usual.

Saturday, Nov. 19.—Very ill. Shelley and Jane go out to call at Mrs. Knapp's;[65] she receives Jane kindly; promises to come and see me. I go to bed early. Charles Clairmont calls in the evening, but I do not see him.

Sunday, Nov. 20.—Still very ill; get up very late. In the evening Shelley reads aloud out of [Stewarton's] the "Female Revolutionary Plutarch." Hogg comes in the evening; gives us a laughable account of Dr. Lamb and Mrs. Newton.[66] Get into an argument about virtue, in which Hogg makes a sad bungle—quite muddled on the point, I perceive.

Monday, Nov. 21.—Rose very late. Read in the "Female Revolutionary Plutarch." In the evening talk. Charles Clairmont comes, and stays with us till 10; he tells us no particular news. The good people of Skinner Street are now tolerably indifferent about Jane.

Tuesday, Nov. 22.—[*Shelley*]—Turner comes in the morning; he goes to France; talks concerning Jane in a manner which is afterwards explained. Shelley goes to Lambert's place; proposes a *post obit* for Godwin's debt; comes home. Jane goes out with Shelley to buy dresses. In the evening Charles Clairmont calls; he tells us that Turner told Godwin we should send Jane back in four days; talks some inconceivable nonsense, but seems on the whole friendly and kind.

64 Of Hogg's *Alexy Haimatoff,* published anonymously in the *Critical Review* for December, 1814. See entry for Jan. 3, 1815.

65 In whose home it was proposed that Claire should live. See Claire's letter of May 28, 1815, to Fanny Godwin (Dowden, I, 519).

66 Dr. William Lambe and Mrs. John Frank Newton, vegetarians.

PERCY BYSSHE SHELLEY

From a pencil sketch by E. E. Williams
November 27, 1821

Courtesy of Mrs. George A. Plimpton

Wednesday, Nov. 23.—[*Shelley*]—Mary walked. Jane went to the Minerva Library. Mary quite recovered. Read. Sit up late.

Thursday, Nov. 24.—[*Shelley*]—Clara very ill; send for Dr. Currie. Clara's illness, an inflammation of the liver. Shelley reads to Mary [Wieland's] "Peregrine Proteus." Bleed Clara in the evening; slight spasm in the side. Hogg comes.

Friday, Nov. 25.—[*Shelley*]—Dr. Currie recommends leeches; they succeed, and Clara is better. Read "Persian"[67] and "Peregrine"; "Peregrine" an exceedingly profound irony against Christ.

Saturday, Nov. 26.—[*Mary*]—Work all day. Shelley finishes "Peregrine." We walk out to Pike's; he is not at home. Work in the evening. Shelley reads [Paine's] "Rights of Man." Clara in an ill humour. She reads "The Italian" [by Ann Radcliffe]. Shelley sits up and talks her into reason.

Sunday, Nov. 27.—Read "The Italian," and talk all day—a very happy day indeed. Hogg comes in the evening; he is sadly perverted, and I begin to lose hopes; his opinion of honour and respect for established customs condemn him in the courts of philosophy.

Monday, Nov. 28.—Finish "The Italian." Walk a little way with Shelley; he goes to Tahourdin's[68] and other lawyers' holes. I return, and work all the evening. A refusal comes from Sir John Shelley. Shelley very tired. Jane reads some of "Adolphus' Lives" aloud.

Tuesday, Nov. 29.—Work all day. Shelley reads the "Fairy Queen" aloud. He goes to Parker's with Clara. In the evening Hogg comes. We have an argument upon the Love of Wisdom, and Free Will and Necessity; he quite wrong, but quite puzzled; his arguments are very weak.

Wednesday, Nov. 30.—Work all day. Heigh-ho! Clara and Shelley go before breakfast to Parker's. After breakfast Shelley is as badly off as I am with my work, for he is out all day with those detested lawyers. In the evening Shelley and Jane go in search of Charles Clairmont; they cannot find him. Read [C. B. Brown's] "Philip Stanley"; very stupid.

Thursday, Dec. 1.—Finish "Philip Stanley." Expect Marianne de St. Croix;[69] she does not come—*grace au Dieu.* Work. Shelley and Clara go in search of Charles Clairmont; they return with him. Hogg comes. Shelley and Clara walk home with Charles Clairmont. Talk about heaps of things, but do not argue tonight.

Friday, Dec. 2.—Work all morning. Jane reads aloud. Shelley out among the bad all morning. Books come from Hookham. Shelley reads

67 Not further identified.

68 Shelley's lawyer.

69 See note to Jan. 2, 1815, entry.

"Prud'homme" aloud to us, and Spencer[*sic*]. Go to bed early. Tahourdin calls.

Saturday, DEC. 3.—Unwell; take medicine; lie down. Read some of Miss [Joanna] Bailley's plays. Tahourdin calls in the evening. Shelley reads "Moore's Journal" aloud.

Sunday, DEC. 4.—Read "Moore's Journal" all day. Shelley reads Diogenes Laertius. Walk about dusk a few times round the Square. Hogg comes in the evening. I like him better to-night than before, but still I fear he is *un enfant perdu.*

Monday, DEC. 5.—Very unwell. Shelley and Clara go out all day to heaps of people. Very unwell indeed! Work. Rather better in the evening. Read [Wieland's] "Agathon," part of which I like, but it is not so good as "Peregrine."

Tuesday, DEC. 6.—Very unwell. Shelley and Clara walk out, as usual, to heaps of places. Read "Agathon," which I do not like so well as "Peregrine." Shelley reads "Moore's Journal." In the evening an affecting or affected letter from Miss Marianne de St. Croix. A letter from Hookham, to say that Harriet has been brought to bed of a son and heir [on November 30]. Shelley writes a number of circular letters of this event, which ought to be ushered in with ringing of bells, &c., for it is the son of his *wife.* Hogg comes in the evening; I like him better, though he vexed me by his attachment to sporting. A letter from Harriet confirming the news, in a letter from a *deserted wife!!* and telling us he has been born a week.

Wednesday, DEC. 7.—Clara and Shelley go out together; Shelley calls on the lawyers and on Harriet, who treats him with insulting selfishness; they return home wet and very tired. Read "Agathon"; I like it less today; he discovers many opinions which I think detestable. Work. In the evening Charles Clairmont comes. Hear that Place[70] is trying to raise 1,200*l.* to pay Hume on Shelley's *post obit;* affairs very bad in Skinner Street—fear of a call for the rent; all very bad. Shelley walks home with Charles Clairmont; goes to Hookham's about the 100*l.* to lend my Father; Hookham out. He returns, very tired. Work in the evening.

Thursday, DEC. 8.—Shelley and Clara go to Hookham's; get the 90*l.* for my Father; they are out, as usual, all morning. Finish "Agathon"; I do not like it; Wieland displays some most detestable opinions; he is one of those men who alter all their opinions when they are about 40, and then think it will be the same with every one, and that they are themselves the only proper monitors of youth. Work. When Shelley and Clara return, Shelley goes to Lambert's; out. Work. In the evening Hogg

[70] Francis Place, Godwin's friend.

comes; talk about a great number of things; he is more sincere this evening than I have seen him before. Odd dreams.

Friday, DEC. 9.—Shelley goes to Lambert's. Read "Moore's Journal." Shelley writes to Marianne de St. Croix. Work. Charles Clairmont calls in the morning. In the evening work, and read "Moore's Journal." Charles Clairmont drinks tea with us. Shelley unwell.

Saturday, DEC. 10.—Talk about the Will. Read "Moore's Journal." Work. In the evening Shelley reads "Mungo Park's Travels" aloud.

Sunday, DEC. 11.—Read Drummond;[71] talk. After dinner walk with Shelley to Pike's; read the newspaper. Clara's whim. Read [Thomas] Pennant's "View of Hindostan."[72] Hogg comes; talk of law; of the different intercourse of sexes, &c. Charles Clairmont calls; I do not see him.

Monday, DEC. 12.—Talk with Shelley; he and Clara go to Longdill's. Read Drummond, p. 28; read [Barrow's] "Embassy to China." In the evening work. Shelley reads "Mungo Park's Travels." He goes to sleep at half-past 7. Jane reads Mirabeau's Life out of "Adolphus."

Tuesday, DEC. 13.—Call at Pike's with Shelley; return home alone. Shelley goes to Tahourdin's; out. Read "Embassy to China"; finish it in the evening. Read "Mungo Park's Travels."

Wednesday, DEC. 14.—Read and finish "Mungo Park's Travels"; they are very interesting, and if the man were not so prejudiced, they would be a thousand times more so; but those institutions must always have Christians. Walk out with Shelley; he reads Suetonius all day. Dine early; after dinner Clara and Shelley go to Tahourdin's. Very weak and unwell. In the evening read Milton's "Letter on Education." Hogg comes; no argument, and not an interesting conversation; but he gives a funny account of Shelley's Father, particularly of his vision and the matrimonial morning; conversation annexed thereunto.

Thursday, DEC. 15.—Shelley finishes Suetonius. Very unwell indeed all day. Shelley and Clara go to Peacock's. Unwell; my eyes ache. Read [C. B. Brown's] "Jane Talbot"; very stupid book; some letters so-so; but the old woman in it is so abominable, the young woman so weak, and the young man (the only sensible one in the whole) the author of course contrives to bring to idiotcy at the end.

Friday, DEC. 16.—Still ill; heigh-ho! Finish "Jane Talbot." [Joseph] Hume[73] calls at half-past 12; he tells us of the great distresses at Skinner Street; I do not see him. Hookham calls; hasty[74] little man; he does not

71 Doubtless Sir William Drummond's *Academical Questions* (1805), which Shelley had read earlier in the year.

72 *The View of Hindoostan, Western and Eastern, of India extra Gangem, China and Japan, of the Malayan Islands, New Holland, and the Spicy Islands* (1798–1800, 4 vols.).

73 Godwin's creditor.

74 Doubtless a misreading of "nasty."

stay long. In the evening Hogg comes. Shelley and Clara are at first out; they have been to look for Charles Clairmont; they find him, and walk with him some time up and down Ely Place. Shelley goes to sleep early; very tired. We talk about flowers and trees in the evening—a country conversation.

Saturday, DEC. 17.—Very ill. Shelley[75] and Clara go to Pike's; when they return, Shelley goes to walk around Square. Talk with Shelley. In the evening he sleeps, and I lie down on the bed. Jane goes to Pike's at 9. Charles Clairmont comes, and talks about several things. Mrs. Godwin did not allow Fanny to come down to dinner on her receiving a lock of my hair. Fanny, of course, behaves slavishly on the occasion. He goes at half-past 11. Go to bed at 12. Odd dream about Hogg.

Sunday, DEC. 18.—Better, but far from well. Pass a very happy morning with Shelley. Charles Clairmont comes at dinner time, the Skinner Street folks having gone to dine at the Kennie's.[76] Jane and he take a long walk together. Shelley and I are left alone. Hogg comes after Clara and her brother return. Charles Clairmont flies from the field on his approach. Conversation as usual. Get worse towards night.

Monday, DEC. 19.—[*Shelley*]—Mary rather better this morning. Jane goes to Hume's about Godwin's bills; learn that Lambert is inclined, but hesitates. Hear of a woman—supposed to be the daughter of the Duke of Montrose—who has the head of a hog. Suetonius is finished; and Shelley begins the "Historia Augustana" [by Blackwell]. Charles Clairmont comes in the evening; a discussion concerning female character. Clara imagines that I treat her unkindly. Mary consoles her with her all-powerful benevolence. I rise (having already gone to bed), and speak with Clara; she was very unhappy; I leave her tranquil.

Tuesday, DEC. 20.—[*Mary*]—Shelley goes to Pike's; take a short walk with him first. Unwell. A letter from Harriet, who threatens Shelley with her lawyer. In the evening read [Lessing's] "Emilia Galotti." Hogg comes. Converse of various things. He goes at 12.

Wednesday, DEC. 21.—[*Shelley*]—Mary is better. Shelley goes to Pike's, to the Insurance Offices, and the lawyer's; an agreement entered into for 3,000*l.* for 1,000*l.* A letter from Wales, offering *post obit.* Shelley goes to Hume's. Mary reads Miss Baillie's plays in the evening. Shelley goes to bed at 8, Mary at 11.

Thursday, DEC. 22.—[*Shelley*]—Mary wakes early. Delightful talk. Shelley and Clara go to Pike's; to the Insurance Offices. Meet Lambert, who brings [Maimbourg's] "History of Arianism." After dinner Shelley and Clara go to Lawrence's. In the evening Hogg comes. He describes

75 S&M, "Jane."

76 Probably James Kenney, the dramatist.

an apparition of a lady,[77] whom he had loved, appearing to him after her death; she came in the twilight summer night, and was hardly visible; she touched his cheek with her hands, and visited him many successive nights; he was always unaware of her approach, and passed many waking hours in expectation of it. Interesting conversation interrupted by Clara's childish superstition. Hogg departs at 12.

Friday, Dec. 23.—[*Shelley*]—Shelley reads Bryan Edward's "History of the West Indies." Mary reads "Ethwald,"[78] and eats oranges. In the evening Shelley reads aloud the "View of the French Revolution" [by Mary Wollstonecraft] for a short time. Hookham comes, and drinks tea with us. Read "View of the Revolution."

Saturday, Dec. 24.—[*Mary*]—Read "View of French Revolution." Walk out with Shelley, and spend a dreary morning waiting for him at Mr. Peacock's. In the evening Hogg comes. I like him better each time; it is a pity that he is a lawyer; he wasted so much time on that trash that might be spent on better things.

Sunday, Dec. 25.—Christmas Day. Have a very bad side ache in the morning, so I rise late. Charles Clairmont comes, and dines with us. In the afternoon read Miss Baillie's plays. Hogg spends the evening with us; conversation, as usual.

Monday, Dec. 26.—[*Shelley*]—The sweet Maie asleep; leave a note with her. Walk with Clara to Pike's, &c. Go to Hampstead, and look for a house; we return in a return chaise; find that Laurence has arrived, and consult for Mary; she has read Miss Bailie's plays all day. Mary better this evening. Shelley very much fatigued; sleeps all the evening. Read [Voltaire's] "Candide."

Tuesday, Dec. 27.—[*Mary*]—Not very well; Shelley very unwell. Read "De Montfort,"[79] and talk with Shelley in the evening. Read "View of the French Revolution." Hogg comes in the evening; talk of heaps of things. Shelley's odd dream.

Wednesday, Dec. 28.—Shelley and Clara out all the morning. Read "French Revolution" in the evening. Shelley and I go to Gray's Inn to get Hogg; he is not there; go to Arundel Street; can't find him. Go to Garnerin's Lecture on electricity, the gasses, and the phantasmagoria; return at half-past 9. Shelley goes to sleep. Read "View of French Revolution" till 12; go to bed.

Thursday, Dec. 29.—Charles Clairmont comes in the morning; do

[77] Mary relates this tale in an essay "On Ghosts," published in the *London Magazine* for March, 1824 (IX, 253–56; tale on pp. 254–55). (See notes for Aug. 18, 1816, and Oct. 20, 1818.)

[78] S&M, "Ethwah," almost certainly an error for *Ethwald,* a play by Joanna Baillie.

[79] A play by Joanna Baillie.

not see him. Shelley goes to auction. Read "View of the French Revolution." Hear Jane talk nonsense about Hogg. In the evening Shelley and Jane go to Garnerin's lecture. Finish "View of French Revolution." Read some of Kirke White's Letters; slavish beyond all measure. Begin "History of West Indies," by Bryan Edwards. Shelley and Jane return a little before 10; there was no lecture to-night.

Friday, Dec. 30.—Shelley and Jane go out as usual. Read Bryan Edwards' "Account of West Indies." They do not return till past 7, having been locked into Kensington Gardens; both very tired. Hogg spends the evening with us.

Saturday, Dec. 31.—[*Shelley*]—The poor Maie was very weak and tired all day. Shelley goes to Pike's and Hume's and Mrs. Peacock's;[80] returns very tired and sleeps all the evening. The Maie goes to sleep early. New Year's Eve.

List of Books read in 1814[81]

MARY

*(Those marked * Shelley has read also.)*

*Letters from Norway. [By Mary Wollstonecraft, 1796.]
*Mary. A Fiction. [By Mary Wollstonecraft, 1788.]
*Wordsworth's Excursion. [1814.]
*Madoc. By Southey. 2 vols. [1805.]
*Curse of Kehama. [By Robert Southey, 1810.]
*Sorcerer. A Novel. [By Veit Weber, tr. by Robert Huish, 1795.]
*Political Justice. 2 vols. [By William Godwin, 1793.]
*The Monk. By [M. G.] Lewis. 4 vols. [1796.]
*Thalaba. 2 vols. [By Robert Southey, 1801.]
*The Empire of the Nairs. [By James Henry Lawrence, 1811.]
*Queen Mab. [By Percy B. Shelley, 1813.]
*St. Godwin. [A parody on Godwin's St. Leon, by Edward Du Bois, 1800.]
*Wrongs of Women. 2 vols. [By Mary Wollstonecraft, 1798.]
Caleb Williams. 3 vols. [By William Godwin, 1794.]
*Zadig. [By Voltaire, 1747.]
*Life of Alfieri. By Himself. 2 vols.
*Essay on Sepulchres. [By William Godwin, 1809.]
*Louvet's Memoirs. [By Jean B. Louvet de Couvray, London, 1795.]

80 T. L. Peacock lived with his mother.

81 Miss Grylls notes (p. 273) that all the book lists "from 1814 to 1818" are in the first eight pages of Volume II of the MS journal (R. Glynn Grylls, *Mary Shelley, A Biography* [London, Oxford University Press, 1938]; hereafter referred to as Grylls).

Carnot's Memorial. [Error for Lazare N. M. Carnot, Mémoire au Roi, 1814.]
*Lives of the Revolutionists. By [John] Adolphus. 2 vols. [4 vols., 1799.]
*Edgar Huntley. 3 vols. [By Charles Brockden Brown, 1801.]
*Peregrine Proteus. 2 vols. [By Christoph M. Wieland, 1791; tr. by W. Tooke, 1796.]
*The Italian. 3 vols. [By Ann Radcliffe, 1797.]
*Prince Alexy Haimatoff. [By Thomas Jefferson Hogg, 1813.]
Philip Stanley. By [Charles Brockden] Brown.
Miss Bailly's Plays. [Joanna Baillie.]
*[Dr. John] Moore's Journal. [During a Residence in France, 2 vols., 1793–94.]
*Agathon. [By Christoph M. Wieland, 1766; tr. by John Richardson, 4 vols., 1773.]
*Mungo Park's Travels in Africa. 1st Part. [1799.]
*[Sir John] Barrow's Embassy to China. [2 vols., 1807.]
Milton's Letter to Mr. Hartlib. [Tractate of Education, 1644.]
Emilia Galotti. [By G. E. Lessing, 1772.]
*Bryan Edward's History of the W. Indies. [2 vols., 1793–94.]
*View of the French Revolution. By M[ary] W[ollstonecraft] G[odwin.] [1794.]
*Candide. [By Voltaire, 1759.]
*Kirke White. [Probably The Remains of Henry Kirke White, With an Account of his Life by Robert Southey. 2 vols., 1807.]

SHELLEY

Diogenes Laertius. [Lives of the Philosophers.]
Cicero: Colectanea.
Petronius. [Satyricon.]
Suetonius. [Lives of the Caesars.][82]

[82] The last two titles in S&M (*Barrow* and *Mungo Park*) are repetitions, and are omitted here, as they are by Dowden (I, 506).

1815

ENGLAND

Sunday, JAN. 1, 1815.—[*Shelley*]—Shelley and Mary talk in the morning. A note and present from Hogg to the own Maie [Mary].[1] Charles Clairmont comes. Jane and I walk to Hookham's, and Westminster Abbey, and Mrs. Peacock's. Hogg comes in the evening. Shelley goes to sleep.

Monday, JAN. 2.—[*Mary*]—Write an answer; read "Tales of the Castle."[2] Shelley and Jane out, as usual. Letter from Marianne [de St. Croix];[3] very affecting; wishing to see Shelley. Harriet sends her creditors here; nasty woman. Now we must change our lodgings. Read Bryan Edwards all evening.

Tuesday, JAN. 3rd.—[*Shelley*]—Creditors from Harriet. Shelley goes to Marianne; hears, to his great surprise, that a rich heiress has fallen in love with Peacock, and lives with him; she is very miserable; God knows why. Shelley is, on her account and that of Miss de St. Croix, who is miserable on her own account. Talk over Peacock's adventure; Shelley writes to him in the evening. A parcel comes from Hookham—the "Critical Review" [December, 1814], which has the [Shelley's] critique of [Hogg's] "Prince Alexander Haimatoff" in it.[4] Read Bryan Edwards. Hogg comes. A very pleasant evening.

Wednesday, JAN. 4.—[*Mary*]—Shelley and Jane go out. Letter from Marianne and Ryan.[5] Read Bryan Edwards all day. In the evening Shelley writes notes. Discussion whether Shelley shall go for Hogg, and whether Jane shall go with him. In the meantime Hogg comes; he stays the evening; make an appointment with him.

Thursday, JAN. 5.—Go to breakfast at Hogg's. Shelley leaves us there,

1 For an analysis of the affair between Hogg and Mary which began about this time, see White, I, 391–93, 400–402. Mary's letters are printed in Scott's *Harriet and Mary*, 46–65. See also Mary's *Letters*, I, 7 n.

2 By Madame de Genlis, translated by Thomas Holcroft (1785, 5 vols.).

3 Who was in love with Peacock. For Peacock's mysterious adventure here introduced, see Mary's *Letters*, I, 67–68; White, I, 387–88; and the Halliford edition of *The Works of T. L. Peacock* (ed. by H. F. B. Brett-Smith and C. E. Jones, London, Constable & Co., Ltd., 1924–34, 10 vols.), I, *xxxiii, lx–lxii*.

4 See entry for Nov. 16, 1814.

5 For the possible identity of Ryan, see a full discussion by White (I, 674–76).

and goes to Hume's. When he returns we go to Newman Street; see the statue of Theoclea; it is a divinity that raises your mind to all virtue and excellence; I never beheld anything half so wonderfully beautiful. Return home very ill. Expect Hogg in the evening, but he does not come. Too ill to read.

Friday, JAN. 6.—Walk to Mrs. Peacock's with Clara. Walk with Hogg to Theoclea; she is ten thousand times more beautiful to-day than ever; tear ourselves away. Return to Nelson Square; no one at home. Hogg stays a short time with me. Shelley had staid at home till 2 to see Ryan; he does not come. Goes out about business, and then with Clara to . In the evening Shelley and Clara go to Garnerin's. Write my journal; look over [Southey's] "Roderick." Very unwell. Hogg comes. Shelley and Clara return at 10. Conversation as usual. Shelley reads [Coleridge's] "Ode to France" aloud, and repeats the poem to "Tranquillity." Talk with Shelley afterwards for some time; at length go to sleep. Shelley goes and sits in the other room till 5; I then call him. Talk. Shelley goes to sleep; at 8 Shelley rises, and goes out.

Saturday, JAN. 7.—Shelley breakfasts with Hogg. Clara goes to meet him at Mrs. Peacock's. She sends Hogg here. Shelley and Clara go to several places, and then take a long walk in search of a house. Ryan calls, but I do not see him. See the death of Sir Bysshe [on January 6] in the papers. Hookham calls, and is very gracious. Hogg goes away at 3. Shelley and Clara do not return till near

[*One leaf torn out*][6]

[*Thursday*, JAN. 12.— . . .]—Letter from Peacock to say that he is in prison; the foolish man lived up to Charlotte's expectancies, who turns out to have nothing. Her behaviour is inexplicable. There is a terrible mystery in the affair. His debt is 40*l*. A letter also from Gray, who knows nothing about her. This is a funny man also. Write to Peacock, and send him 2*l*. Hogg dines with me, and spends the evening. Letter from Hookham.

Friday, JAN. 13.—A letter from Clara. While I am at breakfast Shelley and Clara arrive. The will has been opened, and Shelley is referred to Whitton.[7] His Father would not allow him to enter Field Place; he sits before the door, and reads "Comus." Dr. Blocksome comes out; tells him that his father is very angry with him. Sees my name in Milton. Shelley

[6] S&M reads "[*Here some leaves are cut out.*]." Correction from Grylls' MS notes (see preface). Shelley (with Claire) made a trip to Field Place to be present at the reading of Sir Bysshe's will. For Shelley's financial affairs resulting from his grandfather's death, see Dowden, I, 508–11; and White, I, 393–99.

[7] William Whitton, Sir Timothy Shelley's solicitor.

Sidney comes out; says that it is a most extraordinary will. Shelley returns to Slinfold. Shelley and Clara set out, and reach Kingston that night. Shelley goes to Whitton, who tells him that he is to have the income of 100,000*l.* after his Father's death, if he will entail his estate. Hogg dines, and spends the evening with us.

Saturday, JAN. 14.—Shelley and Clara out all day. Forget—

[*Here more is cut out.*]

[*Saturday,* JAN. 28.— . . .] comes. He sleeps here.[8] Clara and Shelley sit up until 2. Shelley very ill; reads Livy (p. 340).

Sunday, JAN. 29.[9]—[?*Shelley*]—Talk. Walk in Kensington Gardens with Clara. On our return find Clairmont.

Ἀυπασματα πολλα της Μαριης—γλυκερον νοημα διδουσι των οφθαλμων ἑαυτης ακτινες μοι νοσουντι. της Μαριης τεκνον αρχει ζην, και περιπατει κινιν προς μηνα.

[*Mary*]—In the evening Shelley, Clara, and Hogg sleep. Read Gibbon ['s History][10] (p. 292). Cannon calls, but we do not see him. Talk, and look over Cannon's papers; he is a very foolish man. Hogg goes at half-past 11. Shelley and Clara explain, as usual.

Monday, JAN. 30.—Work all day. Shelley reads Livy. Talk. In the evening Shelley reads [Milton's] "Paradise Regained" aloud, and then goes to sleep. Hogg comes at 9. Talk and work. Hogg sleeps here.

Tuesday, JAN. 31.—Shelley is out all day. Work, in the evening, Clara to sleep, as usual. Shelley reads Gibbon aloud to me. Hogg comes; he is not well, but will go home to sleep. Work. Hogg goes at half-past 11.

Wednesday, FEB. 1.—Read Gibbon (end of vol. 1). Shelley reads Livy in the evening. Work. Shelley and Clara sleep. Hogg comes, and sleeps here. Mrs. Hill calls.

Thursday, FEB. 2.—Hogg stays with us all day. Clara does not come down till 4. Talk. Another bill from Chartres. Send to [R.] Hayward's[11] and Charles Clairmont. Shelley explains with Clara. Talk with Hogg, and read Gibbon, but very little (30), in the evening. Work, and Shelley reads Gibbon's "Memoirs" aloud. Clara goes to sleep. Hogg goes at half-past 11.

Friday, FEB. 3.—Rise late. Letter from Charles Clairmont, with 5*l.* Shelley and Clara out all day. Whitton agrees to Shelley's terms. The lease has not been sold. Read Gibbon in the evening; talk. Clara goes to sleep, and Shelley reads Gibbon aloud to me (160). Weeks calls. Hogg

8 S&M, "We sleep here." Correction from Grylls's MS notes.

9 S&M, "Jan. 24."

10 Mary read Gibbon's *Decline and Fall* and Memoirs and Letters concurrently. The page numbers indicate her progress in the History.

11 Godwin's solicitor.

comes. Work. Shelley reads Gibbon's "Memoirs" aloud. Hogg goes at half-past 11.

Saturday, FEB. 4.—Read Gibbon. Shelley reads Livy. After dinner read. Hogg comes at 7. Not well; go to bed early, but read Gibbon in bed (416). Hogg sleeps here.

Sunday, FEB. 5.—Read Gibbon. Take a long walk in Kensington Gardens and the Park; meet Clairmont as we return, and hear that my Father wishes to see a copy of the codicil, because he thinks Shelley is acting rashly. All this is very odd and inconsistent; but I never quarrel with inconsistency; folks must change their minds. After dinner talk. Shelley finishes Gibbon's "Memoirs" aloud. Clara, Shelley, and Hogg sleep. Read Gibbon. Shelley writes to [P. W.] Longdill[12] and Clairmont. Hogg ill, but we cannot persuade him to stay; he goes at half-past 11. (500).

Monday, FEB. 6.—Read Gibbon all morning. Shelley reads Livy. Shelley writes and sends letters. After dinner read Gibbon (finish vol. 2). Hogg comes at 9. Work. He goes at half-past 11. Talk a little, and then go to bed.

Tuesday, FEB. 7.—[*Shelley*]—Mary reads Gibbon. Shelley reads Livy. Shelley goes with Clara to Mrs. Peacock's, and meets Clairmont, who delivers a message from Godwin—equivocal, but kind—he wishes to have a copy of the codicil. Pike's; Hayward's; Longdill's. Cannon the most miserable wretch alive—**καταριπτει υπνον ευδαιμονεστατον.**—He stays the evening, vulgar brute; it is disgusting to hear such a beast speak of philosophy, &c. Let refinement and benovelence convey these ideas. Alexy[13] stays. Talk with Clara at night of Greek, &c.

Wednesday, FEB. 8.—[*Mary*]—Ash Wednesday. So Hogg stays all day. We are to move to-day, so Shelley and Clara go out to look for lodgings. Hogg and Jane pack, and then talk. Shelley and Clara do not return till 3; they have not succeeded; go out again; they get apartments at [41] Hans Place; move. In the evening talk, and read Gibbon. Letters. Pike calls; insolent plague. Hogg goes at half-past 11.

Thursday, FEB. 9.—Prate with Shelley all day. After dinner talk; put the things away. Finish Gibbon's Letters; read his History (173). Shelley and Clara sleep, as usual. Hogg does not come till 10. Work and talk. Shelley writes letters. Go to bed. A mess . . .

[*Here a leaf is torn out.*]

[*Monday,* FEB. 13.—(*Shelley*) . . .]—and, after a conversation of uncommon wit and genius, Erasmus exclaimed, "Aut Morus aut diabolus."

[12] Shelley's solicitor.

[13] Hogg; often so called because he was the author of *Alexy Haimatoff.*

More replied, "Aut Erasmus aut nemo." This interview was the foundation of a long and firm friendship.—Euripides, 9th edition; Æschylus; Sophocles. News from Italy of a conspiracy against Austria. Rose calls. Talk with Clara; walk with her. In the evening read Livy, p. 385, 2nd vol., half; 1,200 pages in seventeen days. Desultory reading. Sleep in the evening. Walk with Clara before dinner. Alexy comes at 9. Talk of Greek and French Tragedy. At night read Livy, pp. 385–450. "Seneca."

Tuesday, FEB. 14.—[*Mary*]—The Maie,[14] 3rd vol. of Gibbon, 607—Virgil's "Georgics."

[*Shelley*]—Shelley goes to Longdill's and Hayward's, and returns feverish and fatigued. Maie finishes the 3rd vol. of Gibbon. All unwell in the evening. Hogg comes, and puts us to bed. Hogg goes at half-past 11.

Wednesday, FEB. 15.—[*Shelley*]—Shelley remains at home; reads Livy. Maie reads very little of Gibbon. We read, and are delighted with, "Lara," the finest of Lord Byron's poems. Shelley reads "Lara" aloud in the evening. Hogg comes, and sleeps. Shelley and Maie still unwell.

Thursday, FEB. 16.—[*Shelley*]—Livy, p. 532, "Cumis (a deo minimis etiam rebus prava religio inserit Deus) mures in æde Jovis aurum rosisse," p. 556, 2nd vol. Maie says, that if we had met the Emperor Julian in private life, he would have appeared a very ordinary man. The Fables of Æsop in Greek.

Friday, FEB. 17.—Clara very unwell. Net[15] in the morning.

[*Here a good deal* (*is*) *torn out.*]

[*Wednesday,* FEB. 22.—(*Shelley*) . . .] [Mary] is in labour, and, after a few additional pains, she is delivered of a female child; five minutes afterwards Dr. Clarke comes; all is well. Maie perfectly well, and at ease. The child is not quite seven months; the child not expected to live. Shelley sits up with Maie; much agitated and exhausted. Hogg sleeps here.

Thursday, FEB. 23.—[*Shelley*]—Mary quite well; the child, unexpectedly, alive, but still not expected to live. Hogg returns in the evening at half-past 7. Shelley writes to Fanny, requesting her to come to see Maie. Fanny comes, and remains the whole night, the Godwins being absent from home. Charles comes at 11, with linen from Mrs. Godwin. Hogg departs at 11. 30*l.* from Longdill.

Friday, FEB. 24.—[*Shelley*]—Maie still well; favourable symptoms in the child; we may indulge some hopes. Hogg calls at 2. Fanny departs. Dr. Clarke calls; confirms our hopes of the child. Shelley very unwell.

14 S&M reads "(The Maie, Mary.)—3rd. vol. of Gibbon . . . . Tuesday, Feb. 14.—[*Shelley*]—Shelley goes to . . . ." Correction from Grylls's MS notes.

15 S&M, "Wet." Corrected from Grylls's MS notes.

Shelley finishes 2nd vol. of Livy, p. 657. Hogg comes in the evening. Shelley unwell and exhausted.

Saturday, FEB. 25.—[*Shelley*]—The child very well; Maie very well also; drawing milk all day. Shelley is very unwell. In the evening Hogg comes; he is sleepy, and goes away soon. Shelley is very unwell.

Sunday, FEB. 26.—[*Mary*]—Maie rises to-day. Hogg comes; talk; she goes to bed at 6. Hogg calls at the lodgings we have taken. Read [Madame de Staël's] "Corinne" (42). Shelley and Clara go to sleep. Hogg returns; talk with him till half-past 11. He goes. Shelley and Clara go down to tea. Just settling to sleep when a knock comes to the door; it is Fanny; she came to see how we were; she stays talking till half-past 3, and then leaves the room, that Shelley and Mary may sleep. Shelley has a spasm.

Monday, FEB. 27.—Rise; talk, and read "Corinne." Hogg comes in the evening. Shelley and Clara go out about a cradle. Shelley[16] and Clara go to sleep. Talk with Hogg; he goes at half-past 11.

Tuesday, FEB. 28.—I come down stairs; talk, nurse the baby, read "Corinne," and work. Shelley goes to Dr. Pemberton about his health.

Wednesday, MAR. 1.—Nurse the baby, read "Corinne," and work. Shelley and Clara out all morning. In the evening Peacock comes. Talk about types, editions, and Greek letters all the evening. Hogg comes. They go away at half-past 11. Bonaparte invades France.

Thursday, MAR. 2.—A bustle of moving.[17] Read "Corinne." I and my baby go about 3. Shelley and Clara do not come till 6. Hogg comes in the evening.

Friday, MAR. 3.—Nurse my baby; talk, and read "Corinne." Hogg comes in the evening.

Saturday, MAR. 4.—Read, talk, and nurse. Shelley reads the "Life of Chaucer" [by Godwin]. Hogg comes in the evening, and sleeps.

Sunday, MAR. 5.—Shelley and Clara go to town. Hogg here all day. Read "Corinne," and nurse my baby. In the evening talk. Shelley finishes the "Life of Chaucer." Hogg goes at 11.

Monday, MAR. 6.—Find my baby dead. Send for Hogg. Talk. A miserable day. In the evening read "Fall of the Jesuits."[18] Hogg sleeps here.

Tuesday, MAR. 7.—Shelley and Clara go after breakfast to town. Write to Fanny. Hogg stays all day with us; talk with him, and read the "Fall of the Jesuits" and "Rinaldo Rinaldini."[19] Not in good spirits. Hogg goes at 11. A fuss. To bed at 3.

Wednesday, MAR. 8.—Finish "Rinaldini." Talk with Shelley. In very

16 S&M, "Jane."

17 Apparently to 13 Arabella Road, Pimlico, London.

18 Not further identified.

19 By V. Ulpius, translated from the German by I. Hinckley (1800, 3 vols.).

bad spirits, but get better; sleep a little in the day. In the evening net. Hogg comes; he goes at half-past 11. Clara has written for Fanny, but she does not come.

Thursday, MAR. 9.—Read and talk. Still think about my little baby—'tis hard, indeed, for a mother to lose a child. Hogg and Charles Clairmont come in the evening. Charles Clairmont goes at 11. Hogg stays all night. Read Fontenelle,[20] "Plurality of Worlds" [1686].

Friday, MAR. 10.—Hogg's holidays begin. Shelley, Hogg, and Clara go to town. Hogg comes back soon. Talk and net. Hogg now remains with us.[21] Put the room to rights.

Saturday, MAR. 11.—Very unwell. Hogg goes to town. Talk about Clara's going away; nothing settled; I fear it is hopeless. She will not go to Skinner Street; then our house is the only remaining place, I see plainly. What is to be done? Hogg returns. Talk, and Hogg reads the "Life of Goldoni"[22] aloud.

Sunday, MAR. 12.—Talk a great deal. Not well, but better. Very quiet all the morning, and happy, for Clara does not get up till 4. In the evening read Gibbon (p. 333.), 4th vol. Go to bed at 12.

Monday, MAR. 13.—Shelley and Clara go to town. Stay at home; net, and think of my little dead baby. This is foolish, I suppose; yet, whenever I am left alone to my own thoughts, and do not read to divert them, they always come back to the same point—that I was a mother, and am so no longer. Fanny comes, wet through; she dines, and stays the evening; talk about many things; she goes at half-past 9. Cut out my new gown.

Tuesday, MAR. 14.—Shelley calls on Dr. Pemberton. Net till breakfast. Shelley reads [Sir Thomas Browne's] "Religio Medici" aloud after Hogg has gone to town. Work; finish Hogg's purse. Shelley and I go up stairs and talk of Clara's going; the prospect appears to me more dismal than ever; not the least hope. This is, indeed, hard to bear. In the evening Hogg reads Gibbon to me (p. 393). Charles Clairmont comes in the evening.

Wednesday, MAR. 15.—[*Shelley*]—Shelley has read the "Life of Chaucer," Ockley's "History of the Saracens," Madame de Stael "Sur la littérature," and 113 pages of the 3rd vol. of Livy.

[*Mary*]—Shelley, Clara, and Hogg go to town. Work. In the evening work and talk.

Thursday, MAR. 16.—Work all day. Shelley reads Gibbon to me; walk

20 Bernard le Bovier, Sieur de Fontenelle.

21 Hogg lived with the Shelleys throughout his holidays—until April 17, when he went "to the Courts."

22 Probably *Memoirs* by himself (Paris, 1787).

with Shelley before dinner. In the evening work; finish my gown, and then read Gibbon (p. 518).

Friday, MAR. 17.—Talk in the morning, and read the paper. Go out at 12 to see Lucien Bonaparte's pictures; they are all old masters, and some very beautiful. I liked the Magdalen of La Greuze best; the Four Evangelists of Carlo Dolce. There were two beautiful Claudes and some fine horses by Wouvermans. Come home about 4. After dinner sleep a little, and read Gibbon (p. 553); work. Hogg goes home at half-past 11. To bed at 1.

Saturday, MAR. 18.—Walk out to Park, and get milk. Meet Hogg; come home to breakfast; work. Shelley and Clara go to Longdill's. Work. Hogg reads Gibbon to me. Go to Bullock's Museum; see the birds; return at 4. Work, and Hogg reads Gibbon aloud; finish vol. 4. Shelley and Clara return at 6. After dinner, work, and play at chess; after tea, talk.

Sunday, MAR. 19.—Dream that my little baby came to life again; that it had only been cold, and that we rubbed it before the fire, and it lived. Awake and find no baby. I think about the little thing all day. Not in good spirits. Shelley is very unwell. Read Gibbon. Charles Clairmont comes. Hogg goes to town till dinner time. Talk with Charles Clairmont about Skinner Street. They are very badly off there. I am afraid nothing can be done to save them. Charles Clairmont says that he shall go to America; this I think a rather wild project in the Clairmont style. Play a game at chess with Clara. In the evening Shelley and Hogg play at chess. Shelley and Clara walk part of the way with Charles Clairmont. Play chess with Hogg, and then read Gibbon (p. 87, vol. 5).

Monday, MAR. 20.—Dream again about my baby. Work after breakfast, and then go with Shelley, Hogg, and Clara to Bullock's Museum; spend the morning there. Return, and find more letters for "A.Z."—one from a "Disconsolate Widow."[23] Read a little of Gibbon (p. 114). Shelley reads Livy; he has arrived at vol. 3, p. 307. Play at chess and work in the evening.

Tuesday, MAR. 21.—Talk, and then read Gibbon. Shelley reads Livy, and then reads Gibbon with me till dinner. After dinner play at chess and read. Peacock comes to tea. Work. After he goes away I read Gibbon (p. 275), and Shelley reads Livy (p. 406).

Wednesday, MAR. 22.—Talk, and read the papers. Read Gibbon all day (p. 368). Charles Clairmont calls about Shelley lending 100*l.* We do not return a decisive answer. After dinner read "Hermsprong";[24] look out of window, and play a game at chess; then go and see the wild beasts

[23] Dowden surmises (I, 518) that Claire had advertised "for a situation as a companion."

[24] Robert Bage, *Hermsprong; Or, Man As He Is Not* (1796, 3 vols.).

of Exeter Change. The lion is a very fine one, but unfortunately, sick. There is a very fine panther, who plays with a cannon-ball. The hyena is very frisky, running after its tail. The serval is a most beautiful animal, and they are all, but the lynx, wonderfully tame. Return, have tea, and play another game of chess with Shelley. Shelley reads three pages of Livy to-day.

Thursday, MAR. 23.—Read Gibbon (p. 405). Shelley reads Livy (p. 448). Walk with Shelley and Hogg to Arundel Street. Read "Le Diable Boiteux" [by Le Sage]. Hear that Bonaparte has entered Paris. As we come home meet my Father and Charles Clairmont. Go in to see the live serpent, &c.; there is among them a most curious monkey, a very pretty antelope, a cassowary, and two land tortoises. Charles Clairmont calls; he tells us that Papa saw us, and that he remarked that Shelley was so beautiful, it was a pity he was so wicked. In the evening we read "Le Diable Boiteux," and play at chess. Clara very unwell at night.

Friday, MAR. 24.—Good Friday.—Clara is unwell. Finish "Le Diable Boiteux." Read a little of Gibbon. Hogg goes to town; and Clara walks in the Park. After dinner play a game at chess with Shelley; then read Gibbon. Fanny comes at a little before 9; talk over the politics of Skinner Street and its allies. Walk to Charing Cross with Shelley, to put Fanny in a coach. Hogg comes to meet us. When we return Shelley plays a game of chess with Clara, and I read Gibbon (p. 463). Shelley reads Livy in the day (p. 554).

Saturday, MAR. 25.—Day of Our Lady, the Virgin Mother of God. Work. Shelley reads Livy. Walk to the Serpentine River, and sail paper boats. Shelley has a spasm as we come home. After dinner work, and play a game of chess with Hogg. Shelley plays at chess with Clara. Reads Livy (p. 673), and then goes to sleep.

[*Easter*] *Sunday,* MAR. 26.—Go to the Park, to meet Hogg, with Shelley. After breakfast read Gibbon (p. 582). Shelley reads Livy (p. 789). Charles Clairmont comes, and dines. After dinner play a game at chess with Charles Clairmont, and then walk with him; talk about Izy Baxter and the rest of the Scotch folks. Talk in evening. Shelley and Clara walk through the Park with Charles Clairmont. Talk, and then play at chess with Hogg.

Monday, MAR. 27.—[*Shelley*]—Easter Monday.—Maie finishes 5th vol. of Gibbon. Shelley and Hogg walk to Kensington Gardens; sail boats, and delight in the fine day. In the evening read. Shelley finishes Livy (p. 920, vol. 3) at half-past 12 at night. Maie works all the evening.

Tuesday, MAR. 28.—[*Mary*][25]—Work in the morning, and then walk out to look at house.

25 "[*Mary*]" not in S&M.

SHELLEY'S HOUSE AT BISHOPSGATE, 1815
From a photograph of a drawing by F. Clementson

[*Here a piece is torn out.*]

near 4. After dinner read Gibbon (p. 172), play a game at chess, and work after tea.

Wednesday, MAR. 29.—Read Gibbon all day. At 2 Shelley, Hogg, and Clara walk to the Serpentine. After dinner Clara is very unwell. Read Gibbon. Peacock drinks tea with us. Work. When Peacock

[*Here several leaves are torn out.*]

[*Thursday,* APR. 6.—. . .]—Read "Man as he is."[26] Hogg comes, and reads [Scott's] "Rokeby" to me. Peacock dines with us. In the evening work and talk.

Friday, APR. 7.—Breakfast with Hogg. Go to the British Museum; see all the fine things—ores, fossils, statues divine, &c. Return. Read "Rokeby"; dine. Go up stairs to talk with Shelley. Read and finish "Rokeby."

Saturday, APR. 8.—Peacock comes at breakfast time; Hogg and he go to town. Read [Voltaire's] "L'Esprit des Nations." Settle to go to Virginia Water. Walk with Shelley to Hatchet's; obliged to give up our plan. After dinner read "L'Esprit des Nations" (p. 32); Shelley reads Italian. Read fifteen lines of Ovid's "Metamorphosis," with Hogg.—[*Shelley*]—"The Assassins," Gibbon, chap. lxiv. All that can be known of "The Assassins" is to be found in "Memoires of the Academy of Inscriptions," tom. xvii, pp. 127–170.

Sunday, APR. 9.—Rise at 8. Charles Clairmont comes to breakfast at 10. Read some lines of Ovid before breakfast; after walk with Shelley, Hogg, Clara, and Charles Clairmont to the little pond in Kensington Gardens; return about 2. Charles Clairmont goes to Skinner Street. Read Ovid with Hogg (finish 2nd Fable). Shelley reads Gibbon and [Guarini's] "Pastor Fido" with Clara. In the evening read "L'Esprit des Nations" (p. 72). Shelley reads "Pastor Fido" (p. 102), Gibbon (vol. xii, p. 364), and the Story of Myrrha in Ovid.

Monday, APR. 10.—Read Voltaire before breakfast (p. 87). After breakfast work. Shelley passes the morning with Harriet, who is in a surprisingly good humour. Mary reads 3rd Fable of Ovid; Shelley and Clara read "Pastor Fido." Shelley reads Gibbon (To recollect the "Life of Rienzi"—*norti pocca*). Mrs. Godwin after dinner parades before the windows. Talk in the evening with Hogg about mountains and lakes and London.

Tuesday, APR. 11.—Work in the morning. Receive letters from Skinner Street, to say that Mamma had gone away in the pet, and had staid out all night. Read 4th and 5th Fables of Ovid. After dinner walk to

[26] A novel by Robert Bage (1792, 4 vols.).

the Park and Kensington Gardens. A beautiful evening. After tea, work. Charles Clairmont comes. In

[*Here is a page or more torn out.*]

Saturday, Apr. 15.—Read Ovid till 3. Shelley and Clara finish "Pastor Fido," and then go out about Clara's lottery ticket; draw. Clara's ticket comes up a prize. She buys two desks after dinner. Read Ovid. Charles Clairmont comes. When he goes, read Ovid (95 lines). Shelley and Clara begin [Ariosto's] "Orlando Furioso." A very grim dream.

Sunday, Apr. 16.—Rise late. A parcel from Fanny, in which is a letter from Christie Baxter, received last September, in which she professes friendship, but such friendship! we see how much worth it is. Miss Smith calls, and gossips for about an hour. Draw, and read a few lines of Ovid, after dinner. Shelley and Jane walk. Read a scene or two out of "As You Like It." Go up stairs to talk with Shelley. Read Ovid (54 lines only). Shelley finishes 3rd canto of Ariosto.

Monday, Apr. 17.—Rise at half-past 8. Hogg goes to the Courts. Read Ovid, Peacock comes; tells us of his plan of going to Canada, and taking Marianne; talk of it after dinner. Walk out to Piccadilly. Aftear tea read Ovid (83 lines); Shelley two or three cantos of Ariosto with Clara, and plays a game of chess with her. Read Voltaire's "Essay on the Spirit of Nations."

Tuesday, Apr. 18.—[*Shelley*]—Rise late. Shelley reads Ariosto to Maie. Ovid. Shelley and Clara go out. Clara makes Shelley a present of "Seneca." Buy Good's "Lucretius."[27] Jefferson and the Maie go for bonnets after dinner with Clara. Shelley reads Ovid (Medea, and the description of the Plague).[28] After tea Mary reads Ovid, 90 lines. Shelley and Clara read Ariosto, 7th canto. Mary reads Voltaire, p. 126.

Wednesday, Apr. 19.—[*Mary*][29]—Rise late. Read Ovid. Shelley and Clara read Ariosto. Peacock comes. Read Ovid (90 lines). Read "Essai sur des Nations" (52). After dinner make boats and then walk out with Shelley, Clara, Jane, and Peacock to sail them; return at 8. Charles Clairmont calls. Read over the Ovid to Jefferson. Shelley and Clara finish the 9th canto of Ariosto.

Thursday, Apr. 20.—Shelley reads two cantos of Ariosto. Work. Shelley reads Voltaire, "Essai sur des Nations" (p. 180). After dinner Clara goes to buy things. Shelley, Jefferson, and I walk to Chelsea Hospital.

[27] John Mason Goode's translation into blank verse with "a most elaborate series of annotations" (1805, 2 vols.).

[28] No parentheses in S&M. Medea, in *Metamorphoses,* Book VII, Fables 1–4; the Plague, in *ibid.,* Fable 5.

[29] "[*Mary*]" not in S&M.

After tea read 35 lines of Ovid. Go to sleep soon in the evening. Lord Chancellor decides in Shelley's favour.[30]

Friday, APR. 21.—After breakfast go with Shelley to Peacock's. Shelley goes to Longdill's. Read 3rd canto of [Scott's] the "Lord of the Isles." Return about 2. Shelley goes to Harriet to procure his son, who is to appear in one of the Courts. After dinner, look over W[illiam] W[ordsworth]'s poems. After tea read forty lines of Ovid. Fanny comes, and gives us an account of Hogan's threatened arrest to my Father. Shelley walks home part of the way with her. Very sleepy. Shelley reads one canto of Ariosto.

Saturday, APR. 22.—Read a little of Ovid. Shelley goes to Harriet's about his son. Work. Fanny comes. Talk. Shelley returns at 4; he has been much teased with Harriet. He has been to Longdill's, Whitton's, &c. and at length has got a promise that he shall appear Monday. After dinner Fanny goes. Read sixty lines of Ovid. Shelley and Clara read to the middle of the 14th canto of Ariosto.

Sunday, APR. 23.—After breakfast read Ovid. Shelley reads Ariosto. Jefferson does not come till 3. After dinner finish 130 lines of Ovid, and read them over to Jefferson. Charles Clairmont comes after tea, and does not go away till after 11. Jefferson reads "Don Quixote"; Clara reads Gibbon. Shelley finishes canto 17 of "Orlando Furioso." Read Voltaire's "Essay on Nations" (p. 203).

[*Here several leaves are torn out, containing the visit to Salt Hill.*[31]]

[*Thursday*, MAY 4.—. . .] which is a striking example of the pomposity of the Skinner Street proceeding. Construe Ovid (p. 117); read some cantos of Spenser['s "Faerie Queene"]. Shelley reads Seneca (p. 124).

Friday, MAY 5.—After breakfast go to Marshall's, but do not see him. Go to the Tomb. Shelley goes to Longdill's. Return soon. Read Spenser; construe Ovid. A fine thunder shower. After dinner talk with Shelley; then Shelley and Clara go out. Construe Ovid till 8 (126 lines); read Spenser. Fanny comes; she tells us of Marshall's servant's death. Papa is to see Mrs. Knapp [about Claire] to-morrow. Read Spenser. Walk home with Fanny and with Shelley. Read Spenser (end of 9th canto). Shelley reads Seneca (p. 143).

Saturday, MAY 6.—Rise at half-past 7; breakfast, and go to Covent Garden (Jefferson goes with me part of the way), and do not come home till

[30] A friendly suit had been brought by Shelley to get a legal interpretation of a clause in Sir Bysshe's will, "a clause debarring from the enjoyment of benefits any heir who sought to defeat the purposes of the will."—White, I, 397.

[31] S&M, "Post Hill."

late; arrange the flowers. Read Spenser; finish 1st book and one canto of the 2nd. Shelley comes home; we talk, and, just as we are comfortable, a

[*Here a leaf or more is torn out.*]

Monday, May 8.—Go out with Shelley to Mrs. Knapp; not at home. Buy Shelley a pencil-case. Return at 1. Read Spenser. Go with Shelley again to Mrs. Knapp; she cannot take Clara. Read Spenser after dinner. Clara goes out with Shelley. Talk with Jefferson; write to Marshall. Read Spenser (canto 11). They return at 8. Very tired; go to bed early. Jefferson scolds.

Tuesday, May 9.—Walk out with Clara in the morning to buy things; return; talk with Shelley. Shelley and Clara walk to the Exhibition. Read Spenser; almost finish 2nd book. Construe 80 lines of Ovid. Charles Clairmont comes. Talk.

Wednesday, May 10.—Not very well; rise late. Walk to Marshall's, and talk with him for an hour. Go with Jefferson and Shelley to British Museum—attend most of the statues; return at 2. Construe Ovid. After dinner construe Ovid (100 lines); finish 2nd book of Spenser, and read two cantos of the 3rd. Shelley reads Seneca every day and all day (p. 308).

Thursday, May 11.—Read a few lines of Ovid; then Shelley walks out with Clara. Read Spenser. Make a catalogue of our books. Read a few lines of Ovid, and after dinner fifty lines. Go with Jefferson to see the wild beasts at Exeter Change; they are very beautiful; the poor lion is dead; we see them feed. Returning, it rains very violently, and there is some beautiful sheet lightning. Return; watch the lightning; talk. Shelley reads Seneca (p. 322).

Friday, May 12.—Not very well. After breakfast read Spenser. Shelley goes out with his friend [Claire]; he returns first. Construe Ovid (90 lines); read Spenser. Jefferson returns at half-past 4, and tells us that poor Sawyer is to be hung.[32] These blessed laws! After dinner read Spenser. Read over the Ovid to Jefferson, and construe about ten lines more. Read Spenser (canto 10 of 4th book). Shelley and the lady [Claire] walk out. After tea, talk; write Greek characters. Shelley and his friend have a last conversation.

Saturday, May 13.—Clara goes; Shelley walks with her. Charles Clairmont comes to breakfast; talk. Shelley goes out with him. Read Spenser all day (finish canto 8, book 5). Jefferson does not come till 5. Get very anxious about Shelley; go out to meet him; return; it rains. Shelley returns at half-past 6; the business is finished. After dinner Shelley is very tired, and goes to sleep. Read Ovid (60 lines). Charles Clairmont comes to tea. Talk of pictures.

[32] See Dowden, I, 518 n.

[*Mary*]—A table spoonful of the spirit of aniseed, with a small quantity of spermaceti.

[*Shelley*]—9 drops of human blood, 7 grains of gunpowder, ½ oz. of putrified brain, 13 mashed grave worms.

The Pecksie, Dormouse.[33]

The Maie and her Elfin Knight.

I begin a new Journal with our regeneration.

List of Books read in 1815

MARY

(*Those marked * Shelley has read also.*)

Posthumous Works [of Mary Wollstonecraft, ed. by W. Godwin, 4 vols., 1798] 3 vols.
Sorrows of Werter. [By Goethe, 1774.]
Don Roderick. By Southey. [2 vols., 1814.]
*Gibbon's Decline and Fall. 12 vols. [1783–90.]
Paradise Regained. [By John Milton.]
*Gibbon's Life and Letters. 1st Edition. 2 vols. [Miscellaneous Works, 1796.]
*Lara. [By Lord Byron, 1814.]
New Arabian Nights. 3 vols.
Corinne. [By Madame de Staël, 1807.]
Fall of the Jesuits.
Rinaldo Rinaldini. [By V. Ulpius, tr. by I. Hinckley, 3 vols., 1800.]
Fontenelle's Plurality of Worlds.
Hermsprong [or Man As He Is Not, by Robert Bage, 3 vols., 1796.]
Le Diable Boiteux. [By Alain René Lesage, 1707.]
Man as he is. [By Robert Bage, 4 vols., 1792.]
Rokeby. [By Sir Walter Scott, 1812.]
Ovid's Metamorphoses in Latin.
*Wordsworth's Poems. [Probably Poems, 2 vols., 1815.]
*Spenser's Fairy Queen.
*Life of the Phillips. [By William Godwin, 1809.]
*[Charles J.] Fox's History of James II. [1808.]
The Reflector. [8 numbers, 1811–12, ed. by Leigh Hunt.]
Fleetwood. [By William Godwin, 3 vols., 1805.]
Wieland. [By Charles Brockden Brown.]

[33] S&M, "the Pecksie's doom salve"; corrected by Miss Grylls (p. 49, n. 1) from the original MS. Pecksie, Dormouse, and Maie were pet names for Mary.

Don Carlos. [Either by Thomas Otway (1676) or by Schiller (1787).]
*Peter Wilkins. [By Robert Paltock, 2 vols., 1751.]
Rousseau's Confessions. [1781.]
Leonora. A Poem. [By Gottfried A. Bürger.]
Emile. [By Rousseau, 1768.]
*Milton's Paradise Lost.
*Life of Lady Hamilton. [Memoirs of Lady Hamilton, 2nd ed., 1815; anonymous.]
De l'Allemagne. By Madame de Stael. [1810.]
3 vols of Barruel. [Histoire du Jacobinisme, 1797.]
*Caliph Vathek. [By William Beckford, 1786.]
Nouvelle Heloise. [By Rousseau, 1761.]
*Kotzebue's Account of his Banishment to Siberia. [The Most Remarkable Year in the Life of Kotzebue, Containing his Exile into Siberia. By Himself. Translated by B. Beresford. 3 vols., 1806.]
Waverley. [By Sir Walter Scott, 1814.]
Clarissa Harlowe. [By Samuel Richardson, 7 vols., 1748.]
[William] Robertson's History of America. [2 vols., 1777.]
*Virgil.
*Tale of a Tub. [? By Jonathan Swift.]
*Milton's Speech on Unlicensed Printing. [Areopagitica, 1644.]
*Curse of Kehama. [By Robert Southey, 1810.]
*Madoc. [By Robert Southey, 1805.]
La Bible Expliquée. [La Bible enfin Expliquée, par plusieurs amôniers. By Voltaire. London (Geneva), 1776.]
Lives of Abelard and Heloise. [By Joseph Berington, Birmingham, 1787.]
*The New Testament.
*Coleridge's Poems.
1st vol. of [Baron D'Holbach's] Système de la Nature.
*Castle of Indolence. [By James Thomson, 1748.]
Chatterton's Poems.
*Paradise Regained. [By John Milton.]
Don Carlos. [A repetition? By Thomas Otway (1676) or by Schiller (1787).]
*Lycidas. [By John Milton.]
*St. Leon. [By William Godwin, 1799.]
Shakespeare's Plays (part of which Shelley read aloud).
*Burke's Account of Civil Society. [A Vindication of Civil Society, 1756.]
*Excursion. [By Wordsworth, 1814.]
Pope's Homer's Iliad.
*Sallust.

Micromegas. [By Voltaire.]
*Life of Chaucer. [By William Godwin, 2 vols., 1803.]
Canterbury Tales. [By Chaucer.]
Peruvian Letters. [Madame F. d'I. de H. Graffigny, The Letters of a Peruvian Princess, tr. from French by Wm. Mudford, 1809.]
Voyages Round the World. [By George, Baron Anson, 1748.]
Plutarch's Lives.
*2 vols. of Gibbon.
Ormond. [By Maria Edgeworth.]
Hugh Trevor. [By Thomas Holcroft, 6 vols., 1794–97.]
*[Eugène] Labaume's History of the Russian War. [A Narrative of the Campaign in Russia, tr. from the French (by E. Boyce), London, 1815.]
Lewis's Tales. [Tales of Wonder (2 vols., 1801), or Romantic Tales (4 vols., 1808).]
Castle of Udolpho. [By Ann Radcliffe, 4 vols., 1794.]
Guy Mannering. [By Sir Walter Scott, 1815.]
*Charles XII. By Voltaire. [1731.]
Tales of the East. [By Henry Weber, 3 vols., 1812.]

SHELLEY

Pastor Fido. [By Guarini, 1590.]
Orlando Furioso. [By Ariosto, 1516.]
Livy's History [of Rome].
Seneca's Works.
Tasso's Gerusalemme Liberata. [1581.]
Tasso's Aminta. [1573.]
2 vols. of Plutarch, in Italian.
Some of the Plays of Euripides.
Seneca's Tragedies.
Reveries of Rousseau. [1776–78.]
Hesiod.
Novum Organum. [By Sir Francis Bacon.]
Alfieri's Tragedies.
Theocritus. [Idyls.]
Ossian. [By James Macpherson.]
Herodotus.
Thucydides. [The History of the Peloponnesian War.]
Homer.
[John] Locke on the Human Understanding. [1690.]
Conspiration de Rienzi. [By Joseph François Laignelot.]

History of Arianism. [By Louis Maimbourg, tr. by William Webster, 2 vols., 1728–29.]
[Simon] Ockley's History of the Saracens. [2 vols., 1708–18.]
Madame de Stael sur la Littérature. [1800.]

1816[1]

SWITZERLAND

Sunday, JULY 21.[2]—St. Martin.—We commenced our intended journey to Chamouni at half after 8, having taken horses beforehand. We pass through the Champagne country, which is extended from Mount Salêir to the base of the higher Alps. The country is sufficiently fertile, covered with corn-fields and orchards, and intersected with sudden acclivities, with flat summits. The day was cloudless and excessively hot. The Alps are perpetually in sight, and, as we advance, the mountains which form their outskirts closed in around us. We passed a bridge on a river which discharges itself into the Arve; the Arve itself, much swollen by the rains, flows constantly on the right of the road. As we approach Bonneville, through an avenue composed of a beautiful species of drooping poplar, we observe that the corn-fields on each side are covered with inundation. Bonneville is a neat little town, with no conspicuous peculiarity except the white towers of the prison, an extensive building overlooking the town. At Bonneville the Alps commence, one of which, clothed in forests, rises almost immediately from the opposite bank of the Arve. From Bonneville to Clusis the road conducts through a spacious and fertile plain, surrounded on all sides by mountains, covered, like those of Mellerie, with forests of intermingled pine wood and chestnut. At Clusis the route turns suddenly to the right, following the Arve along the chasm which

1 The journal for May 14, 1815—July 20, 1816, is lost. In June, 1815, Shelley and Mary toured the southern coast of Devon; they were also in Clifton for a while. In August they settled at Bishopsgate, where their second child, William, was born on January 24, 1816, and where they remained until they, with Claire, left for Geneva, sailing from Dover on May 3, 1816. Arriving at Geneva within ten days, they soon took a cottage called Campagne Chapuis (also Mont Alègre) on the opposite side of the lake. Byron resided close by in the Villa Diodati. Byron and Shelley made their trip around the lake during June 23–July 1.

2 Shelley kept his journal of the trip to Chamouni in the form of a letter to Peacock, the opening date of which is July 22, 1816. Mary printed Shelley's letter in her *History of a Six Weeks' Tour* (1817), altering it in various ways by omissions, additions, and changes of expression, probably with Shelley's help. From her own journal she introduced almost verbatim the first half of her entry for July 21. Shelley's letter is printed in the Julian edition (IX, 182–90) from the original MS in the Pierpont Morgan Library.

it seems to have hollowed among the perpendicular mountains. The scene assumes here also a more savage and colossal character; the valley becomes narrow, affording no more space than is sufficient for the river and the road. The pines descend to the banks, imitating with their regular spires the pyramidal crags which lift themselves far above the regions of the forest. The scene, at the distance of half a mile from Clusis, differs from that of Matlock in little else than the immensity of its proportions, and in its untameable, inaccessible solitude. We now saw many goats browsing on the rocks. Near Maglans, within a league of each other, we saw two waterfalls; they were no more than mountain rivulets, but the height from which they fell, at least 200 feet, made them assume a character inconsistent with the smallness of the stream. The first fell in two parts, and struck first on an enormous rock resembling precisely some colossal Egyptian statue of a female deity; it struck the head of the visionary image, and, gracefully dividing, then fell in folds of foam, more like cloud than water, imitating a veil of the most exquisite woof; it united then, concealing the lower part of the statue, and hiding itself in a winding of its channel, burst into a deeper fall, and crossed our route in its path towards the Arve. The other waterfall was more continuous, and larger; the violence with which it fell made it look rather like some shape which an exhalation had assumed than like water, for it fell beyond the mountain, which appeared dark behind it, as it might have appeared behind an evanescent cloud. The character of the scenery continues the same until we arrived at St. Martin. Clouds had overspread the evening, and hid the summit of Mont Blanc; its base was visible from the balcony of the Inn.

Monday, July 22.—Chamounix.—We leave St. Martin on mules at 7 o'clock. The road for a league lay through a plain, at the end of which we were taken to see the cascade. The water here falls 250 feet, dashing and casting a spray which formed a mist around it. When we approached near to it, the rain of the spray reached us, and our clothes were wetted with the quick falling but minute particles of water. This cataract fell into the Arve, which dashed against its banks like a wild animal who is furious in constraint. As we continued our route to Cerveaux, the mountains increased in height and beauty; the summits of the highest were hid in clouds, but they sometimes peeped out into the blue sky, higher one would think than the safety of God would permit, since it is well known that the Tower of Babel did not nearly equal them in immensity. Our route also lay by les Chutes d'Arve, which is neither so high nor grand as the cataract among the mountains; but there is something so divine in all this scenery, that you love and admire it even when its features are less magnificent than usual.

From Cerveaux we continued on a mountainous and rocky path, and passed an Alpine bridge over the Arve. This is one of the loveliest scenes in the world. The white and foamy river broke proudly through the rocks that opposed its progress; immense pines covered the bases of the mountains that closed around it; and a rock covered with woods, and seemingly detached from the rest, stood at the end and closed the ravine.

As we mounted still higher, this appeared the most beautiful part of our journey. The river foamed far below, and the rocks and glaciers towered above; the mighty pines filled the vale, and sometimes obstructed our view. We then entered the Valley of Chamounix, which was much wider than that we had just left, and gave room for cultivated fields and cottages. The mountains assumed a more formidable appearance, and the glaciers approach nearer to the road. Le Glace de Boisson has the appearance at a distance of a foaming cataract; and on a near approach the ice seems to have taken the forms of pyramids and stalagmites. In one village they offered us for sale a poor squirrel, which they had caught three days before; we bought it; but no sooner had I got it in my hand, than he bit my finger, and forced me to let it go; we caught it, however, again, and Shelley carried it some time; it appeared at length resigned to its fate, when we put it on a railing, where it paused an instant, wondering where it was, and then scampered up its native trees.

As we went along we heard a sound like the rolling of distant thunder, and beheld an avalanche rush down a ravine of the rocks; it stopped midway, but, in its course, forced a torrent from its bed, which now fell to the base of the mountain.

We had passed the torrent soon in the morning. The torrents had torn away the road, and it was with difficulty we crossed. Clare went on her mule, I walked, and Mary was carried.

Fatigued to death, we arrived at 7 o'clock at Chamounix.

At the inn at Cerveaux, among other laws of the same nature, there was an edict of the King of Sardinia's prohibiting his subjects from holding private assemblies, on pain of a fine of 12 francs, and, in default of payment, imprisonment. Here, also, we saw some stones picked up in the mountains, and made some purchases.

Tuesday, JULY 23.—Chamounix.—In the morning, after breakfast, we mount our mules, to see the source of the Arveiron. When we had gone about three parts of the way, we descended and continued our route on foot, over loose stones, many of which were of an enormous size. We came to the source, which lies like a [stage?] surrounded on the three sides by mountains and glaciers. We sat on a rock, which formed the fourth, gazing on the scene before us. An immense glacier was on our left, which continually rolled stones to its foot. It is very dangerous to go directly under this. Our guide told us a story of two Hollanders who went, without any guide, into a cavern of the glacier, and fired a pistol there, which drew down a large piece on them. We see several avalanches, some very small, others of great magnitude, which roared and smoked, overwhelming everything as it passed along, and precipitating great pieces of ice into the valley below. This glacier is increasing every day a foot, closing up the valley. We drink some water of the Arveiron, and return. After dinner, think it will rain, and Shelley goes alone to the Glacier of Boison. I stay at home. Read several tales of Voltaire. In the evening I copy Shelley's letter to Peacock.[3]

Wednesday, JULY 24.—To-day is rainy; therefore, we cannot go to Col de Balme. About 10 the weather appears clearing up. Shelley and I begin our journey to Montanvert. Nothing can be more desolate than the ascent of this mountain; the trees in many places have been torn away by avalanches, and some half leaning over others, intermingled with stones, present the appearance of vast and dreadful desolation. It began to rain almost as soon as we left our inn. When we had mounted considerably, we turned to look on the scene. A dense white mist covered the vale, and tops of scattered pines peeping above were the only objects that presented themselves. The rain continued in torrents. We were wetted to the skin; so that, when [we] had ascended halfway, we resolved to turn back. As we descended, Shelley went before, and, tripping up, fell upon his knee. This added to the weakness occasioned by a blow on his ascent; he fainted, and was for some minutes incapacitated from continuing his route.

We arrived wet to the skin. I read [Madame de Genlis's] "Nouvelles Nouvelles," and write my story.[4] Shelley writes part of [a] letter [to Peacock].

Thursday, JULY 25.—This day promises to be fine, and we set out at 9 for Montanvert with *beaucoup de monde* go also. We get to the top at 12, and behold *le Mer de Glace*. This is the most desolate place in the world; iced mountains surround it; no sign of vegetation appears except on the place from which [we] view the scene. We went on the ice; it is traversed by irregular crevices, whose sides of ice appear blue, while the surface is of a dirty white. We dine on the mountain. The air is very cold, yet many flowers grow here, and, among others, the rhododendron,

[3] Shelley to Peacock, July 22 [–Aug. 2], 1816 (Julian edition, IX, 182–90). Mary copied, at this time and later, some of Shelley's "travel" letters to Peacock, realizing their value both as personal and as literary records. Peacock knew of the copies. (See his *Memoirs of Shelley,* Pt. II, *The Life of Shelley,* with Introduction by Humbert Wolfe [London, Dent and Sons, 1933], II, 344.)

[4] *Frankenstein.* The laconic "Write" which appears frequently hereafter refers mainly to this, Mary's first, novel.

or *Rose des Alpes,* in great profusion. We descend leisurely. Shelley goes to see the mine of Amianthe, and finds nothing worth seeing. We arrive at the inn at 6, fatigued by our day's journey, but pleased and astonished by the world of ice that was opened to our view.

Friday, JULY 26.—We determined to return to-day, as it rained, and we could not possibly go to Col de Balme, as we intended. We return the same way by which we had before come, but the valley through which we passed appeared to me a thousand times more beautiful than before. The hills of the Vale of Servoz are covered with pines, intermixed by cultivated lawns. On one mountain that stands in the middle there are the ruins of a castle. We saw, also, the mountain which fell some years ago, and destroyed many *men and cows* (*"des hommes et des vaches,"* as our guide expressed it). Some of the rocks reached to the vale through which we rode.

I talked with the Guide about the manner of living in the country. The women do almost all the work, such as reaping, making hay, &c. The men serve for guides in the summer, which is lucrative, as they are able to put by sometimes about 20 louis for winter exigencies. In the autumn they hunt the chamois, an occupation they delight in. They think themselves lucky if they kill three in the season, which they are glad to sell for 24 or 25 francs, and if they cannot, they eat it themselves in the winter. They hunt hares, foxes, marmots, and wolves. These last they gain more by than by any other animal. They can sell the skins for 12 francs; and the Government has set a price on their heads—12 francs for a small one, 15 francs for a large one, and 18 francs for a female big with young.

They have the custom here of marrying very early. Ducrée [the guide] married at 18 a girl of 16. This was partly introduced by the conscription, which allowed immunities for the fathers of families. In the winter, many of the men go to Paris, and hire themselves as porters at hotels, &c., for the winter here is a starving kind of thing; they can gain little or no money during the whole course of it. They enjoy, however, the benefit here of cheap living, which, in this cold place, must [be] inestimable. What, indeed, could they do if, joined to their poor fare, they had to struggle with the severities of the seasons. Napoleon was no great favourite here, and they are very indifferent about any Government.

Saturday, JULY 27.—It is a most beautiful day, without a cloud. We set off at 12. The day is hot, yet there is a fine breeze. We pass by the Great Waterfall, which presents an aspect of singular beauty. The wind carries it away from the rock, and on towards the north, and the fine spray into which it is entirely dissolved passes before the mountain like a mist.

The other cascade has very little water, and is consequently not so beautiful as before. The evening of the day is calm and beautiful. Evening is the only time that I enjoy travelling. The horses went fast, and the plain opened before us. We saw Jura and the Lake like old friends. I longed to see my pretty babe. At 9, after much inquiring and stupidity, we find the road, and alight at Diodati. We converse with Lord Byron till 12, and then go down to Chapuis, kiss our babe, and go to bed.

Sunday, JULY 28.—Montalegre.—I read Voltaire's "Romans." Shelley reads Lucretius, and talks with Clare. After dinner, he goes out in the boat with Lord Byron; and we all go up to Diodati in the evening. This is the second anniversary since Shelley's and my union.

Monday, JULY 29.—Write; read Voltaire and Quintus Curtius. A rainy day, with thunder and lightning. Shelley finishes Lucretius, and reads Pliny's Letters.

Tuesday, JULY 30.—Read Quintus Curtius. Shelley reads Pliny's Letters. After dinner, we go up to Diodati, and stay the evening.

Wednesday, JULY 31.—Read ten pages of Quintus Curtius, and Rousseau's "Reveries." In the evening we go up to Diodati.

Thursday, AUG. 1.—Make a balloon for Shelley, after which he goes up to Diodati, to dine and spend the evening. Read twelve pages of Curtius. Write, and read the "Reveries" of Rousseau. Shelley reads Pliny's Letters.

Friday, AUG. 2.—I go to the town with Shelley, to buy a telescope for his birthday present. In the evening Lord Byron and he go out in the boat, and, after their return, Shelley and Clare go up to Diodati; I do not, for Lord Byron did not seem to wish it. Shelley returns with a letter from Longdill, which requires his return to England. This puts us in very bad spirits. I read "Reveries" and "Adêle and Théodore" de Madame de Genlis, and Shelley reads Pliny's Letters.

Saturday, AUG. 3.—Finish the 1st vol. of "Adêle," and write. After dinner, write to Fanny, and go up to Diodati, where I read the "Life of Madame Deffand."[5] We come down early, and talk of our plans. Shelley reads Pliny's Letters, and writes letters.

Sunday, AUG. 4.—Shelley's 24th birthday. Write; read "Tableau de famille."[6] Go out with Shelley in the boat, and read aloud to him the 4th book of Virgil. After dinner, we go up to Diodati, but return soon. I read Curtius with Shelley, and finish the 1st volume, after which we go out in the boat to set up the balloon, but there is too much wind; we set it up from the land, but it takes fire as soon as it is up. I finish the

[5] Probably the "Notice historique sur Madame du Deffand" in *Correspondence inédite de Madame du Deffand* (Paris, 1809, 2 vols.).

[6] A play by Denis Diderot, translated "by a lady" as *The Family Picture* (1781).

"Reveries" of Rousseau. Shelley reads and finishes Pliny's Letters, and begins the "Panegyric of Trajan."

Monday, Aug. 5.—Write; read a little of Curtius; read "Adêle and Théodore." In the evening we go up to Diodati.

Tuesday, Aug. 6.—Finish the 2nd volume of "Adêle"; write; read Curtius. In the evening we go up to Diodati. Shelley finishes the "Panegyric of Trajan," and begins Tacitus.

Wednesday, Aug. 7.—Write, and read ten pages of Curtius. Lord Byron and Shelley go out in the boat. I translate in the evening, and afterwards go up to Diodati. Shelley reads Tacitus.

Thursday, Aug. 8.—Read Curtius; out in the boat with Shelley, who reads Tacitus. Translate, and, in the evening, read "Adêle and Théodore."

Friday, Aug. 9.—Write and translate; finish "Adêle," and read a little Curtius. Shelley goes out in the boat with Lord Byron in the morning and in the evening, and reads Tacitus. About 8 o'clock we go up to Diodati. We receive a long letter from Fanny.[7]

Saturday, Aug. 10.—Write to Fanny. Shelley writes to Charles. We then go to town to buy books and a watch for Fanny. Read Curtius after my return; translate. In the evening Shelley and Lord Byron go out in the boat. Translate, and when they return go up to Diodati. Shelley reads Tacitus. A writ of arrêt comes for Polidori,[8] for having "cassé ses lunettes et fait tomber son chapeau" of the apothecary who sells bad magnesia.

Sunday, Aug. 11.—Read and translate. Lord Byron and Shelley go out in the boat. After dinner, they go out again; and we afterwards go to Diodati. Shelley reads Tacitus, and I read Curtius.

Monday, Aug. 12.—Write my story and translate. Shelley goes to the town, and afterwards goes out in the boat with Lord Byron. After dinner, I go out a little in the boat, and then Shelley goes up to Diodati. I translate in the evening, and read "Le Vieux de la Montagne."[9] Shelley,

[7] Fanny Godwin to Mary, July 29, 1816 (Dowden, II, 39–42).

[8] Dr. John William Polidori, Byron's youthful personal physician. Polidori's own account of this incident is as follows: "An apothecary sold some bad magnesia to L[ord] B[yron]. Found it bad by experiment of sulphuric acid colouring it red rose-colour. Servants spoke about it. Appointed Castan to see experiment; came; impudent; refused to go out; collared him, sent him out, broke spectacles. Laid himself on a wall for three hours; refused to see experiments. Saw L[ord] B[yron], told him his tale before two physicians. Brought me to trial before five judges; had an advocate to plead. I pleaded for myself; laughed at the advocate. Lost his cause on the plea of calumny; made me pay 12 florins for the broken spectacles and costs. Magnesia chiefly alumina, as proved by succenate and carbonate of ammonia."—*The Diary of Dr. John W. Polidori,* ed. by W. M. Rossetti (London, Elkin Mathews, 1911), 136.

[9] A French translation of Ludwig Tieck's book.

in coming down, is attacked by a dog, which delays him; we send up for him, and Lord Byron comes down; in the meantime Shelley returns.

Tuesday, AUG. 13.—Go out in the boat with Shelley, and read Curtius; read "Le Vieux de la Montagne," and write. After dinner, Shelley goes out in the boat with Lord Byron, and afterwards we all go up to Diodati. War. Shelley reads Tacitus.

Wednesday, AUG. 14.—Read "Le Vieux de la Montagne"; translate. Shelley reads Tacitus, and goes out with Lord Byron before and after dinner. [M. G.] Lewis comes to Diodati. Shelley goes up there, and Clare goes up to copy. Remain at home, and read "Le Vieux de la Montagne."

Thursday, AUG. 15.—Go out in the boat a little way with Shelley, but it is stormy, and we soon return. A rainy day. Finish the 5th book of Curtius, and write; finish "The Old Man of the Mountain," translate, and read one book of the "Conjuration de Rienzi" [by J. F. Laignelot]. Shelley reads Tacitus, and writes.

Friday, AUG. 16.—Write, and read a little of Curtius; translate; read [Lafontaine's] "Walther"[10] and some of "Rienzi." Lord Byron goes with Lewis to Ferney. Shelley writes, and reads Tacitus.

Saturday, AUG. 17.—Write, and finish "Walther." In the evening I go out in the boat with Shelley, and he afterwards goes up to Diodati. Begin one of Madame de Genlis' novels. Shelley finishes Tacitus. Poli[dori] comes down. Little babe is not well.

Sunday, AUG. 18.—Talk with Shelley, and write; read Curtius. Shelley reads Plutarch in Greek. Lord Byron comes down, and stays here an hour. I read a novel in the evening. Shelley goes up to Diodati, and Monk Lewis.

[*Shelley*][11]—See Apollo's Sexton [Lewis], who tells us many mysteries of his trade. We talk of Ghosts; neither Lord Byron nor Monk G. Lewis seem to believe in them; and they both agree, in the very face of reason, that none could believe in ghosts without also believing in God. I do not think that all the persons who profess to discredit these visitations really discredit them, or, if they do in the daylight, are not admonished by the approach of loneliness and midnight to think more respectably of the world of shadows.

Lewis recited a poem which he had composed at the request of the Princess of Wales. The Princess of Wales, he premised, was not only a

10 August H. J. Lafontaine, *Walther, ou l'enfant du champ de bataille, traduit de'Allemand par Henri V* (Paris, 1816, 4 vols.).

11 This part of the journal, and the entries for Aug. 29–Sept. 5, were published by Mary Shelley, with a few alterations and omissions, in *Essays,* &c. (1840), as a complementary part of the *History of a Six Weeks' Tour.* The fourth tale by Lewis was published by Mary at the end of her essay "On Ghosts" (*London Magazine,* IX [March 1824], 253–56). (See notes to entries for Dec. 22, 1814, and Oct. 20, 1818.)

believer in ghosts, but in magic and witchcraft, and asserted that prophecies made in her youth had been accomplished since. The tale was of a Lady of her Court in Germany:—This lady (Mina)[12] had been exceedingly attached to her husband, and they had made a vow that the one who died first should return after death and visit the other as a ghost. She was sitting one day alone in her chamber, when she heard an unusual sound of footsteps on the stairs; the door opened, and her husband's spectre, gashed with a deep wound across the forehead, and in military habiliments, entered. She appeared startled at the apparition, and the ghost told her that, when he should visit her in future, she would hear a passing-bell toll, and these words distinctly uttered close to her ear, "Mina, I am here." On enquiry, it was found that her husband had fallen in battle on the very day that she was visited by the vision. The intercourse between the Ghost and the woman continued for some time, until the latter had laid aside all terror, and indulged herself in the affection which she had felt for him whilst living. One evening she went to a ball, and permitted her thoughts to be alienated by the attentions of a Florentine gentleman, more witty, more graceful, and more gentle, as it appeared to her, than any person she had ever seen. As he was conducting her to the dance, a death-bell tolled. Mina, lost in the fascination of the Florentine's attentions, disregarded, or did not hear, the sound; a second peal, louder and more deep, startled the whole company, when Mina heard the Ghost's accustomed whisper, and, raising her eyes, saw in an opposite mirror the reflexion of the Ghost standing over her; she is said to have died of terror.

He told us four other stories—all grim:—

I.

A young man who had taken orders had just been presented with a living, on the death of the incumbent. It was in the Catholic part of Germany. He arrived at the parsonage on a Saturday night—it was summer—and waking about 3 o'clock in the morning, and it being already broad day, he saw a venerable-looking man, but with an aspect exceedingly melancholy, sitting at a desk in the window, reading, and two beautiful boys standing near him, whom he regarded with looks expressive of the profoundest grief. Presently he rose from his seat, the boys followed him, and they were no more to be seen. The young man, much troubled, arose, hesitating whether he should regard what he had seen as a dream or as a waking phantasy. To divert his dejection, he walked towards the church, which the sexton was already preparing for the Morning Service. The first sight that struck him was a portrait, the exact resemblance of the man whom he had seen sitting in his chamber.

12 "Minna" in *Essays* (1840).

MER DE GLACE, CHAMOUNI

Engraved by S. Fisher from a drawing by W. H. Bartlett

It was the custom in this district to place the portrait of each minister after his death in the church. He made the minutest enquiries respecting his predecessor, and learned that he was universally beloved as a man of unexampled integrity and benevolence, but that he was the prey of a secret and perpetual sorrow. His grief was supposed to have risen from an attachment to a young lady, with whom his situation did not permit him to unite himself. Others, however, asserted that a connection did subsist between them, and that even she occasionally brought to his house two beautiful boys, the offspring of their connection. Nothing further occurred until the cold weather came, and the new minister desired a fire to be lighted in the stove of the room where he slept. A hideous stench arose from the stove as soon as it was lighted, and, on examining it, the bones of two male children were found within.

II.

Lord Lyttleton and a number of his friends were joined during the chase by a stranger; he was excellently mounted, and displayed such courage, or rather so much desperate rashness, that no other person in the hunt could follow him. The gentlemen, when the chase was over, invited the stranger to dine with them. His conversation was something of a wonderful kind; he astonished, he interested, he commanded the attention of the most inert. As night came on, the company, being weary, began to retire, one by one, much later than the usual hour; the most intellectual among them were retained the latest by his fascination: as he perceived that they began to depart, he redoubled his efforts to retain them. At last, when few remained, he entreated them to stay with him; but all pleaded the fatigue of a hard day's chase, and all at last retired. They had been in bed about an hour, when they were awakened by the most horrible screams, which issued from the stranger's room. Everyone rushed towards it; the door was locked; after a moment's deliberation, they burst it open, and found the stranger stretched on the ground, writhing with agony and weltering in blood. On their entrance he arose, and collecting himself, apparently with a strong effort, entreated them to leave him; not to disturb him; that he would give every possible explanation in the morning. They complied. In the morning his chamber was found vacant, and he was seen no more.

III.

Miles Andrews, the friend of Lord Lyttleton, was sitting one night alone, when Lord Lyttleton came in, and informed [him] that he was dead, and that this was his ghost which he saw before him. Andrews pettishly told him not to play any ridiculous tricks upon him, for he was not in a temper to bear them. The ghost then departed. In the morning Andrew asked his servant at what hour Lord Lyttleton had arrived. The servant said he did not know that he had arrived, but that he would enquire. On enquiry, it was found that Lord Lyttleton had not arrived, nor had the door been opened to anyone during the whole night. Andrews sent to Lord Lyttleton's, and discovered that he had died precisely at the hour of the apparition.

IV.

A gentleman, on a visit to a friend who lived on the skirts of an extensive forest in the east of Germany, lost his way. He wandered for some hours among the trees, when he saw a light at a distance; on approaching it, he was surprised to observe that it proceeded from the interior of a ruined monastery. Before he knocked at the gate, he thought it prudent to look through the window. He saw a multitude of cats assembled round a small grave, four of whom were at that moment letting down a coffin with a crown upon it. The gentleman, startled at this unusual sight, and imagining that he had arrived among the retreat of fiends and witches, mounted his horse and rode away with the utmost precipitation. He arrived at his friend's house at a late hour, who had sat up waiting for him. On his arrival, his friend questioned him as to the cause of the traces of trouble visible in his face. He began to recount his adventure after much difficulty, knowing that it was scarcely possible that his friend should give faith to his relation. No sooner had he mentioned the coffin with the crown upon it, than his friend's cat, who seemed to have been lying asleep before the fire, leaped up, saying, "Then I'm the King of the Cats," and scrambled up the chimney, and was seen no more.

Monday, AUG. 19.—[*Mary*]—Finish "Les Vœux Temeraires,"[13] write, and read "Rienzi." Shelley goes to the town. After dinner, walk and read. Shelley goes out in the boat with Lewis and Lord Byron, and afterwards goes to Diodati; he reads Plutarch.

Tuesday, AUG. 20.—Read Curtius; write; read "Herman d'Unna."[14] Lord Byron comes down after dinner, and remains with us until dark. Shelley spends the rest of the evening at Diodati; he reads Plutarch.

Wednesday, AUG. 21.—Shelley and I talk about my story ["Frankenstein"]. Finish "Herman d'Unna" and write. Shelley reads Milton. After dinner, Lord Byron comes down, and Clare and Shelley go up to Diodati. Read "Rienzi."

[13] By Madame de Genlis; English translation, *Rash Vows* (1799, 3 vols.).
[14] By Professor Kramer; translated from the German (1794, 3 vols.).

Thursday, Aug. 22.—Write, and then go to the town with Shelley to see the cimetière. It is ugly enough, being nothing more than a part of a field inclosed in with palisades. It is a very weary and tiresome walk. After dinner read some of Madame de Genlis' novels. Shelley reads Milton.

Friday, Aug. 23.—Read Curtius; finish the "Nouvelles Nouvelles" de Madame de Genlis. Shelley goes up to Diodati, and then in the boat with Lord Byron, who has heard bad news of Lady Byron, and is in bad spirits concerning it. After dinner read "Rienzi," and Shelley goes on the water, and afterwards to Diodati. Letters arrive from Peacock and Charles.[15] Shelley reads Milton.

Saturday, Aug. 24.—Write. Shelley goes to Geneva. Read. Lord Byron and Shelley sit on the wall before dinner; after, I talk with Shelley, and then Lord Byron comes down and spends an hour here. Shelley and he go up together. Read "Contes Moraux de [Jean François] Marmontel." Shelley reads the "Germania" of Tacitus.

Sunday, Aug. 25.—Write, and read "Contes Moraux." Go down to the side of the lake to watch the waves. Lord Byron comes down. After dinner read "Rienzi." Lord Byron comes down and spends an hour. Clare and Shelley go up to Diodati. Read "Rienzi." Shelley reads "Germania" and "Memoires d'un Detenu."[16]

Monday, Aug. 26.—Read Curtius and "Caroline of Lichtfeld."[17] Hobhouse and Scroop Davis[18] come to Diodati. Shelley spends the evening there, and reads "Germania." Several books arrive, among others Coleridge's "Christabel," which Shelley reads aloud to me before we go to bed.

Tuesday, Aug. 27.—Finish "Caroline of Lichtfeld" and "Marmontel's Tales." Read [Maturin's] "Bertram" and "Christabel," and several articles of the "Quarterly Review." Shelley dines at Diodati, and remains there all the evening. They go out a short time in the boat.

Wednesday, Aug. 28.—Packing. Shelley goes to the town. Work. Polidori comes down, and afterwards Lord Byron. After dinner we go upon the water; pack; and Shelley goes up to Diodati. Shelley reads "Histoire de la Revolution, par Rabault."

Thursday, Aug. 29.—We depart from Geneva at 9 in the morning. The Swiss are very slow drivers; besides which, we have Jura to mount; we therefore go a very few posts to-day. The scenery is very beautiful,

15 Charles Clairmont to Shelley and Mary, August 8, 1816, Bagneres de Bigorre, [France] (S&M, I, 114–27).

16 Either by Riouffe or by Charles Dumont (see Appendix IV).

17 *Caroline of Lichtfield*, a novel by Jeanne I. Bottens, Baroness de Montolieu, translated from the French by Thomas Holcroft (1786, 3 vols.).

18 John Cam Hobhouse (Lord Broughton), and Scrope B. Davies, Byron's intimate friends.

and we see many magnificent views. We pass *La Vattaz* and *Les Rousses,* which, when we passed in the spring, were in the snow. We sleep at Morrez.

Friday, Aug. 30.—[*Shelley*]—We leave Morrez,[19] and arrive in the evening at Dole, after a various day.

Saturday, Aug. 31.—[*Shelley*]—From Dole we go to Rouvray, where we sleep. We pass through Dijon, and after Dijon take a different route to that which we followed on the two other occasions. The scenery has some beauty and singularity on the line of the mountains which surround the Val de Suzon;[20] low, yet precipitous hills, covered with vines or woods, and with streams, meadows, and poplars at the bottom.

Sunday, Sept. 1.—[*Shelley*]—Leave Rouvray; pass Auxerre, where we dine—a pretty town—and arrive at 2 o'clock at Villeneuve le Guiard.

Monday, Sept. 2.—[*Shelley*]—From Villeneuve le Guiard we arrive at Fontainbleau. The scenery around this Palace is wild, and even savage; the soil is full of rocks, apparently granite, which on every side break through the ground; the hills are low, but precipitous and rough; the valleys, equally wild, are shaded by forests. In the midst of this wilderness stands the Palace and town of Fontainbleau. We visited the Palace. Some of the apartments equal in magnificence anything that I could conceive; the roofs are fretted with gold, and the canopies of velvet. From Fontainbleau we passed to Versailles, in the route towards Rouen. We arrived at Versailles at 9.

Tuesday, Sept. 3.—[*Shelley*]—We saw the Palace and gardens of Versailles, and Le Grand et Petit Trianon; they surpass those of Fontainbleau. The gardens are full of statues of the most exquisite workmanship, vases, fountains, and colonnades. In all that essentially belongs to a garden they are extraordinarily deficient. The orangery is a stupid piece of expense; there was one orange tree (not apparently so old) sown in 1442. We saw only the garden and the theatre at the Petit Trianon. The gardens are in the English taste, and exceedingly pretty. The Grand Trianon was open. It is a summer palace, light, yet magnificent. We were unable to devote the time it deserved to the gallery of paintings here. There was a portrait of Madame La Vallière, the repentant mistress of Louis XIV. She was melancholy, but exceedingly beautiful, and was represented as holding a skull, and sitting before a crucifix, pale, and with downcast eyes. We then went to the great Palace. The apartments are unfurnished, but, even with this disadvantage, are more magnificent than those of Fontainbleau. They are lined with marbles of various colours, whose pedestals and capitals are gilt, and the ceiling is richly gilt,

19 S&M has "Moret" in both instances. Correction from *Essays* (1840).
20 S&M, "Val de Jura." Correction from *Essays* (1840).

with compartments of exquisite painting. The arrangement of these precious materials has in it, it is true, something effeminate and royal. Could a Grecian architect have commanded all the labour and money which was expended on Versailles, he would have produced a fabric which the whole world has never equalled. We saw the Hall (la Salle) of Hercules, the balcony where the King and Queen exhibited themselves to the Parisian mob. The people who showed us through the Palace obstinately refused to say anything about the Revolution; we could not even find out in which chamber the rioters of the 10th of August found the King. We saw the Salle d'Opéra, where are now preserved the portraits of the Kings.[21] There was the race of the House of Orleans, with the exception of Égalité, all extremely handsome; there was Madame de Maintenon, and beside her a beautiful little girl, the daughter of La Vallière.

The pictures had been hidden during the Revolution. We saw the Library of Louis XVI. The librarian had held some place in the ancient Court near Marie Antoinette; he returned with the Bourbons, and was waiting for some better situation. He showed us a book which he had preserved during the Revolution; it was a book of paintings representing a Tournament of the Court of Louis XIV, and it seemed that the present desolation of France, the fury of the injured people, and all the horrors to which they abandoned themselves, stung by their long sufferings, flowed, naturally enough, from expenditures so immense as must have been demanded by the magnificence of this tournament. The vacant rooms of this Palace imaged well the hollow show of monarchy. After seeing these things, we departed towards Havre, and slept at Auxerre.[22]

Wednesday, SEPT. 4.—[*Shelley*]—We passed through Rouen and saw the Cathedral, an immense specimen of the most costly and magnificent Gothic; the interior of the church disappoints. We saw the burial-place of Richard Coeur de Lion and his brother. The altar of the church is a fine piece of marble. Sleep at Yvetot.[23]

Thursday, SEPT. 5.—[*Shelley*]—We arrive at Havre, and wait for the packet. In the evening Willy falls out of bed, and is not hurt.

Friday, SEPT. 6.—[*Mary*]—Still at Havre. Engage a passage. Wind contrary. Read "Le Criminel Secret," which is a very curious and striking book; read "Rienzi." We engage with a captain.

Saturday, SEPT. 7.—We depart at 11, the wind not very good. Sick all day.

Sunday, SEPT. 8.—We arrive at Portsmouth at half-past 2. Shelley is not well. Dine and talk.

21 This sentence, required by the sense, is not in S&M; it is added from *Essays* (1840).
22 S&M, "Auxonne." Correction from *Essays* (1840).
23 S&M, "Gretor." Correction from *Essays* (1840).

Monday, SEPT. 9.—We are kept here until 2 o'clock by the Custom-house. Take leave of Shelley,[24] and go as far as Salisbury, on our way to Bath.

Tuesday, SEPT. 10.—Arrive at Bath about 2. Dine, and spend the evening in looking for lodgings. Read Mrs. [Mary] Robinson's "Valcenza."[25]

Wednesday, SEPT. 11.—Look for lodgings; take some,[26] and settle ourselves. Read the 1st vol. of "The Antiquity" [by Scott], and work.

Thursday, SEPT. 12.—Letter from Shelley. Read the "Edinburgh Review" and the 2nd volume of "The Antiquary."

Friday, SEPT. 13.—Letter from Shelley; write to him. Read "Chrononhotonthologus,"[27] put things away, and work.

Saturday, SEPT. 14.—Read [Milman's] "Fazio," "Love and Madness,"[28] and some of "Rienzi"; work; in the evening finish "The Antiquary."

Sunday, SEPT. 15.—Read "Rienzi"; in the evening walk out; read the "Solitary Wanderer."[29] Letter from Shelley; he is with Peacock.

Monday, SEPT. 16.—Write, and read the "Memoirs of the Princess of Bareith";[30] work; Shelley is searching for a house about Marlow.

Tuesday, SEPT. 17.—Read the "Memoirs" aloud; write to Shelley.

Wednesday, SEPT. 18.—Read the "Memoirs." A letter from Shelley. Write.

Thursday, SEPT. 19.—Set out from Bath; travel until 4 o'clock, when I arrive at Maidenhead. Shelley and Peacock are there to meet me. We walk to Marlow. In the evening read the "Letters of Emile" [by Rousseau].

Friday, SEPT. 20.—Walk to the Fisherman's Cliff and Medmenham Abbey; return about 4. Finish the "Letters of Emile," and read a part of [Richardson's] "Clarissa Harlowe."

Saturday, SEPT. 21.—Shelley and Peacock walk out. Read vol. 6 of "Clarissa."

Sunday, SEPT. 22.—Peacock and Shelley walk out. Read vol. 7 of "Clarissa." Shelley reads the "Letters of Emile."

Monday, SEPT. 23.—Read volume 8 of "Clarissa." Shelley and Peacock

24 Shelley went to London.

25 1792, 2 vols.

26 Apparently at 5 Abbey Church Yard. Later Claire took separate lodgings at 12 New Bond Street.

27 A burlesque drama by Henry Carey (1734).

28 A novel by the Rev. Sir Herbert Croft (1780).

29 Charlotte Smith, *The Letters of a Solitary Wanderer,* a novel (1800, 3 vols.).

30 By Frederica Sophia Wilhelmina of Prussia, Margrave of Bareith, Consort of Frederick William of Brandenburg-Bareuth. See Appendix IV.

walk out. I take a short walk with Mrs. P[eacock]. Peacock's Uncle comes in the evening.

Tuesday, SEPT. 24.—Shelley goes up to London. Read [Johnson's] "The Rambler." Shelley reads Montaigne's "Essays." He does not return until 11 o'clock.

Wednesday, SEPT. 25.—Return to Bath with Shelley; we arrive between 8 and 9, and talk of our plans the rest of the evening.

Thursday, SEPT. 26.—Shelley and I walk out in the morning and evening; talk of our plans; work.

Friday, SEPT. 27.—Read Curtius, and work. Read the "Memoirs of the Princess of Bareith" aloud; in the evening walk.

Saturday, SEPT. 28.—Work, and read the "Memoirs" in the evening; walk with Shelley for two or three hours; work. Shelley reads Peter Pindar's [John Wolcot's] book aloud.

Sunday, SEPT. 29.—Read Clarendon[31] all day. Shelley writes to Albe[32] [Byron], and other things; he finishes Lacretelle's "History of the French Revolution." We walk out for a short time after dinner. Shelley reads Lucian.

Monday, SEPT. 30.—Shelley spends the day at Bristol. Read the "Memoirs" aloud, and begin the "Life of Holcroft" [by himself].

Tuesday, OCT. 1.—Shelley reads the "Life of Holcroft" aloud all day. Read the "Memoirs of the Princess de Bareith."

Wednesday, OCT. 2.—Read Clarendon; finish the "Life of Holcroft"; read [Lady C. Lamb's] "Glenarvon" in the evening; write to Fanny.

Thursday, OCT. 3.—Not well. Read "Glenarvon" all day, and finish it.

Friday, OCT. 4.—Read Clarendon; walk out with Shelley; and get letter from Fanny.[33]

Saturday, OCT. 5.—Read Clarendon and Curtius; walk with Shelley. Shelley reads Tasso.

Sunday, OCT. 6.—[*Shelley*]—On this day Mary put her head through the door and said, "Come and look; here's a cat eating roses; she'll turn into a woman; when beasts eat these roses they turn into men and women."

[*Mary*]—Read Clarendon all day; finish the 11th book. Shelley reads Tasso.

Monday, OCT. 7.—Read Curtius and Clarendon; write. Shelley reads "Don Quixote" aloud in the evening.

Tuesday, OCT. 8.—Letter from Fanny [written at Bristol]. Drawing

[31] *History of the Rebellion and Civil Wars in England.*

[32] Shelley to Byron, September 29, 1816 (Julian edition, IX, 197–200).

[33] Fanny Godwin to Mary, October 3, 1816 (Dowden, II, 53–56).

lesson.[34] Walk out with Shelley to the South Parade, read Clarendon, and draw. In the evening work, and Shelley reads "Don Quixote"; afterwards read "Memoirs of the Princess of Bareith" aloud.

Wednesday, OCT. 9.—Read Curtius; finish the "Memoirs of the Princess of Bareith"; draw. In the evening a very alarming letter comes from Fanny.[35] Shelley goes immediately to Bristol; we sit up for him till 2 in the morning, when he returns, but brings no particular news.

Thursday, OCT. 10.—Shelley goes again to Bristol, and obtains more certain trace. Work and read. He returns at 11 o'clock.

Friday, OCT. 11.—He sets off to Swansea. Work and read.

Saturday, OCT. 12.—He returns with the worst account. A miserable day. Two letters from Papa. Buy mourning, and work in the evening.

Sunday, OCT. 13.—Read "Patronage"[36] and the "Milesian Chief";[37] finish 5th volume of Clarendon. Shelley reads "Life of Cromwell" [written by Himself, 1816?].

Monday, OCT. 14.—Finish "Milesian" and "Patronage"; read "Holcroft's Travels."[38] Shelley reads "Life of Cromwell."

Tuesday, OCT. 15.—Read Clarendon, draw, walk, and work. Letter from Papa.[39]

Wednesday, OCT. 16.—Read Clarendon, draw, and walk.

Thursday, OCT. 17.—Drawing lesson. Read "Alphonsine."[40] Shelley reads "Don Quixote" aloud. Walk; read Latin.

Friday, OCT. 18.—Shelley reads Montaigne. Read Clarendon, walk, write.

Saturday, OCT. 19.—Work; write. Shelley reads Montaigne. Read Clarendon. In the evening, Shelley reads "Don Quixote" aloud.

Sunday, OCT. 20.—Write. Shelley attempts going to Oxford, but is stopped by the men dressed in black; he leaves them, however, and returns home. He reads Montaigne. Read Clarendon and "O'Donnel."[41]

Monday, OCT. 21.—Drawing lesson. Clare and Shelley walk out. Read Clarendon, and draw and write. Shelley reads Montaigne and Lucian; reads "Don Quixote" aloud.

34 Mary's first drawing lesson under Mr. West. Lessons were continued regularly on Mondays and Thursdays (except on Mondays of November 4 and 25) through Thursday, December 12. After December 14, routine life at Bath was interrupted by Harriet's death.

35 Fanny committed suicide on the night of October 9 at the Mackworth Arms Inn, Swansea (see Dowden, II, 47–58; and White, I, 469–74).

36 By Maria Edgeworth (1814, 4 vols.).

37 A novel by Charles Robert Maturin (1812, 4 vols.).

38 Thomas Holcroft, *Travels from Hamburgh through Westphalia, Holland, and the Netherlands* (1804, 2 vols.).

39 Godwin to Mary, October 13, 1816 (Dowden, II, 58).

40 By Madame de Genlis; English translation (1807, 4 vols.).

41 By Lady Morgan (1814, 3 vols.).

Tuesday, OCT. 22.—Draw and write; read Clarendon, and finish the 14th book; work in the evening, and read Curtius. Shelley writes, and reads Montaigne and Lucian, and walks.

Wednesday, OCT. 23.—Walk before breakfast; afterwards write, and read Clarendon. Shelley writes, and reads Montaigne. In the evening read Curtius, and work. Shelley reads "Don Quixote" aloud.

Thursday, OCT. 24.—Drawing lesson. Read Clarendon; write; after dinner read Curtius. Shelley reads Montaigne; after tea, he reads "Don Quixote" aloud.

Friday, OCT. 25.—Draw, write, and read Clarendon. Shelley reads Montaigne. Read Curtius. After tea Shelley reads "Don Quixote" aloud.

Saturday, OCT. 26.—[*Shelley*]—Mary writes her book, and reads Clarendon. Description of a Cave, in the "Morning Chronicle." Shelley from this day determines to keep an account of how much food he eats; consumes in the day 22 ounces. Shelley reads Montaigne; writes; walks.

Sunday, OCT. 27.—[*Shelley*][42]—B. 3.07, 12 gr. L. 3 oz. Write Ch. 2½. [*Mary*]—Finish Clarendon's "History." Shelley reads Montaigne. [*Shelley*]—D. 1307. T. 4.07, 4.9. In all 3.0712 gr. L. 307. D. 1.307. T. 407.45= 24.07. [*Mary*]—Read Curtius and "Rienzi." Shelley reads "Don Quixote" aloud.

Monday, OCT. 28.—[*Mary*]—A drawing lesson. Read the Introduction to Sir H. Davy's "Chemistry"; write; in the evening read "Anson's Voyages"[43] and Curtius. Shelley reads "Don Quixote" aloud after tea. Finish "Anson's Voyages" before night.

Tuesday, OCT. 29.—Draw; read Davy's "Chemistry" with Shelley; read Curtius and "Ide's Travels."[44] Shelley reads Montaigne, and "Don Quixote" aloud in the evening.

Wednesday, OCT. 30.—Read Davy's "Chemistry." Letters from Charles. Draw, and write to him. Read "Ide's Travels" and Curtius in the evening. Shelley reads Montaigne, and "Don Quixote" aloud in the evening.

Thursday, OCT. 31.—Drawing lesson. Afterwards Shelley is called for by Mr. Lawes; talk with him. Read "Ide's Travels." Shelley reads "Don Quixote" aloud in the evening.

Friday, NOV. 1.—Shelley is teased all the day by Mr. Lawes. Draw, and read "Don Quixote" in the evening.

Saturday, NOV. 2.—Shelley calls at the "Greyhound." Write; read

[42] S&M does not distinguish different writers in entries of the twenty-seventh and twenty-eighth.

[43] George, Baron Anson, *A Voyage Round the World* (1748).

[44] Evert Ides, *Three Years' Travels from Moscow Over-land to China,* (London, 1705 [published as by E. Ysbrants Ides]).

Davy. In the evening read Curtius and "Les Incas,"[45] and work. Shelley writes a little, and reads Montaigne. Draw.

Sunday, Nov. 3.—Draw, write; read "Les Incas." Shelley reads Montaigne; walks. In the evening read Curtius, and Shelley reads "Don Quixote" aloud.

Monday, Nov. 4.—Draw, write; read Davy; in the evening Curtius and "Don Quixote." Shelley reads Montaigne.

Tuesday, Nov. 5.—Draw, and read "Bryan Perdue."[46] Shelley reads Montaigne and "Don Quixote." Work in the evening.

Wednesday, Nov. 6.—Draw; finish "Bryan Perdue"; write. Not well in the evening. Begin [Richardson's] "Sir C. Grandison."

Thursday, Nov. 7.—Drawing lesson. Walk; read "Sir C. Grandison." Shelley reads Montaigne in the morning, and finishes "Don Quixote" in the evening.

Friday, Nov. 8.—Draw, walk, and read "Sir C. Grandison." Shelley reads Montaigne. Read Curtius, and [Maria Edgeworth's] "Castle Rackrent" aloud. I finish "Castle Rackrent" in the evening.

Saturday, Nov. 9.—Write; read "Grandison"; read Curtius. Shelley reads "Gulliver's Travels" aloud, and Montaigne in the morning.

Sunday, Nov. 10.—Draw; read "Grandison" and Curtius. Shelley reads and finishes Montaigne, to his great sorrow. He reads Lucian.

Monday, Nov. 11.—Drawing lesson. Read "Grandison," write, and read Curtius. Shelley reads Lucian and [Swift's] "Gulliver's Travels" in the evening.

Tuesday, Nov. 12.—Walk, and read "Grandison" and Curtius; work in the evening. Shelley reads Lucian, and goes to bed early.

Wednesday, Nov. 13.—Read "Grandison"; write. Shelley reads Lucian and "Gulliver" in the evening. Work; walk.

Thursday, Nov. 14.—Read "Grandison." Drawing lesson. Walk; read Curtius. Shelley reads Lucian. After tea, work. Shelley reads "Gulliver" aloud.

Friday, Nov. 15.—Write; finish "Grandison"; walk. Shelley reads Locke. Read Curtius after dinner; after tea work. Shelley finishes "Gulliver," and begins "Paradise Lost."

Saturday, Nov. 16.—Draw, write; read old voyages; not well; read Curtius. In the evening Shelley reads 2nd book of "Paradise Lost." Shelley reads Locke.

Sunday, Nov. 17.—Draw, write; read Locke and Curtius. Shelley reads Plutarch and Locke; he reads "Paradise Lost" aloud in the evening. I work.

[45] A poetical tale by Jean François Marmontel (Paris, 1777).

[46] By Thomas Holcroft (1805, 3 vols.).

Monday, Nov. 18.—Drawing lesson. Write, and read Locke. Shelley walks with Clare; reads Locke and Plutarch. Read Curtius; work in the evening. Shelley reads "Paradise Lost" aloud.

Tuesday, Nov. 19.—Walk to the higher Crescent to see the Eclipse, but is too cloudy; see many disconsolate people with burnt glass. Finish 1st book of Locke, read Curtius, and work. Shelley reads Locke, Plutarch, and "Paradise Lost" aloud. Letter from Albe.[47]

Wednesday, Nov. 20.—Draw and write (137); read Locke and Curtius; begin [Richardson's] "Pamela." Shelley reads Locke, and in the evening "Paradise Lost" aloud to me.

Thursday, Nov. 21.—Drawing lesson. Write, read Locke, and walk out; after dinner read Curtius. After tea Shelley reads "Paradise Lost" aloud. Read "Pamela." Little Babe not well. Shelley reads Locke and "Pamela."

Friday, Nov. 22.—Draw, read Locke, and write; walk after dinner; read Curtius. Shelley reads Locke and Curtius, and finishes "Paradise Lost"; reads "Pamela" aloud.

Saturday, Nov. 23.—Babe is not well. Write, draw and walk; read Locke. Shelley reads Locke and Curtius, and "Pamela" aloud in the evening. Elise[48] goes to the play.

Sunday, Nov. 24.—Write, read Locke, and draw; walk after dinner; read Curtius and "Pamela"; work. After tea Shelley reads Curtius.

Monday, Nov. 25.—Write, and read Locke; draw, and walk. Shelley reads Curtius and Plutarch. Read "Pamela," and Shelley reads Gibbon, after tea.

Tuesday, Nov. 26.—Write, draw, and read Locke. Shelley reads Plutarch. Walk; read "Pamela"; after, read Curtius and "Les Incas." Shelley reads Gibbon in the evening; goes out to take a little walk, and loses himself.

Wednesday, Nov. 27.—Write; read Locke and "Pamela"; Curtius after tea. Shelley is not well; he reads Plutarch. Work in the evening, and read "Les Incas."

Thursday, Nov. 28.—Drawing lesson. Write; read "Pamela"; in the evening I finish Curtius. Shelley reads and finishes Plutarch's "Life of Alexander." After tea, Shelley reads the 20th chapter of Gibbon to me.

Friday, Nov. 29.—Write, read Locke, and walk; after dinner, read some of Livy, but am stopped by the badness of the edition. Shelley reads "Political Justice" and the 21st chapter of Gibbon aloud. Read "Pamela."

[47] To which Shelley replied on November 20 (see Julian edition, IX, 204–205).

[48] A Swiss nurse brought with them from Geneva. She remained in their service until early 1819, leaving them at Naples after having married the troublesome Paolo Foggi. She was already in 1816 a mother; her daughter (who remained in Switzerland) was called Aimée.

Saturday, Nov. 30.—Finish "Pamela"; draw, write, read Locke, and walk. Shelley reads "Political Justice" and 22nd chapter of Gibbon. Read two Odes of Horace.

Sunday, Dec. 1.—Letter from Leigh Hunt.[49] Send the present of Mathews. Write; read Locke, and the "Edinburgh Review," and two Odes of Horace. Shelley reads "Political Justice" and Shakespeare, and the 23rd chapter of Gibbon.

Monday, Dec. 2.—Drawing lesson. Write, read Locke, and walk. Shelley reads Roscoe's "Life of Lorenzo de Medicis." Read Lucian, and work in the evening; read several Odes of Horace.

Tuesday, Dec. 3.—Write; draw; read Locke and the "Life of Lorenzo." Shelley reads it, and finishes it. In the evening he reads 25th [24th?] chapter of Gibbon and several Odes of Horace.

Wednesday, Dec. 4.—A letter from Mrs. Godwin to Clare, and to me a letter from Aunt Everina concerning my sister [Fanny]. Write; read the "Life of Lorenzo." Shelley reads the Appendix, and writes to Hayward and Papa; he reads the 25th chapter of Gibbon aloud.

Thursday, Dec. 5.—Shelley sets off for Marlow. Drawing lesson. Write; send a letter to Aunt Everina [and a letter to] Shelley. Read Lucian aloud to Clare;[50] one Ode of Horace; in the evening, the "Quarterly Review" and Locke.

Friday, Dec. 6.—Read Lucian; write; draw; read Horace. Letter from Mrs. Godwin and 100*l.* Write to Mrs. Godwin and Shelley; work; read the "Rights of Women" [by Mary Wollstonecraft].

Saturday, Dec. 7.—Walk; write; read the "Rights of Women"; "Opuscula" of Cicero; read Lucian, and work; draw.

Sunday, Dec. 8.—Write; read "Rights of Women"; "Opuscula."

Monday, Dec. 9.—Drawing lesson. Letters from Mrs. Godwin and Charles Clairmont.[51] Write; finish the "Rights of Women"; begin "Chesterfield's Letters to his Son"; read "Opuscula"; work.

Tuesday, Dec. 10.—Write; read Locke and Chesterfield, "De Senectute," and "The Wanderer."[52]

[49] Shelley's real friendship with Hunt began at this time (see Dowden, II, 59–63; and White, I, 475–79).

[50] S&M reads "Write; send a letter to Aunt Everina. Shelley read Lucian aloud to Clare . . . ." There can be no doubt that the S&M reading is wrong and that the alteration is substantially correct. Shelley left early that morning for Marlow; Mary did write Shelley a letter on the fifth (see *Letters,* I, 13–15); and it was Mary who was at this time reading Lucian, Horace, and Locke. For some days previous, Shelley's principal reading had been Gibbon's History. Dowden also suggests this emendation in his copy of S&M (I, 166).

[51] Charles Clairmont to Shelley and Mary, November 18, 1816, Bagneres de Bigorre (S&M, I, 153–64).

[52] A long poem by Richard Savage (1729).

Wednesday, DEC. 11.—Draw; write; read "The Wanderer"; read "De Senectute" and Chesterfield.

Thursday, DEC. 12.—Letter from Shelley; he has gone to visit Leigh Hunt. A letter from Leigh Hunt. Drawing lesson. Read Chesterfield, Locke, and "De Senectute."

Friday, DEC. 13.—Write; read Locke, "De Senectute," and Chesterfield; draw. Letter from Shelley; he is pleased with Hunt.

Saturday, DEC. 14.—Draw; finish "Senectute"; read Chesterfield. Shelley comes back in the evening.

Sunday, DEC. 15.—Draw. A letter from [Thomas] Hookham with the news of the death of Harriet Shelley.[53] Walk out with Shelley. He goes to town after dinner. Read Chesterfield.

Monday, DEC. 16[–31].—I have omitted writing my Journal for some time. Shelley goes to London and returns; I go with him; spend the time between Leigh Hunt's and Godwin's. A marriage takes place on the 30th[54] of December, 1816. Draw; read Lord Chesterfield and Locke.

List of Books read in 1816

MARY

*(Those marked * Shelley has read also.)*

*[C. P.] Mortiz, Tour in England. [Translated from the German, 1795.]
Tales of the Minstrels. [By Monsieur Le Grand; tr. from French *c.* 1775.]
*[Mungo] Park's Journal of a Journey in Africa. [1815.]
Peregrine Proteus. [By Christoph M. Wieland, 1791; tr. by W. Tooke, 1796.]
*[Byron's] Siege of Corinth. Byron's Parisina. [Both 1816.]
4 vols. of Clarendon's History [of the Rebellion and Civil Wars in England, 3 vols., 1702–1704].
*Modern Philosophers. [By Elizabeth Hamilton, 3 vols., Bath, 1800.]
Opinions of various Writers [Different Authors up]on the Punishment of Death. By B[asil] Montagu. [1809.]
Erskine's Speeches. [The Speeches of the Hon. Thomas Erskine, 4 vols., 1810.]
*Caleb Williams. [By William Godwin, 3 vols., 1794.]

53 T. Hookham to Shelley, December 13, 1816 (Dowden, II, 67–68). Harriet's body had been found in the Serpentine on December 10. For matters relating to Harriet's death, see Dowden, II, 63–74; and White, I, 480–89.

54 S&M reads "29th," which the MS notes of Miss Grylls confirms as the true reading of the MS journal. It is, however, an error; Shelley and Mary were married at St. Mildred's Church, London, on December 30 (see Dowden, II, 72).

*3rd Canto of Childe Harold. [By Lord Byron, 1816.]
Schiller's Armenian. [Der Geisterseher (1789), tr. by William Render as The Armenian, or The Ghost Seer (1800).]
Lady Craven's Letters. [Letters from [Elizabeth] Craven to the Margrave of Anspach in 1785 and 1786, 1814 (2nd ed.).]
Caliste.
Nouvelles Nouvelles. [By Madame de Genlis. Repeated below.]
Romans de Voltaire.
Reveries d'un [Promeneur] Solitaire, de Rousseau. [1776–78.]
Adêle et Théodore. [By Madame de Genlis, 1782.]
*Lettres Persannes de Montesquieu. [1721.]
Tableau de Famille. [By Denis Diderot.]
Le Vieux de la Montagne. [By Ludwig Tieck, a French translation of.]
*Conjuration de Rienzi. [By J. F. Laignelot. A repetition.]
Walther, par [August H. J.] La Fontaine. [A French translation, 4 vols., Paris, 1811.]
Le Vœux Temeraires. [By Madame de Genlis. English translation, Rash Vows, 3 vols., 1799.]
Herman d'Una. [By Prof. Kramer; tr. from German, 3 vols., 1794.]
Nouveaux Nouvelles de Mad. de Genlis. [A repetition; title incorrect.]
Contes Moraux de [Jean F.] Marmontel.
*Christabel. [1816.]
Caroline de Lichtenfeld. [By Jeanne I. Bottens, Baroness de Montolieu; tr. by Thomas Holcroft, 3 vols., 1786.]
*Bertram. [By Charles R. Maturin.]
*Le Criminel Secret.
Vancenza. By Mrs. [Mary] Robinson. [2 vols., 1792.]
Antiquary. [By Sir Walter Scott, 3 vols., Edinburgh, 1816.]
*Edinburgh Review. No. LII. [June 1816, Vol. 26.]
Chrononhotonthologus. [By Henry Carey, 1734.]
*Fazio. [By Henry H. Milman, 1815.]
Love and Madness. [By Sir Herbert Croft, 1780.]
Memoirs of Princess of Bareith.
*Letters of Emile. [By Rousseau, 1762.]
The latter part of Clarissa Harlowe. [By Samuel Richardson, 7 vols., 1748.]
Clarendon's History of the Civil War. [A repetition.]
*Life of Holcroft. [By Holcroft himself, completed by William Hazlitt, 3 vols., 1816.]
*Glenarvon. [By Lady Caroline Lamb, 1816.]
Patronage. [By Maria Edgeworth, 4 vols., 1814.]
The Milesian Chief. [By Charles R. Maturin, 4 vols., 1812.]

O'Donnel. [By Lady Morgan, 3 vols., 1814.]
*Don Quixote. [By Miguel de Cervantes.]
*Vita Alexandri Quintii Curtii.
Conspiration de Rienzi. [By Joseph François Laignelot.]
Introduction to Davy's Chemistry. [?Elements of Chemical Philosophy, 1812.]
Les Incas de [Jean Françoise] Marmontel. [1777.]
Bryan Perdue. [By Thomas Holcroft, 3 vols., 1805.]
Sir C. Grandison. [By Samuel Richardson, 7 vols., 1754.]
*Castle Rackrent. [By Maria Edgeworth, 1800.]
*Gulliver's Travels. [By Jonathan Swift, 1726.]
*Paradise Lost. [By John Milton, 1667.]
*Pamela. [By Samuel Richardson, 2 vols., 1741.]
*3 vols. of Gibbon['s Decline and Fall of the Roman Empire, 12 vols., 1783–90].
1 book of Locke's Essay [Concerning Human Understanding, 1690].
Some of Horace's Odes.
*Edinburgh Review, LIII. [Sept. 1816, Vol. 27.]
Rights of Women. [By Mary Wollstonecraft, 1792.]
De Senectute. By Cicero.
2 vols. of Lord Chesterfield's Letters to his Son. [2 vols., 1774; later editions 4 vols.]
*Story of Rimini. [By Leigh Hunt, 1816.]

SHELLEY

Works of Theocritus, Moschus, &c.
Prometheus of Æschylus (Greek).
Works of Lucian (Greek).
*Telemacho. [François S. de La Mothe Fénelon, Télémaque, 1699.]
La Nouvelle Heloise. [By Rousseau, 1761.]
*[Thomas] Blackwell's History of the Court of Augustus. [3 vols., Edinburgh, 1753–56.]
Lucretius de Rerum Natura.
Epistolæ Plinii.
Annals. By Tacitus.
Several of Plutarch's Lives (Greek).
Germania of Tacitus.
Memoires d'un Detenu. [By Riouffe or Charles Dumont; see 1816, n. 16.]
Histoire de la Revolution. Par Rabault et Lacretelle. [Two separate books.]
Montaigne's Essays.

Tasso. [Gerusalemme Liberata, 1581.]
Life of Cromwell. [? Memoirs of Oliver Cromwell and His Children, Supposed to be Written by Himself, 3 vols., 1816.]
Locke's Essay [Concerning Human Understanding, 1690].
Political Justice. [By William Godwin, 2 vols., 1793.]
Lorenzo de Medicis. [By William Roscoe, 2 vols., 1795.]
Coleridge's Lay Sermon. [The Statesman's Manual . . . A Lay Sermon, 1816.]

1817

ENGLAND

Wednesday, JAN. 1.—Return from London; travel all day; unwell.

Thursday, JAN. 2.—Read "Lord Chesterfield's Letters"; part of the "Lay Sermon" [by Coleridge]. Shelley writes.

Friday, JAN. 3.—Read Lord Chesterfield; write; finish the "Lay Sermon." Shelley writes.

Saturday, JAN. 4.—Read Lord Chesterfield; write; work. Shelley writes.

Sunday, JAN. 5.—Finish Lord Chesterfield; read "Douglas"[1] and [? James Shirley's] "The Gamester"; write. Shelley writes.

Monday, JAN. 6.—Shelley goes to London. Write; read several papers in [Addison's] "The Spectator"; Locke, and "Memoirs of Count Gramont" [by Anthony Hamilton]. Meeting held here; very quiet.

Tuesday, JAN. 7.—Write; read "Life of Clarendon";[2] walk; read a little Latin; work.

Wednesday, JAN. 8.—Write; read Locke; walk; read "Life of Clarendon"; work.

Thursday, JAN. 9.—Walk out all the morning; read [Cicero's] "Somnium Scipionis" and [Smollett's] "Roderick Random."

Friday, JAN. 10.—Write; finish "Roderick Random"; work.

Saturday, JAN. 11.—

Sunday, JAN. 12.—[11–15]—Charles Clairmont.[3]—Four days of idle-

[1] Probably the tragedy by John Home.

[2] By himself: Edward Hyde, Earl of Clarendon (1759).

[3] Evidently refers to a letter from Charles, who was in France.

SHELLEY'S HOUSE AT MARLOW, 1817

Reprinted by permission from the Illustrated London News, *August 6, 1892*

ness.[4] Letters from Shelley;[5] he is obliged to stay in London. Read "Comus"; "Knights of the Swan";[6] 1st volume of Goldsmith's "Citizen of the World."

Thursday, JAN. 16.—Read [Richard] Cumberland's "Memoirs"; work.

Friday, JAN. 17.—Read "Memoirs"; walk out, and work.

Saturday, JAN. 18.—Read "Memoirs," and work.

Sunday, JAN. 19.—Finish the "Memoirs of Cumberland"; read [Johnson's] "The Rambler."

Monday, JAN. 20.— Read Junius. Rain all day. Work.

Tuesday, JAN. 21.—Walk out, work, and read ["Letters of] Junius"; read "Amadis."[7]

Wednesday, JAN. 22.—Read Junius, "Somnium Scipionis," and work; read "Amadis of Gaul."

Thursday, JAN. 23.—Read and finish Junius; finish "Somnium Scipionis"; work; read "Amadis."

Friday, JAN. 24.—My William's birthday. How many changes have occurred during this little year; may the ensuing one be more peaceful, and my William's star be a fortunate one to rule the decision of this day.[8] Alas! I fear it will be put off, and the influence of the star pass away. Read the "Arcadia" [by Sir Philip Sidney] and "Amadis"; walk with my sweet babe.

Saturday, JAN. 25.—An unhappy day. I receive bad news, and determine to go up to London. Read the "Arcadia" and "Amadis." Letter from Mrs. Godwin and William [Godwin, Jr.].

Sunday, JAN. 26.—Journey to town. Mrs. Godwin and William at the inn to meet me.

Monday, JAN. 27.—Read "The Rehearsal" [by the Duke of Buckingham]; in the evening visit Hunt's. Shelley is not very well.

Tuesday, JAN. 28.—Read the "Journey to the World Underground";[9] return to the Godwins; read "The Rehearsal"; go with Shelley to [Basil] Montague's; he is frightened with a letter concerning Hunt, but it is all nothing.

[4] Claire's baby Alba (renamed Allegra in 1818) was born on January 12, which accounts for Mary's "idleness" and neglect of her journal. Mary's reticence concerning Claire, especially her connection with Byron, is emphatically indicated by her failure to record the birth of Claire's child, which she even hides from prying eyes under "Four days of idleness." In fact, Mary is very cautious about recording any personal matters.

[5] Shelley to Mary, January 11, 1817 (Dowden, II, 97–98; Julian edition, IX, 215–16); and Shelley to Mary, [undated] (Dowden, II, 98–99; Julian edition, IX, 217–18).

[6] By Madame de Genlis; translated by the Rev. Beresford (1796, 3 vols.).

[7] Vasco de Lobeira, *Amadis de Gaul,* translated by Robert Southey.

[8] A reference to the Chancery proceedings concerning Shelley's children by Harriet. For a history of the Chancery suit, see Dowden, II, 76–95; and White, I, 489–97.

[9] A novel by Ludwig, Baron Holberg; English translation, 1742.

Wednesday, JAN. 29.—Read "The Restoration" [by the Duke of Buckingham]. Shelley is out, but nothing takes place. I wish "Blue Eyes"[10] was with me. Go to the Play—"Jealous Wife"[11] and "The Ravens."[12] P. Pilcher[13] dines.

Thursday, JAN. 30.—Shelley and Godwin call on [Henry, Lord] Brougham. William Godwin goes to school. Read the "Arcadia"; see Marshall and Peter; come to Hunt's, and remain the night there; read Hunt's Journal,[14] which is extremely interesting.

Friday, JAN. 31.—Write the Journal; read the "Arcadia." Shelley goes to town with Hunt.

Saturday, FEB. 1.—Read the "Arcadia" and the "World Underground." Shelley dines at Skinner Street. In the evening Hunt, Mrs. Hunt, and I go to the Opera—[Mozart's] "Figaro."[15] I am very much pleased. We sleep at Godwin's.

Sunday, FEB. 2.—A disagreeable conversation with Mrs. Godwin in the morning. Shelley goes to Hunt's. Read [Scott's] "Tales of my Landlord"; walk with Papa; write out Shelley's Declaration [in the Chancery proceedings].[16]

Monday, FEB. 3.—Read "Tales of my Landlord"; dine at Hunt's, and sleep. P. Pilcher at Godwin's.

Tuesday, FEB. 4.—Hear Hunt's music; dine with Hunt, Mrs. Hunt, and Miss K[ent][17] at Godwin's; sleep at Hunt's.

Wednesday, FEB. 5.—Read "Tales of my Landlord"; walk on the Heath. Messrs. Keats and Reynolds[18] sup at Hampstead.

Thursday, FEB. 6.—Finish "Tales of my Landlord"; hear Hunt's music; go to town; read Beaumont's "Hermaphroditus";[19] sup with Godwin, and have a pleasant conversation with him.

Friday, FEB. 7.—Out all day with Mrs. Godwin; read the "Arcadia"; return to Hunt's; talk with Mrs. Hunt in the evening.

10 William, her child, often so called.

11 A comedy by George Colman, produced at Drury Lane on February 12, 1761; published in 1761.

12 Isaac Pocock, *The Ravens; or, The Force of Conscience,* a melodrama, produced at Covent Garden on January 28, 1817 (Allardyce Nicoll, *A History of Early Nineteenth Century Drama, 1800–1850* [Cambridge, The University Press, 1930, 2 vols.], II, 374).

13 A Marlow friend.

14 *The Examiner* for January 26 (see Dowden, II, 84).

15 *Le Nozze di Figaro (The Marriage of Figaro).*

16 See Dowden, II, 86–88; and White, I, 494–95.

17 Elizabeth (Bessy) Kent, Mrs. Hunt's sister.

18 John Keats and his friend John Hamilton Reynolds, who, with Shelley, had been praised by Hunt in his famous "Young Poets" article in the December 1, 1816, *Examiner.*

19 A poem, *Salmasis and Hermaphroditus* (1602).

Saturday, FEB. 8.—Shelley and Hunt go to London to attend the Chancery. Read the "Arcadia"; dine and spend the evening at H[orace] Smith's. The suit is again put off.

Sunday, FEB. 9.—Walk with Shelley and Hunt to [Lord] Brougham's in the morning; after dinner, read the "Arcadia." Several of Hunt's acquaintances come in the evening. Music. After supper, a discussion until 3 in the morning with [William] Hazlitt concerning Monarchy and Republicanism.

Monday, FEB. 10.—Read the "Arcadia"; go to Godwin's. Lambs [Charles and Mary] call there.

Tuesday, FEB. 11.—Read the "Arcadia." Shelley attends Chancery; he hears that the question will not come on, and quits the Court; it is argued afterwards, but no judgment given. Mr. Hunt and Miss Kent dine at Godwin's. We go to the play—see the "Merchant of Venice." See Miss L[amb] there. Return to Hunt's to sleep.

Wednesday, FEB. 12.—Not well; read the "Arcadia." Shelley goes to the Godwins. J[ohn] and G[eorge] Keats drink tea and sup.

Thursday, FEB. 13.—Read the "Arcadia" all day; remain at Hunt's.

Friday, FEB. 14.—Read the "Arcadia" and [Beaumont and Fletcher's] "Cupid's Revenge." Shelley reads the "Arcadia." He is out all day with Mrs. Hunt.

Saturday, FEB. 15.—Finish the "Arcadia." Shelley goes to town. Mr. Keats calls. Walk out. Miss Kent is ill.

Sunday, FEB. 16.—Walk out with Shelley. Mr. and Mrs. Hazlitt, B. Montagu, and Godwin dine; in the evening, others come in. Music.

Monday, FEB. 17.—Not well; read the "Martial Maid" and the "Wild Goose Chase" of Beaumont and Fletcher.

Tuesday, FEB. 18.—Walk out with Mrs. and Mr. Hunt. Clare and William arrive. Conversation and music in the evening.

Wednesday, FEB. 19.—Walk out with Hunt; go to Skinner Street with William and Clare; return at 7. Several people sup at the Hunts'.

Thursday, FEB. 20.—Shelley and Hunt go to town. Walk to Clare's; read "The Round Table" [by William Hazlitt].

Friday, FEB. 21.—Read "The Round Table"; go to Clare; read after dinner. Mrs. Hunt frightens us by staying out late.

Saturday, FEB. 22.—Arrange Hunt's flowers; read; go to Shout's,[20] and to the play with Mr. and Mrs. Hunt and Elise—[John Gay's] "Beggars' Opera," "Bombastes Furioso,"[21] and the "Flight of the Zephyr."

Sunday, FEB. 23[–APR. 9].—We remain at Hunt's some time longer,

[20] A sculptor's.

[21] A burlesque by William Barnes Rhodes (1810).

and then Shelley, William, Clare,[22] and I depart for Marlow. Shelley returns Monday [March 3].[23] I read "The Rambler" and "Amadis." I go up to town the following day;[24] see Manuel and the picture of Brutus. I return Thursday [? March 13], and the following week we enter our house [on March 18]. Write every day; read [Scott's] "Waverley," Pliny's Letters, "Political Justice," and Milton's "Tenure of Kings and Magistrates." Shelley reads "Waverley," "Tales of my Landlord," and several of the works of Plato. Godwin comes down [April 2] and we go on the water [April 3 and 5] with him. Sunday [April 6] he returns. We go to Maidenhead with him. It is drearily cold. In the evening the Hunts come. Mrs. Hunt is very unwell. —— comes. C[laire] has been with us a week before.[25]

Thursday, Apr. 10.—Correct "Frankenstein." Shelley reads "Alcestis." A little turmoil in the evening. Mrs. Hunt is very unwell.

Friday, Apr. 11.—Correct "Frankenstein"; work. Shelley reads Wordsworth aloud in the evening.

Saturday, Apr. 12.—Correct "Frankenstein"; walk; read Pliny; work.

Sunday, Apr. 13.—Correct "Frankenstein"; read "Political Justice"; walk with Shelley and Pilcher, and see a white owl. After tea, Shelley reads Spenser aloud.

Monday, Apr. 14.—Correct "Frankenstein"; walk after dinner; go in the boat to Temple. Shelley reads Spenser in the evening.

Tuesday, Apr. 15.—Correct "Frankenstein"; read Pliny. Shelley goes to Henley. Walk after dinner; work.

Wednesday, Apr. 16.—Correct "Frankenstein"; not well; work, and talk with Mrs. Hunt. Shelley reads the Bible.

Thursday, Apr. 17.—Correct "Frankenstein"; read Pliny; work. Shelley reads "History of the French Revolution" [by Rabaut St.-Étienne?].

Friday, Apr. 18.—Transcribe; after dinner, walk to Little Marlow with Shelley and Pilcher.

Saturday, Apr. 19.—Transcribe; go on the water with Willy and Shelley, and the others walk by the river-side.

22 An error for Elise, for it is evident that Claire remained in London until after the Marlow house was occupied by the Shelleys on March 18.

23 See Mary's letters of March 2 and 5 written at Marlow (*Letters,* I, 18–23).

24 Probably an error for Monday, [March 10].

25 The full text probably would read: "Alba comes. Claire has been with us since a week before." It is clear that Claire and her child did not come to Marlow until the Shelleys were settled in their house. In order to avoid local gossip, Claire probably came down shortly before Godwin's arrival, and Alba was probably brought down by the Hunts.

In her MS notes Miss Grylls states that the original journal reads: "S. comes. C. has been with us a week now." The "S." must be a misreading, for Shelley had not been away recently.

Sunday, APR. 20.—Transcribe; after dinner, walk in the garden.

Monday, APR. 21.—Transcribe. In the evening, Shelley finishes reading "Macbeth."

Tuesday, APR. 22.—Transcribe; walk to the wood; work. Shelley reads "History of the French Revolution," and goes to Medmenham with Mrs. Hunt and Pilcher.

Wednesday, APR. 23.—Transcribe; read Pliny; finish 3rd book; go out in the boat with Shelley and Willy. Shelley reads "History of the French Revolution," and Spenser aloud in the evening.

Thursday, APR. 24.—Transcribe all day, and, after tea, read Pliny, and walk. Shelley reads a canto of Spenser.

Friday, APR. 25.—Transcribe all day. After tea, Shelley reads two cantos of Spenser.

Saturday, APR. 26.—

Tuesday, APR. 29.—Transcribe, and correct "Frankenstein"; read Pliny; walk. The piano arrives. Shelley reads Spenser aloud, and finishes the 1st and begins the 2nd book.

Wednesday, APR. 30.—

Saturday, MAY 3.—Transcribe; read Pliny; walk out. On May 3rd, a letter. Shelley reads "History of the French Revolution."

Sunday, MAY 4.—

Friday, MAY 9.—Read Pliny; transcribe; read "Clarke's Travels." Shelley writes, and reads Apuleius and Spenser in the evening.

Saturday, MAY 10.—

Tuesday, MAY 13.—Finish transcribing; read Pliny and "Clarke's Travels." Shelley writes his Poem ["Laon and Cythna"]; reads "History of the French Revolution" and Spenser aloud in the evening.

Wednesday, MAY 14.—Read Pliny and Clarke. Shelley reads "History of the French Revolution," and corrects "Frankenstein." Write Preface. Finis.

Thursday, MAY 15.—Read Pliny and Clarke; walk in the garden. Shelley reads "History of the French Revolution," and walks; he reads Spenser in the evening.

Friday, MAY 16.—

Monday, MAY 19.—Read Pliny and "Clarke's Travels." Shelley reads "History of the French Revolution," and Spenser in the evening. Think of going to Henley on ———. A letter.

Tuesday, MAY 20.—Read Apuleius. Shelley reads Spenser aloud.

Wednesday, MAY 21.—Read Apuleius. Shelley reads Spenser aloud.

Thursday, MAY 22.—We depart from Marlow[26] at half-past 10. The

[26] Mary's main purpose in going to London was to arrange for the publication of *Frankenstein*. She lodged at Godwin's house.

day is cloudy, but pleasant, and the banks of the Thames delightful. Sleep at Kingston.

Friday, MAY 23.—A very fine day. We arrive in London about 2. Godwin dines at [John Philpot] Curran's. Go to the Opera with Shelley—[Mozart's] "Don Giovanni."

Saturday, MAY 24.—Go to the Exhibition. (Canova's Sculptures; Turner's Landscape; the Bard; Portrait of Salamé, like Albe.) Read "Anna St. Ives."[27] Ogilvie calls.

Sunday, MAY 25.—Read Suetonius, and finish "Anna St. Ives." Hogg and Ogilvie dine; Hazlitt comes in the evening.

Monday, MAY 26.—Read Suetonius, and Defoe on the Plague; walk with Godwin. Shelley leaves us [for Marlow]. Read Defoe. In the evening, walk to Somers Town. [John] Murray likes "Frankenstein."

Tuesday, MAY 27.—Finish Defoe; read Suetonius; finish Cæsar; read and finish [John Wilson's] "City of the Plague"; go to the theatre—[John Brown's] "Barbarossa."

Wednesday, MAY. 28.—Read Suetonius, and Miss Edgeworth's "Comic Dramas." F[anny] Holcroft's Novel ["Fortitude and Frailty"]. Godwin sups with Hazlitt at Dr. Wolcot's. Write to W. G.;[28] read 3rd canto of "Childe Harold."

I am melancholy with reading the 3rd canto of "Childe Harold." Do you not remember, Shelley, when you first read it to me? One evening after returning from Diodati. It was in our little room at Chapuis.[29] The lake was before us, and the mighty Jura. That time is past, and this will also pass, when I may weep to read these words, and again moralise on the flight of time.

Dear Lake! I shall ever love thee. How a powerful mind can sanctify past scenes and recollections! His is a powerful mind; and that fills me with melancholy, yet mixed with pleasure, as is always the case when intellectual energy is displayed. I think of our excursions on the lake. How we saw him when he came down to us, or welcomed our arrival, with a good-humoured smile. How vividly does each verse of his poem recall some scene of this kind to my memory! This time will soon also be a recollection. We may see him again, and again enjoy his society; but the time will also arrive when that which is now an anticipation will be only in the memory. Death will at length come, and in the last moment all will be a dream.

27 By Thomas Holcroft (1792, 7 vols.).

28 Possibly an error for M. H. (Marianne Hunt, who was then at Marlow). William Godwin, Jr., could be indicated if he were away from home.

29 Not recorded in the journal.

Am I not very melancholy? Godwin is out, and I shall finish the canto, although I fear it will not raise my spirits.

Thursday, MAY 29.—Finish F. Holcroft's Novel; read Suetonius; talk with Godwin. Shopping. Read the "Quarterly Review." Marshall dines with us. Godwin dines at Curran's.

Friday, MAY 30.—Marshall breakfasts with us. Shopping. Read the "Quarterly Review." After dinner, walk with Papa to the New Bridge, and sup at [Charles] Lamb's. Cards.

Saturday, MAY 31.—Shopping. Return to Marlow. Shelley and Mrs. Hunt not well.

Sunday, JUNE 1.—Read [Thomas Moore's] "Lalla Rookh"; not well all day.

Monday, JUNE 2.—Not well; work. Shelley reads Homer, and writes.

Tuesday, JUNE 3.—Letter from Dublin. Work; walk out. Shelley reads Homer.

Wednesday, JUNE 4.—Begin Tacitus; walk out with Shelley; sit to Mrs. Hunt in the evening. Shelley reads "St. Helena Manuscript."[30]

Thursday, JUNE 5.—Read Tacitus; walk in the garden with Shelley; after dinner, sit to Mrs. Hunt. Shelley reads "Histoire de la Revolution Française," and two cantos of Spenser in the evening.

Friday, JUNE 6.—Read Tacitus and "St. Helena Manuscript"; walk in the garden. In the evening, Shelley reads Spenser aloud.

Saturday, JUNE 7.—

Saturday, JUNE [7–]14.—Finish the 1st book of Tacitus; become unwell; read "Davis's Travels in America." Godwin's "Cursory Strictures." "Reply to the attacks of Dr. [Samuel] Parr";[31] write to I[sabel] B[axter]. Shelley reads "Histoire de la Philosophie Moderne"[32] and Spenser aloud. Longdill comes down, and spends Friday night [June 13] here.

Sunday, JUNE 15.—Read Tacitus; walk in the garden.

Monday, JUNE 16.—Read Tacitus; go on the water in the evening with Shelley, Elise, and William; read Buffon in the evening.

Tuesday, JUNE 17.—Read Tacitus; go in the boat to Medmenham Abbey; spend the day there; return on the ass.

Wednesday, JUNE 18.—Shelley, Hunt, Mary Anne, Miss Kent, and the children go to Clifton Woods. Finish 2nd book of Tacitus, and read Buffon's "Histoire Naturelle." Shelley reads Arrian. Watson acquitted; read his trial. "Frankenstein" sent back;[33] send it to Godwin.

[30] By J. Fréderic Lullin de Chateauvieux (London, 1817, published anonymously).

[31] Two pamphlets by Godwin: *Cursory Strictures on Lord Chief Justice Eyre's Charge to the Grand Jury* (1794) (anonymous); and *Thoughts Occasioned by Dr. Parr's Spital Sermon, being a Reply to the Attacks of Dr. Parr,* &c. (1801). (The *Spital Sermon* was an attack on *Political Justice.*) S&M, "Godwin's cursory strictures."

[32] By title only in Appendix IV.

[33] By John Murray.

Thursday, JUNE 19.—Work. Shelley goes to Hambledon. Read a little of Tacitus.

Friday, JUNE 20.—Work; read Tacitus. Shelley writes, and reads Arrian.

Saturday, JUNE 21.—Letter from I[sabel] B[axter].[34] Shelley is out all day; he writes, and reads Arrian. Read Tacitus. Shelley reads the 1st act of the "Faithful Shepherdess" [by John Fletcher] aloud.

Sunday, JUNE 22.—Shelley reads Arrian. Read Tacitus.

Monday, JUNE 23.—I remain with Marianne [Hunt] all day, who scrapes the statues. Shelley reads Arrian's "Historia Indica."

Tuesday, JUNE 24.—The statues. Shelley reads Arrian.

Wednesday, JUNE 25.—Hunt, Marianne, Shelley, and Thornton depart for London. Read "Sleeper Awakened" in the "Arabian Nights"; walk out.

Thursday, JUNE 26.—Read Tacitus and Buffon.

Friday, JUNE 27.—Read Tacitus and [Rousseau's] "Julie."

Saturday, JUNE 28.—Read "Julie." Shelley returns at midnight.

Sunday, JUNE 29.—Read "Julie." Talk with Shelley.

Monday, JUNE 30.—Read "Julie." Shelley reads Homer. He is not well.

Tuesday, JULY 1.—Read "Julie." Shelley very unwell; he reads Homer.

Wednesday, JULY 2.—Finish "Julie"; read Tacitus. Shelley reads Homer. He is better.

Thursday, JULY 3.—Read Tacitus; finish 3rd book; read Buffon. Shelley reads Homer.

Friday, JULY 4.—Read Tacitus. Shelley reads Homer.

Saturday, JULY 5.—

Tuesday, JULY 8.—Read Tacitus; the "Persian Letters" [by Montesquieu]. Shelley reads Homer, and writes; reads a canto of Spenser and part of the "Gentle Shepherdess" aloud.

Wednesday, JULY 9.—Read Tacitus and Buffon. Shelley reads Homer and Plutarch.

Thursday, JULY 10.—Read Tacitus. Shelley reads Spenser aloud. Read Buffon.

Friday, JULY 11.—Shelley reads Homer's Hymns. Finish 5th book of Tacitus. Shelley reads Spenser aloud.

Saturday, JULY 12.—Write from Pliny; read Tacitus. Shelley reads Homer's Hymns. Miss Kent and the [Hunt] children depart. William Cambden. Work.

Sunday, JULY 13.—Read Tacitus. Shelley reads "Prometheus Desmotes" [of Æschylus], and I write it. He reads Homer's Hymns.

[34] S&M, "J. B."

Monday, JULY 14.—Read Tacitus; transcribe; work. Books arrive from London.

Tuesday, JULY 15.—

Tuesday, JULY [15]–22.—Read Tacitus; "Clarke's Travels"; transcribe for Shelley. Shelley writes; reads several of the Plays of Æschylus, and Spenser aloud in the evening.

Wednesday, JULY 23.—

Saturday, JULY [23–]26.—Read Tacitus; read Miss [Maria] Edgeworth's "Harrington" and "Ormond"; [C. B. Brown's] "Arthur Mervyn." Shelley reads the "Agamemnon" of Æschylus, and walks to Hampden and Virginia Water. Hogg is in Marlow.

Sunday, JULY 27.—

Thursday, JULY [27–]31.—Read Tacitus and "Clarke's Travels." Shelley goes to Egham; he reads Æschylus and [Elphinstone's] "Travels in the Kingdom of Caubul." Read "Rasselas"; make jellies, and work. Hogg returns to London, talking of ducks and women. A disagreeable letter from Isabel.

Friday, AUG. 1.—

Tuesday, AUG. [1–6][35] 5.—Work; read Tacitus. A letter from Longdill with the Master's decision—against us. Shelley finishes the Plays of Æschylus; finishes the "History of Caubul"; writes; reads three chapters of Gibbon aloud. Monday Shelley's birthday; he is 25.

Wednesday, AUG. 6.—

Saturday, AUG. 9.—Shelley reads Gibbon aloud. Write the Journal of our travels.[36] Work; not well.

Sunday, AUG. 10.—

Wednesday, AUG. [10–]13.—Shelley writes; reads Plato's "Convivium" ["The Symposium"]; Gibbon aloud. Read several of Beaumont and Fletcher's Plays. Write Journal of our first travels.

Thursday, AUG. 14.—

Sunday, AUG. [14–]17.—Read the Plays [of Beaumont and Fletcher]; write. Shelley finishes 5th volume of Gibbon; begins reading aloud [Ben Jonson's] "Cynthia's Revels"; writes, and reads the "Œdipus" of Sophocles.

Monday, AUG. 18.—

Saturday, AUG. [18–]24.—Read a little of Tacitus; several of Beaumont and Fletcher's Plays. Shelley reads [Ben Jonson's] "Volpone" and

[35] This entry also includes August 6, for it was on that date that Longdill's letter, dated the fifth, was received. For Longdill's letter, see *Shelley Memorials,* ed. by Lady [Jane] Shelley (London, Smith, Elder and Co., 1859), 75–76. See also Mary's letter of August 6, 1817, to Mrs. Hunt (*Letters,* I, 27–29). For the Master's decision, see Mary's *Letters,* I, 28 n., and Dowden, II, 91–94.

[36] Published as *History of a Six Weeks' Tour* (1817).

"The Alchemist" aloud, and begins "Lalla Rookh." Work. A letter from Lackington, [Allen & Co.].[37]

Sunday, Aug. 25.—

Friday, Aug. [25–]29.—Finish the 11th book of Tacitus; read some of Beaumont and Fletcher's Plays; work. Shelley writes. Read some of the Plays of Sophocles, and "Antony and Cleopatra" of Shakespeare, and "Othello" aloud. Hookham comes to Marlow; I do not see him.

Saturday, Aug. 30.—My birthday.

Monday, Sept. 1.—Mr. Baxter[38] arrives. Read the "Fall of Sejanus" [by Ben Jonson]. Shelley walks with Mr. Baxter.

Tuesday, Sept. 2.—[Clara is born.]

Friday, Sept. [2–]19.—I am confined Tuesday, 2nd. Read "Rhoda,"[39] "Pastor's Fireside,"[40] "Missionary," "Wild Irish Girl,"[41] "The Anaconda,"[42] [Lady C. Lamb's] "Glenarvon," 1st volume of "Percy's Northern Antiquities."[43] Bargain with Lackington concerning "Frankenstein." Letter from Albe.[44] An unamiable letter from Godwin about Mrs. Godwin's visits. Mr. Baxter returns to town Thursday, 4th. Shelley writes his Poem; his health declines. Friday, 19th, Hunts arrive.

Saturday, Sept. 20.—

Monday, Sept. [20–]29.—Shelley finishes his Poem ["Laon and Cythna"], and goes up to town with Clare, Tuesday, 23rd. Hunts quit us on Thursday [Sept. 25]; Clare returns Friday [Sept. 26]; and Mr. Baxter quits us Monday [Sept. 29]. Read [Ben Jonson's] "Catiline's Conspiracy"; "Strathallan."[45]

Tuesday, Sept. 30.—

Sunday, [Sept. 30–] Oct. 5.—Shelley remains in town; much teased. Friday evening [Oct. 3] he comes down, and goes up again Saturday morning [Oct. 4]. Read Fielding's[46] "Amelia," [Smollett's] "Sir Launcelot Greaves," a little of Tacitus, [Thomas Moore's] "Twopenny Postbag" [1813].

Thursday, Oct. 9.—Read [Godwin's] "St. Leon" aloud; read "Davis's Travels in America"; Tacitus; work, and walk.

37 Which Shelley answered on August 22 (see Julian edition, IX, 240).

38 William T. Baxter, Isabel's father.

39 A novel, published anonymously (1816, 3 vols.).

40 A novel by Jane Porter (1817, 3 vols.).

41 By Lady Morgan, *The Missionary* (1811, 3 vols.); *The Wild Irish Girl* (1806, 3 vols.).

42 Not further identified.

43 Thomas Percy (1770, 2 vols.).

44 Which Shelley answered on September 24 (see Julian edition, IX, 245–47).

45 A novel by Alicia Lefanu (1816, 4 vols.).

46 S&M reads: ". . . and goes up again. Saturday morning, read Fielding's . . .", which is obviously wrong. See Mary's letter of October 5 to Shelley (*Letters,* I, 38–40).

Friday, Oct. 10.—

Sunday, Oct. [10–]12.—Walk out; work. Shelley comes down on Friday evening [Oct. 10]. Read, and finish "Miseries of Human Life";[47] write out letters from Geneva.[48] Shelley transcribes his Poem. On Saturday [Oct. 11] walk out with him and Willy. Peacock drinks tea here. Shelley goes away Sunday evening [Oct. 12]. Transcribe.

Monday, Oct. 13.—

Tuesday, Oct. 14[–21.]—Read Tacitus and "Les Lettres d'une Peruvienne";[49] walk; work. Shelley and Godwin come down Sunday evening [Oct. 19]. On Monday [Oct. 20][50] go to Hampden in a gig with Papa. See Hampden's Monument. The gig breaks down. The scenery between Hampden and the Harrow is very beautiful. Tuesday, we talk about various things. Curran dies, Tuesday, 14th.

Wednesday, Oct. 15 [error for 22].—Shelley and Godwin depart. Arrange the Library; transcribe "Frankenstein."

Thursday, Oct. 16 [error for 23].—

Monday, [Oct. 24–] Nov. 3.—Shelley comes down on Friday [Oct. 24] with [Walter] Coulson,[51] who stays until Sunday [Oct. 26]. Talk with him. Peacock drinks tea here. Shelley remains until the next Sunday [Nov. 2], writing,[52] reading, and walking. Write the translation of Spinosa from Shelley's dictation. Translate [Apuleius's] "Cupid and Psyche"; read Tacitus and "Rousseau's Confessions."

Tuesday, Nov. 4.—Read Tacitus; translate Apuleius; read "Rousseau's Confessions"; write to Mr. Baxter, and invite Christy [Baxter];[53] walk, and work.

Wednesday, Nov. 5.—Write; read a little of Tacitus; write to Shelley and William Godwin; walk; read "Rousseau's Confessions."

Thursday, Nov. 6.—Write to Shelley; translate Apuleius; read "Rousseau's Letters." The Princess Charlotte dies.

Friday, Nov. 7.—Read "Rousseau's Letters"; translate; pack up.

Saturday, Nov. 8.—Go to London with Elise; spend the day at Skinner Street.

[47] A novel by James Beresford (1806–1807, 2 vols.).

[48] For the *Six Weeks' Tour.*

[49] Madame Françoise Graffigny, *Les Lettres d'une Péruvienne Princesse,* a novel (1747).

[50] Godwin's diary establishes these dates (see Dowden, II, 155).

[51] Dowden (II, 155) describes Coulson as "a young *élève* of Jeremy Bentham, reporter for the *Chronicle,* afterwards editor of the *Globe,* a Cornishman, and himself a giant Cormoran of encyclopædic knowledge."

[52] S&M reads, ". . . Sunday. Writing, ..." Correction from the MS notes of Miss Grylls.

[53] See Mary to Christie Baxter, November, 1817 (*Letters,* I, 45).

Sunday, Nov. 9.—Call on the Hunts; finish "Rousseau's Letters." Godwin calls, and Mr. Baxter.[54]

Monday, Nov. 10.—Read Dante; call on the Hunts. Papa calls, and Mr. [Charles] Ollier [Shelley's publisher].

Tuesday, Nov. 11.—Read Lamb's "Specimens"; walk to Hunt's in the evening with Shelley. Papa and Mr. Ollier drink tea with us. Shelley begins a Pamphlet.[55]

Wednesday, Nov. 12.—Shelley finishes his Pamphlet. Walk to Hunt's; read Dante; finish Lamb's "Specimens"; walk to Mr. Ollier's; read "Zapolya."[56]

Thursday, Nov. 13.—Translate Apuleius; write to Isabel. Papa dines with us. Dr. Curry call. Mr. Baxter and Mr. [David] Booth spend the evening with us.

Friday, Nov. 14.—Translate; dine at Hunt's. Music in the evening.

Saturday, Nov. 15.—Translate; walk to Ollier's and Hookham's. Mr. and Mrs. Godwin dine here. Read Shelley's Pamphlet.

Sunday, Nov. 16.—Translate; dine at Godwin's; read [Molière's] "George Dandin."

Monday, Nov. 17.—Hookham and Hunts dine here. Coulson comes in the evening.

Tuesday, Nov. 18.—Spend the day at Hunt's. Mr. and Mrs. Godwin dine here. Hunt, Keats, and Coulson calls.

Wednesday, Nov. 19.—Return to Marlow. Read "Mathilde,"[57] &c.

Thursday, Nov. 20.—Walk; read "Family of Montorio."[58]

Friday, Nov. 21.—Finish the "Family of Montorio"; read Tacitus.

Saturday, Nov. 22.—Walk; read Tacitus and "Le Testament";[59] work.

Sunday, Nov. 23.—Read "Le Testament"; finish 13th book of Tacitus.

Monday, Nov. 24.—

Saturday, Nov. 29.—I read Tacitus; three of Hume's Essays, 8, 9, 10; some of the "German Theatre";[60] write; walk. Shelley reads "Political Justice" and two cantos of his Poem.

Sunday, Nov. 30.—Shelley finishes reading his Poem aloud. Read from the "German Theatre"; walk; work. Peacock spends the evening here.

54 Shelley and Mary were lodging at 19 Mabledon Place.

55 *An Address to the People on the Death of the Princess Charlotte. By the Hermit of Marlow* (1817, printed for Charles Ollier). See Dowden, II, 156–60; and White, I, 544–46.

56 A dramatic poem by S. T. Coleridge (1817).

57 Either Sophie Cottin's *Mathilde* (Paris, 1800–1801, 4 vols.), or Madame de Souza's *Eugène et Mathilde* (Paris, 1811, 3 vols.).

58 Charles R. Maturin, *Fatal Revenge, or the Family of Montorio* (1807, 3 vols.).

59 By François Villon?

60 Probably Benjamin Thompson, *The German Theatre* (1800–1801).

Monday, Dec. 1.—Shelley finishes "Political Justice." Read Tacitus and Hume; work; in the evening, read [Godwin's] "Mandeville."

Tuesday, Dec. 2.—Read "Mandeville" all day, and finish it. Shelley reads "Mandeville."

Wednesday, Dec. 3.—Walk out with Shelley. Write letters.[61] Shelley writes.

Thursday, Dec. 4.—Write; read Tacitus and 19th Essay of Hume; walk out; transcribe Peacock's Poem.

Friday, Dec. 5.—Write; read Tacitus; walk; copy [T. L. Peacock's] "Rhododaphne." Shelley reads [Paine's] "Rights of Man."

Saturday, Dec. 6.—Write; read Essays of Hume, 19, 20, 21; walk; copy "Rhododaphne." Hogg comes in the evening.

Sunday, Dec. 7.—Write; finish the 1st part of Hume's Essays; copy "Rhododaphne."

Monday, Dec. 8.—Copy "Rhododaphne." Shelley reads and finishes "Coleridge's Literary Life."

Tuesday, Dec. 9.—Write; read "Laon and Cythna"; copy "Rhododaphne."

Wednesday, Dec. 10.—Finish copying "Rhododaphne"; read one Essay of Hume; walk.

Thursday, Dec. 11.—Walk; read Essays of Hume, 2, 3, 4, 5. Shelley reads Hume.

Friday, Dec. 12.—Read Essays of Hume, 6, 7, 8, 9, 10; finish the 14th book of Tacitus; walk. Shelley reads Berkeley.

Saturday, Dec. 13.—Read "Laon and Cythna"; work. Shelley reads Berkeley, and part of "Much Ado about Nothing," aloud. Read Essays of Hume, 11, 12, 13.

Sunday, Dec. 14.—Read 14th Essay of Hume; write; walk. Shelley reads Berkeley. Ollier comes down.

Monday, Dec. 15.—Work; walk; alterations for "Cythna."[62]

Tuesday, Dec. 16.—Ollier goes up. Finish "Cythna"; work; finish 1st volume of Hume. Shelley reads Lady Morgan's "France."

Wednesday, Dec. 17.—Read "The Little Thief";[63] work. Shelley reads "France."

Thursday, Dec. 18.—Walk; write. Shelley reads "France."

Friday, Dec. 19.—Shelley reads "France." Read "Romans de Voltaire"; Hume; walk.

Saturday, Dec. 20.—Write; walk; read Hume. Shelley reads "France." Godwin comes in the evening.

[61] Mary to W. T. Baxter, December 3, 1817 (*Letters,* I, 45–46).

[62] See Dowden, II, 162–67; White, I, 547–52; and F. L. Jones, "The Revision of *Laon and Cythna,*" *Journal of English and Germanic Philology,* XXXII (July, 1933), 366–72.

[63] John Fletcher, *The Night-Walker, Or the Little Thief.*

Sunday, Dec. 21.—Read "France"; walk.

Monday, Dec. 22.—Read Tacitus; 100 lines of the "Georgics." Godwin goes up to town. Shelley walks, and reads 1st book of "Paradise Lost" in the evening. Mr. Francis calls with news of [William] Hone's third acquittal.[64]

Tuesday, Dec. 23.—Read Tacitus; walk. Shelley reads Gibbon. Finish "France."

Wednesday, Dec. 24.—Read Tacitus and Hume. Shelley reads Gibbon. Read "Georgics," 194.

Thursday, Dec. 25.—Christmas Day.—Read Tacitus and Hume. Shelley reads Gibbon. Walk.

Friday, Dec. 26.—Read Tacitus and Hume. Shelley reads Gibbon. Walk. Horace Smith comes in the evening.

Saturday, Dec. 27.—Work. Shelley reads Gibbon. Talk.

Sunday, Dec. 28.—Read Tacitus and "The Three Brothers."[65] Shelley reads Gibbon. Horace Smith goes.

Monday, Dec. 29.—Read Tacitus; finish "The Three Brothers"; walk. Shelley reads Gibbon.

Tuesday, Dec. 30.—Finish the 15th book of Tacitus; read Hume; write to Isabel.[66] Shelley reads Gibbon, and a book of "Paradise Lost."

Wednesday, Dec. 31.—Read Tacitus; walk. Shelley reads Gibbon. Frantin comes.

List of Books read in 1817

MARY

*(Those marked * Shelley has read also.)*

2 vols of Lord Chesterfield's Letters. [2 vols., 1774; later edns. 4 vols.]
*Coleridge's Lay Sermon. [1817.]
Memoirs of Count Grammont. [By Anthony Hamilton, 1714.]
Somnium Scipionis. [By Cicero.]
Roderick Random. [By Tobias Smollett, 2 vols., 1748.]
Comus. [By John Milton, 1637.]
Knights of the Swan. [By Madame de Genlis; tr. by Rev. Beresford, 3 vols., 1796.]
[Richard] Cumberland's Memoirs. [2 pts., 1806–1807.]
Junius's Letters. [2 vols., 1772.]

64 See White, I, 552, 746.

65 A novel by Joshua Pickersgill (1803, 4 vols.).

66 On the same day Mary added a postscript to Shelley's letter to W. T. Baxter (see Mary's *Letters,* I, 46).

Journey to the World Underground. [By Ludwig, Baron Holberg; tr. 1742.]
Duke of Buckingham's Rehearsal, and the Restoration.
Countess of Pembroke's Arcadia. By Sir P. Sidney.
Round Table. By W. Hazlitt. [2 vols., Edinburgh, 1817.]
Cupid's Revenge
Martial Maid
Wild Goose Chase } Beaumont and Fletcher
*Tales of my Landlord. [By Sir Walter Scott, 1816.]
Rambler. [By Samuel Johnson.]
*Waverley. [By Sir Walter Scott, 1814.]
Amadis de Gaul. [By Vasco de Lobeida; tr. by Robert Southey.]
Epistolæ Plinii Secundi.
*Story of Psyche in Apuleius.
Anna St. Ives. [By Thomas Holcroft, 7 vols., 1792.]
Vita Julii Cæsaris. Suetonius.
*Defoe on the Plague. [A Journal of the Plague Year, 1722.]
*[John] Wilson's City of the Plague. [1816.]
Miss [Maria] Edgeworth's Comic Dramas. [1817.]
Fortitude and Frailty. By [Fanny] Holcroft.
3rd canto of Childe Harold. [By Lord Byron, 1816.]
Quarterly Review.
*Lalla Rookh. By T. Moore. [1817.]
*[John] Davis's Travels in America. [Travels of Four Years and a Half in the United States of America, 1803.]
*Godwin's Miscellanies. [? The Enquirer: Reflections on Education, Manners, and Literature, in a series of Essays, 1797.]
*Spenser's Fairy Queen.
*Manuscrit venu de St. Helêne. [By J. Fréderic Lullin de Chateauvieux, London, 1817.]
Buffon's Théorie de la Terre.
Beaumont and Fletcher's Plays.
*Volpone, Cynthia's Revels, The Alchemist, Fall of Sejanus, Catiline's Conspiracy. [By Ben Jonson.]
La Nouvelle Héloise. [By Rousseau, 1761.]
Lettres Persiennes. [Lettres Persanes (1721), by Montesquieu.]
Miss [Maria] Edgeworth's Harrington and Ormond. [3 vols., 1817 (2nd ed.).]
Arthur Mervyn. [By Charles Brockden Brown, 1799–1800.]
*Antony and Cleopatra. Othello. [By Shakespeare.]
Missionary. [By Lady Morgan, 3 vols., 1811.]
Rhoda. [Published anonymously, 3 vols., 1816.]

Wild Irish Girl. [By Lady Morgan, 3 vols., 1806.]
Glenarvon. [By Lady Caroline Lamb, 1816.]
The Anaconda.
Pastor's Fireside. [By Jane Porter, 3 vols., 1817.]
Amelia. [By Henry Fielding, 4 vols., 1752.]
Sir Launcelot Greaves. [By Tobias Smollett, 2 vols., 1762.]
Strathallan. [By Alicia Lefanu, 4 vols., 1816.]
Twopenny Postbag. [By Thomas Moore, 1813.]
Anti-Jacobin Poetry. [Poetry of the Anti-Jacobin, 2nd ed., 1800.]
Miseries of Human Life. [By James Beresford, 2 vols., 1806–1807.]
*[Thomas] Moore's Odes and Epistles. [1806.]
Les Lettres d'une Peruvienne [Princess. By Madame F. d'I. de H. Graffigny.]
Confessions et Lettres de Rousseau. [1781.]
*[Charles] Lamb's Specimen's [of English Dramatic Poets, 1808].
Molière's George Dandin. [1668.]
Le Testament. [? By François Villon, 1456 and 1461.]
Family of Montorio. [By Charles R. Maturin, 3 vols., 1807.]
Querelles de Famille. [Bu August H. J. Lafontaine; tr. 3 vols., 1811.]
German Theatre. [By Benjamin Thompson, 6 vols., 1800.]
Eugenie and Mathilde. [Eugène et Mathilde, by Madame de Souza, 3 vols., Paris, 1811.]
*Mandeville. [By William Godwin, 3 vols., 1817.]
*Laon and Cythna. [By Percy B. Shelley, 1817.]
*Lady Morgan's France. [2 vols., 1817.]
The Three Brothers. [By Joshua Pickersgill, 4 vols., 1803.]
1st vol. of Hume's Essays.
Annalium C. Cornelii Taciti.

SHELLEY

Symposium of Plato
Plays of Æschylus
Plays of Sophocles
Iliad of Homer
Arrian's Historia Indica
Homer's Hymns
} Greek

Histoire de la Révolution Française. [By Lacretelle or Rabaut St.-Étienne.]
Apuleius. [The Golden Ass.]
Metamorphoses (Latin). [By Ovid.]
Coleridge's Biographia Literaria. [2 vols., 1817.]
Political Justice. [By William Godwin, 2 vols., 1793.]

HORACE SMITH

Engraved by Finden from a portrait by Maskerrier

Rights of Man. [By Thomas Paine, 1791–92.]
Elphinstone's Embassy to Caubul. [2 vols., 1815.]
Several vols. of Gibbon['s Decline and Fall of the Roman Empire].

1818

ENGLAND

Thursday, JAN. 1.—Read Tacitus; walk; write to Isabel [Mrs. Booth]; read Hume. Shelley reads Gibbon.

Friday, JAN. 2.—Read Tacitus. Shelley reads Gibbon, and walks out.

Saturday, JAN. 3.—Unwell. Shelley unwell. Peacock passes the day here. Hogg comes in the evening.

Sunday, JAN. 4.—Shelley unwell. Talk with him.

Monday, JAN. 5.—Talk with Shelley. He is better.

Tuesday, JAN. 6.—Shelley reads 1st and 6th book of the "Æneid." Walk a little way with him.

Wednesday, JAN. 7–[19].—Read 2nd book of "Æneid"; read "Dr. Clarke's Travels." They read Tacitus, "Clarke's Travels," Gibbon, [Scott's] "Guy Mannering," Terence, and Hume, till the 19th, when Hogg goes.

Tuesday, JAN. 20.—Shelley translates Homer's Hymns. Godwin and William Godwin [Jr.] arrive.[1]

Thursday, JAN. 22.—Godwin and his son William go.

Friday, JAN. 23.—Shelley has ophthalmia again. Play at chess with him; read Clarke.

Saturday, JAN. 24.—Read 6th book of Virgil to Shelley; read Clarke; walk out, and see a lovely rainbow.

Sunday, JAN. 25.—Carter[2] calls. Walk with Shelley and Peacock.

Thursday, JAN. 29.—Shelley, Clare, and Peacock go up to town. Read Sterne['s "Tristram Shandy"], and the 2nd canto of "Childe Harold."

Friday, JAN. 30[–FEB. 4].—Read "Tristram Shandy," Clarke, [Scott's] "Rob Roy," &c., till Thursday [Feb. 5].

Thursday, FEB. 5.—Shelley and Clare return in the evening.

Friday, FEB. 6.—Pack the books; play at chess with Shelley.

[1] There are "minor entries" for January 21 and 26 in the MS journal, according to the MS notes of Miss Grylls.

[2] Doubtless the Mr. Carter who occupied the house after the Shelleys left. On this day, according to Claire's diary, the Marlow house was sold (Dowden, II, 179 n.).

Saturday, FEB. 7[–10].—Shelley goes up to London [Feb. 7]. Pack; read "Henry Monteagle,"[3] [Byron's] "Giaour," "Corsair," "Lara"; and pack up till Tuesday, 10th, when we leave Marlow; and go to the Opera in the evening—[Mozart's] "Don Giovanni."

Wednesday, FEB. 11.—Look for lodgings;[4] spend the evening at Hunt's. [Peacock, Hogg, and Keats were present.][5]

Thursday, FEB. 12[–15].—Go to the Indian Library, and the Panorama of Rome. On Friday, 13th, spend the morning at the British Museum, looking at the Elgin Marbles. On Saturday, 14th, go to Hunt's. Clare and Shelley [with Peacock and Hogg] go to the Opera. On Sunday, 15th, Mr. Bransen,[6] Peacock, and Hogg dine with us.

Monday, FEB. 16.—Go to the play with Peacock. [Saw Milman's "Fazio," a tragedy, and "Harlequin Gulliver," a pantomime.]

Tuesday, FEB. 17.—In the morning, go to see the casts from Phidias. Hogg spends the evening here.

Wednesday, FEB. 18[–25].—Spend the day at Hunt's. On Thursday, 19th, dine at Horace Smith's, and copy Shelley's Eclogue.[7] On Friday, 20th, copy Shelley's critique on "Rhododaphne."[8] Go to the Apollonicon with Shelley. On Saturday, 21st, copy Shelley's critique, and go to the Opera in the evening. Spend Sunday [Feb. 22] at Hunt's. On Monday, 23rd, finish copying Shelley's critique, and go to the play in the evening —"The Bride of Abydos." On Tuesday [Feb. 24], go to the Opera—[Mozart's] "Figaro." On Wednesday [Feb. 25], Hunt dines with us. Shelley is not well.

Sunday, MAR. 1[–8].—Read Montaigne. Spend the evening at Hunt's. On Monday, 2nd, Shelley calls on Mr. Baxter. Isabel Booth is arrived, but neither comes nor sends. Go to the play in the evening with Hunt and Marianne, and see a new comedy damned.[9] On Thursday, 5th, Papa calls, and Clare visits Mrs. Godwin. On Sunday, 8th, we dine at Hunt's, and meet Mr. [Vincent] Novello.[10] Music.[11]

[3] Probably a misreading of *Helen Monteagle,* a novel by Alicia Lefanu (1818, 3 vols.).

[4] They lodged at 119 Great Russell Street, Bloomsbury Square.

[5] The bracketed additions for February 11, 12, and 16 are taken from Dowden (II, 183), who derived them from Claire's diary.

[6] Dowden's spelling (II, 183) is "Bramsen" (from Claire's diary).

[7] *Rosalind and Helen,* as yet incomplete.

[8] The review of Peacock's poem was given to Hunt for insertion in the *Examiner,* but it remained unpublished until 1880, when H. B. Forman included it in Shelley's *Prose Works* (White, I, 556, 748).

[9] *The Castle of Glyndower,* at the Drury Lane Theatre (Dowden, II, 184 n.).

[10] A musician.

[11] The MS journal has a short "unimportant entry" for March 8, say Miss Grylls's MS notes, which probably refer to the last part of this entry dated March 1.

Monday, MAR. 9.—Christening the Children.[12] Horace Smith calls; he spends the evening here, with Godwin and Peacock. After they are all gone, Hunt comes, with Miss Kent; they go at 12.

Tuesday, MAR. 10.—Packing. Hunt and Marianne spend the day with us. Mary Lamb calls. Papa in the evening. Our adieus.

Wednesday, MAR. 11.—Travel to Dover.[13]

Thursday, MAR. 12.—FRANCE. Discussion of whether we should cross. Our passage is rough. A sick lady is frightened, and says the Lord's Prayer. We arrive at Calais, for the third time.

Friday, MAR. 13.—Spend the morning in preparations,[14] and then quit Calais. The country is uninteresting; but the weather is delightful, and, after the sun has set, the horned moon, Orion, and his brethren lend us their light. The gates of St. Omer are shut, and a woman from the other side the moat shrieks out a demand of who the invaders are. She carries the reply to the Commander, and returns in about half an hour, heading a party of about a dozen soldiers, and, upon a promise of *remembering the guard,* lets us through three tremendous gates, when we arrive at a magnificent hotel, and rest for the night.

Saturday, MAR. 14.—We pass through a dismal country, with very disagreeable postillions, and sleep at Douay.

Sunday, MAR. 15.—Sleep at La Fêre.

Monday, MAR. 16[–21].—Shelley reads Schlegel[15] aloud to us. We sleep at R[h]eims on Tuesday, 17th, after a hard day's journey. We sleep at St. Dizier on Wednesday, 18th. We arrive at more pleasant country; hills covered with vines, while the road winds with the River Marne through the valley. We sleep at Langres on Thursday, 19th. We set out late. Shelley reads Schlegel aloud; and we travel on in a pleasant country, among nice people. We sleep at Dijon. On Saturday, 21st, we are detained three hours at Macon by the breaking of a spring of the caleche. Shelley reads Schlegel aloud. We arrive at Lyons at half past 11.

Sunday, MAR. 22.—A fine pleasant day. We agree with a voiturier to take us to Milan, and then walk out by the side of the river until its confluence with the Saone. We can see from here Jura and Mont Blanc, and the whole scene reminds us of Geneva. After dinner, our voiturier comes, and we have a long conversation with him about the state of Lyons, and passed events in it. He was here in the revolutionary times.

[12] At the parish church of St. Giles-in-the-Fields. Claire's child, heretofore called Alba, was christened as Clara Allegra (Dowden, II, 183).

[13] Claire's diary for March 11 and 12 is printed by Dowden (II, 186–87), who also gives other extracts for March 30 and April 1, 1818 (II, 191–92).

[14] Including the purchase of a carriage, according to Claire's diary (Dowden, II, 187 n.).

[15] Probably *On Dramatic Art and Literature* (see Appendix IV).

After this, we ride out by the river-side, and see the moon rise, broad and red, and behind the Alps. Shelley writes to Lord Byron.

Monday, MAR. 23[–25.]—Walk out in the morning. After dinner, we ride to the Isle de Barbe, where there is a fête. In the evening we go to the Comedie, which is very amusing. Tuesday [March 24], a rainy day; pack. On Wednesday, 25th, we set out from Lyons, and advance towards the mountains whose white tops are seen at a distance. We sleep at Tour du Pin.[16]

Thursday, MAR. 26.—[*Shelley*][17]—We travel towards the mountains, and begin to enter the valleys of the Alps. The country becomes covered again with verdure and cultivation, and white châteaux and scattered cottages, among woods of old oak and walnut trees. The vines are here peculiarly picturesque; they are trellised upon immense stakes, and the trunks of them are moss-covered and hoary with age. Unlike the French vines, which creep lowly on the ground, they form rows of interlaced bowers, which, when the leaves are green, and the red grapes are hanging among those hoary branches, will afford a delightful shadow to those who sit upon the moss underneath. The vines are sometimes planted in the open fields, and sometimes among orchards of lofty apple and pear trees, the twigs of which are just becoming purple with the bursting blossoms.

We dined at Les Echelles, a village at the foot of a mountain of the same name, the boundaries of France and Savoy. Before this we had stopped at Pont Beauvoisin, where the legal limits of the French and Sardinian dominions are placed. We here heard that a Milanese had been sent all the way back to Lyons, because his passport was unauthorized by the Sardinian Consul, a few days before, and that we should be subjected to the same treatment. We, in respect to the character of our nation I suppose, were suffered to pass. Our books, however, were, after a long discussion sent to[18] Chambery, to be submitted to the Censor, a Priest who admits nothing of Rousseau, Voltaire, &c., into the dominions of the King of Sardinia. All such books are burned.[19] After dinner, we ascended Les Echelles, winding along a road cut through perpendicular rocks of immense elevation, by Charles Emmanuel, Duke of Savoy, in 1582. The rocks, which cannot be less than 1000 feet in perpendicular height, sometimes overhang the road on each side, and almost shut out the sky. The scene is like that described in the "Prometheus" of Æschylus;

16 S&M, "Tour de Piu"; corrected by Dowden (II, 189).

17 Mary printed this entry in *Essays* (1840) as a footnote to the first of the Letters from Italy.

18 S&M, "at"; "sent to" in *Essays*.

19 This sentence is not in S&M; taken from *Essays*.

vast rifts and caverns in granite precipices; wintry mountains, with ice and snow above; the loud sounds of unseen waters within the caverns; and walls of toppling rocks, only to be scaled, as he describes, by the winged chariot of the Ocean Nymphs.

Under the dominion of this tyranny, the inhabitants of the fertile valleys bounded by these mountains are in a state of the most frightful poverty and disease. At the foot of this ascent were cut into the rocks at several places stories of the misery of the inhabitants, to move the compassion of the traveller. One old man, lame and blind, crawled out of a hole in the rock, wet with the perpetual melting of the snows above, and dripping like a shower bath.

The country as we descended to Chambery continued as beautiful, though marked with somewhat of a softer character than before, where we arrived a little after night-fall.

Friday, MAR. 27.—[*Mary*]—SAVOY.—Remain at Chambery all day; it rains. Elise's mother, father-in-law, and little girl come to see her.[20]

Saturday, MAR. 28.—Approach the highest Alps; we see the sun rise on them; and as we advance we are enclosed by them. We follow the windings of a river, and find the scenery exceedingly beautiful. It will be much finer in summer, when the leaves are out. [They slept this night at St. Jean Maurienne.][21]

Sunday, MAR. 29.—We advance higher among the mountains, and the snows encroach upon the road. The scene is far more desolate, and there is something dreadful in going on the edge of an overhanging precipice. We cross an Alpine bridge [Pont du Diable] thrown across a chasm. We sleep at the foot of Cenis.

Monday, MAR. 30.—We cross Cenis. The road is excellent where the snows have not accumulated on it. We arrive at Susa, and go to see a triumphal arch in honour of Augustus. A pretty woman shows it to us. It was a scene to have pleased Hunt.

Tuesday, MAR. 31.—Journey all day through a pleasant and cultivated country. Sleep at Turin.

Wednesday, APRIL 1.[22]—Spend the day at Turin; walk about the town. Go to the Opera in the evening; we do not know the name of it, and cannot make out the story. The two principal singers are very good.

Thursday and Friday, APR. 2 and 3.—Travel all day.

Saturday, APR. 4.—Travel all day, and arrive at Milan in the evening.

Sunday, APR. 5.—Walk about the town, and visit the Cathedral, which

20 See note to Nov. 23, 1816, entry. Claire describes Elise as "a very superior woman of about thirty" (Dowden, II, 190 n.).

21 Dowden's addition (II, 190).

22 Claire's longer diary entry is printed by Dowden (II, 192).

is very fine. Go to the Opera in the evening; the opera we cannot hear,[23] but the ballet of "Othello" [by Vigano] is very beautiful.

Monday, Apr. 6.—Read [Tasso's] "Aminta" with Shelley. He reads [Manso's] "Vita del Tasso."

Tuesday, Apr. 7.—Write letters; read Molière's Plays; go to the Opera —the same as before.

Wednesday, Apr. 8.—Read Molière; walk out; write letters.

Thursday, Apr. 9.—Shelley and I journey towards Como. The weather is beautiful, and the country we pass through continued gardens. We arrive at Como about 3, and after dinner go out on the Lake, which is narrow, but very beautiful. The mountains come precipitously down to the Lake, and are covered with chestnut woods. In the evening read an Italian translation of [Richardson's] "Pamela."

Friday, Apr. 10.—In the morning we go out on the Lake to look for a house, with a person we are recommended to by Signor Marietta. We see a very nice house, but out of repair, with an excellent garden, but full of serpents. On our return from the Villa Lanzi, we leave our companion, and set out for the Tremezzina. Nothing can be more divine than the shores of this lovely lake. We go to look at the house of a M. Sommariva, and are joined by the master, who makes his apologies that he cannot accompany us in our search. We sleep at an inn here.

Saturday, Apr. 11.—We look at a house beautifully situated, but too small; and afterwards, crossing the Lake, at another magnificent one, which we shall be very happy if we obtain. We then return to Como. Nothing can be more divine than the shores—partly bare, partly overgrown with laurels. We visit a very fine waterfall, and the Pliniana. The wind is against us, and the Lake rather rough. We arrive at Como about 5. Shelley has finished the "Life of Tasso," and reads Dante. Read "Pamela." A thunderstorm.

Sunday, Apr. 12.[24]—

Sunday, Apr. [12–]19.—Return on Sunday [April 12] to Milan. Ride out on the Corso. Nothing particular happens during the week. Read and finish the Italian "Pamela," begin [Richardson's] "Clarissa Harlowe" in Italian. Shelley reads and finishes Dante's "Purgatorio." Write to Charles and Aunt Everina. A letter from Peacock. Shelley writes to him and to Albe.[25]

23 See Mary to L. & M. Hunt, April [6–8], 1818 (*Letters,* I, 48).

24 For Claire's interesting entry for April 12 about a "Curious adventure," see Dowden, II, 196.

25 The letter to Peacock is obviously that dated Milan, April 20, 1818 (Julian edition, IX, 296–300). Peacock answered it on May 30 and in part on July 5 (Halliford edition of Peacock's *Works,* VIII, 192–94, 196–99). The letter to Byron was written on April 13 (Julian edition, IX, 295–96).

Monday, Apr. 20.—Walk out, and read "Clarissa Harlowe." Shelley reads "Hamlet." In the evening go to the Opera—"Il Rivale di se Stesso," and "Il Spada di Renetti." We are very much delighted and amused.

Tuesday, Apr. 21.—Read "Mandeville." A letter from Albe. Go to the Opera in the evening.

Wednesday, Apr. 22.—Shelley unwell; he reads the "Paradiso"; writes to Albe.[26] Read "Mandeville." Merryweather calls.

Thursday, Apr. 23.—Finish "Mandeville." In the evening walk out. Clare reads the "Memoirs of Madame Manson" to us.

Friday, Apr. 24.—Walk out; read the "Aristippus" of Wieland. Shelley reads [Scott's] "Rob Roy." Italian Master[27] in the evening. Albe! Albe everywhere!

Saturday and Sunday, Apr. 25 and 26.—Read "Aristippus"; write Italian exercises; read 1st Ode of Horace; and walk out.

Monday, Apr. 27.—Clare's birthday. Letter from Albe. Read "Aristippus."

Tuesday, Apr. 28.—Alba [Allegra] goes with Elise [to Byron at Venice]. Finish "Aristippus." Italian exercises.

Wednesday, Apr. 29.—Go to the Opera in the evening. Packing.

Thursday, Apr. 30.—Packing. Shelley writes to Hogg, Peacock, and Horace Smith, and to [Byron].[28]

Friday, May 1.—Set out from Milan;[29] sleep at Piacenza. The country is pleasant and fertile.

Saturday, May 2.—Sleep at Parma. The country becomes more fertile and picturesque; the horizon is bounded by the Apennines, but we travel along a fertile plain, chiefly cornfields, planted with trees, up which the vines are trained, and then festooned from one tree to another. Parma is a dear town. Read [Wieland's] "Les Abderites." Shelley finishes "Aristippe."

Sunday, May 3.—Sleep at Modena. We approach the mountains.

Monday, May 4.—Dine at Bologna, and from thence, leaving the fertile plains, we ascend the mountains, and sleep in a solitary inn among them.

Tuesday, May 5.—Our day is passed in passing the mountains. We sleep at the Barberine. The south side of the Apennines is more picturesque, and clothed with chestnut woods.

26 Shelley to Byron, April 22, 1818 (Julian edition, IX, 301–303).

27 Signor Mombelli (Dowden, II, 198).

28 Shelley to Hogg, April 30, 1818 (Julian edition, IX, 305–307); Shelley to Peacock, April 30, 1818 (*ibid.,* IX, 308); Shelley to Byron, April 30, 1818 (*ibid.,* IX, 304–305). The letter to Hogg, Dowden (II, 200–201) prints as "to a Friend (probably Horace Smith)."

29 Claire's account of the journey to Pisa is printed by Dowden (II, 203–205).

Wednesday, MAY 6.—We descend along the vale of the Arno, which is very beautiful. Sleep at La Scala, an inn merely.

Thursday, MAY 7.—Arrive at Pisa.[30] Walk out, and am made low-spirited by the sight of the criminals, chained and guarded, who work in the streets.

Friday, MAY 8.—A letter from Elise. Walk out, and in the evening go to the top of the Leaning Tower, and visit the Cathedral. Prepare to quit Pisa.

Saturday, MAY 9.—Journey to Leghorn. After we arrive,[31] walk out. A stupid town. We see the Mediterranean. Read a French translation of Lucian. Mrs. Gisborne calls in the evening, with her husband;[32] she is reserved, yet with easy manners.

Sunday, MAY 10.—Read translation of Lucian. Shelley reads Euripides. Call on Mrs. Gisborne. In the evening, walk on the Mole; meet Mrs. Gisborne; a long conversation with her about my Father and Mother.

Monday, MAY 11[–16].—Read Lucian. Shelley reads Manso's "Life of Tasso." Walk out in the evening with Mr. and Mrs. Gisborne.

This is repeated through the week.

Sunday, MAY 17.—Read and finish [Carlo] Gozzi's Play of "Zobeide." Walk out with Mrs. Gisborne and Mr. Beilby. Shelley reads the "Hippolitus" of Euripides.

Monday, MAY 18[–29].—Read the "Melarance"[33] of Gozzi. Italian exercises and lesson. Walk in the evening with Mr. and Mrs. Gisborne. She tells me a strange story that happened to her concerning a mad girl.

Read, write, work, and walk out with the same party as before. Finish copying the Cenci MS. on Monday, 25th. On Tuesday, 26th, Shelley sets off for the Baths of Lucca.[34] On Thursday, 28th, Shelley returns. In the evening, walk to see Henry Reveley's[35] steam engine with him and Mr. and Mrs. Gisborne.

Saturday and Sunday, MAY 30 and 31.—Walk with Shelley and Mr. and Mrs. Gisborne. In the evenings, read 6th canto of Ariosto with Shelley and "Mille et Une Nuits."

Monday, JUNE 1.—Read 7th canto of Ariosto, and "Mille et Une Nuits." In the evening, walk out with Mr. and Mrs. Gisborne.

30 They lodged at the Tre Donzelle (Dowden, II, 205).

31 For a few days they lodged at the Acquila Nera; then took apartments (White, II, 14).

32 Maria and John Gisborne. Maria was an old friend of Mary's mother and father, and after the death of her first husband, Mr. Reveley, had rejected a proposal of marriage by Godwin, whose wife, Mary Wollstonecraft, had died in giving birth to Mary.

33 *L'Amore delle Tre Melarance* (1761).

34 To look for a house.

35 Mrs. Gisborne's son by her first husband.

Tuesday, JUNE 2.—Shelley reads the "Philoctetes" of Sophocles. Read 2nd and 3rd acts of [Terence's] "Phormio"; "Mille et Une Nuits." Cold dismal weather. Walk in the evening with Shelley, Clare, and Mr. and Mrs. Gisborne.

Wednesday, JUNE 3.—Shelley reads "Electra" and "Ajax" [of Sophocles]. Read 8th canto of Ariosto and the 4th act of "Phormio"; finish "Mille et Une Nuits"; read the "Zaïre," and the "Alzire" of Voltaire. It rains all day.

Thursday, JUNE 4.—Read 9th canto of Ariosto; finish "Phormio." Shelley reads "Ajax." In the evening walk out with Shelley, Clare, and Mr. and Mrs. Gisborne.

Friday, JUNE 5.—Read 10th canto of Ariosto; the "Mahomet" of Voltaire. In the evening, walk to Mrs. Partridge[36] with Shelley, Clare, Henry Reveley, and Mr. and Mrs. Gisborne. Mr. Beilby calls.

Saturday, JUNE 6[–10].—Read 11th canto of Ariosto, and "Merope" and "Semiramis" of Voltaire. In the evening, take a short walk with Shelley, Mr. and Mrs. Gisborne, and Henry Reveley.

We read, work, and walk with the Gisbornes, Clare, and Henry Reveley, till Wednesday, 10th, when we take leave of Mr. and Mrs. Gisborne and Henry Reveley.

Thursday, JUNE 11.—Travel to Bagni di Lucca, and settle ourselves a little in our house [Casa Bertini]. Walk out in the evening. Signor Chiappa[37] calls.

Friday, JUNE 12.—Shelley unwell.

Saturday, JUNE 13.—Read 17th canto of Ariosto, and Gibbon. Shelley reads the "Memorabilia" [of Xenophon]. Walk out, and read 250 lines of the 8th book of the "Æneid."

Sunday, JUNE 14.—Read 18th canto of Ariosto, and Gibbon. Shelley reads "Memorabilia." Walk out. Shelley reads aloud six eclogues from the "Shepherd's Calendar" [by Spenser].

Monday, JUNE 15.—Read 19th canto of Ariosto, and Gibbon. Shelley reads the "Memorabilia." Letters written to Hunt, Mrs. Gisborne, Peacock,[38] Walter Scott, &c. Shelley reads a part of the "Shepherd's Calendar" aloud in the evening.

36 An aunt of Benjamin Robert Haydon, English painter (see Mary's *Letters,* I, 52 & n.).

37 Probably Signor G. B. del Chiappa and the owner of the Shelleys' house (Dowden, II, 211 n.).

38 These letters apparently were written on various dates, and are probably the following: (1) Mary to L. & M. Hunt, Leghorn, May 13, 1818 (*Letters,* I, 50–52); (2) Mary to Mrs. Gisborne, Bagni di Lucca, June 15, 1818 (*ibid.,* I, 52–54); (3) Shelley to Peacock, Livorno, June 5, 1818 (Julian edition, IX, 309–10). From the letters themselves it is clear that all of Shelley's 1818 letters to Peacock through July 25 have survived and are (with this entry) accounted for by the journal.

Tuesday and Wednesday, JUNE 16 and 17.—Read 20th and 21st cantos of Ariosto, and Gibbon. Shelley finishes the "Memorabilia" of Xenophon. He finishes the "Shepherd's Calendar"; reads "The Clouds" of Aristophanes. Signor Chiappa calls in the evening.

Thursday, JUNE 18.—Read 22nd canto of Ariosto, and Gibbon. Shelley reads Gibbon and "The Clouds." Read two Odes of Horace in the evening. Walk out with Shelley.

Friday, JUNE 19.—Read 23rd canto of Ariosto, and Gibbon, and the 3rd Ode of Horace. Shelley finishes "The Clouds"; reads Hume's England aloud in the evening. Take a long and delightful walk.

Saturday, JUNE 20.—Read 24th canto of Ariosto, Gibbon, and 4th and 5th Odes of Horace. Shelley reads the "Plutus" of Aristophanes, and Gibbon; in the evening, he reads Hume's History aloud.

Sunday, JUNE 21.—Read 25th canto of Ariosto, Gibbon, and 6th and 7th Odes of Horace. Shelley reads the "Lysistrœ" of Aristophanes, finishes Gibbon, and reads Hume's England in the evening.

Monday, JUNE 22.—Read 26th canto of Ariosto, Gibbon, and the 8th, 9th, 10th, and 11th Odes of Horace. Shelley reads Aristophanes and "Anacharsis."[39] Walk in the evening. Hear Hume's England read aloud after tea.

Tuesday, JUNE 23.—Read 27th canto of Ariosto, Gibbon, and 12th and 13th Odes of Horace. Shelley reads Aristophanes and "Anacharsis."

Wednesday, JUNE 24.—Read 28th canto of Ariosto, Gibbon, and Horace. Shelley reads Aristophanes and "Anacharsis." Signor Chiappa calls in the afternoon.

Thursday, JUNE 25.—Read 29th canto of Ariosto, finish Gibbon, and read Horace. Shelley reads Aristophanes and "Anacharsis." Walk out. Letters from England.[40] Hume's England read aloud in the evening.

Friday, JUNE 26.—Read 30th canto of Ariosto, Livy, Horace, and [Ben Jonson's] "Every Man in his Humour." Shelley reads Aristophanes and "Anacharsis."

Saturday, JUNE 27.—Read 31st canto of Ariosto, Livy, Horace, and [Ben Jonson's] "Epicœne, or the Silent Woman." Shelley reads Aristophanes and "Anacharsis."

Sunday, JUNE 28.—Read 32nd canto of Ariosto, Livy, Horace, and [Ben Jonson's] "Volpone." Shelley reads Aristophanes and "Anacharsis."

Monday, JUNE 29.—Read 33rd canto of Ariosto, Livy, Horace, and the "Magnetick Lady" [by Ben Jonson]. Shelley reads Aristophanes and "Anacharsis," and Hume's History aloud in the evening, after our walk.

39 By Abbé J. J. Barthélemy.

40 Probably Godwin to Mary, June 1, 1818 (S&M, I, 279–80); and Godwin to Shelley, June 8, 1818 (*ibid.*, I, 281–83).

Tuesday, JUNE 30.—Go with Shelley on horseback to *Il Prato Fiorito,* a flowery meadow at the top of one of the high Apennines. Read "Anacharsis." Shelley reads "Anacharsis."

Wednesday, JULY 1.—Read 34th canto of Ariosto, Livy, Horace, and "Anacharsis."

Thursday, JULY 2.—Read 35th canto of Ariosto, Livy, Horace, and "Anacharsis." Shelley reads Aristophanes and "Anacharsis." He writes to Hunt. Letter from Papa.[41]

Friday, JULY 3.—Read 36th canto of Ariosto, Livy, Horace, "Anacharsis." Walk out in the evening. After tea, Signor Chiappa calls.

Saturday, JULY 4.—Read 37th canto of Ariosto, Virgil, and [Wieland's] "Peregrinus Proteus." Shelley rides to Lucca in the evening.

Sunday, JULY 5.—Shelley returns from Lucca; he reads "Anacharsis"; and at 10 o'clock go to the Casino.

Monday, JULY 6.—Read 38th canto of Ariosto; finish the 1st book of Livy. Shelley reads Aristophanes and "Anacharsis."[42]

Thursday, JULY 9.—Read 41st canto of Ariosto, Horace, and "Anacharsis." Shelley translates the "Symposium" [of Plato], and reads the "Maid's Tragedy" of Beaumont. He reads Hume's England aloud in the evening.

Friday, JULY 10.—Read 42nd canto of Ariosto, Livy, "Anacharsis," Horace, and Shakespere's "Coriolanus." Shelley translates the "Symposium," and reads [Beaumont and Fletcher's] "Philaster" and Hume's England aloud in the evening. Clare's letter to Elise.

Saturday, JULY 11.—Claire's letter to Elise [and then list of reading].[43]

Sunday, JULY 12.—Ride out in the morning; read a part of the 43rd canto of Ariosto, and "Anacharsis"; go to the Casino in the evening. Shelley translates the "Symposium," and reads a part of it to me. He reads the "Laws of Candy" [by John Fletcher and Philip Massinger].

Monday, JULY 13.—Read a part of the 43rd canto of Ariosto, Livy, Horace, and "Anacharsis." Shelley translates the "Symposium," and reads Hume's England aloud in the evening.

Tuesday, JULY 14.—Finish the 43rd canto of Ariosto; read Livy and "Anacharsis." Shelley translates the "Symposium"; he reads a part to me, and Hume's England in the evening. Ride out before breakfast.

Wednesday, JULY 15.—Read 44th canto of Ariosto, Livy, Horace, and "Anacharsis." Shelley translates the "Symposium," and reads the "Wife

[41] Godwin to Mary, June 20, 1818 (S&M, I, 290A–B).

[42] In the MS journal are "minor entries" for July 7 and 8, says Miss Grylls in her MS notes.

[43] Entry not in S&M; taken from the MS notes of Miss Grylls.

for a Month" [by John Fletcher]. We ride out in the morning. After tea, Shelley reads Hume's England.

Thursday, JULY 16.—Read 45th canto of Ariosto; finish the 2nd book of Livy; read Horace and "Anacharsis." Shelley translates the "Symposium," and reads Herodotus.

Friday, JULY 17.—Shelley and Clare set out for Lucca. Ride out, and meet them returning, Clare having fallen off.[44] Read a part of the 46th canto of Ariosto, Livy, Horace, and "Anacharsis." Shelley finishes the translation of the "Symposium," and reads Herodotus; walks out in the evening to his bath.

Saturday, JULY 18.—Shelley and Clare go to Lucca. Read Livy, Horace, and "Anacharsis." Ride out in the evening. Shelley reads Herodotus.

Sunday, JULY 19.—Finish [Ariosto's] "Orlando Furioso"; read "Anacharsis."

Monday, JULY 20.—Shelley finishes correcting the "Symposium," and I begin to transcribe it. Read Livy and "Anacharsis." Shelley reads Herodotus and Hume's England aloud in the evening.

Tuesday, JULY 21.—Read Livy and "Anacharsis," and transcribe the "Symposium." A rainy day. Shelley reads Herodotus and Hume's England aloud in the evening.

Wednesday, JULY 22.—Read Livy and "Anacharsis," and transcribe the "Symposium." Shelley reads Herodotus and Hume's England aloud in the evening.

Friday, JULY 24.—Transcribe the "Symposium"; read "Anacharsis" and Horace. Shelley reads Herodotus. Ride out in the evening.

Saturday, JULY 25.—Read Livy; transcribe the "Symposium." Shelley reads Herodotus. Read "Anacharsis." We ride out after dinner; and in the evening Shelley reads Hume's England aloud.

Sunday, JULY 26.—Read 1st act of [Tasso's] "Aminta"; Livy; finish "Anacharsis"; transcribe the "Symposium." Shelley reads Herodotus. Shelley writes letters to Papa, Horace Smith, and Peacock.[45]

Monday, JULY 27.—Finish 2nd book of Livy; read 3rd act of "Aminta"; transcribe the "Symposium." Shelley reads Herodotus. We go to a Festa di Ballo in the evening.

Tuesday, JULY 28.—Finish the "Aminta"; read Livy; transcribe the "Symposium"; read the "Revolt of Islam." Shelley reads Herodotus.

44 On this occasion Shelley and Claire did not get to Lucca, as is proved by Shelley's letter of July 25, 1818, to Peacock, which states, "I have ridden over to Lucca, once with Clare, and once alone" (Julian edition, IX, 313). White (II, 21) is in error in stating that there were "two visits to Lucca" by Shelley and Claire.

45 Shelley to Peacock, July 25, 1818 (Julian edition, IX, 313–16); Shelley to Godwin, July 25, 1818 (*ibid.*, IX, 316–18). Peacock replied on August 30 (*Works,* Halliford edition, VIII, 202–204).

Wednesday, JULY 29.—Read Livy; the "Bartholomew Fair" of Ben Jonson; walk in the evening. Shelley reads Herodotus and Hume in the evening.

Thursday, JULY 30.—Read Livy and the "Tale of a Tub" of Ben Jonson; transcribe the "Symposium." Shelley reads Herodotus and Hume in the evening.

Friday, JULY 31.—Read Livy; "The Case is Altered" of Ben Jonson; transcribe the "Symposium." Shelley reads Herodotus and Hume in the evening.

Saturday, AUG. 1.—Read Livy; the "Revolt of Islam"; 1st canto of Tasso['s "Gerusalemme Liberata"]. Shelley reads Herodotus and Hume's England aloud in the evening. Transcribe the "Symposium."

Sunday, AUG. 2.—Read 2nd canto of Tasso; Livy; transcribe the "Symposium." Shelley finishes Herodotus. Ride out in the evening, and after supper go to the Casino.

Monday, AUG. 3.—Read 3rd canto of Tasso; Livy; transcribe the "Symposium"; finish the "Revolt of Islam." Shelley reads the "Persæ" of Æschylus, and "Eustace's Travels." He reads Hume's England after tea.

Tuesday, AUG. 4.—Read the 4th canto of Tasso; work; read "Letters and Thoughts";[46] Plato, "Phædrus," p. 380; Horace. Shelley reads "Phædrus" of Plato. Walk in the evening. Shelley reads Hume's England in the evening.

Wednesday, AUG. 5.—Read 5th canto of Tasso; work. Shelley reads "Phædrus," "Eustace's Travels," and Hume's England in the evening.

Thursday, AUG. 6.—Read a part of the 6th canto of Tasso; finish transcribing the "Symposium"; work. Shelley reads "Richard III" in the evening.

Friday, AUG. 7.—Read a part of the 7th canto of Tasso, Livy, Montaigne, and Eustace. Shelley reads Theocritus and "Richard III" aloud in the evening. Ride out.

Saturday, AUG. 8.—Read Livy, Montaigne, Horace. Shelley reads Theocritus and Horace. Ride in the evening. Shelley reads "Richard III" aloud in the evening. Clare falls from her horse.

Sunday, AUG. 9.—Finish 7th canto of Tasso; read Livy and Montaigne; read; and after tea go to the Casino. Shelley reads Theocritus.

Monday, AUG. 10.—Read 8th canto of Tasso, Livy, and Montaigne; ride out. Shelley reads Theocritus and "Henry VIII" aloud in the evening.

Tuesday, AUG. 11.—Read 9th canto of Tasso, Livy, Montaigne, and Horace. Shelley reads Theocritus and Virgil's "Georgics." After tea, he reads aloud and finishes the Play of "Henry VIII."

[46] Possibly [? William Beckford], *Letters and Observations, Written in a Short Tour through France and Italy* (Salsbury, 1786).

Wednesday, Aug. 12.—Read 10th canto of Tasso; Livy, Montaigne, Horace. Shelley reads Theocritus and the "Georgics." After tea, he begins the 5th volume of Hume.

Thursday, Aug. 13.—Read 11th canto of Tasso; Livy, Montaigne, Horace. Shelley reads Theocritus. Ride out. After tea, he reads Hume aloud.

Friday, Aug. 14.—Copy Shelley's Eclogue;[47] read Horace. In the evening, ride out. A letter from Elise.

Saturday, Aug. 15.—Copy Shelley's Eclogue; read Livy. Shelley reads the "Georgics." Ride out. Shelley reads Hume in the evening.

Sunday, Aug. 16.—Finish transcribing Shelley's Eclogue. Shelley is not well. He reads Lucian. Another letter from Elise.

Monday, Aug. 17.—Work. Shelley and Clare depart for Venice.[48] Read 12th canto of Tasso, and two acts of "Troilus and Cressida."

Tuesday, Aug. 18.—Read Livy; 13th canto of Tasso; finish "Troilus and Cressida"; read three books of Pope's "Homer." Walk in the evening.

Wednesday, Aug. 19.—Read 14th canto of Tasso, and Pope's "Homer."

Thursday, Aug. 20.—Read Livy, 15th canto of Tasso, and Pope's "Homer."

Friday, Aug. 21.—Little Clara is not well. Read Livy, 16th canto of Tasso, and Pope's "Homer."

Saturday, Aug. 22.—Read Livy, 17th canto of Tasso, and Pope's "Homer." Not well.

Sunday, Aug. 23.—Very unwell. Read Pope's "Homer." A letter from Shelley.[49]

Tuesday, Aug. 25.—The Gisbornes come.[50]

Thursday, Aug. 27.—Mr. Gisborne read 18th canto of Tasso to me. Read the "Symposium" to Mrs. Gisborne.

Friday, Aug. 28.—Finish reading the "Symposium" to Mrs. Gisborne. Walk out in the evening. A letter from Shelley.[51] Consultation.

Saturday, Aug. 29.—Bustle. Paolo goes to Lucca. Walk out in the evening.

Sunday, Aug. 30.—My birthday (21). Packing.

Monday, Aug. 31.—Travel to Lucca with Mrs. Gisborne; she then

47 *Rosalind and Helen,* which Shelley, at Mary's request, completed at the Baths of Lucca.

48 For the history of August 17–November 4, see Dowden, II, 221–40; and White, II, 28–40, 56.

49 Shelley to Mary, Florence, [August 20, 1818] (Julian edition, IX, 322–24).

50 The MS journal has a brief "reading" entry for August 26, according to the MS notes of Miss Grylls.

51 Shelley to Mary, Venice, [August 23, 1818] (Julian edition, IX, 325–30).

leaves me. Go on to Florence, where we arrive late. The day is hot, but the evening is delightful.

Tuesday, SEPT. 1.—Remain at Florence all day. Read "Hymns," "Epithalamium," &c., of Spenser. Ride about the city.

Monday, SEPT. [2–]14.—In four days, Saturday 5th, arrive at Este.[52] Poor Clara [the baby] is dangerously ill. Shelley is very unwell, from taking poison in Italian cakes. He writes his Drama of "Prometheus." Read seven cantos of Dante. Begin to translate "A Cajo Gracco" of Monti, and "Measure for Measure."

Tuesday, SEPT. 15.—Read Livy.[53]

Wednesday, SEPT. 16.—Read the "Filippo" of Alfieri. Shelley and Clare go to Padua. He is very ill from the effects of his poison.

Thursday, SEPT. [22–]24.—This is the Journal of misfortunes. Shelley writes; he reads "Œdipus Tyrannus" to me. On Tuesday, September 22, he goes to Venice. On Thursday [Sept. 24], I go to Padua with Clare; meet Shelley there. We go to Venice with my poor Clara, who dies the moment we get there. Mr. Hoppner[54] comes, and takes us away from the inn to his house.

Friday, SEPT. 25.—Remain at the Hoppners'. Shelley calls on Lord Byron. He reads the 4th canto of "Childe Harold."

Saturday, SEPT. 26.—An idle day. Go to the Lido, and see Albe [Byron] there.

Sunday, SEPT. 27.—Read 4th canto of "Child Harold." It rains. Go to the Doge's Palace, Ponté di Sospire,[55] &c. Go to the Academy with Mr. and Mrs. Hoppner, and see some fine pictures. Call at Lord Byron's, and see the Fornarina.[56]

Monday, SEPT. 28.—Go with Mrs. Hoppner and Cavaliere Mengaldo to the Library. Shopping. In the evening, Lord Byron calls.

Tuesday, SEPT. 29.—Leave Venice, and arrive at Este at night. Clare is gone with the children to Padua.

Wednesday, SEPT. 30.—The chicks return.[57] Transcribe [Byron's] "Mazeppa." Go to the Opera in the evening.[58]

52 S&M reads "Saturday, Sept. 5.—Arrive at Este." Correction from MS notes of Miss Grylls. At Este they occupied Casa Capucini (or I Capuccini), Byron's villa among the Euganean Hills.

53 Not in S&M; addition made from the MS notes of Miss Grylls, who says that the MS journal notes "other reading each day to Saturday the 19th."

54 R. Belgrave Hoppner, British consul-general at Venice. For a while he and his wife had charge of Allegra.

55 "Ponte dei Sospiri" in Dowden (II, 231).

56 Margarita Cogni. "Farmaretta" in S&M.

57 William and Allegra return to Este from Padua, with Claire.

58 This sentence is evidently misplaced or inadequately explained, for there was no opera to attend at Este.

OCTOBER [1–4].—Transcribe "Mazeppa," copy the Ode, and send them to Venice. Read [Alfieri's] "Saul." Shelley reads Malthus ["On the Principle of Population."].

Monday, OCT. 5.—Read Livy; finish the Tragedies of Alfieri. Walk out with Shelley. He reads Malthus, and "Cymbeline" aloud in the evening.

Tuesday, OCT. 6.—Read Livy, the "Tempest," and "Two Gentlemen of Verona." Shelley finishes Malthus, and reads "Cymbeline" aloud.

Wednesday, OCT. 7.—Read "Vita di Alfieri" [by himself], and Livy. Shelley goes to Padua. Reads "Cymbeline" to me in the evening.

Thursday, OCT. 8.—Read "Vita di Alfieri," and Livy. Shelley reads "Winter's Tale" aloud to me.

Friday, OCT. 9.—Read "Vita di Alfieri," and half 9th book of Virgil. Shelley reads "Winter's Tale" aloud. Walk in the evening.

Saturday, OCT. 10.—Finish "Vita di Tasso," read "Timon of Athens"; work. Shelley finishes the "Winter's Tale."

Sunday, OCT. 11.—Read "Timon of Athens." Pack. Travel with Shelley, William, and Elize to Padua.

Monday, OCT. 12.—Arrive at Venice at 2 o'clock. Read "All's Well that Ends Well." Spend the evening at Mr. Hoppner's.

Tuesday, OCT. 13.—Work. Call at Mr. Hoppner's; spend the day there. Shelley goes to Albe in the evening.

Tuesday, OCT. [14–]20.—Remain at Venice. Dine at the Hoppners' every day. Read "Women" of Maturin,[59] "The Fudge Family,"[60] [Byron's] "Beppo," &c. Go with Mr. and Mrs. Hoppner to see the Opera of "Othello"—a wretched piece of business. Shelley begins the "Republic of Plato."

The Chevalier Mengaldo spends the evening at the Hoppners', and relates several ghost stories—two that occurred to himself.[61]

When the Chevalier was at the University, and very young, on returning home to pass the vacation, he heard that the inhabitants of the town had been frightened by the mighty visitation of a ghost, who traversed the town from one end to the other; so much to their terror, that no one would venture out after dark. The Chevalier felt a great curiosity to see the ghost, and stationed himself at the window of a house of one

59 Charles R. Maturin; a novel (1818, 3 vols.).

60 Thomas Moore, *The Fudge Family in Paris* (1818).

61 The first two of these tales were printed in *Shelley Memorials* (pp. 104–106). The second tale was reproduced by Mary almost exactly from the journal in an essay "On Ghosts" (*London Magazine,* IX [March 1824], 253–56). The essay contains this account of the Chevalier Mengaldo: "The Italian was a noble, a soldier, . . . he had served in Napoleon's armies from early youth, and had been to Russia, had fought and bled, and been rewarded."—p. 255. (See notes to Dec. 22, 1814, and Aug. 18, 1816, entries.)

BAY OF NAPLES AND MOUNT VESUVIUS
Engraved by E. Benjamin from a painting by G. Arnald, A.R.A.

of his friends, by which the shadow always passed. Twelve o'clock struck; no ghost appeared. One; half-past one. The Chevalier grew sleepy, and determined to return home. The town chiefly consisted, like most country towns, of one long street; and as the Chevalier, on his road home, was at one end of it, he saw at the other something white, like a rabbit or greyhound, that appeared to advance towards him. He perceived that as it advanced it grew larger and larger, and appeared to take a human form. The Chevalier could now no longer doubt but that it was the ghost, and felt his courage fail him, although he strove to master it as well as he could. The figure, as it approached, grew gigantic, and the Chevalier crouched behind a column as it passed, which it did with enormous footsteps. As it passed, it appeared all dressed in white; the face was long and white, and its hand appeared of itself capable of covering the whole body of Mengaldo.

The Chevalier, when he was in the army, had a duel with a brother officer, and wounded him in the arm. He was very sorry at having wounded the young man, and attended him during its cure; so that when he got well they became firm and dear friends. Being quartered, I think, at Milan, the young officer fell desperately in love with the wife of a musician, who disdained his passion. The young man became miserable, and Mengaldo continually advised him to ask leave of absence—to hunt, to pay a visit, and in some way to divert his passion. One evening the young man came to Mengaldo, and said, "Well, I have asked leave of absence, and am to have it early to-morrow morning; so lend me your fowling-piece and cartridges, for I shall go to hunt for a fortnight." Mengaldo gave it him; and among his bird-shot were some bullets, put there for safety, in case, while hunting, he should be attacked by a wolf, &c.

The young man said, "Tell the lady I love that our conversation has been chiefly about her to-night, and that her name was the last I spoke." "Yes, yes," said Mengaldo; "I will say anything you please; but do not talk of her any more—you must forget her." On going away, the young man embraced Mengaldo warmly; but the latter saw nothing more in it than his affection, combined with melancholy, in separating himself from his mistress.

When Mengaldo was on guard that night, he heard the report of a gun. He was first troubled and agitated by it, but afterwards thought no more of it, and, when relieved from guard, went to bed, although he passed a restless and sleepless night. In the morning early, some one knocked at the door. The man said he had got the young officer's leave of absence, and had taken it to his house; a servant had opened the door, and he had gone upstairs; but the officer's room-door was locked, and no one answered to his knocking; but something oozed through under the door that appeared like blood. Mengaldo was dreadfully terrified; he hurried to his friend's house, burst open the door, and found him stretched on the ground; he had blown out his brains, and his head and brains were scattered about the room, so that no part of the head remained on the shoulders. Mengaldo was grieved and shocked, and had a fever in consequence, which lasted some days. When he was well, he got leave of absence, and went into the country, to try to divert his mind.

One evening, at moonlight, he was returning home from a walk, and passing through a lane with a hedge on both sides, so high that he could not see over it. As he walked along, he heard a rustling in the bushes beside him, and the figure of his friend issued from the hedge and stood before him, as he had seen him after his death, without his head. This figure he saw many times afterwards, always in the same place. It was impalpable to the touch, and never spoke, although Mengaldo often addressed it. Once he took another person with him. The same rustling was heard; the same shadow stepped forth. His companion was dreadfully terrified; he tried to cry, but his voice failed him, and he ran off as quickly as he could.

The third story belongs to one of the noblest families of the Frioul, of the name of ——, many years ago, when the Count and Countess were residing at their Castle of San Salvatore:—

The Countess was a very jealous woman; and one day as she sat at her toilet, the Count being in the room, she perceived, by means of a large mirror, some signs of intelligence pass between her husband and her maid; but she dissimulated, and said nothing. Shortly after, a fair was given at the town there, to which all the servants of the Castle resorted. The Count was from home, and the Countess sent all the servants to the fair except the maid, whom she commanded to follow her. She led her upstairs, where some men were ready to execute her orders. They placed her against a place prepared in the wall, and walled her up, notwithstanding her shrieks and entreaties. When the servants returned, and the girl was inquired for, the Countess said that she had sent her to a relation several miles off, and she was thought of no more.

When the Father of the Count was about to die, a figure appeared dressed in white robes by his bed-side; her countenance was white also; but he recognised the features of the girl who had formerly attended on the Countess. Ever since that time this shade has always appeared to some one of the House before any death or misfortune.

One of the servants of the Castle saw her not many years back. He was at that time Huntsman, and following the chase. One morning, just at daybreak, the game, followed by the hunters, ran up a declivity, and then descended the other side. The Huntsman was the last; and when the party were all out of sight on the other side of the hill, he saw the Donna Bianca advancing towards him. He dropped his gun; he strove to cry, but he could not; he strove to fly, but his steps were involuntarily towards, instead of away from, the ghost. As he approached, she motioned him away with her hand, and then, passing by him, disappeared. When she had gone, his gun had disappeared with her; but it would have been useless to him if he had found it, for he never hunted again.

Wednesday, Oct. 21.—Dine at Hoppners' with Mengaldo. Go to the Comedy in the evening—stupid beyond measure. Shelley spends the evening with Albe.

Thursday, Oct. 22.—Go again to the Comedy with the same party. Shelley spends the evening with Albe.

Friday, Oct. 23.—Read "Macbeth." Walk out with Mr. and Mrs. Hoppner and Mengaldo in the Public Gardens. Mengaldo gives me an account of his campaigns in Russia.

Saturday, Oct. 24.—Write to Mrs. Hunt.[62] Dine at the Hoppners. Read the "Quarterly." Shelley goes to Este.

Sunday, Oct. 25.—Read the "Life of Virgil." Walk out with Mr. and Mrs. Hoppner. Go to the Theatre with them.

Monday, Oct. 26.—Go to Lido with Mrs. Hoppner. Read [Scott's] "Black Dwarf" [1816].

Tuesday, Oct. 27.—Read the "Hecyra" of Terence. Dine at the Hoppners.

Wednesday, Oct. 28.—Finish Terence. Mr. H[oppner] very unwell.[63]

Thursday, Oct. 29.—Work; go out in the gondola. Shelley returns with Allegra. Call on the Hoppners.

Saturday, Oct. 31.—Take leave of the Hoppners. Travel to Padua.

Sunday, Nov. 1.—Return to Este. Read Mrs. C. Smith's novel of "Emmeline."[64]

Wednesday, Nov. 4.—Prepare for our journey. Read [Fielding's] "Joseph Andrews."

Thursday, Nov. 5.—Go as far as Rovigo. Bad roads and cloudy weather.

Friday, Nov. 6.—Very bad roads; our horses could hardly draw the

[62] In her letter of March 12, 1819, to Mrs. Hunt, Mary says of this letter: "I wrote you a long one from Venice but the laudable love of gain . . . caused the hotel keeper to charge the postage & to throw the letter into the fire."—*Letters,* I, 63.

[63] Not in S&M; taken from the MS notes of Miss Grylls.

[64] Miss Grylls's MS notes indicate that the MS journal has brief "reading entries" for November 2 and 3.

carriage; we get oxen where we can. Pass by a farm-house filled with the finest oxen in the world. Sleep at Ferrara.

Saturday, Nov. 7.—Remain all day at Ferrara. Visit the Public Library, where we see the arm-chair and inkstand of Ariosto, his handwriting, and also that of Tasso. Visit the carcere of Tasso. Read Montaigne. Shelley reads Plato's "Republic."

Sunday, Nov. 8.—We travel through a marshy uninteresting country, on a rainy day. Sleep at Bologna. Shelley reads 4th canto of Ariosto aloud to me. Read Montaigne.

Monday, Nov. 9.—Shelley and I spend this day in looking at pictures; we see many exquisitely beautiful of the first masters—a Christ of Correggio, St. Cecilia of Raphael, a great many of Guido, Franceschini, Domenichino, and Caracci. Shelley reads Plato's "Republic." Finish 11th book of Horace; read Montaigne.

Tuesday, Nov. 10.—We visit again the Academia delle Belle Arte, and then make a pilgrimage to the Madonna di Luca, on the hill. A delightful day, and very pleasant ride. Shelley writes to Peacock.[65] Read Montaigne.

Wednesday, Nov. 11.—We travel through pretty English country, and sleep at Faenza.

Thursday, Nov. 12.—The country is the same as the day before—pretty, and very English. I am very tired. Read Montaigne. Sleep at Cesena.

Friday, Nov. 13.—Pass the Rubicon. See a Roman bridge and triumphal arch, both of the Augustan age, at Rimini. Sleep at Catholica.

Saturday, Nov. 14.—Pass through Pesaro and Fano. Begin to wind among and ascend the Apennines. Sleep, or do not sleep, for we do not undress, at a miserable inn at Fossombrone.

Sunday, Nov. 15.—Pass along the banks of the Metaurus, which are exceedingly beautiful. See Monte Asdrubale. Pass along a road made by the Consul Æmilius, and a passage cut through the rock. The scene is fine and Promethean, but not so fine, I think, as Les Echelles, in Savoy. Sleep miserably at Scheggia.

Monday, Nov. 16.—We are still among the Apennines, which are not so beautiful as the day before, having the hilly confined aspect those mountains generally have. The scenery becomes more beautiful towards nightfall. Sleep at Foligno.

Tuesday, Nov. 17.—Sleep at Spoleto, where we visit a magnificent aqueduct, built, they say, by the Romans, and repaired by the Goths; it is thrown across a deep narrow valley. Pass by the Clitumnus and its Temple.

65 Shelley to Peacock, Bologna, Monday, [November 9 and 10, 1818] (Julian edition, IX, 342–48).

Wednesday, Nov. 18.—We sleep at Terni. Visit the celebrated waterfall [of the Velino], first from below, where we see it as a fine painting, and afterwards from above, where it is more beautiful than any painting—the thunder, the abyss, the spray, the graceful dash of water lost in the mist below—it put me in mind of Sappho leaping from a rock, and her form vanishing as in the shape of a swan in the distance. As we return home, we behold Venus, brighter, and nearly as large, as the moon in her first quarter.

Thursday, Nov. 19.—We wind among the Apennines; and in the evening the scenery is beautifully wooded. Sleep at Nepi.

Friday, Nov. 20.—We travel all day the Campagna di Roma—a perfect solitude, yet picturesque, and relieved by shady dells. We see an immense hawk sailing in the air for prey. Enter Rome. A rainy evening. Doganas and cheating innkeepers. We at length get settled in a comfortable hotel.

Saturday, Nov. 21.—Visit St. Peter's; the outside of the church disappoints us; we do not think it so fine as St. Paul's; the inside is wonderfully magnificent; and the approach, the square (surrounded by colonnades), the beautiful fountains, the obelisk, form altogether the most splendid piazza I ever saw. Read Montaigne.

Sunday, Nov. 22.—Visit the Capitol, the Coliseum, the Forum, the Pantheon, St. Peter's, &c. The Coliseum is much finer than I expected; the whole of the ruins do not disappoint in grandeur and beauty, but in quantity. Read Montaigne. Go to the Opera in the evening—the worst I ever saw.

Monday, Nov. 23.—Visit Monte Cavallo, Baths of Diocletian, Santa Maria degli Angeli, Santa Maria Maggiore, Le Sette Salle delle Terme di Tito, and again the Coliseum and Forum. Read Montaigne, and write to Papa.

Tuesday, Nov. 24.—Go to the Coliseum with William. Sketch. Shelley goes with Clara to the Vatican. Read Montaigne.

Wednesday, Nov. 25.—Sketch in the Coliseum and the Temple of Peace. Read Montaigne. Shelley begins [writing] the "Tale of the Coliseum."

Thursday, Nov. 26.—Visit Santo Paolo Fuori delle Mura, a barn of a church, supported by the loveliest Corinthian columns of a lilac-tinted marble, taken by that hateful wretch Constantine from the tomb of Hadrian. See the tomb of Cestius, of Cæcila Metella, &c.; and afterwards the fountains of Trevi and Navona.

Friday, Nov. 27.—Shelley departs for Naples. Read Montaigne. Walk to the Coliseum and the Forum. Prepare for our journey. A letter from Mrs. Hoppner; answer it.

Saturday, Nov. 28.—Travel to Velletri. We pass first over the Campagna di Roma, crossed in two places by an immense aqueduct. Afterwards, as we approach the sea, the country becomes hilly and woody, and exceedingly beautiful. We coast along just on the borders of the hills, among the trees, and at every opening we see the plain bordering the sea, and the sea itself, about two miles off; some rocky islands appear in it not very far from the shore. Read Montaigne.

Sunday, Nov. 29.—Cross the Pontine Marshes. There are no houses or villages to be seen in the whole extent, if you except three miserable post-houses. The people you meet have all a savage appearance; they appear to gain their livelihood by sporting, or robbing, where they dare. We meet many soldiers as patrols, both on foot and on horseback. Just before we enter Terracina, we leave the Marshes; bold bare rocks rise around us, and we hear the roaring of the sea. The inn is situated on the beach, and from its windows we see the Promontory of Circe, and, on the rocks behind, the ruins of the Temples of Jupiter and Apollo. Read Montaigne.

Monday, Nov. 30.—We leave Terracina at daybreak, and travel along a road at the foot of a range of bare bleak hills. As we approach Gaeta, the little plain at the foot of the hills is covered with a wood of olives, festooned by vines. By the roadside, overlooking the Bay of Gaeta, we see the Tomb of Cicero, near the place where he was murdered, in the midst of the olive wood; it is a tower of two stories, smaller at the top than at the bottom, and overgrown with weeds. About a mile further on, we arrive at the Mole. The inn where we lodge is situated in the middle of the bay, where the land projects a little into the sea; it overlooks a garden planted with orange and olive trees. This garden is close to the sea, so that the olive trees dip their branches into the sea. I never saw a more picturesque bay; the land almost meets around; and the bold promontory to the right is enlivened by the town and Castle of Gaeta situated upon it. The whole bay is sanctified by the fictions of Homer, and the garden in particular by the ruins of the Villa of Cicero, which overlooks the sea. A Poet could not have a more sacred burying place than in an olive grove on the shore of a beautiful bay, sheltered by the range of bleak hills, which contrast with the beautiful wooded plains at their feet. From his Villa he beheld the sun rise behind one mountainous promontory to the left, pass over the sea, and set behind the mountains which form the promontory on the right. In the middle, between the promontories, is a rocky island several miles off. The waves of the sea broke close under the windows of his villa, which was perhaps then shaded, as it is now, by an olive grove, and scented by orange and lemon trees. His Tomb, which I have mentioned, is at the distance of a mile from this villa. After twice embarking, and being twice driven to shore by the wind (such a wind as this of to-day, which blew fiercely from sea to land), he was carried in a litter through the woods, when overtaken by the soldiers. Read Montaigne.

Tuesday, DEC. 1.—A long and fatiguing journey. We arrive at Naples about 6 o'clock. We see the flames of Vesuvius as we drive along.

Thursday, DEC. 3.—Work, and walk out in the Royal Gardens, on which our lodgings [250 Riviera di Chiaia] look out. Shelley reads Livy.

Saturday, DEC. 5.—Go to Herculaneum.[66] Visit the Theatre, which is all there is to see of the town. Visit the Museum at Portici, which only contains the stucco paintings taken from the walls of the Ancient Cities. Shelley reads Livy. I finish 6th book; read Montaigne.

Sunday, DEC. 6.—Read [Le Sage's] "Gil Blas"; walk in the Gardens.

Monday, DEC. 7.—Ride out in the town. Read "Gil Blas."

Tuesday, DEC. 8.—Go on the sea with Shelley. Visit Cape Miseno, the Elysian Fields, Avernus, Solfatara. The Bay of Baiæ is beautiful; but we are disappointed by the various places we visit.

Wednesday, DEC. 9.—Read Livy, "Claire d'Albe,"[67] "Gil Blas." Walk in the Gardens. Shelley reads Livy.

Thursday, DEC. 10.—Read Livy, and "Adele de Senange."[68] Shelley reads Livy.

Friday, DEC. 11.—Finish "Gil Blas"; read Livy.

Saturday, DEC. 12.—Read [Madame de Staël's] "Corinne," and Livy. Shelley reads Livy.

Sunday, DEC. 13.—Read "Corinne," and Livy. Shelley reads "Corinne." Go to the Opera in the evening.

Monday, DEC. 14.—Finish "Corinne," and 7th book of Livy. Shelley reads "Corinne." Walk in the Gardens.

Tuesday. DEC. 15.—Read Livy. Visit Virgil's Tomb, and the Grotto of Pausilippo. Shelley reads "Corinne."

Wednesday, DEC. 16.—Go up Vesuvius, and see the rivers of lava gush from its sides. We are very much fatigued, and Shelley is very ill. Return at 10 o'clock.

Thursday, DEC. 17.—We read Livy. Walk in the Gardens. Beautiful lightning in the evening.

Friday, DEC. 18.—We read Livy. Write out Shelley's Poem ["Prometheus Unbound"].

Saturday, DEC. 19.—Spend the morning at the Studii, and see the

66 For a connected account of Shelley's sightseeing in and about Naples, see White, II, 62–66.

67 A novel by Sophie Cottin (1808, 2 vols.). S&M reads "d'Alve."

68 By Madame de Souza (Paris, 1768).

most beautiful statues. Shelley writes letters.[69] Finish copying his Poem. Read Livy.

Sunday, DEC. 20.—Finish 8th book of Livy; read Montaigne; correct "Frankenstein."

Monday, DEC. 21.—Read the "Georgics." Walk in the Gardens.

Tuesday, DEC. 22.—Go to Pompeii. We are delighted with this ancient city. Read Montaigne. Shelley reads Livy.

Wednesday, DEC. 23.—Read the "Georgics." Shelley reads Livy.

Thursday, DEC. 24.—Finish 1st book of the "Georgics." Shelley begins reading Winkelmann's "Histoire de l'Art" to me in the evening.[70]

Sunday, DEC. 27.—Finish 2nd book of the "Georgics." Clare is not well. Shelley reads Winkelmann. Walk in the Gardens.

Monday, DEC. 28.—Read the "Georgics." Shelley reads Livy and Winkelmann to me. Visit Virgil's Tomb.

Tuesday, DEC. 29.—Work. Read two cantos of Dante with Shelley. He reads Livy and Winkelmann aloud.

Thursday, DEC. 31.—Shelley reads Winkelmann aloud to me.

List of Books read in 1818

MARY

[E. D.] Clarke's Travels [in Various Countries of Europe, Asia, and Africa, 6 vols. 1810–23.]
Æneid. [By Virgil.]
Terence.
Hume's Dissertation on the Passions. [Four Dissertations, 1757.]
Sterne's Tristram Shandy. [9 vols., 1759–67.]
[Sterne's] Sentimental Journey [2 vols., 1768] and Letters.
2 vols. of Montaigne. [Essais.]
[August W. von] Schlegel on the Drama. [Lectures on Dramatic Art and Literature, tr. by J. Black, 1815.]
Rhododaphne. [By Thomas Love Peacock, 1818.]
Aminta of Tasso. [1573.]
Œuvres de Molière.
2 books of the Odes of Horace.
Aristippe [1800–1801], and Les Abderites [1774] de [Christoph M.] Wieland.

69 On the nineteenth Shelley probably finished his letter of December [17 or 18, 1818] to Peacock (Julian edition, X, 12–20, where it is incorrectly dated [22nd] from the postmark).

70 In the MS journal are brief reading entries ("Livy and Winckelmann read aloud every day") for December 25 and 26, according to the MS notes of Miss Grylls.

French Translations of Lucian.
[Vincenzo] Monti's Tragedies.
Orlando Furioso. [By Ariosto, 1532.]

1819

ITALY

Friday, JAN. 1.—Work; read Dante. Spend the evening at Madame Falconet's. Shelley reads Livy.

Saturday, JAN. 2.—Read Dante. Shelley reads Winkelmann aloud. Spend the morning at the Studii.

Sunday, JAN. 3.—Shelley reads Livy, and Winkelmann aloud. Read Dante and Sismondi ["Histoire des Républiques Italiennes"].

Monday, JAN. 4.—Finish 3rd "Georgic." Shelley reads Livy.

Tuesday, JAN. 5.—Read Sismondi and Dante. Shelley finishes Livy. Ride out.

Wednesday, JAN. 6.—Read "Georgics," Sismondi, and Dante. Shelley reads Plutarch's "Lives."

Thursday, JAN. 7.—Read "Georgics," and Dante.

Friday, JAN. 8.—Read "Georgics," and Dante. Shelley reads Euripides.

Saturday, JAN. 9.—Finish the "Georgics"; read 25th and 26th cantos of Dante.

Sunday, JAN. 10.—Read Livy, Dante, and Sismondi.

Monday, JAN. 11.—Read Livy, Dante, and Sismondi. Shelley reads Euripides.

Tuesday, JAN. 12.—Allegra's birthday. Read Dante and Livy.

Wednesday, JAN. 13.—Read Dante, "History of Two Viziers,"[1] Sismondi.

Thursday, JAN. 14.—

Wednesday, JAN. 20.—Finish the "Inferno" of Dante, and the 9th book of Livy. Shelley and I read Sismondi.

Thursday, JAN. 21.—

Saturday, JAN. 23.—Read Sismondi. Shelley writes letters.[2]

[1] Not further identified.

[2] On the twenty-third Shelley probably wrote at least a portion of his long letter to Peacock (Julian edition, X, 20–28), conjecturally dated January 24 by Ingpen (for no apparent reason; the Naples postmark is dated January 26).

Sunday, JAN. 24.—

Saturday, JAN. 30.—Read Sismondi.

Sunday, JAN. 31.—

Thursday, FEB. 4.—Read Sismondi; finish 10th book of Livy.

Friday, FEB. 5.—

Wednesday, FEB. 10.—Read Sismondi and "Faublas."[3] On Wednesday, go to Caserta.

Thursday, FEB. 11.—Read Sismondi. Go the Lago d'Agnano and the Caccia d'Astroni.

Friday and Saturday, FEB. 12 and 13.—Read Sismondi, and the "Purgatorio."

Sunday, FEB. 14.—Go to the Caccia d'Astroni. M. Rosmilly[4] dines with us.

Monday, FEB. 15.—

Monday, FEB. 22.—Read Sismondi. Go out on the Mascherada. Walk in the Gardens.

Tuesday, FEB. 23.—A rainy day. Set off for Pæstum. Sleep at Salerno.

Wednesday, FEB. 24.—Go to Pæstum. Stopt at a river five miles from Pæstum, and obliged to walk. A dull day; but a fine evening until sunset, when it begins to rain again.

Thursday, FEB. 25.—Return to Naples. Visit Pompeii on our road. Finish Sismondi.

Friday, FEB. 26.—Visit the Studii.

Saturday, FEB. 27.—Pack.

Sunday, FEB. 28.—Leave Naples at 2 o'clock. Sleep at Capua. Vincenzo drives. A most tremendous fuss.

Monday, MAR. 1.—Travel to Gaeta.

Tuesday, MAR. 2.—Remain the whole day at Gaeta, playing at chess, and strolling about the woods and by the sea-shore.

Wednesday, MAR. 3.—Sleep at Terracina. A most wonderful contrast between this place and Gaeta.

Thursday, MAR. 4.—Sleep at Velletri. A most fatiguing day's journey.

Friday, MAR. 5.—After passing over the beautiful hills of Albano, and traversing the Campagna, we arrive at the Holy City again, and see the Coliseum again.[5]

[3] Jean B. Louvet de Couvray, *The Chevalier de Faublas* (English translation, 1793, 4 vols.).

[4] Possibly Dr. Roskilly, Shelley's physician, mentioned by Charles MacFarlane (see White, II, 64–65, 66).

[5] They lodged at the Villa di Parigi.

All that Athens ever brought forth wise,
All that Afric ever brought forth strange,
All that which Asia ever had of prize,
Was here to see. Oh, marvellous great change!
Rome living was the world's sole ornament;
And dead, is now the world's sole monument.

Saturday, MAR. 6.—Read the 1st volume of [Godwin's] "Mandeville."

Sunday, MAR. 7.—Move to our lodgings [in the Palazzo Verospi, 300 Corso]. A rainy day. Visit the Coliseum. Read the Bible.

Monday, MAR. 8.—Visit the Museum of the Vatican. Read the Bible.

Tuesday, MAR. 9.—Shelley and I go to the Villa Borghese. Drive about Rome. Visit the Pantheon. Visit it again by moonlight, and see the yellow rays fall through the roof upon the floor of the Temple. Visit the Coliseum.

Wednesday, MAR. 10.—Visit the Capitol, and see the most divine statues. Lord Guildford calls.

Thursday, MAR. 11.—Read the Bible.

Friday, MAR. 12.—Go to hear Messe [Mass], and the Padre Pacifico, with the Signora Dionigi.[6] See the Pope. Visit the Capitol.[7]

Saturday, MAR. 13.—Read the Bible. Lord Guildford calls. Walk to the Baths of Caracalla. Meet the Pope. See the Arch of Janus, &c. I am dreadfully tired. Write to Marianne.[8] Read Montaigne.

Sunday, MAR. 14.—Read Montaigne, the Bible, and Livy. Walk to the Coliseum. Shelley reads Winkelmann.

Monday, MAR. 15.—Write; read Montaigne and Livy. Go to the Villa Albano and the Villa Borghese. Shelley reads Lucretius.

Tuesday, MAR. 16.—Visit the Cœlian Mount. Read the Bible, Livy, and Montaigne. Shelley reads Lucretius.

Wednesday, MAR. 17.—Write. Visit Porta Maggiore, the Temple of Minerva Medici, the Gardens of the Quirinal, Monte Cavallo, Villa Borghese, and Terme di Tito. Read Montaigne.

Thursday, MAR. 18.—Write; read Montaigne and Livy. Go to Cestius' Tomb and the Borghese Gardens.

Friday, MAR. 19.—Write; read Montaigne and Livy. Go to the Villa Pamfili and the Villa Borghese. Clare's singing lesson.

[6] Incorrectly spelled "Dionizi" throughout S&M; correction made hereafter without notice. Signora Marianna Dionigi (1756–1826), "a distinguished painter, antiquary, authoress, and member of academies innumerable, now in her elder years . . . but a centre of intellectual culture in Rome, and able to gather many strangers to her *conversazioni.*"—Dowden, II, 255.

[7] Claire's diary for March 12–16, 28 is printed by Dowden (II, 257–58).

[8] Mary to Marianne Hunt, March 12, 1819 (*Letters*, I, 63–64). Mary probably began the letter on the twelfth and finished it on the thirteenth.

Saturday, MAR. 20.—Write; read Livy and Montaigne. Visit the Palazzo Rospigliosi. Visit the Signora Dionigi.

Sunday, MAR. 21.—Visit the Palazzo Spada. See the Statue of Pompey, at the base of which Cæsar died. Read Montaigne.

Monday, MAR. 22.—Visit the Farnesina, and Villa Lanzi. Read Montaigne. Dr. Bell[9] calls. Finish 21st book of Livy. Shelley reads Lucretius.

Tuesday, MAR. 23.—Read Livy and Montaigne; draw. Go to the Gardens Borghese.

Wednesday, MAR. 24.—Drawing Master.[10] Read Livy and Montaigne. Shelley reads Euripides. Visit the Vatican. See the Pictures of Raphael.

Thursday, MAR. 25.—Draw; read Livy. Visit the Palazzo Giustiniani. Visit the Signora Dionigi. Shelley goes to Mr. Torlonia.[11]

Friday, MAR. 26.—Draw; read Montaigne. Visit the Vatican. Shelley reads the "Medea" of Euripides.

Saturday, MAR. 27.—Drawing lesson. Finish Montaigne. Walk in the Borghese Gardens. Read Livy.

Sunday, MAR. 28.—Draw. Ride. Visit the Signora Dionigi.

Monday, MAR. 29.—Drawing lesson. Dr. and Mrs. Bell call. In the evening, go and hear the "Miserere."

Tuesday, MAR. 30.—Draw all day. Ride to the Borghese Gardens. Shelley goes to hear the "Miserere" in the evening. Shelley reads Plutarch's "Life of Marius."

Wednesday, MAR. 31.—Drawing lesson. Call on Mr. Bell. Ride to the Borghese Gardens. Read "Hamlet." Shelley read "Life of Marius."

Thursday, APR. 1.—Walk to the Capitol. Go to the Vatican with Shelley and Willmouse. Read "Romeo and Juliet." Shelley reads the "Hippolitus" of Euripides.

Friday, APR. 2.—Go out with Signora Dionigi to see the Pavilion of the Emperor. Read and finish 22nd book of Livy. The Entry of the Emperor. Read "King Lear"; draw.

Saturday, APR. 3.—Drawing lesson. Go to sketch at the Baths of Caracalla. Read "Othello."

Sunday, APR. 4.—Draw; read "Julius Cæsar." Walk in the Borghese Gardens. Shelley visits the Signora Dionigi.

Monday, APR. 5.—Drawing lesson. Read "King John," and Livy. Letters from England.[12] Visit the Pictures of Raphael at the Vatican. After dinner walk to the Coliseum.

[9] Dr. J. Bell, a well-known English physician.

[10] Mary notes twenty-nine lessons in all (the last on June 1), usually on Monday, Wednesday, and Saturday of each week until May 14, when they become more frequent.

[11] Of Messrs. Torlonia & Company, bankers.

Tuesday, Apr. 6.—Drawing. Sit to the Signor Delicati [an artist]. Walk in the Borghese Gardens.

Wednesday, Apr. 7.—Drawing lesson. Ride out. Read Livy. Go in to the Signora Dionigi in the evening.

Thursday, Apr. 8.—Write to Mrs. Gisborne. In the evening, see the Cross lighted at St. Peter's. Read "Forsyth's Tour."[13]

Friday, Apr. 9.—Finish "Forsyth's Tour." Walk with Shelley to the Coliseum. In the evening, go to the Lavada and Supper of the Pellerine.

Saturday, Apr. 10.—Draw. Sketch in the Borghese Gardens. Read Livy.

[*Easter*] *Sunday*, Apr. 11.—Spend the morning in St. Peter's, seeing the Funzioni. Read Livy, and the "Merry Wives of Windsor." Go to see the lighting of the Cupola and the Girandola, in the evening, with the Signora Dionigi and Mr. Davies.

Monday, Apr. 12.—Drawing lesson. Draw in the Borghese Gardens. Visit the Signora Dionigi.[14]

Tuesday, Apr. 13.—Draw in the Borghese Gardens. Signor Chiappa calls. Read Livy. In the evening, Mr. Davies calls.

Wednesday, Apr. 14.—Drawing lesson. Visit Monte Cavallo. Finish the 23rd book of Livy. Visit the Signora Dionigi.

Thursday, Apr. 15.—Draw all the morning in the Gardens Borghese. Walk to the Coliseum. Read "Huon de Bordeaux," and "Roman de la Chevalerie."[15]

Friday, Apr. 16.—Paint; read Livy. Draw in the Borghese Gardens. The Neapolitan and his Sister[16] walk about with us. After dinner, Shelley reads the 1st book of "Paradise Lost" to me. Visit the Signora Dionigi.

Saturday, Apr. 17.—Drawing lesson. Read Metastasio. Shelley reads "Paradise Lost" aloud. Visit the Signora Dionigi in the evening.

Sunday, Apr. 18.—Draw. Signor Delicati comes. Afterwards, ride to the Vatican, and walk through it. In the evening, visit the Signora Dionigi.

Monday, Apr. 19.—Drawing lesson. Signor Delicati comes. Ride to the Borghese Gardens. Mr. Bell calls. Read Metastasio.

Tuesday, Apr. 20.—Draw. Signor Delicati comes. Read Metastasio.

12 From Leigh Hunt, dated March 9, 1819 (*The Correspondence of Leigh Hunt*, ed. by his Eldest Son [Thornton Hunt], [London, Smith, Elder and Co., 1862, 2 vols.], I, 126–30); answered by Mary on April 6, 1819 (*Letters*, I, 65–67). And from Peacock; answered by Shelley on April 6, 1819 (Julian edition, X, 45–49. Ingpen's note on p. 45 is in error: by "16th" in the postscript Mary meant Peacock's "Letter No. 16.").

13 Joseph Forsyth, *Remarks on Antiquities, Arts, and Letters during an Excursion in Italy in the Years 1802 and 1803* (1813).

14 Extracts from Claire's diary for April 12–18 are printed by White (II, 89–90).

15 Not further identified.

16 Musicians of Arpino, named Fanelli.

Go to the Feast of the Capitol in the evening with Mr. Davies. Shelley is very unwell.

Wednesday, Apr. 21.—Drawing lesson. Walk with Shelley to the Capitol. Go to the Gardens Borghese. Read Metastasio. Shelley reads the   of Shakespeare. Signora Dionigi calls.

Thursday, Apr. 22.—Draw. Signor Delicati comes. Visit the Palazzo Colonna, and see the picture of Beatrice Cenci. Ride to the Borghese Gardens. Read Livy. Visit the Signora Dionigi.

Friday, Apr. 23.—Draw. Signor Delicati comes. Go to the Borghese Gardens.

Saturday, Apr. 24.—Drawing lesson. Signor Delicati comes. Go to the Trinita, and to the Coliseum. The Albini, &c. spend the evening in our room.

Sunday, Apr. 25.—Read Shelley's Drama ["Prometheus Unbound"]. Signor Delicati comes. Mr. Bell calls. Spend the evening with Signora Dionigi, and see Colonel Calicot Finch.[17]

Monday, Apr. 26.—Drawing lesson. A rainy day. Work. Visit the Signora Dionigi in the evening.

Tuesday, Apr. 27.—Spend the morning with Miss [Amelia] Curran.[18] Go and see the German Exhibition. Visit Signora Dionigi. Read Livy.

Wednesday, Apr. 28.—ψηττα λιψαι. Drawing lesson. Go to the Vatican with Miss Curran. Read Livy.

Thursday, Apr. 29.—Paint. Go with Miss Curran to the Borghese Gardens and to the Coliseum. Read Livy.

Friday, Apr. 30.—Paint. Signor Delicati comes. Spend the rest of the morning with Miss Curran. In the evening, work.

Saturday, May 1.—Drawing lesson. Read Livy, and "Romans Chevaleresques."[19]

Sunday, May 2.—Paint; finish 24th book of Livy. Call on Miss Curran.

Monday, May 3.—Paint. Call on Miss Curran. Read "Bib de Chevalerie."[20] Lesson.

Tuesday, May 4.—Paint. Spend the rest of the morning with Miss Curran. Read Livy.

17 Robert Finch (1783–1830), parson, traveler, scholar, antiquarian, philanthropist—a most extraordinary man, in many ways ridiculous. The name "Calicot" was applied to him (privately) by the Shelleys, who borrowed it from Thomas Moore's *The Fudge Family in Paris;* the title "Colonel" was assumed by Finch. See Elizabeth Nitchie, *The Reverend Colonel Finch* (New York, Columbia University Press, 1940).

18 The artist daughter of John Philpot Curran. She painted portraits of Mary, Claire, William, and Shelley.

19 Not further identified. Probably the same as the *Roman de la Chevalerie* of April 15.

20 Not further identified.

Wednesday, MAY 5.—Lesson. Read Livy and Chrysostome. Walk out with Miss Curran.

Thursday, MAY 6.—Read Livy; draw. Adventure of Shelley at the Postoffice.[21] Read the "Visions of Quevedo."[22]

Friday, MAY 7.—Draw. Shelley sits to Miss Curran. Change our lodgings.[23] Walk. Read Bocaccio.

Saturday, MAY 8.—Draw. Finish 25th book of Livy; read Bocaccio.

Sunday, MAY 9.—Draw. Walk with Miss Curran on the banks of the Tiber. Read Livy and Bocaccio.

Monday, MAY 10.—Work. Drawing lesson.

Tuesday, MAY 11.—Draw; work. Walk with Miss Curran; spend the evening with her. Walk on the Trinita. Visit the Casa Cenci.

Wednesday, MAY 12.—Drawing lesson. Work. Read Bocaccio. Miss Curran spends the evening with us.

Thursday, MAY 13.—Go to Tivoli with Miss Curran and spend the day there. It rains as we return. Read the "Decamerone."

Friday, MAY 14.—Work. Drawing lesson. Read Livy, and the "Decamerone." Shelley writes his Tragedy ["The Cenci"]. Will sits to Miss Curran.

Saturday, MAY 15.—Work, and draw. Walk to the Capitol and Monte Cavallo. Read the "Decamerone."

Sunday, MAY 16.—Drawing lesson. Read the "Decamerone," and Livy.

Monday, MAY 17.—Draw; read the "Decamerone," and Livy. Walk out.

Tuesday, MAY 18.—Drawing lesson. Finish 26th book of Livy; read the "Decamerone." Spend the evening with Miss Curran.

Wednesday, MAY 19.—Drawing lesson. Read the "Decamerone." Spend the evening with Miss Curran, who is ill.

Thursday, MAY 20.—Drawing lesson. Read the "Decamerone."

Friday, MAY 21.—Draw; read the "Decamerone."

Saturday, MAY 22.—Draw; finish the "Decamerone." Miss Curran calls. Drawing lesson.

Sunday, MAY 23.—Draw; read Livy. Shelley spends the day at Albano.

Monday, MAY 24.—Drawing lesson. Read Livy. Walk.

Tuesday, MAY 25.—Draw. William is not well. Read Livy.

Wednesday, MAY 26.—Drawing lesson. Read Livy.

[21] See White, II, 178 and 589, n. 6.

[22] Francisco Gomez de Quevedo.

[23] They moved to "65 Via Sistina, L'Ultimo Casa sulla Trinita dei Monti," as Claire notes in her diary, probably to be near Miss Curran, who lived at 64 Via Sistina. (Neither Dowden nor White notes this change of residence at Rome.)

Thursday, MAY 27.—Draw; finish 27th book of Livy. Walk to the Coliseum.

Friday, MAY 28.—Sit to Miss Curran. William gets better in the evening. Read Livy.

Saturday, MAY 29.—Read Livy, [Cervantes's] "Persiles and Sigismunda." Drawing lesson. Miss Curran calls.

Sunday, MAY 30.—Read Livy, and "Persiles and Sigismunda." Draw. Spend the evening at Miss Curran's.

Monday, MAY 31.—Read Livy, and "Persiles and Sigismunda." Draw. Walk in the evening.

Tuesday, JUNE 1.—Drawing lesson. Read Livy. Walk by the Tiber. Spend the evening with Miss Curran.

Wednesday, JUNE 2.—See Mr. Vogel's pictures. William becomes very ill in the evening.

Thursday, JUNE 3.—William is very ill, but gets better towards the evening. Miss Curran calls.

Friday, JUNE 4.[24]—

Wednesday, AUG. 4.—LEGHORN—I begin my Journal on Shelley's birthday. We have now lived five years together; and if all the events of the five years were blotted out, I might be happy; but to have won, and then cruelly to have lost, the associations of four years, is not an accident to which the human mind can bend without much suffering.

Since I left Rome[25] I have read several books of Livy, "Antenor,"[26] "Clarissa Harlowe," the "Spectator," a few novels, and am now reading the Bible, and Lucan's "Pharsalia," and Dante. Shelley is today 27 years of age. Write; read Lucan and the Bible. Shelley writes the "Cenci," and reads Plutarch's "Lives." The Gisbornes call in the evening. Shelley reads "Paradise Lost" to me. Read two cantos of the "Purgatorio."

Thursday, AUG. 5.—Write; read the "Edinburgh Review." Shelley reads Plutarch's "Lives," and two cantos of the "Purgatorio." The Gisbornes in the evening.

Friday, AUG. 6.—Read the "Quarterly Review," and [Coleridge's]

[24] William died at noonday on June 7, and was buried in the Protestant Cemetery. The Shelleys left Rome on June 10, arrived at Leghorn on the seventeenth, remained there a week, and then removed to Villa Valsovano, a house near the sea, about halfway between Leghorn and Monte Nero. Claire's summary of June 7–24 is quoted by Dowden (II, 269).

Following the blank June 4 entry, S&M has: "(The Journal ends here.—P. B. S.)." The MS notes of Miss Grylls state that there is no such entry by Shelley in the MS journal.

[25] S&M, "home"; an obvious error.

[26] Etienne François de Lantier, *Voyages d'Antenor en Grèce et en Asie* (2nd ed., ? 1797); translated as *Travels of Antenor* (1799, 3 vols.).

PISA

Arno Bridge and the "Tre Donzelle"
(first building on the left)

Courtesy of Newman Ivey White

"Remorse." An unhappy day. Shelley reads one act of the "Alchemist" [by Ben Jonson] to the Gisbornes in the evening. Read two cantos of the "Purgatorio."

Saturday, AUG. 7.—Write; finish the 5th book of Lucan;[27] read the Bible, and with Shelley two cantos of the "Purgatorio." Visit Mrs. Gisborne. Shelley reads aloud the 2nd act of the "Alchemist." He writes his Tragedy.

Sunday, AUG. 8.—Read the Bible; write. Shelley reads the "Alchemist" aloud. He finishes his Tragedy.

Monday, AUG. 9.—Write; read the "New Inn" of Ben Jonson, and two cantos of Dante with Shelley. He reads the "Alchemist" aloud in the evening. The Gisbornes sup with us.

Tuesday, AUG. 10.—Write; read the "Poetaster" [by Ben Jonson], and two cantos of Dante with Shelley. He finishes the "Alchemist." Walk with Mrs. Gisborne.

Wednesday, AUG. 11.—Write; read Lucan, and the "Wife for a Month" [by John Fletcher], and two cantos of the "Purgatorio" with Shelley. He reads "Philaster," and copies his Tragedy. The Gisbornes in the evening.

Thursday, AUG. 12.—Nothing more written until

Friday, AUG. [12–]20.—Copy Shelley's Tragedy. We receive Hunt's picture.[28] Finish the "Purgatorio." Shelley reads Beaumont and Fletcher's Plays, and the "Revolt of Islam" aloud in the evening. See the Gisbornes every night. On Wednesday, 19th, write to Mrs. Hoppner.

Saturday, AUG. 21[–28].—Write; read Beaumont and Fletcher, Dante, and Lucan. Shelley reads the Greek Tragedians and Bocaccio. On Tuesday [Aug. 24], he writes to Peacock.[29] This day [Aug. 28] I write to Mrs. Hunt.[30] Shelley reads "Paradise Lost" aloud.

Saturday, SEPT. 4.—Copy. Charles Clairmont[31] comes to us. Read the "Paradiso," and Beaumont and Fletcher, and finish the 7th book of Lucan. Shelley reads Bocaccio, the Greek Tragedians, and Calderon. The Gisbornes visit us.

Sunday, SEPT. 5.—

27 S&M has "Lucian" in entries for August 7, 11, 21—obvious errors for "Lucan," whose *Pharsalia* Mary was reading.

28 "It was a half-length chalk drawing by Wildman, Thornton Hunt's drawing-master." —Julian edition, X, 75 n. See Mary's *Letters,* I, 76.

29 Shelley to Peacock, August [24], 1819 (Julian edition, X, 72–74, dated [probably 22nd]).

30 Mary to Mrs. Hunt, August 28, 1819 (*Letters,* I, 75–78).

31 He had been in Spain for fifteen months; he left the Shelleys for Vienna about November 10.

Sunday, Sept. [10–]12.—Finish copying my Tale.[32] Copy Shelley's "Prometheus."[33] Work. Read Beaumont and Fletcher's plays. On Friday [Sept. 10], Shelley sends his Tragedy to Peacock.[34] On Sunday [Sept. 12], Mr. Gisborne sets out for England. Shelley reads Calderon with Charles Clairmont, and Boccaccio.

Monday, Sept. 13.—Read Lucan; finish the 8th book. Read Beaumont and Fletcher. Visit Mrs. Gisborne. Shelley reads Boccaccio aloud, and Calderon with Charles Clairmont.

Tuesday, Sept. 14.—Read Lucan. Visit Mrs. Gisborne. Shelley reads Calderon, and Boccaccio aloud in the evening. Read 23rd and 24th cantos of Dante with him.

Wednesday, Sept. 15.—Read Lucan. Shelley reads Calderon, and Ben Jonson's "Sad Shepherd" aloud in the evening. Read 24th canto of Dante with him. Mrs. Gisborne in the evening. Shelley writes to Torlonia.

Thursday, Sept. 16.—Read Lucan. Shelley reads Calderon, Dante with me, and finishes the "Sad Shepherd" aloud in the evening. Madame de Plantis and Zoide[35] drink tea with us.

Friday, Sept. 17.—Finish 9th book of Lucan. Read Fletcher and Dante with Shelley. He reads the "Trionfe della Morte" [of Petrarch] aloud in the evening, and Calderon with Charles Clairmont and Mrs. Gisborne.

Wednesday, Sept. 22.—Work. Read Beaumont and Fletcher, and Dante. Shelley reads Calderon, and talks about the steam engine.[36]

Thursday, Sept. 23.—Read the "Chances" [by John Fletcher]. Work. Shelley and Charles Clairmont go to Florence. Shelley's Poem goes to Hunt,[37] and a letter to Peacock.[38]

Wednesday, Sept. [24–]29.—Finish Lucan's "Pharsalia." Read Fletcher. Pack; work. Spend much time with Mrs. Gisborne. Shelley returns on Saturday evening [Sept. 25] from Florence; he is very unwell.

Thursday, Sept. 30.—Take leave of Mrs. Gisborne. Travel to Pisa. See Mrs. M[ason].[39] Read Massinger.

[32] Possibly her *Mathilda,* which was never published. See the journal entries for August 6 and September 4, 1821. See also Mary's *Letters,* I, 156; and Elizabeth Nitchie, "Mary Shelley's *Mathilda:* An Unpublished Story and Its Biographical Significance," *Studies in Philology,* XL (July, 1943), 447–62.

[33] Act IV, written at Leghorn.

[34] Shelley to Peacock, September 9, 1819 (Julian edition, X, 81–82). The actual sending of the letter and MS was probably on the tenth.

[35] Madame Merveilleux du Plantis and her daughter. This lady kept the lodging house in which the Shelleys took an apartment when they moved to Florence (October 2).

[36] The steam engine was being built by Henry Reveley, Mrs. Gisborne's son, an engineer.

[37] *The Masque of Anarchy,* with a letter to Hunt, according to Mary's letter of September 24 to Hunt (*Letters,* I, 80–82).

[38] Shelley to Peacock, September 21, 1819 (Julian edition, X, 82–84).

Friday, OCT. 1.—Visit Mrs. M[ason]. Travel to Empoli. Read Massinger.

Saturday, OCT. [2–]9.—Arrive at Florence [Oct. 2].[40] Read Massinger. Shelley begins Clarendon; reads Massinger, and Plato's "Republic." Clare has her first singing lesson on Saturday. Go to the Opera, and see a beautiful ballet.

Sunday, OCT. 10.—Read Horace; work. Shelley reads Beaumont and Fletcher, and Plato.

Monday, OCT. 11.—Read Horace, work. Go to the Gallery. Shelley finishes the 1st volume of Clarendon. Read the "Little Thief" [by John Fletcher].

Tuesday, OCT. 12.—Read Horace; work. Shelley reads Clarendon aloud. Letters from Mrs. Gisborne and Hunt.[41]

Wednesday, OCT. 13.—Read Horace, and [Mateo Alemán's] the "Life of Guzman d'Alfarache" [1790]. Shelley reads Clarendon aloud. He spends the morning at the Gallery.

Thursday, OCT. 14.—Finish "Guzman d'Alfarache"; read Horace. Work; walk. Letters from Peacock and Hunt.[42] Write to Mrs. Gisborne[43] and Mrs. M[ason].

Wednesday, OCT. [15–]20.—Finish the 1st book of Horace's "Odes." Work; walk; read, &c. On Saturday [Oct. 16], letters are sent to England.[44] On Tuesday [Oct. 19], one to Venice.[45] Shelley visits the Galleries. Reads Spenser, and Clarendon aloud.

Sunday, OCT. 24.—Read 2nd book of Horace; read "Undine,"[46] &c. Shelley finishes 3rd volume of Clarendon aloud, and reads "Peter Bell."[47] He reads Plato's "Republic."

Thursday, OCT. [25–]28.—Work; read; copy [Shelley's] "Peter Bell." Monday night [Oct. 25], a great fright with Charles Clairmont. Shelley reads Clarendon aloud, and Plato's "Republic." Walk. On Thursday

39 Lady Mountcashell, the common-law wife of George William Tighe. They lived in Pisa at Casa Silva under the name of Mason and had two daughters, Nerina and Laura (or Laurette). (See Dowden, II, 315–18.)

40 They lodged at Palazzo Marini, 4395 Via Valfonda.

41 For Mrs. Gisborne's letter (undated, but should be [Leghorn, October 11, 1819]), see S&M, II, 418–20. Probably Hunt to Mary, [London], September 12, 1819 (S&M, II, 405–407).

42 Probably Hunt to Shelley and Mary, [London,] September 20, 1819 (S&M, II, 411–13).

43 Mary's letter does not survive, but Shelley's letter of October 13 or 14 to Mrs. Gisborne is in the Julian edition (X, 91–94).

44 Shelley to C. & J. Ollier, October 15, 1819 (Julian edition, X, 95–96).

45 Shelley to Mr. Dorville, vice-consul at Venice, October 18, 1819 (Julian edition, X, 97).

46 By F. H. Karl, Baron de La Motte-Fouqué (1811).

47 Either by Wordsworth or by John Hamilton Reynolds.

[Oct. 28], the protest from the Bankers. Shelley writes to them,[48] and to Peacock, Longdill, and H. Smith.

Saturday, Oct. 30.—Read Horace; work. Shelley reads Clarendon aloud. Writes "Peter Bell."

Tuesday, Nov. 2.—Read Horace; work. Finish copying "Peter Bell [the Third]," which is sent.[49] Shelley finishes 4th volume of Clarendon; reads Plato.

Friday, Nov. 5.—Read Horace; [Anthony Hamilton's] "Memoires du Comte Grammont." Shelley writes his letter concerning [Richard] Carlile.[50] Shelley reads Madame de Stael's Account of the Revolution, and Clarendon aloud.

Saturday, Nov. 6.—Read Horace, and "Lettres de Sevignè." Shelley sends his letter concerning Carlile, and writes to Peacock. He reads Plato's "Republic," and Clarendon aloud.

Sunday, Nov. 7.—Finish 3rd book of Horace's "Odes"; read Madame de Sevignè's Letters, and Fletcher's "Love's Pilgrimage." Shelley reads Plato's "Republic," and Clarendon aloud.

Monday, Nov. 8.—Read Horace, and Madame de Sevignè; write. Shelley reads Plato, and Clarendon aloud. Walk on the Terrace.

Tuesday, Nov. 9.—Read Madame de Sevignè. Bad news from London.[51] Shelley reads Clarendon aloud, and Plato. He writes to Papa.

Friday, [Nov. 10–] Dec. 31.—I have not kept my Journal all this time; but I have little to say, except that on the morning of Friday, November 12, little Percy Florence was born. We have seen a good deal of Mr. and and Mrs. Meadows, Miss Stacey and her party, and Louise.[52] I read little else than Madame de Sevignè's Letters. Shelley reads St. Luke aloud to us, and to himself the New Testament. Visit the Galleries, Pitti Palace, &c.

I now begin a new year—may it be a happier one than the last unhappy one.[53]

48 Shelley to Brookes & Company, October 30, 1819 (Julian edition, X, 101–102). Shelley's finances remained complicated until December 23. For further details, see Mary's *Letters,* I, 87, and Shelley's letters to Reveley and the Gisbornes (Julian edition, X, 100, 131, 132, 135–36). For the connection with Henry Reveley's steamboat, see Dowden, II, 303–306; and White, II, 164.

49 Sent to Hunt, with a letter dated November 2, 1819 (Julian edition, X, 103–104).

50 Addressed to Leigh Hunt, dated November 3, 1819, and intended for insertion in the *Examiner* (Julian edition, X, 105–19). See Dowden, II, 289–90; and White, II, 166–68.

51 About Godwin's financial affairs, see White, II, 162–63.

52 Miss Sophia Stacey, ward of Mr. Robert Parker, who was the husband of one of Sir Timothy Shelley's sisters; and Miss Corbet Parry-Jones (see Helen Rossetti Angeli, *Shelley and His Friends in Italy* [London, Metheun & Co., 1911], 95–105; and White, II, 172–75). Louise was a daughter of Madame du Plantis, owner of the house in which the Shelleys lived.

53 This sentence is not in S&M. Miss Grylls prints it (p. 119) from the original MS journal.

1820

ITALY

Saturday, Jan 1.—Read Livy; work. Shelley reads the Bible, Sophocles, and the Gospel of St. Matthew to me.

Sunday, Jan. 2.—Read Livy. Walk in the Cascine. Pass a part of the evening down stairs with Mrs. Meadows. Talk of our plans with Shelley.

Monday, Jan. 3.—Read Livy. Walk to see the pictures of Salvator Rosa. Shelley reads [Byron's] "Don Juan" aloud in the evening; he goes to the theatre with Mr. Tomkins.[1] Mrs. Meadows visits me.

Tuesday, Jan. 4.—Read "Don Juan"; work; walk. Letters from Mrs. Mason and Mrs. Gisborne.

Wednesday, Jan. 5.—Read Livy; work; read [Byron's] "Mazeppa." Shelley reads Sophocles, and St. Matthew aloud to me. Translate S[pinoz]a.

Thursday, Jan. 6.—Walk out; work. Mr. Tomkins drinks tea with us. We pass the evening with Mrs. Meadows.

Friday, Jan. 7.—Read Livy; work. Shelley is ill.—

Saturday, Jan. 8.—Read Livy; translate S[pinoz]a; work. Shelley reads St. Matthew aloud. A letter from Hunt; &c.

Sunday, Jan. 9.—Read Livy; translate S[pinoz]a. Shelley reads the Bible, Sophocles, and St. Matthew aloud.

Monday, Jan. 10.—Read the Bible. Go to the Pitti Palace with Mr. Meadows. Sit with Mrs. Meadows in the evening.

Tuesday, Jan. 11.—Read the Bible, and Livy. Write to Mrs. Gisborne and Mr. Mason.

Wednesday, Jan. 12.—Write to Miss Stacey and to Charles [Clairmont]. Translate S[pinoz]a. Work in the evening. Shelley reads the "Tempest" aloud, and the Bible and Sophocles to himself. Shelley writes to Hunt.

Thursday, Jan. 13.—Walk out with Mrs. Meadows. They spend the evening with us. Shelley reads the "Tempest" aloud, and the Bible and Sophocles to himself.

Friday, Jan. 14.—Work. Finish the Book of Proverbs. Shelley reads the Bible, and Sophocles; finishes the "Tempest" aloud to me.

Saturday, Jan. 15.—Finish translating the 1st chapter of S[pinoz]a;

[1] An amateur painter (see Dowden, II, 312 n.).

read Livy. Shelley reads the Bible, and Sophocles; the "Hercules" ["Trachiniæ"] of Sophocles aloud to me. Mr. and Mrs. Meadows spend the evening with us.

Sunday, JAN. 16.—Translate S[pinoz]a with Shelley.

Friday, JAN. 21.—Shelley reads Sophocles, the Bible, and "King John," and "1st Part of Henry IV" aloud. Finish 30th book of Livy. Finish Proverbs, Ecclesiastes, and Solomon's Song. Go to the Gabinetto di Fisica. Work.

Saturday, JAN. 22.—Go to the Tribune at the Gallery. Work. Shelley reads "Henry IV" aloud.

Sunday, JAN. 23.—Read Livy; translate S[pinoz]a. Shelley reads the Bible and "Muller's Universal History." Spend the evening with Mrs. Meadows.

Monday, JAN. 24.—Walk with Shelley. Work, pack, &c.

Tuesday, JAN. 25.—Pack. Percy Florence baptized.[2] Shelley unwell.

Wednesday, JAN. 26.—Go to Empoli very uncomfortably in a boat, and the rest of the way much jolted in a carriage. Arrive at Pisa.[3]

Thursday, JAN. 27.—PISA—Spend the day with Mr. Mason. Read "Travels before the Flood."[4]

Friday, JAN. 28.—A rainy day. Look for lodgings. Finish "Travels before the Flood." Shelley calls on Mr. Mason and Signor G———o. Read Pamphlets.

Saturday, JAN. 29.—Spend the day at Mr. Mason's. Go into our lodgings [Casa Frasi, on the Lung 'Arno]. Read Pamphlets.

Sunday, JAN. 30.—Finish the Pamphlets. After dinner, go to Mr. Mason's; drink tea there. Begin [Rousseau's] "Julie."

Monday, JAN. 31.—Read "Julie." Shelley goes to Leghorn. Mr. Mason and N[erina] call.

Tuesday, FEB. 1.—Ride out with Mr. Mason. Write; read "Julie."

Wednesday, FEB. 2.—Ride out with Mr. Mason. Work. Read "Julie." Shelley returns; he reads Isaiah aloud to me.

Thursday, FEB. 3.—Read "Julie." Walk. Dine at Mr. Mason's, and spend the evening there.[5]

Thursday, FEB. [4–]10.—Finish "Julie"; read the "Fable of the Bees."[6]

[2] By Mr. Harding, an English clergyman.

[3] Claire's diary for January 26 is quoted by Dowden (II, 313). They put up at the Tre Donzelle.

[4] Author unidentified. See Appendix IV.

[5] In his copy of S&M, Dowden copied these entries from Claire's diary: "Feb. 5.— . . . Vacca calls and says I am scrophulous and I say he is ridiculous. Feb. 8.—In the evening go to the Opera with Laurette, Shelley and Signor Zanetti. La Ceverentola di Rossini. Many masks."

[6] By Bernard De Mandeville (1714).

Visit and ride out with Mr. Mason. Shelley and Clare go to the Opera [on Feb. 8]. Shelley finishes reading Isaiah to me, and begins Jeremiah. He reads Las Casas on the Indies, Æschylus and Athenæus.

Friday, FEB. 11.—Shelley reads Las Casas, and Jeremiah aloud. Read the "Fable of the Bees." Call on Mr. Mason.

Sunday, FEB. 13.—Read "Fable of the Bees." Letter from Miss S[tacey]. After dinner, call on Mr. Mason. Shelley reads Jeremiah aloud in the evening.

Monday, FEB. 14.—Read Livy and the "Fable of the Bees"; read Las Casas. Shelley reads Plato, and spends the day at Casa Silva.

Tuesday, FEB. 15.—Read "Fable of the Bees." Spend the day after 12 at Casa Silva. Last day of the Carnival. Write to Hunt.

Wednesday, FEB. 16.—Read Livy and "Fable of the Bees." Shelley reads Plato, and Jeremiah aloud. Ride out with Mr. Mason. King's death.[7]

Thursday, FEB. 17.—Read Livy and "Fable of the Bees." Shelley reads Plato. Ride out with Mr. Mason, and spend the evening there. Yesterday a letter from Longdill.

Friday, FEB. 18.—Finish 32nd book of Livy; read "Fable of the Bees." Ride out with Mr. Mason. Shelley reads and finishes Jeremiah.

Saturday, FEB. 19.—Read Livy and "Fable of the Bees." Shelley reads "Henry IV" aloud; he reads Plato.

Sunday, FEB. 20.—Read Livy and "Fable of the Bees." Spend the evening at Casa Silva. Talk concerning the Irish Rebellion.

Monday, FEB. 21.—Read Livy, and the "Fable of the Bees." Shelley reads "Solis' History of Mexico." Walk out, and call at Casa Silva.[8] Shelley reads "Henry IV" in the evening.

Tuesday, FEB. 22.—

Wednesday, FEB. 23.—

Thursday, FEB. 24.—

Friday, FEB. [22–]25.—Read Livy, and "Fable of the Bees." Copy Shelley's Poems. Shelley reads "History of Mexico," and "Henry IV" aloud. Drink tea once at Casa Silva; call there. News of the Duc de Berri's assassination. Rainy weather. Shelley unwell.

Saturday and Sunday, FEB. 26 and 27.—Days of idleness and nursing. Dine and spend the evening at Casa Silva. Read "Fable of the Bees."

Monday, FEB. 28.—Mr. and Mrs. Gisborne spend the day with us. Call on Mrs. Mason. N[erin]a ill.[9] Our new servant comes.[10]

Thursday, MAR. 2.—Call at Casa Silva. Shelley reads "Henry V." Let-

[7] George III died on January 29.

[8] The home of Mr. and Mrs. Mason, in the Via Mala Gonella.

[9] With the measles, writes Dowden in his copy of S&M.

[10] In his copy of S&M, Dowden copied Claire's diary for "Feb. 29 [Leap Year]. In the evening go to an Accademia of Music—Many buffa songs by a priest."

ter from Papa. Answer it. Catarina goes to the hospital.

Friday, MAR. 3.—Shelley goes to Leghorn. Finish "Fable of the Bees." Read [Ben Jonson's] "Catiline's Conspiracy." Ride with Mr. Mason.

Saturday, MAR. 4.—Read [Paine's] "Common Sense." Ride with Mr. Mason.

Sunday, MAR. 5.—Read [Paine's] "Letter to the Abbé Raynal,"[11] &c. Ride with Mr. Mason. Finish 33rd book of Livy; begin the "Age of Reason" [by Paine].

Monday, MAR. 6.—Read "Age of Reason"; write. Shelley returns from Leghorn. Ride with Mr. Mason.

Tuesday, MAR. 7.—Call at Casa Silva. Read the "Utopia" [of Sir Thomas More]; write. Shelley reads "Henry VI" aloud.

Thursday, MAR. 9.—Read the "Utopia." Ride out. Percy has the measles. Shelley reads Hobbes, and Ezekiel aloud.

Friday, MAR. 10.—Finish the "Utopia"; read Livy. Ride out with Mr. Mason. Shelley reads Hobbes. Conspiracy to kill all the English Ministers. Shelley reads Tobit aloud.

Saturday, MAR. 11.—Finish the "Age of Reason." Ride with Mr. Mason. Shelley reads [Ben Jonson's] the "Fall of Sejanus" aloud, and "Hobbes on Man."

Sunday, MAR. 12.—Read "Rights of Man"; write; ride.

Monday, MAR. 13.—Read "Rights of Man"; ride. Shelley reads Hobbes, and "Catiline's Plot" aloud.

Tuesday, MAR. 14.—Move to other lodgings.[12] Write. Read "Rights of Man."

Wednesday, MAR. 15.—Read "Rights of Man." Call at Casa Silva. Shelley reads Hobbes; finishes "Catiline's Plot."

Thursday, MAR. 16.—Read "Rights of Man." Shelley reads Hobbes. Call at Casa Silva.

Friday, MAR. 17.—Read "Rights of Man." Translate S[pinoz]a with Shelley. Drink tea at Casa Silva. Shelley reads Hobbes.

Tuesday, MAR. 21.—Translate S[pinoz]a with Shelley. Read "Lettres Cabalistiques."[13] Shelley finishes the "Leviathan" of Hobbes; reads the Bible aloud. Visit Casa Silva.

Wednesday, MAR. 22.—Translate S[pinoz]a; read "Lettres Cabalistiques." Shelley reads Ezekiel aloud, and "Political Justice."

Sunday, MAR. 26.—Translate S[pinoz]a. Shelley reads one canto and a half of Virgil aloud; he reads "Political Justice." Read Tasso. Visit at Casa Silva.

[11] By Thomas Paine (1782).

[12] Apparently to a more spacious apartment on the top floor of Casa Frasi.

[13] By Jean B. de Boyer, Marquis d'Argens (1769).

Monday, MAR. 27.—Translate S[pinoz]a. Shelley reads, and I also, "Voltaire's Memoirs" by himself.

Tuesday, MAR. 28.—Translate S[pinoz]a. Spend the evening at Casa Silva.

Wednesday, MAR. 29.—Translate S[pinoz]a. Shelley reads the "Æneid" aloud.

Thursday, MAR. 30.—Translate S[pinoz]a. Call at Casa Silva. Shelley finishes aloud the 3rd book of the "Æneid."

[*Good*] *Friday,* MAR. 31.—Go in the morning to Casa Silva. Read Machiavelli['s], "History of Castruccio Castracani."[14] Translate S[pinoz]a. Shelley reads part of the 4th book of the "Æneid" aloud. Read "Condorcet's Life of Voltaire."[15] Shelley reads Locke.

Saturday, APR. 1.—Translate S[pinoz]a; read "Life of Voltaire"; finish "Life of Castruccio"; Shelley reads "Political Justice." Finish 4th book and all we mean to read of 5th book of Virgil. Visit at Casa Silva. Shelley reads Locke.

[*Easter*] *Sunday,* APR. 2.—Translate S[pinoz]a. Shelley reads "Life of Voltaire," and [Mrs. Barbauld's] "Evenings at Home." Visit at Casa Silva; see Tatty.[16] Shelley reads "Wisdom of Solomon" aloud in the evening. Shelley reads Locke.

Tuesday, APR. 4.—Visit at Casa Silva. A letter from Papa. Shelley ill. Translate S[pinoz]a. Shelley reads "Political Justice," and Locke.

Wednesday, APR. 5.—Translate S[pinoz]a. Visit at Casa Silva.

Thursday, APR. 6.—Write to Papa. Translate S[pinoz]a. Visit at Casa Silva.

Friday, APR. 7.—Write;[17] translate S[pinoz]a. Drink tea at Casa Silva with Tatty.

Saturday, APR. 8.—Translate S[pinoz]a; write. Spend the evening at Casa Silva.

Sunday, APR. [9–]23.—Write; read—I am sure I forget what. Visit Casa Silva. The Gisbornes visit us.[18] Shelley reads Locke. He goes to

14 Mary evidently read both Machiavelli's *Life of Castruccio Castracana* and Niccolò Tegrimi's *Vita di Castruccio Castracana degli Antelminelli,* the first biography of Castruccio. The list for 1820 indicates only one life by Segreno, which is evidently a misreading of the MS for Tegrimi.

15 By the Marquis de Condorcet; English translation (1790, 2 vols.).

16 Familiar name for Mr. Mason (Tighe).

17 About this time Mary began writing *Castruccio, Prince of Lucca* (published in 1824 as *Valperga*).

18 They were there on April 20, on which day Shelley wrote to Hogg, "I am now reading with her [Mrs. Gisborne] the 'Agamemnon' of Æschylus."—Julian edition, X, 159. Ingpen has misdated letter CCCCLXVI (p. 161), Shelley to J. M. Gisborne; April 23 should be April 13. The correct date is important in that the Gisbornes' visit, which Shelley is expecting, was already over before the twenty-third.

Leghorn. Letters from Papa.[19] Write to him. Babe vaccinated. Translate S[pinoz]a. Intend to be regular now, I hope.[20]

Monday, Apr. 24.—Finish "Brydone's Travels";[21] read Livy; write. Call at Casa Silva; stay the evening there.

Tuesday, Apr. 25.—Write. Shelley reads Virgil in the evening. Call at Casa Silva.

Wednesday, Apr. 26.—Write. Shelley finished 8th book of Virgil. Read Ovid.

Thursday, Apr. 27.—Write; read [Defoe's] "Robinson Crusoe." Shelley reads Virgil, 9th book, in the evening.

Friday, Apr. 28.—Go to Leghorn.[22] Spend the day with the Gisbornes. Return at night.

Saturday, Apr. 29.—An uncomfortable day. Read "Robinson Crusoe."

Sunday, Apr. 30.—Another uncomfortable day. A letter from Madame H[oppner].[23] Read "Robinson Crusoe." Spend the evening at Casa Silva.

Monday, May 1.—Write; finish 34th book of Livy; read "Robinson Crusoe."

Tuesday, May 2.—Write; read Livy, and "Robinson Crusoe." Shelley finishes [Plato's] "Phædrus"; reads Virgil to me in the evening.

Wednesday, May 3.—Write; finish P———e; read Livy, and "Robinson Crusoe." Spend the evening at Casa Silva.

Thursday, May 4.—Read Livy and Ovid; finish 10th book of Virgil with Shelley; read "Robinson Crusoe."

Friday, May 5.—Read Livy; write. Shelley spends the evening at Casa Silva.

Saturday, May 6.—Finish 35th book of Livy; write. Shelley reads Fletcher's Tragedy of "Bonduca" aloud to me in the evening.

Sunday, May 7.—Write. Spend the evening at Casa Silva. Read "Robinson Crusoe."

Monday, May 8.—Write; read "Robinson Crusoe." Shelley finishes the Tragedy of "Bonduca" to me in the evening.

Tuesday, May 9.—Write; read Livy, and "Robinson Crusoe." Shelley reads "Phædon," having read "Phædrus." Reads the Tragedy of "Thierry and Theodoret" [by Beaumont and Fletcher] to me.

Wednesday, May 10.—Read Livy; write. Shelley finishes [reading the] Tragedy [of "Thierry and Theodoret"] to me. Walk with him.

19 Godwin to Mary, March 30, 1820 (S&M, III, 488A–B).

20 That is, regular in writing her journal.

21 Patrick Brydone, *A Tour Through Sicily and Malta* (1773, 2 vols.).

22 With Shelley, to take leave of the Gisbornes, who were departing for England on May 2.

23 It was, Claire says in her diary, "concerning green fruit and God."

Thursday, May 11.—Write; read "Astronomy" [in the Encyclopedia]; finish "Robinson Crusoe." Shelley reads aloud in the evening.

Friday, May 12.—Write—S[helley] reading aloud in the evening.[24]

Saturday, May 13.—Write. Shelley reads aloud. Read Livy.

Sunday, May 14.—Write. Spend the evening at Casa Silva.

Monday, May 15.—Write; read [Thomas Day's] "Sandford and Merton."[25]

Tuesday, May 16.—Read "Sandford and Merton," and "Astronomy." Write.

Wednesday, May 17.—Read "Astronomy"; write. Walk with Shelley.

Thursday, May 18.—Read Livy, and "Sandford and Merton." Call at Casa Silva.

Friday, May 19.—Read "Astronomy"; write. Go out.

Saturday, May 20.—Read Livy. Shelley reads to me Spenser and Virgil.

Sunday, May 21.—Write; read Livy. Not well. Drink tea at Casa Silva. Read "Vindication of the Rights of Woman" [by Mary Wollstonecraft].

Monday, May 22.—Shelley goes to Casciano. Read and finish "Vindication of the Rights of Woman"; finish "Sandford and Merton."

Tuesday, May 23.—Read Boswell's "Life of Johnson." Visit Casa Silva.

Wednesday, May 24.—Write; read Livy, and Boswell's "Life of Johnson." Ride out with Mr. Mason.

Thursday, May 25.—Shelley returns from Casciano. Write; read Livy, and Boswell's "Life of Johnson."

Friday, May 26.—Finish 36th book of Livy; read Boswell's "Life of Johnson." Drink tea at Casa Silva. Shelley writes to H. Smith. Vases sent.[26] Shelley reads Theocritus.

Saturday, May 27.—Read Livy, and "Life of Johnson." Visit Casa Silva. Shelley not well.

Sunday, May 28.—Read Livy, and "Life of Johnson"; write.

Monday, May 29.—Read Livy; finish "Life of Johnson."

Tuesday, May 30.—Read Livy, and "Astronomy." Shelley reads "Paradise Regained" aloud. Write.

Wednesday, May 31.—Read Livy, and Virgil, with Shelley. Call at Casa Silva.

Thursday, June 1.—Finish 38th book of Livy; read "Posthumous Letters" [of Mary Wollstonecraft]; walk.

24 In S&M this entry is blank; the addition is made from the MS notes of Miss Grylls.

25 1783–89, 3 vols.

26 "Alabaster vases from the antique," sent to Horace Smith as a present. See Shelley to J. & M. Gisborne, May 26, 1820 (Julian edition, X, 175).

Friday, JUNE 2.—Read Livy, and "Posthumous Letters"; write. Tatty calls.

Saturday, JUNE 3.—Write; translate S[pinoz]a with Shelley. Drink tea at Casa Silva; Tatty there. Read "Memoirs [of Mary Wollstonecraft" by Godwin].

Sunday, JUNE 4.—Write; finish 39th book of Livy; read "Letters from Norway" [by Mary Wollstonecraft].

Monday, JUNE 5.—Read "Letters from Norway"; write; read Livy; walk. Shelley reads "Paradise Regained" aloud.

Tuesday, JUNE 6.—Finish "Letters from Norway"; read Livy. Shelley finished "Paradise Regained."

Wednesday, JUNE 7.—Read Livy, and [Mary Wollstonecraft's] "Mary, a Fiction." Call at Casa Silva. Shelley not well. Our box comes.

Thursday, JUNE 8.—A better day than most days and good reason for it, though Shelley is not well. Clare away at Pugnano. Read [Scott's] "Legend of Montrose" and the "Indicators" [of Leigh Hunt].

Friday, JUNE 9.—Read [Scott's] "Bride of Lammermoor."

Saturday, JUNE 10.—Read [Scott's] "Ivanhoe." Shelley goes to Casciano. Write.

Sunday, JUNE 11.—Write; finish "Ivanhoe." Shelley returns.

Monday, JUNE 12.—Paolo . Dine and spend the evening at Casa Silva; sleep there.

Tuesday, JUNE 13.—Read [Godwin's] "Fleetwood." Shelley goes to Leghorn, and returns.

Wednesday, JUNE 14.—Read "Fleetwood." Pack. Read [Goldsmith's] "Vicar of Wakefield."

Thursday, JUNE 15.—Pack. Go to Leghorn.[27]

Friday, JUNE 16.—Finish "Fleetwood."

Saturday, JUNE 17.—Babe unwell. We are unhappy and discontented.

Sunday, JUNE 18.—Babe well. Read [Godwin's] "Caleb Williams."

Monday, JUNE 19.—Read "Caleb Williams." Shelley reads Euripides.

Tuesday, JUNE 20.—Write; finish "Caleb Williams." Shelley reads Euripides.

Wednesday, JUNE 21.—Read Sterne's "Sentimental Journey."

Thursday, JUNE 22.—Walk to the sea.

Friday, JUNE 23.—Write and read. Shelley reads Euripides.

Saturday, JUNE 24.—Read the "Quarterly."

Sunday, JUNE 25.—Read the "Quarterly"; finish 11th book of Virgil

[27] They occupied the Gisbornes' house, Casa Ricci. The residence in Leghorn was occasioned by Shelley's wish to be near his lawyer, Federico del Rosso, through whom he was attempting to silence his old servant Paolo Foggi, who was spreading scandalous stories about the Shelleys and was trying to blackmail them.

with Shelley. I am now better; before, I was too much oppressed and too languid to do anything.

Monday, June 26.—Finish 40th book of Livy; finish Virgil. Shelley reads "Ricciardetto" [by Niccolò Fortiguerra] to me.

Tuesday, June 27.—Read Livy, Shelley reads Greek Romances.

Wednesday, June 28.—Finish 41st book of Livy; begin Lucretius with Shelley. He reads Greek Romances.

Thursday, June 29.—Read Livy, and [Catherine] Macaulay's "History of England"; and Lucretius with Shelley. He reads Greek Romances and "Ricciardetto" aloud in the evening.

Friday, June 30.—Read Livy. Letter from Papa. Read Lucretius with Shelley. He reads "Ricciardetto" aloud. Read "History of England."

Saturday, July 1.—Read Livy; write and read [Shelley's] letters to Hogg, Mrs. Gisborne, Papa, and Mr. Hamilton.[28] Shelley reads "Ricciardetto" aloud.

Sunday, July 2.—Finish 43rd book of Livy; read "History of England." Shelley reads Greek Romances.

Monday, July 3.—Read Livy and "History of England." Shelley reads "Ricciardetto" aloud. Finish 1st book of Lucretius with Shelley.

Tuesday, July 4.—Greek exercises; read Livy and "History of England." Shelley reads Lucretius with me, and "Ricciardetto" aloud.

Wednesday, July 5.—Read Livy; write; read Lucretius with Shelley. He reads Greek Romances, and "Ricciardetto" aloud.

Thursday, July 6.—Finish 44th book of Livy. Read Lucretius with Shelley. He reads Greek Romances, and "Ricciardetto" aloud.

Friday, July 7.—Read Livy, Greek, and Lucretius. Shelley reads "Ricciardetto."

Saturday, July 8.—Read Livy; Greek; and finish 2nd book of Lucretius with Shelley. He reads "Ricciardetto" aloud.

Sunday, July 9.—Finish Livy. Read Greek, and Lucretius. Shelley reads "Ricciardetto," and Greek Romances.

Monday, July 10.—Read "Middleton's Cicero,"[29] Greek, and Lucretius. Shelley reads "Ricciardetto" aloud.

Tuesday, July 11.—Read Greek, 1st Oration of Cicero, and Lucretius. Shelley reads "Ricciardetto" aloud.

Wednesday, July 12.—Read Greek; finish 1st Oration of Cicero, and the 3rd book of Lucretius; read Mrs. Macaulay, and "Ricciardetto."

[28] Shelley to Hogg, July 1, 1820 (*Shelley at Oxford,* ed. W. S. Scott [London, The Golden Cockerel Press, 1944], 62); Shelley to J. & M. Gisborne, June 30, 1820 (Julian edition, X, 179–82); Shelley to Samuel Hamilton, July 1, 1820 (*ibid.,* X, 184–85).

[29] Conyers Middleton, *Life of Cicero* (1741).

Thursday, July 13.—Write; read Greek, "History of England," and Lucretius. Shelley finishes Greek Romances.

Friday, July 14.—Read Greek, "History of England," and Lucretius. Shelley finishes his translation of Homer's "Hymn to Mercury." Walk.

Saturday, July 15.—Greek. Shelley goes to Pisa. Read 2nd Oration of Cicero, and "History of England."

Sunday, July 16.—Read Greek, and "History of England."

Monday, July 17.—Shelley returns. Write. Read Greek, and "Ricciardetto."

Tuesday, July 18.—Read Greek, and "History of England"; write; read Lucretius. Shelley begins "History of England."

Wednesday, July 19.—Read Greek, Cicero, and Lucretius.

Thursday, July 20.—Mr. Mason, Laurette, and Miss Field[30] spend the day with us. Read Greek.

Friday, July 21.—Read Greek; finish the Oration for Roscius.

Saturday, July 22.—Read Greek, the Oration for Roscius the Comedian, and "History of England."

Sunday, July 23.—Read Greek, 1st Oration of Verres, and "History of England."

Monday, July 24.—Read Greek.

Tuesday, July 25.—Shelley returns [from Pisa]. Read Greek.

Wednesday, July 26.—Read Greek, and "Ricciardetto."

Thursday, July 27.—Read Greek; finish 4th book of Lucretius. Read "Ricciardetto."

Friday, July 28.—Read Greek. Shelley goes to Pisa.

Saturday, July 29.—Read Greek, and "History of England."

Sunday, July 30.—Read Greek; walk; write.

Monday, July 31.—Ill the whole day.

Tuesday, Aug. 1.—Read Greek. Shelley returns; walk with him. He reads Apollonius Rhodius. Pack.

Wednesday, Aug. 2.—Read Greek; walk. The weather is too hot for study.

Thursday, Friday, and Saturday, Aug. 3, 4, and 5.—Read Greek. Pack, &c. Leave Leghorn [Aug. 4]. Visit Casa Silva.[31]

Thursday, Aug. 10.—Write a story for Laurette. Walk on the mountains, Le Buche delle Fate. The weather is warm and delightful.

Friday, Aug. 11.—In the evening we go to Lucca. The country is delicious, and we have a very pleasant ride.

Saturday, Aug. 12.—Shelley goes to Monte San Pelegrino. Walk about Lucca. Go up the Campanile, Casa Guinzi, Chiesa di San Francesco

[30] Companion or tutor in the Masons' home (White's index).

[31] They went to the Baths of Pisa (San Giuliano) on the fifth and settled in Casa Prinni.

Martino, the Patron Saint of Lucca. Ride round the walls. Return to San Giuliano [Baths of Pisa]. A delightful evening.

Sunday, AUG. 13.—Shelley returns. Call on La Tantini.

Monday, AUG. 14.—Read Muratori['s] "Antichità d'Italia,"[32] and Greek. Walk with Shelley. W[rites] W[itch of] A[tlas].

Tuesday, AUG. 15.—Read Muratori, and Greek. W. W. A.

Wednesday, AUG. 16.—Read Muratori, and Greek. Walk. W. W. A. finished.

Thursday, AUG. 17.—Read Muratori, and Greek.

Friday, AUG. [18–]25.—Read Greek, Muratori, and Lucretius. Walk. Clare goes to Pisa [on Aug. 22]. On 24th, Mrs. Mason comes for the day [Claire returns with her].[33] Shelley writes an Ode to Naples; reads Mrs. Macaulay; finishes Apollonius Rhodius; begins "Swellfoot the Tyrant," suggested by the pigs at the fair of St. Giuliano. Reads the "Double Marriage" [of Beaumont and Fletcher] aloud.

Tuesday, AUG. 29.—Read Muratori, and Greek; finish Lucretius; walk.

Wednesday, AUG. 30.—Read Muratori, Greek, Queen's Letter,[34] and "Swellfoot."

Thursday, AUG. 31.—Read Muratori, and Greek. Shelley and Clare go to Leghorn.

Friday, SEPT. 1.—Read Muratori, Greek, and Irish book.[35]

Saturday, SEPT. 2.—Read Muratori, Greek, and Irish book.

Sunday, SEPT. 3.—Read Muratori, Greek, and Irish Book. Shelley returns.

Monday, SEPT. 4.—Read Muratori, Greek, and "Rebellion of Ireland."[36] Shelley finishes Mrs. Macaulay, and reads the "Republic" of Plato. Ride to Pisa.

Tuesday, SEPT. 5.—Read Muratori, Greek, and "Rebellion of Ireland." Walk.

Wednesday, SEPT. 6.—Read Muratori, Greek, and "Rebellion of Ireland." Walk up Lucca Mountains.

Friday, SEPT. 8.—Read Muratori, and Greek; finish "Rebellion of Ireland." Ride towards Calci.

Saturday, SEPT. 9.—Read Muratori, Greek, and with Shelley the 1st Epistle of Horace. Walk. Shelley reads the "Republic" of Plato.

32 Lodovico Antonio Muratori.

33 MS notes by Dowden in his copy of S&M.

34 Not further identified.

35 The 1820 list suggests that this was a book of travels.

36 Edward Hyde, Earl of Clarendon, *The History of the Rebellion and Civil Wars in Ireland* (Dublin, 1719–20). (After 1816 published as a fourth volume to the three-volume *Civil Wars in England.*)

Sunday, Sept. 10.—Read Muratori, and Greek, walk up the Mountain with Shelley. Shelley reads aloud [Fletcher and Massinger's] "Lovers' Progress."

Monday, Sept. 11.—Read Muratori, and Greek. Walk.

Tuesday, Sept. 12.—Go to Pisa; go to Campo Santo, Leaning Tower, &c.

Wednesday, Sept. 13.—Finish Muratori; read Greek, and "Travels of Rolando."[37] Shelley reads "Robertson's America," and begins Boccaccio aloud.

Thursday, Sept. 14.—Read Villani,[38] "Travels of Rolando," and Greek.

Friday, Sept. 15.—Walk up a mountain with Shelley. Read Villani, and Greek.

Saturday, Sept. 16.—Mr. Mason visits us. Read Greek. Begin the "Georgics" with Shelley. Shelley reads Boccaccio in the evening.

Sunday, Sept. 17.—Read Villani, Greek, and Boccaccio in the evening. Shelley not well.

Monday, Sept. 18.—Read Greek, and Boccaccio in the evening. Go to Pisa.

Tuesday, Sept. 19.—Read Villani, and Greek. A thunder storm. Shelley reads "History of Charles V," by Robertson.

Wednesday, Sept. 20.—Read Villani; write. Read Boccaccio, and Greek.

Thursday, Sept. 21.—Read Villani, and Greek; write. Read Boccaccio. Shelley reads "Antient Metaphysics" [by Lord Monboddo].

Friday, Sept. 22.—Read Sismondi and Boccaccio. Shelley reads "Antient Metaphysics." Write. Vaccà[39] calls.

Saturday, Sept. 23.—Read Sismondi, Greek, and Petrarch. Shelley reads "Gillies' Greece," and "Antient Metaphysics." Write. Shelley dines at Pisa.

Sunday, Sept. 24.—Read Sismondi, and Greek; write. Read "Troilus and Cressida" in the evening.

Monday, Sept. 25.—Read Sismondi, and Greek; write. Read "Troilus and Cressida."

Tuesday, Sept. 26.—Read Villani, and Greek; write. Read "Troilus and Cressida."

Sunday, [Sept. 27–]Oct. 1.—Write. Read Sismondi. Shelley goes to

37 By L. F. Jauffret; translated from the French (1804, 4 vols.).

38 Giovanni Villani (1280?–1348), *Historia Fiorentine,* a chronicle history of the city of Florence.

39 Andrea Vaccà Berlinghieri, noted physician and surgeon. One of the chief motives for the removal to Pisa was Shelley's desire to consult Vaccà about his health.

FRANCESCO PACCHIANI

Leghorn, and returns. Read Boccaccio, and Greek. Shelley reads Herodotus, "Gillies' Greece," and "Antient Metaphysics."

Monday, Oct. 2.—Write. Read Sismondi.

Tuesday, Oct. 3.—Write. Read Sismondi, and Greek.

Tuesday, Oct. 10.—Write. Ride to Pisa. Walk. The Gisbornes return [from England].

Thursday, Oct. 12.—Write. Read Sismondi. Ride to Pisa. Read "Georgics," and Boccaccio.

Friday, Oct. 13.—Ride to Vico Pisano. A delightful day.

Saturday, Oct. 14.—Shelley goes to Pisa with Tatty. Write; walk. Read "Don Juan."

Sunday, Oct. 15.—A rainy day. Write. Shelley returns. Read "Family Sermons."[40]

Monday, Oct. 16.—Go to Leghorn.

Tuesday, Oct. 17.—Write. Read "Prometheus Unbound." Shelley goes to Leghorn, and returns very late.

Wednesday, Oct. 18.—Rain till 1 o'clock. At sunset the arch of cloud over the west clears away; a few black islands float in the serene; the moon rises; the clouds spot the sky; but the depth of heaven is clear. The nights are uncommonly warm. Write. Shelley reads [Keats's] "Hyperion" aloud. Read Greek.

My thoughts rise and fade in solitude;
  The verse that would invest them melts away
  Like moonlight in the heaven of spreading day.
How beautiful they were, how firm they stood,
Flecking the starry sky like woven pearl!

Thursday, Oct. 19.—Ride to Pisa. Read Keats' Poems. Henry Reveley calls. Walk. Read Greek. Wind N. N. W., cloudy, the sun shining at intervals. The spoils of the trees are scattered about, and the chestnuts are much browner than a week ago. In the evening the moon, with Venus just below her, sails through the clouds, but shines clearly where they are not.

Friday, Oct. 20.—Shelley goes to Florence.[41] Write. Read Greek. Wind N. W., but more cloudy than yesterday, yet sometimes the sun shines out; the wind high. Read Villani.

Saturday, Oct. 21.—Rain in the night and morning; very cloudy; not an air stirring; the leaves of the trees quite still. After a showery morning, it clears up somewhat, and the sun shines. Read Villani, and ride to Pisa.

[40] Not further identified.

[41] He accompanied Claire, who was to live in Florence in the house of Professor Bojti.

Sunday, OCT. 22.—Rainy night and rainy morning; as bad weather as is possible in Italy. A little patience, and we shall have St. Martin's summer. At sunset the arch of clear sky appears where it sets, becoming larger and larger, until, at 7 o'clock, the dark clouds are alone over Monte Nero; Venus shines bright in the clear azure; and the trunks of the trees are tinged with the silvery light of the rising moon. Write, and read Villani. Shelley returns with [Thomas] Medwin. Read Sismondi.

Monday, OCT. 23.—Rainy night and morning. At noon a N. W. wind rises, and somewhat disperses the clouds; the sun shines out at intervals; it clouds over again. Read Villani; write.

Tuesday, OCT. 24.—Rainy night and morning; it does not rain in the afternoon. Shelley and Medwin go to Pisa. Walk; write.

Wednesday, OCT. 25.—Rain all night. The banks of the Serchio break, and by dark all the baths are overflowed. Water four feet deep in our house. The weather fine.

Saturday, [OCT. 26–]NOV. 4.—Having had an inflammation in my eyes, my Journal and everything else has been neglected. After the flood, the rainy weather ceases for a time. Thursday, Friday, Saturday, and Sunday [Oct. 26–29] are fine, though cloudy. On Saturday, Oct. 28, we engage lodgings,[42] to which we remove on Sunday [Oct. 29]. Letters from [?Claire], complaining of dulness. Medwin reads "Dramatic Scenes,"[43] to us, and a part of his Journal in India.[44] Thursday, Friday, and Saturday [Nov. 2–4] are clear beautiful days. Walk. S. T. goes on ill. Inexplicable conduct of the Gisbornes.[45]

Sunday, NOV. 5.—Henry Reveley. Write. Read very little. Walk. Mrs. Medwin [?Mason] ill.

Monday, NOV. 6.—A cloudy day. Walk; write. Visit Mrs. Medwin [?Mason]. Henry Reveley here. Medwin reads a part of his Journal aloud.

Tuesday, NOV. 7.—A bad day. Write. Read [Thomas Erskine's] "Armata," and Homer.

Wednesday, NOV. 8.—A beautiful day; cloudless and warm. Write; walk. Read Homer.

Saturday, NOV. 11.—Write. Read [Madame de Staël's] "Corinne." Walk. Read Homer. Days with cloud, and rain rain.

Sunday, NOV. 12.—Percy's birthday. A divine day; sunny and cloudless; somewhat cold in the evening. It would be pleasant enough living

[42] Casa Galetti in Pisa.

[43] By Bryan W. Procter [Barry Cornwall] (1819).

[44] Medwin's journal was apparently in MS.

[45] The Shelleys were greatly offended when the Gisbornes, on their return from England, failed to stop and see them. The Gisbornes had come through or near the Baths of Pisa; and even when they were again at home in Leghorn, they made no immediate effort to see the Shelleys. Mary and Shelley's letters register high indignation.

in Pisa if one had a carriage, and could escape from one's house to the country without mingling with the inhabitants; but the Pisans and the Scolari, in short, the whole population, are such, that it would sound strange to an English person if I attempted to express what I feel concerning them—crawling and crab-like through their sopping[46] streets. Read "Corinne." Write.

Monday, Nov. 13.—Finish "Corinne." Write. My eyes keep me from all study; this is very provoking.

Tuesday, Nov. 14.—Write. Read Homer, Targione,[47] and Spanish. A rainy day. Shelley reads Calderon.

Thursday, Nov. [20–]23.—Write. Read Greek and Spanish. M[edwin] ill. On Monday [Nov. 20], walk. Play at chess. [Claire returns from Florence on the twenty-first.][48]

Friday, Nov. 24.—Read Greek, Villani, and Spanish with M[edwin]. Bill against the Queen thrown out in the Lords. Pacchiani[49] in the evening. A rainy and cloudy day.

Friday, Dec. 1.—Read Greek, "Don Quixote," Calderon, and Villani. Pacchiani comes in the evening. Visit La Viviani.[50] Walk. Sgricci[51] is introduced. Go to a funzione on the death of a Student.

Saturday, Dec. 2.—Write an Italian letter to Hunt.[52] Read "Œdipus" [of Sophocles], "Don Quixote," and Calderon. Pacchiani and a Greek Prince call—Prince Mavrocordato.[53] Delightful weather.

Sunday, Dec. 3.—Read Greek, Calderon, and "Don Quixote." Visit Emilia. Mr. Taaffe[54] in the evening. A cloudy day.

Monday, Dec. 4.—Read "Don Quixote," and Greek. Walk out. A delightful day.

46 S&M, "sapping"; an obvious error, I think, considering the days of rain noted on November 11.

47 Giovanni Targione-Tozzetti, probably his *Viaggi in Toscana* (1768–69) (see Mary's *Letters,* I, 227).

48 Extracts from Claire's diary for November 23—December 13 are printed by White (II, 239–41).

49 Francesco Pacchiani, professor at the University of Pisa, who introduced all the new people who suddenly appear in the journal (see Dowden, II, 359–61; and White, II, 241–43).

50 Emilia Viviani (see E. Viviani della Robbia, *Vita di una Donna* [Emilia Viviani] [Florence, G. E. Sansoni, 1936]; Dowden, II, 369–83; and White, II, 247–70).

51 Tommaso Sgricci, the most famous *improvvisatore* of his day (see Dowden, II, 366–68; White, II, 243–44; and Mary's *Letters,* I, 117, 122).

52 Mary to Hunt (in Italian), December 3, 1820 (*Letters,* I, 115–19, Italian text and translation).

53 Prince Alexander Mavrocordato, two years older than Shelley and the center of a small group of Greek exiles (see Dowden, II, 361–63).

54 John Taaffe, Irish poet and writer of a Commentary on the *Divine Comedy* (see Dowden, II, 363–65).

Tuesday, Dec. 5.—Ride to Ponte Serchio. Read Greek. Sgricci in the evening. Cloudy, but mild.

Wednesday, Dec. 6.—Read Greek, and "Don Quixote." Ride out. A warm cloudy day. Shelley reads.

Thursday, Dec. 7.—Read Greek. Call on the Princess Argiropoli.[55] Sgricci dines with us. Foggi[56] calls in the evening.

Friday, Dec. 8.—Read Greek. Walk.

Saturday, Dec. 9.—Read Greek and Spanish with Emilia Viviani in the evening.

Sunday, Dec. 10.—Read Greek. The Greeks call. Call on Mrs. Mason. Read "Don Quixote."

Monday, Dec. 11.—Read Greek, Spanish, and Calderon. Pacchiani in the evening.

Tuesday, Dec. 12.—Read Greek. Copy the "Witch of Atlas." Sgricci in the evening.

Wednesday, Dec. 13.—Read Greek. Not well. Read [Leigh Hunt's] "Indicators." Pacchiani in the evening.

Thursday, Dec. 14.—Read Greek, and "Indicators." Pacchiani in the evening.[57]

Friday, Dec. 15.—Read Villani. Call on Mr. Mason. Rain ever since Monday. It holds up this morning, but begins again at sunset. Read "Magnet."[58] Mr. Taaffe in the evening.

Tuesday, Dec. 19.—Read Greek. Copy for Shelley. Read Villani. Call on Emilia Viviani. Mr. Mason, Mr. Taaffe, and Pacchiani call. Beautiful day.

Wednesday, Dec. 20.—Read Greek. Call on the Princess Argiropoli and Emilia. Prince Mavrocordato calls, and Pacchiani. Go to the theatre, and hear the Improvise of Sgricci, a most wonderful and delightful exhibition.[59] He poured forth a torrent of poetry clothed in the most beautiful language.

[*Thursday,* Dec. 21.—Records calling on Emilia and visits from Mavrocordato and Sgricci, and about his performance.][60]

Friday, Dec. 22.—Read Greek. Walk. Call on Mr. Mason. Mavrocordato before tea, and after, Pacchiani and Sgricci. Shelley very unwell. Winter begun to-day.

[55] Cousin of Prince Mavrocordato.

[56] S&M, "Fazzi"; corrected by Dowden (II, 359). Signor Foggi was a friend of the Gisbornes.

[57] Claire adds in her diary, "He is indecent."—Dowden's copy of S&M, III, 550.

[58] Not further identified. Claire's diary for December 15 reads: "Shelley is magnetised and begs them not to ask him questions, because he shall say what he ought not."

[59] The subject was "Iphigenia in Tauris."

[60] This entry (not in S&M) is taken from the MS notes of Miss Grylls.

Saturday, Dec. 23.—Pacchiani goes to Florence [with Claire]. Read Greek. Call on Emilia.

Sunday, Dec. 24.—Read Greek, and "Sintram."[61] Shelley not well.

Monday, Dec. 25.—Read Greek. Prince Mavrocordato calls. Sgricci and Mr. Taaffe in the evening.

Tuesday, Dec. 26.—Warm, sunny, and soft. Read Greek. Call on Emilia. Sgricci to dinner.

Wednesday, Dec. 27.—Read a book of Tasso to Shelley. Call on Mr. Mason and Emilia. Cloudy, but without rain.

Thursday, Dec. 28.—Read Greek. A rainy day, and cold.

Friday, Dec. 29.—Read Greek. Call on Emilia. Write letters.[62]

Saturday, Dec. 30.—Read Greek. Emilia Viviani and Mr. Taaffe in the evening. A cold cloudy day.

Sunday, Dec. 31.—A clear day, with a bleak tramontane. Read Greek. Ride out. Emilia Viviani and Prince Mavrocordato in the evening. Read Æsop.

List of Books read in 1820

MARY

*(Those marked * Shelley has read also.)*

The remainder of Livy. [History of Rome.]
*The Bible until the end of Ezekiel.
*Don Juan. [Cantos I–II. By Lord Byron, 1819.]
*Travels before the Flood. [2 vols., 1796.]
La Nouvelle Heloise. [By Rousseau, 1761.]
The Fable of the Bees. [By Bernard De Mandeville, 1714.]
[Thomas] Paine's Works.
Utopia. [By Sir Thomas More.]
*Voltaire's Memoirs. [London, 1784.]
*The Æneid and Georgics. [By Virgil.]
[Patrick] Brydone's Travels. [A Tour Through Sicily and Malta, 2 vols., 1773.]
Robinson Crusoe. [By Daniel Defoe, 1719.]
Sandford and Merton. [By Thomas Day, 3 vols., 1783–89.]
*Astronomy in the Encyclopaedia.
Vindication of the Rights of Woman. [By Mary Wollstonecraft, 1792.]
*Boswell's Life of Johnson. [1791.]

[61] F. H. Karl, Baron de la Motte-Fouqué, *Sintram and His Companions,* translated from the German by J. C. Hare (1820).

[62] Mary to Hunt, December 29, 1820 (*Letters,* I, 121–25); Mary to Mrs. Gisborne, December 29 [30, 1820] (*ibid.,* I, 126).

Paradise Regained and Lost. [By John Milton.]
Letters From Norway [1796] and Posthumous Works. [Ed. by W. Godwin, 4 vols., 1798. By Mary Wollstonecraft.]
Ivanhoe [1820], Tales of my Landlord. [Probably 3rd series, 1819. By Sir Walter Scott.]
Fleetwood [1805], Caleb Williams. [1794. By William Godwin.]
*Ricciardetto. [By Niccoló Fortiguerra.]
*Mrs. [Catherine] Macaulay's History of England. [8 vols., 1763–83.]
*Lucretius. [De Rerum Natura.]
The first 3 Orations of Cicero.
[Lodovico A.] Muratori, Antichità d'Italia.
Travels and Rebellion in Ireland. [Probably two books, the second being: Edward Hyde, Earl of Clarendon, The History of the Rebellion and Civil Wars in Ireland, Dublin, 1719–20.]
Segreno's Life of Castruccio. [Probably error for: Niccoló Tegrimi, Vita di Castruccio Castricani degli Antelminelli.]
*Boccaccio Decamerone.
*Keats' Poems. [Lamia, Isabella, The Eve of St. Agnes, and Other Poems, 1820.]
*Armata. [A Fragment, 1817. By Thomas, Baron Erskine.]
Corinne. [By Madame de Staël, 1807.]
The First Book of Homer, Œdipus Tyrannus [by Sophocles], a little Spanish, and much Italian.

SHELLEY

The New Testament.
[Johannes von] Muller's Universal History. [3 vols., 1811; tr. by J. C. Prichard, 1818.]
[Thomas] Hobbes. [Mainly the Leviathan, 1651.]
Political Justice. [By William Godwin, 1793.]
Locke
[William] Robertson's America [1777] and History of Charles V. [3 vols., 1769.]
Antient Metaphysics. [By James Burnett, Lord Monboddo, 6 vols., Edinburgh, 1779–99.]
[John] Gillies' Greece. [2 vols., 1786.]
Solis' History of Mexico [1684]. Several of the Plays of Calderon.
Sophocles.
Plato's Republic, Phædon, Phædrus. Euripides.
Greek Romances.
Apollonius Rhodius. [Argonautica.]

1821

ITALY

Monday, JAN. 1.—Read Greek. A rainy day and cold. Miss Finch[1] in the evening. Read Horace.

Tuesday, JAN. 2.—Read Greek. Walk out. Emilia Viviani. Madame Tantini,[2] with letters.

Wednesday, JAN. 3.—Read Greek, and Tasso. Prince Mavrocordato, and afterwards Pacchiani. Write to Clare.

Thursday, JAN. 4.—Read Greek. 3rd book of Tasso. Walk out. T. Medwin in the evening.

Friday, JAN. 5.—Read Greek. Emilia Viviani. Mr. Taaffe calls. Sgricci. Accademia. At Lucca to-night.[3] Fine in the morning; rain after 12.

Saturday, JAN. 6.—Read Greek, and Villani. Finish copying for Shelley. Mr. Taaffe and Foggi in the evening. Rain at night.

Sunday, JAN. 7.—Read Greek, and Villani. Walk out. Emilia Viviani.

Monday, JAN. 8.—Read Greek. Emilia Viviani. Shelley at Casa Silva.

Tuesday, JAN. 9.—Rainy, but warm weather; on the days when it does not rain, a mild sirocco blows. Damp all day; warm rain every night, and lightning. Read Greek, and Voltaire's Tales. Mr. Taaffe in the evening.

Wednesday, JAN. 10.—Read Greek. Shelley reads fragments of Æschylus. Pacchiani calls. Shelley ill.

Thursday, JAN. 11.—Read Greek. In the evening go with Pacchiani, [the baby, Percy Florence, and Maria, the nurse] to Lucca.

Friday, JAN. 12.—At Lucca. Sgricci calls. Call on Madame Bernardini.[4] Go with her to the Accademia: subject, "Ignez di Castro."

Saturday, JAN. 13.—Return to Pisa. Call on Emilia Viviani, Sgricci, and afterwards Pacchiani: all in the evening.

Sunday, JAN. 14.—Read [Scott's] the "Abbot." Write to Clare.[5] Pacchiani calls.

1 Possibly an error for Miss Field, friend of the Masons.

2 She and her husband were among the Shelleys' Italian friends in Pisa.

3 Sgricci performed at Lucca. White (II, 244) is mistaken in thinking that the Shelleys attended this exhibition.

4 Marchesa Eleonora Bernardini of Lucca.

5 Mary to Claire, January [14 and 15], 1821 (*Letters,* I, 126–30). The letter gives an excellent account of the trip to Lucca and of Sgricci's performance.

Friday, JAN. [15–]19.—The Williams' arrive.[6] Call on them, and they come here. Go to the Duke of Chablaise. Pacchiani and Sgricci and Mr. Taaffe call. Signora Bernardini. Contessa dei Conti. Mr. Mason. Read "Œdipus Tyrannus [of Sophocles]. Emilia Viviani pays her visit here. Prince Mavrocordato, &c.

Saturday, JAN. 20.—Walk all day. Williams, Sgricci, and Mr. Taaffe.

Sunday, JAN. 21.—Walk with Prince Mavrocordato. Call on the Viviani. Go to the Opera with the Williams' in the evening.

Monday, JAN. 22.—The Williams' and Medwin go to Leghorn. Read Greek. Call on the Viviani. Prince Mavrocordato after dinner. Sgricci. Accademia in the evening: the subject the "Quattro Etadi," and the tragedy "La Morte d'Ettore."[7] He [Sgricci] visits our box after the end of the tragedy.

Tuesday, JAN. 23.—Shelley goes to Leghorn. Ride out with Mr. Mason. Read Greek. Call on Emilia Viviani. A Greek lesson with Prince Mavrocordato. After his departure Sgricci comes. Shelley returns at half-past ten.

Wednesday, JAN. 24.—Sgricci calls to take leave. Pacchiani calls. The Williams' and Bowens'[8] dine with us. Prince Mavrocordato and Foggi in the evening.

Thursday, JAN. 25.—Read Greek. Pacchiani, La Conti and Biondi[9] call. Call on the Taddisli and Emilia Viviani. Finish "Œdipus Tyrannus." Mr. Taaffe in the evening.

Friday, JAN. 26.—Read Greek. Write. Call on Emilia Viviani and the Williams'. Read Æsop. Henry Reveley in the evening. Send Shelley's article to Clare.[10]

Saturday, JAN. 27.—Read Greek. Call on Mrs. Taaffe and Emilia Viviani. Ever since Friday we have had no rain. The air was at first warm, is now below freezing every morning, but every day, on the Lung' Arno, there is a warm, delightful temperature, like the last day of April in England.

Sunday, JAN. 28.—Read Greek. The Williams' dine with us. Walk

[6] Edward Ellerker Williams and his wife Jane. They landed at Leghorn on January 13, and were in Pisa by the sixteenth, on which day Mrs. Williams dined with the Shelleys. At that time Shelley had not yet seen Edward. (Shelley to Claire, [January 16, 1821], Julian edition X, 229–30.) See Dowden, II, 386–87; and White, II, 282–83.

[7] *The Death of Hector.*

[8] Williams' "friend Captain Bowen who has spent £1100 of prize money in shewing two sisters Italy—a rough English sailor." (For this and more, see Mary to Claire, January 21, 1821, *Letters,* I, 131.)

[9] S&M, "Riondi." Luigi Biondi, who married Emilia Viviani on September 8, 1821 (White, II, 319).

[10] "This I suppose to be the *Blackwood* articles on Shelley."—Dowden's note in his copy of S&M, III, 580.

out. Emilia Viviani in the morning; in the evening, Prince Mavrocordato and Henry Reveley.

Monday, JAN. 29.—Read Greek. Write to Clare. Pacchiani goes to Florence. Call on Emilia Viviani. Mr. Taaffe and Henry Reveley in the evening.

Tuesday, JAN. 30.—Read Greek. Dante's "Vita Nuova." Walk on the Argine. The Williams' and Prince Mavrocordato in the evening.

Wednesday, JAN. 31.—Read Greek. Call on Emilia Viviani. Shelley reads the "Vita Nuova" aloud to me in the evening.

Thursday, FEB. 1.—Read Greek. Walk out with the Williams'. Prince Mavrocordato and M. Costar call. In the evening the Prince comes again, and Henry Reveley calls.

Friday, FEB. 2.—Read Greek. Write. Emilia Viviani walks out with Shelley in the evening. The Opera, with the Williams' ("Il Matrimonio Segreto"[11]).

Saturday, FEB. 3.—Read Greek. Walk with Shelley. In the evening Prince Mavrocordato and Mr. Taaffe.

Sunday, FEB. 4.—Read Greek. Walk. The Williams' to dinner.

Monday, FEB. 5.—Read Greek. Call on Emilia Viviani. Walk out on the Leghorn Road. In the evening the Williams', Prince Mavrocordato, and Mr. Taaffe.

Tuesday, FEB. 6.—Read Greek. Sit to Williams. Call on Emilia Viviani. Prince Mavrocordato in the evening. A long metaphysical argument.

Wednesday, FEB. 7.—Read Greek. Sit to Williams. In the evening the Williams', Prince Mavrocordato, and Mr. Taaffe.

Thursday, FEB. 8.—Read Greek (no lesson). Sit to Williams, and after dinner walk out with him. Write; read Greek.

Friday, FEB. 9.—Read Greek all day. In the evening Shelley at Mrs. Mason's. The Williams' and Prince Mavrocordato.

Saturday, FEB. 10.—Read Greek, and "Vita Nuova." Walk out with the Williams'. In the evening Mr. Taaffe.

Sunday, FEB. 11.—Read Greek (no lesson). Walk out with the Williams'. Call on Emilia Viviani. In the evening the Williams'.

Monday, FEB. 12.—Read Greek (no lesson). Finish the "Vita Nuova." In the afternoon call on Emilia Viviani. Walk. Mr. Taaffe calls.

Tuesday, FEB. 13.—Read Greek. The Williams' to dine, and in the evening Prince Mavrocordato. Walk with Williams.

Wednesday, FEB. 14.—Read Greek. Visit Emilia Viviani. Mr. Taaffe in the evening.

[11] Music by Cimarosa; libretto by Bertatti; based on Colman's *The Clandestine Marriage* (Nicoll, *Early Nineteenth Century Drama,* II, 553).

Thursday, Feb. 15.—Read Greek. Walk with Williams. Spend the evening at Casa Silva.

Friday, Feb. 16.—Read Greek (no lesson). Visit Emilia Viviani. Shelley at Casa Silva. Alone in the evening.

Saturday, Feb. 17.—Read Greek. Ride out with Mrs. Mason. Walk with the Williams'. Prince Mavrocordato in the evening.

Sunday, Feb. 18.—Visit Emilia Viviani. Read Greek. Walk.

Monday, Feb. 19.—Read Greek. Walk. The Williams' in the evening.

Tuesday, Feb. 20.—Read Greek. Call on Emilia Viviani. Shelley begins "King Lear" in the evening. Mr. Taaffe calls.

Wednesday, Feb. 21.—Read Greek (no lesson). Walk with E. Williams; he spends the evening with us.

Thursday, Feb. 22.—Read Greek. The Williams' to dine with us. Walk with them. Il Diavolo[12] Pacchiani calls. Shelley reads "The Ancient Mariner" aloud.

Friday, Feb. 23.—Read Greek. Ride to the Baths with the Williams'. In the evening the Williams'. Prince Mavrocordato and M. Costar.

Saturday, Feb. 24.—Read Greek. A cloudy mizzling day, with a fine sunset. Visit Emilia Viviani.

Sunday, Feb. 25.—Read Greek. Call on Emilia Viviani. The Williams' in the evening. A cloudy day without rain.

Monday, Feb. 26.—Read Greek (no lesson). Call on Emilia Viviani, and on the Williams' in the evening. A cloudy morning, but beautiful afternoon.

Tuesday, Feb. 27.—A fine day, with a tramontana. Medwin goes. Read Greek. The Williams' in the evening. Walk with them.

Wednesday, Feb. 28.—Read Greek (no lesson). Call on Emilia Viviani. Mr. Taaffe in the evening; a cloudy damp sirocco.

Thursday, March 1.—Read Greek. Prince Mavrocordato dines with us. A rainy day. Begin the "Defence of Poetry," by Sir Philip Sydney.

Friday, March 2.—Read Greek (no lesson). Walk with the Williams', they and Mr. Taaffe in the evening. A rainy morning and fine afternoon.

Saturday, Mar. 3.—Read Greek (no lesson). Walk with the Williams'. Read Horace with Shelley in the evening. A delightful day.

Sunday, Mar. 4.—Read Greek. Write letters. The Williams' to dine with us. Walk with them. Williams relates his history. They spend the evening with us, with Prince Mavrocordato and Mr. Taaffe.

Monday, Mar. 5.—Read Greek. Move to our new lodgings [Casa Aulla]. Dine with the Williams'.

Tuesday, Mar. 6.—Read Greek. Walk. Housework. The Williams' and Mr. Taaffe in the evening.

[12] Popular name for Pacchiani.

Wednesday, MAR. 7.—Read Greek. Walk with Williams. A dull windless sirocco.

Thursday, MAR. 8.—Read Greek (no lesson). Call on Emilia Viviani. E. Williams calls. Shelley reads "The Case is Altered," of Ben Jonson, aloud in the evening. A mizzling day and rainy night; that beautiful weather is now ended which we enjoyed almost uninterruptedly for two months, usually the coldest in the year; at one time indeed it froze at night and morning, though the sunbeams were warm and vivifying in the middle of the day; sometimes a tramontana blew, but in general a temperate warmth pervaded the atmosphere, except during the heats of February. March winds and rains are begun, the last puff of winter's breath—the eldest tears of a coming spring; she ever comes in weeping and goes out smiling.

Friday, MAR. 9.—Read Greek. A beautiful day. Walk with Shelley. Mr. Taaffe and the Williams' in the evening.

Saturday, MAR. 10.—Read Greek (no lesson). A heavenly day. Call on the Williams'; walk with him.

Sunday, MAR. 11.—Read Greek. Sir P. Sydney's "Defence of Poetry." A mizzling sirocco; the Williams' and Prince Mavrocordato to dine with us. In the evening the Williams' and Mr. Taaffe.

Monday, MAR. 12.—Read Greek (no lesson). Finish the "Defence of Poetry." Copy for Shelley;[13] he reads to me the "Tale of a Tub" [of Ben Jonson]. A delightful day after a misty morning.

Tuesday, MAR. 13.—Read Greek. Walk with Shelley. Visit Emilia Viviani. The Williams' and Mr. Taaffe in the evening. A divine day.

Wednesday, MAR. 14.—Read Greek (no lesson). Copy for Shelley. Walk with Williams. Prince Mavrocordato in the evening. I have an interesting conversation with him concerning Greece. The second bulletin of the Austrians published. A sirocco, but a pleasant evening.

Thursday, MAR. 15.—Read Greek. Copy for Shelley. Visit Emilia Viviani. Walk with Shelley. In the evening Prince Mavrocordato, the Williams', and Mr. Taaffe. Rain in the night and morning; a tolerable afternoon; at sunrise a tramontana rises.

Friday, MAR. 16.—Read Greek. Copy for Shelley. Walk with Williams. Mrs. Williams confined.[14] News of the revolution of Piedmont, and the taking of the citadel of Candia by the Greeks. A beautiful day, but not hot.

[13] Shelley's *Defence of Poetry.*

[14] Rosalind Williams was born. In his journal Williams wrote: "It was about 9 o'clock in the evening, on the Friday, the 16th of March, 1821, that I heard of this event, having retired to S[helley]'s to avoid the confusion and feelings such scenes occasion. M[ar]y brought me the news."—*Journal of Edward E. Williams,* with Introduction by Richard Garnett (London, Elkin Mathews, 1902), 16.

Saturday, MAR. 17.—Read Greek. Copy for Shelley. A pleasant walk with Williams. The day divine. A slight tramontana. Mr. Taaffe in the evening.

Sunday, MAR. 18.—Read Greek. Copy for Shelley. A sirocco and mizzle. Bad news from Naples. Walk with Williams. Prince Mavrocordato in the evening.

Monday, MAR. 19.—Read Greek. Copy for Shelley. Walk with Williams. A violent misty maestrale. Mr. Taaffe in the evening. Read his "Notes to Dante."[15]

Tuesday, MAR. 20.—Read Greek. Finish copying for Shelley. Walk with Williams. A clear maestrale.

Wednesday, MAR. 21.—Read Greek. Alex. Mavrocordato. Call on the Williams'. In the evening Williams, Mr. Taaffe, and Alex. Mavrocordato. A cloudy and mizzling day.

Thursday, MAR. 22.—Read Greek. Mr. Taaffe's "Comments." Walked with Williams. Shelley at Casa Silva. A rainy night and morning; one loud clap of thunder comes, the wind changes, and a fine clear maestrale blows all day.

Friday, MAR. 23.—Read Greek. Mr. Taaffe's "Comments." Walk with Williams. Call on Emilia Viviani. Williams and Mr. Taaffe in the evening. A cloudy day but a fine sunset.

Saturday, MAR. 24.—Read Greek. Alex. Mavrocordato. Walk with Shelley. Call on Emilia Viviani and Mrs. Williams. Alex. Mavrocordato and Mr. Taaffe in the evening. A sunny day, with tramontana.

Sunday, MAR. 25.—Read Greek. Call on Emilia Viviani, along with Williams. The Opera in the evening, with Williams and Laurette. A fine day.

Monday, MAR. 26.—Read Greek. Alex. Mavrocordato. Finish the "Antigone" [of Sophocles]. A mizzling day. Spend the evening at the Williams'.

Tuesday, MAR. 27.—Read Greek. Alex. Mavrocordato. Shelley goes to Lucca. A mizzling day and fine evening. Shelley returns. Mr. Taaffe in the evening.

Wednesday, MAR. 28.—Read Greek. Alex. Mavrocordato. Call on Emilia Viviani. Walk with Williams. Mr. Taaffe in the evening. A fine day, though changeful as to clouds and wind. The State of Massa declares the constitution. The Piedmontese troops are at Sarzana.

Thursday, MAR. 29.—Read Greek. Walk out with Williams. Williams in the evening. A cloudy day.

[15] In MS. The first volume of Taaffe's "Comment on the *Divine Comedy*" was, Dowden says (II, 365), published later by John Murray.

Friday, MAR. 30.—Read Greek. Walk with Williams. A libeccio. Mr. Taaffe in the evening. Shelley at Mrs. Mason's.

Saturday, MAR. 31.—Read Greek. Call on Emilia Viviani. Read Mr. Taaffe's "Comments on Dante." Walk with Williams and Shelley. Alex. Mavrocordato and Mr. Taaffe in the evening.

Sunday, APR. 1.—Read Greek. Alex. Mavrocordato calls with news about Greece.[16] He is as gay as a caged eagle just free. Call on Emilia Viviani. Walk with Williams; he spends the evening with us.

Monday, APRIL 2.—Read Greek. Alex. Mavrocordato calls with the Proclamation of Ipsilanti. Write to him. Ride with Shelley into the Cascini. A divine day, with a north-west wind. The theatre in the evening. Tachinardi.

Tuesday, APR. 3.—Read Greek. Walk with Williams. A divine morning. A sirocco rises in the afternoon; it blows hard at night. In the evening Alex. Mavrocordato. Shelley at Casa Silva.

Wednesday, APR. 4.—Write to Hunt.[17] Read Greek. Mr. Taaffe and Williams in the evening. A cloudy, windy day.

Thursday, APR. 5.—Write, &c. Shelley and Williams go to Pugnano. Alex. Mavrocordato calls. Walk with Alex. Mavrocordato and Williams. Mr. Taaffe in the evening. A fierce west wind all day.

Friday, APR. 6.—Read Greek. Call on Jane Williams and Emilia Viviani. A sirocco.

Saturday, APR. 7.—Bad news from Alex. Mavrocordato. Walk with Williams. An east wind.

Sunday, APR. 8.—Read Greek. The Williams' to dine. Walk with Williams; he and Mr. Taaffe in the evening.

Monday, APR. 9.—Read Greek. Campetti calls, and Alex. Mavrocordato. After dinner walk with Alex. Mavrocordato and Williams. In the evening Mr. Taaffe and Alex. Mavrocordato.

Tuesday, APR. 10.—Read Greek, and "Osservatore Fiorentino."[18] Walk with Williams. In the evening Williams and Alex. Mavrocordato.

16 See Mary and Shelley to Claire, [April 2, 1821] (Julian edition, X, 250–51); Dowden, II, 394–95; and Mary's *Letters* (Mary's part only), I, 136–37.

17 Hunt's letter of March 1, 1821, to Shelley (*The Correspondence of Leigh Hunt,* I, 161–63) was received on April 4. Hunt wrote: "Poor Keats! have you yet heard of him? They send word from Rome that he is dying." Mary's letter of April 5, [1821] to Mrs. Gisborne (*Letters,* I, 137–38) shows that the Shelleys had not yet heard of Keats's death at Rome on February 23.

18 *L'Osservatore Fiorentino sugli edifizi della sua patria, per servire alla storia della medesima* [By M. Lastri] (Firenze, 1776–78, 2 vols.); (3rd edition, "eseguita sopra quella del 1797, riordinata e compiute dall'autore [M. Lastri], coll' aggiunta di varie annotazioni del professore G. del Rosso" [Firenze, 1821, 8 vols.]). According to Mary's note in the *Poetical Works* (1839), Shelley's *Ginevra* was founded "on a story to be found in the first volume" of this book.

Wednesday, APR. 11.—Read Greek, and "Osservatore Fiorentino." A letter[19] that overturns us. Walk with Shelley. In the evening the Williams' and Mr. Taaffe.

Thursday, APR. 12.—Read Greek, and "Osservatore Fiorentino." Shelley rides to Pugnano. In the evening Mr. Taaffe and Alex. Mavrocordato. All this time we have abominable libeccio siroccos, rain and wind.

Friday, APR. 13.—Read Greek. Alex. Mavrocordato calls. "Osservatore Fiorentino." Walk with the Williams'. Shelley at Casa Silva in the evening. An explanation of our difficulty.[20]

Saturday, APR. 14.—Read Greek. (Alex. Mavrocordato). Finish the "Osservatore Fiorentino." Henry Reveley to dinner. A divine evening. After tea Henry Reveley, Mr. Taaffe, and Alex. Mavrocordato.

Sunday, APR. 15.—Read Greek. Targioni. Henry Reveley dines and goes to Leghorn with Shelley and Williams. In the afternoon call on Mrs. Mason. In the evening Alex. Mavrocordato. A divine day. The evening somewhat clouded.

Monday, APR. 16.—Write. Targioni. Read Greek. Mrs. Williams to dinner. In the evening Mr. Taaffe. A wet morning, in the afternoon a fierce maestrale. Shelley, Williams, and Henry Reveley try to come up the canal to Pisa; miss their way, are capsized, and sleep at a contadino's.[21]

Tuesday, APR. 17.—Read Greek. Targioni. Villani. Walk with the Williams'; they spend the evening with us. Rain in the morning; a maestrale in the evening.

Wednesday, APR. 18.—Villani. Read three Odes of Anacreon. Shelley and Williams go to the Baths. Alex. Mavrocordato in the evening, with news from Greece. A bad day, but a good sunset, with a slight maestrale.

Thursday, APR. 19.—Read Greek. Alex. Mavrocordato. Villani. Shelley goes to the Baths. Reads Plato. A cloudless day, but tramontana.

Friday, APR. 20.—Read Greek. Villani. Ride to the Baths. The Williams' in the evening. A fine day, but tramontano, which makes the evening cold.

[19] The letter was from Horace Smith to Shelley, March 28, 1821 (S&M, III, 598–600, misdated April 3), informing Shelley that his income had been stopped (see White, II, 284–85, 610). Nat L. Kaderly makes an important correction to the usual history of this complication in Shelley's affairs by showing that Dr. Hume did not seek action against Shelley for the sum of £ 30 due him for one quarter, but for £ 120 due and unpaid (through no real fault of Shelley) for one year's maintenance of Shelley's children (see Kaderly's "The Stoppage of Shelley's Income in 1821," *Modern Language Notes,* LIX [December, 1944], 545–47).

[20] Horace Smith's (lost) letter of April 3, 1821.

[21] See Dowden, II, 398–400; and White, II, 286–87.

Saturday, Apr. 21.—Read Greek. Villani. Walk with the Williams'. Write. Mr. Taaffe in the evening. Medesimo tempo.

Sunday, Apr. 22.—Read Greek. Villani. Write. Walk with the Williams', who spend the evening with us. Mr. Taaffe.

Monday, Apr. 23.—Read Greek. Villani. Write. Shelley dines at Casa Silva. Walk with Alex. Mavrocordato and the Williams'. Mr. Taaffe calls in the evening. Fine weather, increasing in heat.

Tuesday, Apr. 24.—Read Greek. Alex. Mavrocordato. Hume. Villani. Walk with the Williams'. Alex. Mavrocordato calls in the evening, with good news from Greece. The Morea free. Mr. Taaffe calls. A warm day, but a libeccio.

Wednesday, Apr. 25.—Hume. Villani. Read Greek. Call on Emilia Viviani. Walk with Williams. In the evening the Williams' and Alex. Mavrocordato. A warm libeccio.

Thursday, Apr. 26.—Villani. Write. The Gisbornes arrive [for a visit]. Walk with Williams; he and Mr. Taaffe in the evening. A divine day, the first perfectly summer.

Friday, Apr. 27.—Read Greek. Alex. Mavrocordato. Write. Read Villani. Walk. Mr. Taaffe, the Williams', and Foggi in the evening.

Saturday, Apr. 28.—Read Greek. Write. Alex. Mavrocordato. Read Villani. Call on Emilia Viviani. Alex. Mavrocordato in the evening.

Sunday, Apr. 29.—Read Greek. Walk. The Williams' and Mr. Taaffe in the evening.

Monday, Apr. 30.—Read Greek. Write. The Gisbornes go with Shelley and Williams [to Leghorn]. Walk. Henry Reveley comes in the evening with the boat.[22] Shelley returns.

Tuesday, May 1.—Read Greek. Call on Emilia Viviani. Walk. Williams and Henry Reveley to dinner. Henry Reveley in the evening.

Wednesday, May 2.—Read Greek. Villani. Shelley and Henry Reveley sail. A violent shower. Alex. Mavrocordato and Mr. Taaffe in the evening.

Thursday, May 3.—Read Villani. Go out in boat; call on Emilia Viviani. Walk with Shelley. In the evening Alex. Mavrocordato, Henry Reveley, Danielli,[23] and Mr. Taaffe.

Friday, May 4.—Read Greek (Alex. Mavrocordato). Read Villani. Shelley goes to Leghorn by sea, with Henry Reveley. Call on Emilia Viviani. In the evening Mr. Taaffe and Alex. Mavrocordato.

Saturday, May 5.—Alex. Mavrocordato calls. Read Greek. Read Villani. Call on Emilia Viviani. Shelley returns. Alex. Mavrocordato in the evening.

[22] The boat had been undergoing repairs at Leghorn since the accident of April 16.
[23] One of Emilia Viviani's suitors.

Sunday, MAY 6.—Read Greek. Reviews. Call on Emilia Viviani. Shelley goes to the Williams'.[24] In the evening Danielli and Mr. Taaffe.

Monday, MAY 7.—Reviews. Call on Emilia Viviani and Mrs. Mason. In the evening go with Mr. Taaffe to the D[uke] of Chablais. Alex. Mavrocordato in the evening.

Tuesday, MAY 8.—Packing. Read Greek (Alex. Mavrocordato). Shelley goes to Leghorn. In the evening walk with Alex. Mavrocordato to Pugnano. See the Williams'; return to the Baths.[25] Shelley and Henry Reveley come. The weather quite April; rain and sunshine, and by no means warm.

Wednesday, MAY 9.—A fine day. Arrange. Write letters. Read Greek. Shelley goes to Pisa. Mr. Taaffe calls.

Thursday, MAY 10.—Translate Italian. Read Greek. Go to the Williams'; spend the evening there. *θρεψεις λεαινας σκυμνον.*

Friday, MAY 11.—Write. Read Greek. Walk with Shelley; he reads some of the tales of Sachetti aloud in the evening. Thunder in the distance, but a fine day, and not hot.

Saturday, MAY 12.—Write. Read Greek. Williams dines with us. Go to Pisa in the boat. Call at the convent [to see Emilia Viviani]. Shopping, &c. Meet Alex. Mavrocordato. Return to the Baths. A delightful day, and very cool.

Sunday, MAY 13.—Write Italian. The Williams' come and spend the day. Walk to the Blache delle Fate.[26]

Monday, MAY 14.—Write. Read Greek. Letter-writing.[27] Walk with Shelley; he reads [Ben Jonson's] "Every Man in his Humour" aloud in the evening. A cold day; rain in the morning; a beautiful evening, but cool.

Tuesday, MAY 15.—Write. Read Greek. Muratori. Walk with Babe.

Wednesday, MAY 16.—Write. After dinner go to the Williams'. Walk up a mountain with them. A delightful evening. The Prince [Mavrocordato] comes in his new dress; return with him to the Baths.

Thursday, MAY 17.—Write. Read Greek. Walk. A delightful day. Shelley not well.

Friday, MAY 18.—Write. Read Greek. Shelley goes to Pisa, and sees Vaccà. Henry Reveley comes in the evening. A fine day.

Saturday, MAY 19.—A cloudy day but agreeable. Write. Read Greek. Spend the evening with the Williams'.

24 About May 1 the Williamses had moved to "the beautiful villa of Marchese Poschi, at Pugnano, about seven miles and a half from Pisa."—*Journal of E. E. Williams,* 16.

25 The Shelleys moved to the Baths of Pisa on May 8, though Mary does not make this clear.

26 Called La Buche delle Fate in the entry for August 10, 1820.

27 Mary to Amelia Curran, May 14, 1821 (*Letters,* I, 142–43).

THOMAS MEDWIN

Reproduced by permission of the Oxford University Press from Medwin's revised Life of Shelley, *ed. by H. Buxton Forman, 1913*

Sunday, MAY 20.—A very fine, clear day. Write Greek. Williams dines with us. Walk with him. His play.[28] Shelley finishes "Every Man in his Humour."

Monday, MAY 21.—A cloudy day; a mizzle in the morning. Write. Read Greek. Go to Pisa. Visit Emilia Viviani and Casa Silva. Return to the Baths with Alex. Mavrocordato.

Tuesday, MAY 22.—Walk with the Prince in the morning. Write. Read Greek. Dine with Alex. Mavrocordato at the Williams'.

Wednesday, MAY 23.—Write. Read Greek. Shelley goes to Pisa; finishes [Pope's] the "Rape of the Lock" to me in the evening. Libeccio.

Thursday, MAY 24.—Write. Read Greek. The Williams' and Mr. Taaffe to dinner. Walk. Libeccio.

Friday, MAY 25.—Write. Dine at the Williams'. Shelley and Williams go down the Serchio to the sea.

Saturday, MAY 26.—Write. Read Greek. Walk. Shelley reads Pope's "Essay on Criticism" aloud.

Sunday, MAY 27.—Write. Read Greek. Letters from Alex. Mavrocordato.[29] Williams to dinner. Return with him to Pugnano.

Monday, MAY 28.—Write. Read Greek. Walk. Alex. Mavrocordato calls. A cold tramontana.

Tuesday, MAY 29.—Write. Read Greek. The Williams' walk with me. A fine day with a fresh wind.

Wednesday, MAY 30.—Write. Go to Pisa to Emilia Viviani and Casa Silva. Fine weather with a fresh wind. Shelley goes to sleep at the Williams'.

Thursday, MAY 31.—Read Greek. Walk. Shelley returns at midnight from his tour to Brentina. Write to Papa and C. Clairmont. Summer is now about to begin.

Friday, JUNE 1.—Write. Read Greek. The Williams' come. Walk. Shelley goes to Pisa. Mr. Taaffe calls.

Saturday, JUNE 2.—Write. Read Greek. Shelley goes to Pisa. Walk to Pisa with Williams.

Sunday, JUNE 3.—The Williams' to dinner. Write. Read Greek. Walk with the Williams'.

Monday, JUNE 4.—Write. Read Greek. Walk to the Williams'. Shelley at Pisa. He does not return until midnight. A thunderstorm.

Tuesday, JUNE 5.—A rainy day. Walk in the evening.

Wednesday, JUNE 6.—Write. Go to the Williams'. A fine day.

[28] *The Promise; or A Year, a Month, and a Day.*

[29] S&M has eight letters (in French) from Mavrocordato to Mary. The (two) letters received by Mary on May 27 are at III, 628–30.

Thursday, JUNE 7.—Read Greek. Alex. Mavrocordato calls. A fine day. Walk with Shelley. Bunaditto aloud in the evening. Mr. Taaffe calls.

Friday, JUNE 8.—Write. Read Greek. Go to Pisa with Williams. Call at Casa Silva. Meet Alex. Mavrocordato.

Saturday, JUNE 9.—Write. Go to the Williams' in the evening. Fine day, but windy; cloudy; libeccio.

Sunday, JUNE 10.—Write. Read Greek. Go to Pisa after dinner. A cloudy libeccio.

Monday, JUNE 11.—Shelley goes to Pisa. Write. Read Greek. Mr. Taaffe calls. A very cool day.

Tuesday, JUNE 12.—Write. Read Greek. The Williams' to dinner. A fine day, but libeccio.

Wednesday, JUNE 13.—A bad rainy day. Read Greek. Write. Shelley goes to Pisa.

Thursday, JUNE 14.—A fine day, though cool. Old plays.[30] Dine at the Williams'. Greek.

Friday, JUNE 15.—Old plays. Alex. Mavrocordato calls. Rain in the morning; fine in the evening. Walk with Williams to Pisa. Mr. Taaffe calls.

Saturday, JUNE 16.—Read Old Plays. Shelley goes to Pisa. Mr. Taaffe calls. Read Greek. A bad rainy day.

Sunday, JUNE 17.—Write. Read Greek. A rainy morning, but a fine though cold afternoon. Go to Pugnano. Old Plays.

Monday, JUNE 18.—Shelley goes to Pisa. Write. Call on the Conti. Read Malthus ["On the Principle of Population," 1798].

Tuesday, JUNE 19.—Write. Read Malthus. Mr. Taaffe and Granger[31] call.

Wednesday, JUNE 20.—Shelley goes to Pisa. Read Malthus. Walk to Pugnano.

Thursday, JUNE 21.—Read "Treatise on Magic," and Malthus. [?Claire][32] dines with us. Shelley reads the first book of [Chaucer's] "Troilus and Cressida" aloud in the evening. Mr. Taaffe and Granger call.

Friday, JUNE 22.—Go to Pisa. Call on Emilia Viviani and on the P. P. Argyropulo. Dine at Casa Silva. Read Malthus.

Saturday, JUNE 23.—Abominably cold weather—rain, wind, and cloud, —quite an Italian November or a Scotch May. Shelley and Williams go

30 Possibly *Ancient British Drama* (ed. by Walter Scott, 1810, 3 vols.). In his letter of February 22, 1821, to Ollier (Julian edition, X, 243), Shelley requested that "The 'Old English Drama,' 3 vols.," be sent to him.

31 Apparently a friend of Mr. Taaffe; spelled "Grainger" by Shelley in his letter of July 4, 1821, to Taaffe (Julian edition, X, 282).

32 Dowden says (II, 418), "on June 21 Claire spent the day with her [Mary] at the Baths."

to Leghorn. Write. Read and finish Malthus. Begin the "Answer" [by Godwin].[33] Jane spends the day here, and Edward returns in the evening. Read Greek.

Sunday, JUNE 24.—Write. Read the "Answer to Malthus." Finish it. Shelley at Leghorn.

Monday, JUNE 25.—Little Babe not well.[34] Shelley returns. The Williams' call. Read Old Plays. Vaccà calls.

Tuesday, JUNE 26.—Babe well. Write. Read Greek. Shelley not well. Mr. Taaffe and Granger dine with us. Walk with Shelley. Vaccà calls. Alex. Mavrocordato sails [for Greece.]

Wednesday, JUNE 27.—Shelley at Pisa. Write. Read Greek. Go to Pugnano. Vaccà calls.

Thursday, JUNE 28.—Write. Read Greek. Read [?Henry] Mackenzie's Works. Go to Pugnano in the boat. The warmest day this month. Fireflies in the evening.

Friday, JUNE 29.—Write. Read Greek. The Williams' to dinner. Read "Edgeworth's Life."[35]

Saturday, JUNE 30.—Write. Read Greek. Write to Alex. Mavrocordato. Spend the evening at Pugnano.

Sunday, JULY 1.—Write. Dine at Pugnano. Walk up the hill. Read "Edgeworth's Life." Fine weather now.

Monday, JULY 2.—Write. Read "Edgeworth's Life."

Tuesday, JULY 3.—The Williams' dine with us. Write. Read "Philoctetes" [of Sophocles].

Wednesday, JULY 4.—Finish "Philoctetes." Write.

Thursday, JULY 5.—Write. Read Homer, and Old Plays.

Friday, JULY 6.—Write. Read Homer, and Old Plays. Go to Pugnano in the evening. Shelley calls on Count Nazawly.[36]

Saturday, JULY 7.—Write. Read Homer, and "Diary of an Invalid."[37] Shelley goes to Pisa. Go to the Casino in the evening. Tolerable weather, but cold.

Sunday, JULY 8.—Write. Read Homer, and "Diary of an Invalid." The Williams' dine with us.

Monday, JULY 9.—Write. Read Homer. Go to Pugnano in the evening.

Tuesday, JULY 10.—Write. Finish the first book of the "Odyssey." Read Old Plays. The Williams' in the evening.

33 William Godwin, *Of Population. An Answer to Mr. Malthus's Essay* (1820).

34 The trouble was "a fever produced by teething" (Mary's *Letters,* I, 145).

35 *Memoirs of Richard Lovell Edgeworth, Concluded by Maria Edgeworth* (1820, 2 vols.).

36 Spelled "Magawly" by Shelley, who wrote to John Taaffe on July 4, 1821: "I thank you for . . . bringing me acquainted with the Count Magawly."—Julian edition, X, 281.

37 By Henry Matthews (1819).

Wednesday, JULY 11.—The Cicala[38] for the first time, and the first real fine summer day. Write. Read Homer and Old Plays. Call on Madame Tantini; and the Casino in the evening.

Thursday, JULY 12.—Write. Read Homer. Dine at Pugnano. Read Shelley's "Adonais."

Friday, JULY 13.—Write. Read Homer, and Old Plays. Walk with Shelley.

Saturday, JULY 14.—Write. Read Homer. Go to Pugnano.

Sunday, JULY 15.—Write. Read Homer and Mrs. Hutchinson's "Memoirs."[39] Shelley dines at Casa Silva.

Monday, JULY 16.—Write. Read Mrs. Hutchinson's "Memoirs." The Williams' to dinner.

Tuesday, JULY 17.—Write. Read Homer. Finish Mrs. Hutchinson's "Memoirs." Mr. Mason calls. Walk. Read Old Plays.

Wednesday, JULY 18.—Write. Read Homer and "Ludlow's Memoirs."[40] Go to Pugnano in the evening.

Thursday, JULY 19.—Read Tegrino.[41] Shelley goes to Pisa. Go to Pugnano; sleep there.

Friday, JULY 20.—Read Homer. Walk, &c.

Saturday, JULY 21.—Read Homer. Walk, &c.

Sunday, JULY 22.—Read Homer. Walk, &c. Shelley dines at Pisa. Return to the Baths [from Pugnano].

Monday, JULY 23.—Clare here. Go to Casino in the evening.

Tuesday, JULY 24.—Williams' to dinner. Write. Read Homer.

Wednesday, JULY 25.—Write. Dine at Casa Silva. Read "Ludlow's Memoirs." Shelley goes to Leghorn.

Thursday, JULY 26.—The Gisbornes here. In the evening call on the Mastiani.

Friday, JULY 27.—The Gisbornes here. Go to Pugnano in the boat.

Saturday, JULY 28.—Read to Mrs. Gisborne. The Williams' come, and Madame Mastiani.

Sunday, JULY 29.—The Williams' in the evening. Count Nazawly calls. The Gisbornes and Shelley depart for Florence.[42]

38 An insect, heard for the first time in the summer.

39 Mrs. Lucy Hutchinson, *The Memoirs of the Life of Colonel Hutchinson,* with a fragment of a "Life" of Herself (1806).

40 Edmund Ludlow (1698–99).

41 Evidently a misreading of the MS journal. The right name is probably Niccolò Tegrimi (1448–1527), author of the first biography of Castruccio Castracana. (See note to Mar. 31, 1820 entry.)

42 The Gisbornes were on their way to England; Shelley went to Florence to look for a house for Horace Smith.

Monday, JULY 30.—The Williams' all day. Sit to Edward. Finish third book of Homer. Call on Madame Tantini.

Tuesday, JULY 31.[43]—Williams here; sit to him; return with him to Pugnano.

Wednesday, AUG. 1.—Williams here; not well; sit to him. Read Homer.

Thursday,[44] AUG. 2.—Williams. Shelley returns. A letter with news.[45] Jane comes to dinner.

Friday, AUG. 3.—Williams. Shelley dines at Pisa. After dinner go to Casa Silva. Shelley departs [for Ravenna].

Saturday, AUG. 4.—Williams all day. Read Homer. Walk. Call on Madame Tantini. Williams finishes my miniature. Shelley's birthday. Seven years are now gone; what changes! what a life! We now appear tranquil; yet who knows what wind—but I will not prognosticate evil; we have had enough of it. When Shelley came to Italy, I said all is well if it were permanent; it was more passing than an Italian twilight. I now say the same. May it be a Polar day; yet that, too, has an end.

Sunday, AUG. 5.—Read Homer. Dine at Pugnano. Read Edward's play ["The Promise"].

Monday, AUG. 6.—Read "Matilda"[46] to Edward. After dinner go with him to Pugnano in the boat. Read Homer.

From AUG.[47] 6 to AUG. 31.—Shelley goes to Ravenna [on the third]. Read two books of Homer. some days. Shelley returns.[48] Go often to Pugnano. Edward with us every morning. The Guiccioli[49] arrives; see her. My portrait painted;[50] Shelley's begun. Walk to meet Clare every morning at 6.[51] Copy C[astruccio] P[rince] of L[ucca].[52]

Saturday, SEPT. 1.—Copy C. P. of L. Edward paints. Shelley reads Kant. The Guiccioli calls, and La Conti.

Sunday, SEPT. 2.—Copy. Call on La Conti. Edward paints. Go to Pugnano in the evening.

Monday, SEPT. 3.—Copy. Dine at Pugnano. Tanetti there. Singing.

43 Shelley's letter to Mary from Florence (Julian edition, X, 293–94) is dated Tuesday, which Ingpen designates as [August 1] instead of the correct date [July 31].

44 S&M, "Tuesday."

45 The letter was from Byron, informing Shelley of his intention of leaving Ravenna and inviting him there for a visit.

46 See note to entry for Sept. 12, 1819.

47 S&M, "July."

48 Shortly before the twenty-second.

49 Countess Teresa Guiccioli, Byron's mistress.

50 A miniature by Williams, finished on August 4 and given by Mary to Shelley as a birthday present.

51 Claire was probably staying either with the Williamses at Pugnano, or with Mrs. Mason at Pisa.

52 S&M, "C. P. of Z."; also in Sept. 1 entry.

Tuesday, SEPT. 4.—Copy. The Williams' with us. Read "Matilda" to Jane. Go with them to Pugnano, and return in the Baroccino.

Wednesday, SEPT. 5.—Copy. Go to Pisa to vist the Guiccioli. Clare arrives. Read "Anastasius" [by Thomas Hope].[53]

Thursday, SEPT. 6.—Copy. Williams in the morning. Finish [Scott's] "Kenilworth."

Friday, SEPT. 7.—Copy. The Williams' to dinner.

Saturday, SEPT. 8.—Journey to Spezzia [with Shelley and Claire]. Dine on the road under trees. Arrive at La Spezzia.

Sunday, SEPT. 9.—Read "Anastasius." Go out on the Bay; ride about there.

Monday, SEPT. 10.—Return to Massa. Visit Carrara. A moonlight walk.

Tuesday, SEPT. 11.—A rainy day; return home. Dine at Pugnano.

Wednesday, SEPT. 12.—The Williams' to dine with us. A fine day.

Thursday, SEPT. 13.—Go to Pisa.

Friday, SEPT. 14.—Clare and Shelley go to Pisa. Edward to bathe here. The Guiccioli calls.

Saturday, SEPT. 15.—O———. Trip to Vico Pisano with the Williams'.

Monday, SEPT. 17.—The Williams' to dinner. Go to Pisa with them.

Tuesday, SEPT. 18.—Picnic on the Pugnano Mountain. Music in the evening. Sleep there.

Wednesday, SEPT. 19.—Shelley goes to Pisa. Edward bathes here. Finish "Anastasius." The Guiccioli calls.

Thursday, SEPT. 20.—Williams to dinner. Go with Jane to Pisa.

Monday, SEPT. 24.—Go to Pisa with Jane.

Tuesday, SEPT. 25.—Go to Pisa with Edward. Call on the Guiccioli. Pugnano in the evening.

Thursday, SEPT. 28.—Edward here. Copy. Go to Pugnano after dinner. Copy.

Friday, SEPT. 29.—Go to Pisa with Jane. The Williams' dine here.

Saturday, SEPT. 30.—Copy. Clare calls. Shelley goes to Pisa.

All October is left out, it seems. We are at the Baths, occupied with furnishing our house, copying my novel, &c., &c.[54]

Thursday, Nov. 1.—Go to Florence.[55] Copy. Ride with Guiccioli. Albe [Lord Byron] arrives.[56]

53 A novel (1819, 3 vols.).

54 In her diary for October 25 Claire notes, "Mary removing to Pisa" from the Baths of Pisa. Williams's journal for the same date says (p. 19), "The Shelleys go into their new house." The Shelleys occupied an apartment "at the top of the Tre Palazzi di Chiesa" (Mary to Mrs. Gisborne, November 30, 1821, *Letters*, I, 150). The Williamses took a lower flat in the same house.

55 This probably should read, "Claire goes to Florence."

Friday, Nov. 2.—Copy. Read [Byron's] "Cain." Shelley calls on Albe. Mr. Taaffe calls.

Saturday, Nov. 3.—Copy. Call on the Guiccioli. Walk.

Sunday, Nov. 4.—The Williams' arrive.[57] Copy. Call on the Guiccioli.

Monday, Nov. 5.—Williams calls on Albe. A rainy day. Copy. P[ietro] G[amba].[58]

Tuesday, Nov. 6.—Copy. Albe calls. P[ietro] and T[eresa] G[uiccioli].

Wednesday, Nov. 7.—Copy.

Thursday, Nov. 8.—Call on the Guiccioli. Ride out with her, and meet Albe. She and Taaffe in the evening.

Saturday, Nov. 10.—Walk. Copy. Read the "German's Tale."[59] Ride with Countess Guiccioli. She and Pietro in the evening. Mr. Spooner calls.

Thursday, Nov. [11–]15.—Copy. Read [Godwin's] "Caleb Williams" to Jane. Ride with the Guiccioli. Shelley goes on translating S[pinoz]a with Edward.[60] Medwin arrives [on Nov. 14]. Taaffe calls. Argyropulo calls. Good news from the Greeks.

Friday, Nov. 16.—Finish "Caleb Williams" to Jane. Copy. Ride with the Guiccioli. Medwin to dinner.

Tuesday, Nov. 28.—Ride with the Guiccioli. Suffer much with rheumatism in my head.

Wednesday, Nov. 29.—† I mark this day because I begin my Greek again, and that is a study which ever delights me. I do not feel the bore of it, as in learning another language, although it be so difficult, it so richly repays one; yet I read little, for I am not well. Shelley and the Williams' go to Leghorn;[61] they dine with us afterwards with Medwin. Write to Clare.

Thursday, Nov. 30.—Correct the novel. Read a little Greek. Not well. Ride with the Guiccioli. The Count Pietro in the evening.

Saturday, Dec. 1.—Read "The History of Shipwrecks."[62] Not well. Correct the novel. The Williams' and Medwin the evening.

56 Byron occupied the Palazzo Lanfranchi, "the finest palace on the Lung' Arno," according to Shelley (Julian edition, X, 318).

57 They moved from Pugnano to Pisa.

58 Brother of Teresa Guiccioli.

59 "Kruitzner or the German's Tale," Vol. IV of *The Canterbury Tales* (1797–1805, 5 vols.), by Harriet Lee. It was dramatized as *Werner* by Byron, who had begun work on it by December 21, 1821, according to Williams's *Journal* (p. 30).

60 See *Journal of E. E. Williams,* 25–26.

61 In his *Journal* (pp. 27–28) Williams relates an interesting incident which occurred in Leghorn on this occasion.

62 Possibly Sir John G. Dalyell, *Shipwreck and Disasters at Sea* (Edinburgh, 1812, 3 vols.; published anonymously).

Sunday, DEC. 2.—Read "The History of Shipwrecks." Read Herodotus with Shelley. Ride with La Guiccioli. Pietro and her in the evening.

Monday, DEC. 3.—Write letters. Read Herodotus with Shelley. Finish C. A.[63] to Jane. Taaffe calls. He says that his Turk is a very moral man, for that when he began to tell a scandalous story he interrupted him immediately, saying, "Ah! we must never speak thus of our neighbours." Taaffe would do well to take the hint.

Tuesday, DEC. 4.—Read Herodotus with Shelley in the evening. First with the Williams', and then call on the Guiccioli. Read Tacitus.

Wednesday, DEC. 5.—Read Milton on Divorce.[64] Walk with the Williams' to the Garden. A divine day. Spend the evening at M. Mason's. Read Tacitus.

Thursday, DEC. 6.—Read Homer. Walk with Williams. Spend the evening with them. Call on T. Guiccioli with Jane, while Taaffe amuses Shelley and Edward.[65] Read Tacitus. A dismal day.

Friday, DEC. 7.—Letter from Hunt and Bessy. Walk with Shelley. Buy furniture for them, &c. Walk with Edward and Jane to the Garden, and return with T. Guiccioli in the carriage. Edward reads the "Shipwreck of the 'Wager' "[66] to us in the evening.

Saturday, DEC. 8.—Get up late and talk with Shelley. The Williams' and Medwin to dinner. Walk with Edward and Jane in the Garden. Return with T. Guiccioli. T. Guiccioli and Pietro in the evening. Write to Clare. Read Tacitus.

Sunday, DEC. 9.—Go to church at Dr. Nott's.[67] Walk with Edward and Jane to the Garden. In the evening first Pietro and Teresa, afterwards go to the Williams'.

Monday, DEC. 10.—Out shopping. Walk with the Williams' and T. Guiccioli to the Garden. Medwin at tea. Afterwards we are alone, and after reading a little Herodotus, Shelley reads Chaucer's "Flower and the Leaf," and then Chaucer's "Dream"[68] to me. Read Tacitus. A divine, cold, tramontana day.

Tuesday, DEC. 11.—Rise late. Walk with Edward, and then ride with

63 Probably should be C. W. for *Caleb Williams,* though the entry for November 16 reads "Finish 'Caleb Williams' to Jane."

64 *The Doctrine and Discipline of Divorce* (1643).

65 By telling them about the poet Monti's going to bed for the winter (Williams's *Journal,* 29–30).

66 Probably a part of "The History of Shipwrecks."

67 George Frederick Nott (1767–1841). The services were held on the ground floor of the Tre Palazzo. See entries for December 16, 1821; February 24, March 3, and April 10, 1822. See White, II, 339–40.

68 According to Williams's *Journal* (p. 30), Shelley read *Chaucer's Dream* aloud again on December 20.

the Guiccioli. She spends the evening here with Edward and Jane and Medwin. Shelley reads aloud after tea. Read Herodotus with him. At night read Tacitus.

Wednesday, DEC. 12.—Read [Scott's] "Ivanhoe." Walk with the Williams'. While we are with them Shelley hears a rumour of a man to be burnt at Lucca.[69] Calls on Lord Byron with Medwin.

Thursday, DEC. 13.—Read "Ivanhoe." Out shopping. Work. Edward and Jane in the evening. Shelley at M. Mason's. Mr. Taaffe calls. We find the burning story to be all false.

Friday, DEC. 14.—Read Homer. Work. Shelley reads Lord Byron's "Heaven and Earth" in the evening.[70]

Saturday, DEC. 15.—Read Homer and [Scott's] "Waverley." Work. Ride with T. Guiccioli. In the evening I go to the Williams'.

Sunday, DEC. 16.—Read "Waverley." Go to church. Walk to the garden with Edward and Jane. They spend the evening with us. Shelley goes to M. Mason's. Medwin dines at Mrs. Beauclerk's.

Monday, DEC. 17.—Shelley, Williams, and Medwin dine with Taaffe at Lord Byron's. T. Guiccioli calls. Dine with Jane, and spend the evening there.

Tuesday, DEC. 18.—Rain and wind commences. Spend the evening at Casa Silva. Read Homer and [Scott's] the "Antiquary."

Wednesday, DEC. 19.—Rain and wind. Shelley goes out in the boat. Read the "Antiquary." Walk with Jane.

Thursday, DEC. 20.—Go in the carriage with T. Guiccioli. The Williams' in the evening. Read [Scott's] "Rob Roy."

Wednesday, DEC. 26.—Shelley dines with Lord Byron. Call on the Greek,[71] and Lady Synnot. Ride out with T. Guiccioli. Go to the Opera, &c., &c.

69 See Dowden, II, 450–51; and White, II, 339.

70 On this date Williams wrote: "In the evening went to S[helley], who read aloud a poem of Lord B.'s, which he had only finished the day before. It is called 'Heaven and Earth, a Mystery.' "—*Journal,* 30.

71 The Argyropuli did not sail with Mavrocordato on June 26; they left Pisa for Florence on February 28, 1822.

1822[1]

ITALY

Sunday, JAN. 13.—Read [Rousseau's] "Emile." Walk with Jane and ride with T. Guiccioli. The Opera in the evening with the Williams', Benno, and Bartolini.[2]

Monday, JAN. 14.—Read "Emile." Call on T. Guiccioli and see Lord Byron. [Edward John] Trelawney arrives.

Tuesday, JAN. 15.—Read "Emile." Walk with the Williams' and E. Trelawney to the Garden. They all dine with us. The Opera in the evening.[3]

[1] The unrecorded days of December 27, 1821—January 12, 1822, are partially covered by the *Journal of E. E. Williams* (1902). The *Journal* also supplies many important facts not recorded by Mary, whose entries are usually very brief—an indication of how busy she was rather than of a lack of interest in her journal. Mary printed most of Williams's journal from April 28 to the end on July 4 in her edition of the *Essays,* &c. (1840) as a long footnote to Letters 63 and 66 of the "Letters from Italy." (It is worth noting that the following entries which she prints are not printed in the *Journal* as published in 1902: May 12 [the May 9–12 entries in the 1902 edition should be May 8–11], May 15, 22.) Richard Garnett published additional extracts in *The Fortnightly Review* for June, 1878; and Mary's and Garnett's extracts were combined and printed by H. B. Forman in his edition of Shelley's *Prose Works* (1880; IV, 310–25). Dowden printed other hitherto unpublished extracts in 1886.

[2] Lorenzo Bartolini, sculptor, who was making a bust of Byron.

[3] Extracts from the *Journal of E. E. Williams* (pp. 35–36): *"Tuesday, January 15th.* Trelawny called, and brought with him the model of an American schooner, on which it is settled with S[helley] and myself to build a boat thirty feet long, and T[relawny] writes to Roberts at Genoa to commence on it directly.

"Saturday, January 19th. Accompanied T[relawny] in his tilbury as before. Called on Lord B[yron] who wishes to have a boat on the model of ours now building at Genoa, intending to enter into a competition with us in sailing. Played with him till evening, dined with S.'s and go to the new opera, Henry the Fifth, a dull insipid concern.

Sunday, January 20th: Fine. Mary and Jane in a carriage, and Trelawny and myself in the tilbury, proceed to Pugnano, and ascend a short distance up Monte Maggiore, where after a tiffin we practice firing at a half-crown, which T. hits three times. Return about half past four, and dine with the Shelleys on the side of a wild boar which Captain Hay sent from the Maremma. Pass the evening there.

"Wednesday, January 23rd. Fine. S. breakfasts here. . . . Trelawny called, and tying his horse to the knocker while he wrote a note, the animal, trying to get away, broke the harness, &c., and deprived us of our ride. . . . Called on Lord B., and walked with Mary and Jane.

"Thursday, January 24th. . . . Dined with Lord B., and met there a Captain Scott, and the same party as before. Lord B. receives a volume containing 'Sardanapalus', 'The Two Foscari', and 'Cain.' . . .

"Saturday, January 26th. S. sent us some beautiful but too melancholy lines ('The Serpent is shut out from Paradise', &c.)."

Wednesday, JAN. 16.—Work. Walk with the same party; they dine with Albe. Dine with Jane. Read Albe's tragedy ["Werner"] to her.

Thursday, JAN. 17.—Copy. Walk with Jane. The Opera in the evening with the Williams' and E. Trelawney.

Friday, JAN. 18.—Copy. Walk with Jane. Spend the evening with her. Late, Taaffe, Trelawney, Edward, and Shelley come.

Saturday, JAN. 19.—Copy. Walk with Jane. The Opera in the evening. Trelawney is extravagant—un giovane stravagante—partly natural and partly perhaps put on, but it suits him well, and if his abrupt but not unpolished manners be assumed, they are nevertheless in unison with his Moorish face (for he looks Oriental yet not Asiatic) his dark hair, his Herculean form, and then there is an air of extreme good nature which pervades his whole countenance, especially when he smiles, which assures me that his heart is good. He tells strange stories of himself, horrific ones, so that they harrow one up, while with his emphatic but unmodulated voice, his simple yet strong language, he pourtrays the most frightful situations; then all these adventures took place between the age of thirteen and twenty. I believe them now I see the man, and, tired with the everyday sleepiness of human intercourse, I am glad to meet with one, who, among other valuable qualities, has the rare merit of interesting my imagination. The *crew* and Medwin dine with us.

Sunday, JAN. 20.—Ride with Jane to Pugnano. The *crew* and Medwin dine with us. T. Guiccioli and Pietro in the evening.

Monday, JAN. 21.—Walk with Jane. Copy. The Corsair crew and Medwin dine at Williams'. Spend the evening here. Write to Clare.

Tuesday, JAN. 22.—Walk with Jane. Copy. She dines with me; the rest dine with Trelawney, and join us in the evening with Taaffe.

Wednesday, JAN. 23.—Copy. Walk. E. Trelawney dines with us; go with him to Mrs. Beauclerc's in the evening.

Thursday, JAN. 24.—Copy. Read [Byron's] "Sardanapalus." E. Trelawney and Edward call; they dine at Lord Byron's; Jane dines with me. T. Guiccioli in the evening.

Friday, JAN. 25.—Finish copying. E. Trelawney and Edward call, and the Baron Lutzerode. Go to Mrs. Beauclerc's in the evening.

Saturday, JAN. 26.—Write to William [Godwin, Jr.]. Walk with Jane. Trelawney and the Williams' dine with us. Read the "Two Foscari" [of Byron].

Sunday, JAN. 27.—Read Homer. Walk. Dine at the Williams'. The Opera in the evening. Ride with T. Guiccioli.

Monday, JAN. 28.—The Williams' breakfast with us. Go down to Bocca d' Arno in the boat with Shelley and Jane. Edward and E. Trelawney meet us there; return in the gig; they dine with us; very tired.

Tuesday, JAN. 29.—Work. Walk with Jane. Read Homer. Ride with T. Guiccioli. To the Opera in the evening with Edward and Jane. Trelawney sits with us until late.

Wednesday, JAN. 30.—Read Homer and Tacitus. Ride with T. Guiccioli. E. Trelawney and Medwin to dinner. The Baron Lutzerode in the evening.

> But as the torrent widens towards the ocean,
> We ponder deeply on each past emotion.

Read the 1st vol. of the "Pirate" [by Scott].

Thursday, JAN. 31.—Read Homer. Work. Walk with Jane. In the evening, call on the Guiccioli.

Friday, FEB. 1.—Read the second volume of the "Pirate." Edward with me in the morning. Walk to the Garden [with Jane and Edward to meet Lord Byron]. Edward, Jane, Trelawney, and Medwin to dinner. Taaffe, Baron von Lutzerode, and Mr. Spooner call.

Saturday, FEB. 2.—Go through the Pine Forest to the sea with Shelley and Jane. [Return about three o'clock.] Read the third volume of the "Pirate." In the evening go to the Williams'.

Sunday, FEB. 3.—Read Homer. Walk to the Garden with Jane. Return with Medwin to dinner. Trelawney in the evening. A wild day and night; some clouds in the sky in the morning, but they clear away. A south wind.

Monday, FEB. 4.—Read Homer. Breakfast with the Williams'. Edward, Jane, and Trelawney go to Leghorn. Walk with Jane. Southey's letter concerning Lord Byron.[4] Write to Clare. In the evening Jane, the Gambas and Taaffe.

Tuesday, FEB. 5.—Read Homer. Read Tacitus. Read "Emile" and first canto of Dante. Walk with Jane on the Leghorn road and ride with T. Guiccioli. Edward and Trelawney return in the evening.[5]

[4] Southey's letter, dated Keswick, January 5, 1822, in *The Courier* (printed in Byron's *Works,* Letters and Journals, ed. by R. E. Prothero [London, John Murray, 1898–1901, 6 vols.], VI, 389–92). Byron immediately sent a challenge to Southey through Douglas Kinnaird, who did not forward it.

[5] Extracts from the *Journal of E. E. Williams* (pp. 37–40): "*Tuesday, February 5th.* T. wrote definitively to Roberts.

"*Thursday, February 7th.* Fine. Left Pisa at eleven with S. for Spezzia, in order to look for a summer residence. The Governor being absent, we departed without any signature to our passports. Bad road for most part as far as Pietra Santa. At this place we suffered the caleche to precede us, while we sauntered carelessly after it to avoid the detention which the police would have occasioned. The guard hailed the carriage, but suffered us to pass unquestioned. The scenery from this place to Massa is truly Arcadian. . . .

"*Friday, February 8th.* Fine. Grand and sublime scenery. Left Massa at half past eight. Crossed the Magra near Sarzana, and arrived at Spezzia at three o'clock. At Sarzana we

Wednesday, FEB. 6.—Read second canto of Dante. Walk with Jane. Trelawney to dinner. T. Guiccioli and her brother call. In the evening to the Opera.

Thursday, FEB. 7.—Read Homer, Tacitus, and "Emile." Shelley and Edward depart for La Spezzia. Walk with Jane, and to the Opera with her in the evening. With E. Trelawney afterwards to Mrs. Beauclerc's ball. During a long long evening in mixed society how often do one's sensations change, and, swift as the west wind drives the shadows of clouds across the sunny hill or the waving corn, so swift do sensations pass, painting—yet, oh! not disfiguring—the serenity of the mind. It is then that life seems to weigh itself, and hosts of memories and imaginations, thrown into one scale, make the other kick the beam. You remember what you have felt, what you have dreamt; yet you dwell on the shadowy side, and lost hopes and death, such as you have seen it, seem to cover all things with a funeral pall. The time that was, is, and will be, presses upon you, and, standing the centre of a moving circle, you "slide giddily as the world reels." You look to Heaven and would demand of the everlasting stars that the thoughts and passions which are your life may be as everliving as they. You would demand of the blue empyrean that your mind might be as clear as it, and that the tears which gather in your eyes might be the shower that would drain from its profoundest

called on Mr. Lucciardi, to whom Vacca had given us letters. He again introduced us by these means to a Canon at Spezzia, who accompanied us in a boat to the western shores of the bay, but without offering the slightest hope that we could be accommodated with a house or houses. We looked into every hovel, but in vain. Dined and slept at Spezzia.

"*Saturday, February 9th.* Fine. Beautiful day. Rose early and took boat for Lerici. On going ashore to see some fishermen drag their net, an old man among them said he knew of some houses, and would accompany us. He showed us many; but two pleased us particularly. Walked a long distance in search of others, but found nothing. Returned in the boat to Spezzia, and left that place again for Sarzana, to enquire about the two houses which we had seen. Arrived at Sarzana at six o'clock, where we dined and slept. *Aquila Nera,* a clean inn—not very dear.

"*Sunday, February 10th.* Fine. Signor Luciardi called and told us that Madame Catani's house was positively not to be had, but that the one on the beach would be let for 100 crowns a year. Went to Lerici in the afternoon, and took a boat across the bay to see a house opposite Porto Venere. Returned to Sarzana to dinner, and slept there.

"*Monday, February 11th.* Fine. Left Sarzana at nine o'clock. Arrived to dinner at Via-Reggio at three, and at Pisa at 7. Dreadful road.

"*Tuesday, February 12th.* Consulted with S. about a new tragedy. T. called and brought with him R[obert]s' drawing of Lord B.'s boat.

"*Monday, February 18th.* Jane unwell. S. turns physician. Called on Lord B., who talks of getting up Othello. Laid a wager with S. that Lord B. quits Italy before six months. Jane put on a Hindostanee dress, and passed the evening with Mary, who had also the Turkish costume.

"*Sunday, February 24th.* Fine. Claire calls. . . . Call on Lord B., beat him at billiards, and played till evening with Trelawny. The S.'s, M., and T. dine here.

"*Monday, February 25th.* Fine. Claire leaves us for Florence."

depths the springs of weakness and sorrow. But where are the stars? Where the blue empyrean? A ceiling clouds that, and a thousand swift consuming lights supply the place of the eternal ones of Heaven. The enthusiast suppresses her tears, crushes her opening thoughts, and—But all is changed; some word, some look excite the lagging blood, laughter dances in the eyes and the spirits rise proportionably high.

> "The Queen is all for revels, her light heart,
> Unladen from the heaviness of state,
> Bestows itself upon delightfulness."

Friday, Feb. 8.—Sometimes I awaken from my visionary monotony and my thoughts flow until, as it is exquisite pain to stop the flowing of the blood, so it is painful to check expression and make the overflowing mind return to its usual channel. I feel a kind of tenderness to those, whoever they may be (even though strangers), who awaken the train and touch a chord so full of harmony and thrilling music, when I would tear the veil from this strange world and pierce with eagle eyes beyond the sun; when every idea, strange and changeful, is another step in the ladder by which I would climb the———

Read "Emile." Jane dines with me, walk with her, E. Trelawney and Jane in the evening. Trelawney tells us a number of amusing stories of his early life. Read third canto of "L'Inferno."

They say that Providence is shown by the extraction that may be ever made of good from evil, that we draw our virtues from our faults. So I am to thank God for making me weak. I might say, "Thy will be done," but I cannot applaud the permitter of self-degradation, though dignity and superior wisdom arise from its bitter and burning ashes.

Saturday, Feb. 9.—Read "Emile." Walk with Jane, and ride with T. Guiccioli. Dine with Jane. Taaffe and T. Medwin call. I retire with E. Trelawney, who amuses me as usual by the endless variety of his adventures and conversation.

Sunday, Feb. 10.—Read "Emile," Homer, and fourth canto of "L'Inferno." Walk with Jane and ride with T. Guiccioli. E. Trelawney dines with me. To the Opera with him and Jane in the evening.

Monday, Feb. 11.—Read Homer and "Emile." Walk. Jane and T. Medwin dine with me. Edward and Shelley return in the evening.

Tuesday, Feb. 12.—Read Homer, Tacitus, and "Emile." Walk. Pietro and Taaffe call. Call on the Williams'.

Wednesday, Feb. 13.—Read Homer and "Anastasius." Walk with Jane. Trelawney in the evening.

Thursday, Feb. 14.—Read Homer and [Hope's] "Anastasius." Walk with the Williams' in the evening. "Nothing of us but what must suffer a sea change."

Friday, FEB. 15.—The tigers are tamed, and Lady Noel dies.[6] Ride with T. Guiccioli. The Williams' and Trelawney dine with us. Read Homer and "Anastasius."

Saturday, FEB. 16.—Read Homer and "Anastasius." Walk with Jane. T. Medwin and Trelawney dine and spend the evening with us.

Sunday, FEB. 17.—Finish "Anastasius." Walk with the Williams'. Ride with T. Guiccioli. Dine at Williams'. The Veglione in the evening.

Monday, FEB. 18.—Read Homer. Walk with the Williams'. Jane, Trelawney, and Medwin in the evening.

Tuesday, FEB. 19.—Read [Mary Wollstonecraft's] "Letters from Norway." Call on the Greeks. Walk with Shelley. Ride with T. Guiccioli. To the Veglione in the evening with Jane, Trelawney, and Shelley.

Wednesday, FEB. 20.—Shelley and Trelawney go to Leghorn; they return late to dinner.

Thursday, FEB. 21.—Read Homer with Jane. Clare arrives.

Friday, FEB. 22.—Talk with Clare.[7] Spend the evening at the Williams'. Mrs. Ramsay calls.

Saturday, FEB. 23.—Talk with Clare. Walk with Jane. They all dine with us.

Sunday, FEB. 24.—Go to church. Call on Mrs. Beauclerc. Walk with Jane, and dine there.

Monday, FEB. 25.—What a mart this world is! Feelings, sentiments—more invaluable than gold or precious stones—are the coin, and what is bought? Contempt, discontent and disappointment, if indeed the mind be not loaded with drearier memories. And what say the worldly to this? Use Spartan coin, pay away iron and lead alone, and store up your precious metal. But alas! from nothing, nothing comes, or, as all things seem to degenerate, give lead and you will receive clay—the most contemptible of all lives, is where you live in the world and none of your passions or affections are called into action. I am convinced I could not live thus, and as Sterne says, that in solitude he would worship a tree, so in the world I should attach myself to those who bore the semblance of those qualities which I admire. But it is not this that I want; let me love the trees, the skies and the ocean, and that all encompassing spirit of which I may soon become a part—let me, in my fellow creature, love that which is,—and not fix my affection on a fair form endued with imaginary at-

[6] Lady Byron's mother.

[7] Claire was greatly agitated and had determined to leave Italy. See Claire's letter of February 18, 1822, to Byron (Dowden, II, 484–86), and Mary's urgent letter of February 10, [1822] to Claire (*Letters,* I, 157).

tributes; where goodness, kindness and talent are, let me love and admire them at their just rate, neither adorning, or diminishing, and, above all, let me fearlessly descend into the remotest caverns of my own mind, carry the torch of self-knowledge into its dimmest recesses: but too happy if I dislodge any evil spirit or enshrine a new deity in some hitherto uninhabited nook.

Read [Mary Wollstonecraft's] "Wrongs of Woman," and Homer. Clare departs. Walk with Jane. Ride with T. Guiccioli. Spend the evening at Mrs. Mason's.

Tuesday, FEB. 26.—Read Homer, and "Wrongs of Woman." Walk with Jane, and ride with T. Guiccioli. T. Guiccioli dines with us.

Wednesday, FEB. 27.—Read letters. Walk with Edward. Ride with T. Guiccioli. In the evening the Williams' and T. Guiccioli.

Thursday, FEB. 28.—Take leave of the Argyropulos.[8] Walk with Shelley. Ride with T. Guiccioli. Read letters. Spend the evening at the Williams'. Trelawney there.

Friday, MAR. 1.—An embassy. Work. My first Greek lesson. Walk with Edward. In the evening work.

Saturday, MAR. 2.—Read Homer. Walk with Jane. Spend the evening at Mrs. Beauclerc's.[9]

[8] They were going to Florence.

[9] Extracts from the *Journal of E. E. Williams* (pp. 40–50): "*Saturday, March 2nd.* Met S. in his boat. Sailed back with him.

"*Friday, March 8th.* Dined with Lord B. During dinner S. repeated some of the finest lines of 'Childe Harold,' and Lord B., after listening to a stanza, cried, 'Heavens, S., what infinite nonsense are you quoting?'

"*Thursday, March 14th.* S. and T. sailed in the boat, and on our return, in passing the bridge, were hailed by the Custom House officers. Not, however, paying any attention to them (we have frequently passed without interruption), they seized the boat, threatened to imprison our servant, and without our paying fifty livres they declare it shall become their property. S. wrote to the minister of police about it. [Boat ordered to be given up.]

"*Wednesday, March 20th.* Called on B. Kinnaird did not think it necessary to present Lord B.'s challenge to fight Southey, and therefore this contemptible affair is dropped for the moment. Walked with Shelley along the banks of the Arno. Took our writing materials, and while S. translated Calderon's 'Cyprian,' I wrote some revisions.

"*Thursday, March 21st.* Fine. Wrote a few lines. Trelawny called. He has heard from Roberts that S.'s boat will be launched to-day. T. writes to R. to send her round to Viareggio, when they will me[e]t her, and proceed to Genoa to bring Lord B.'s schooner round. Mary and Jane accompany T. and myself in the boat up the Arno. Trelawny dined. Went to the theatre. Saw Charles XIIth. A tolerable actor in Charles.

"*Sunday, March 24th.* Fine. Mary sends in, asking us to accompany her to Viareggio, but are deterred from going by finding the morning too far advanced to enable us to return this evening. Walked with Trelawny and S. upon the Argine. Called on Lord B.

"At home, writing till five o'clock. Went to dine at S.'s, and after sitting for a considerable time waiting for their return home, I was surprised at the lateness of the evening. Trelawny at length came in, and told us that Lord B.'s party, consisting of himself, Shelley, Captain Hay, Count Gamba (the son), and Taaffe were riding, and the Countess with

EDWARD ELLERKER WILLIAMS

From a sketch by himself

Courtesy of the British Museum

Mrs. S[helley], were behind in the carriage, when a mounted dragoon dashed through their party and touched Taaffe's horse as he passed, in an insolent and defying manner. Lord B. put spurs to his horse, saying that he should give some account of such insolence. S.'s horse, however, was the fleetest, and coming up to the dragoon he crossed and stopped him till the party arrived, but they had now reached the gate where a guard was stationed, and finding himself so well supported, he drew his sword, and after abusing them all as cursed English (maledetti Inglesi) began to cut and slash to the right and left, and what signified it to him if he had the blood of all the English robbers—saying he arrested them all. 'Do that if you can,' said Lord B., and dashed through the guard with young Count Gamba, and reached home to bring arms for what he expected would turn to a serious scuffle. The dragoon, finding the rest of the party intended to force their way, made a desperate cut at Shelley, who took off his cap, and warding the blow from the sharp part of the sabre, the hilt struck his head and knocked him from his horse; the fellow was repeating a cut at S. when down, when Captain Hay parried with a cane he had in his hand, but the sword cut it in two, and struck Captain H.'s face across the nose. A violent scene now took place, and the dragoon tried to get into town and escape, when Lord B. arrived, and half drawing a sword-stick to show that he was armed, the fellow put up his sword and begged of Lord B. to do the same. It was now dark, and after walking a few paces with Lord B. he put his horse into a gallop and endeavoured to get off, but on passing Lord B.'s house, a servant had armed himself with a pitchfork, and speared him as he passed. He fell from his horse and was carried to the hospital. The wound is in the abdomen.

"Trelawny had finished his story when Lord B. came in, the Countess fainting on his arm, S. sick from the blow, Lord B. and the young Count foaming with rage. Mrs. S. looking philosophically upon this interesting scene, and Jane and I wondering what the devil was to come next. A surgeon came, and Lord B. took him with the Countess home, where she was bled and soon came round. Taaffe next entered, and after having given his deposition at the Police Station, returned to us with a long face, saying that the dragoon could not live out the night. All soon sallied forth again to be the first to accuse, and according to Italian policy not wait to be accused. All again return, mutually recriminated and recriminating. 9 o'clock. The report already in circulation about Pisa is that a party of peasants having risen in insurrection, made an attack upon the guard, headed by some Englishmen, that the guard maintained their ground manfully against an awful number of the armed insurgents, that they were at length defeated—one Englishman, whose name was Trelawny, left dead at the gate, and Lord B. mortally wounded, who is now telling me the tale—and I drinking brandy and water by his side.

"Ten o'clock. How the attack ought to have been conducted is now agitating. All appear to me to be wrong. 11 o'clock—disperse to our separate homes.

"Monday, March 25th. Cloudy. At 7 this morning an officer from the police called here, demanding my name, country, profession, and requesting to have an account of my actions between the hours of 6 and 8 yesterday evening. My servants told him I was then asleep, but that they could inform him that I was engaged in a very bloody scene between those hours.

" 'Then he must come to the Police office.' 'Ask him,' said I, 'if I am to bring the scene or the whole play as far as I have written.' 12 o'clock S. calls. The wounded dragoon much worse. Hear that the soldiers are confined to their barracks, but they swear to be revenged on some of us. The Countess G. better, as well as Captain Hay. A report is now abroad that Taaffe is the assassin, and is now confined in Lord B.'s house, guarded by bull-dogs, &c., to avoid the police. This he overheard himself while walking down the Lung Arno. T. and I think it necessary to go armed. A skate strap is therefore substituted for a pistol belt, and my pistols so slung to T.'s waist.

"2. [o'clock] Sallied forth very much stared and pointed at. Called on Lord B. Heard that extreme unction had been administered to the dragoon, whose wound is considered mortal. A deposition is drawn up, and sent with all the signatures concerned to the Police.

"The Grand Duke is expected to-night.

"4 o'clock. The dragoon dying. Half-past 4. All armed with sword-sticks, pistols, &c.,

mount as usual amidst a great crowd that surround the door. Nothing new on their return except a great crowd to see them dismount.

"10 o'clock. T. called here after having been with Lord B. The dragoon much worse.

"The Grand Duke arrived.

"Tuesday, March 26th. Cloudy. I hurry to breakfast. S. received a note from a lady last night, desiring him not to venture near her house after dark, for the friends of the dragoon were on the look out for him, although they did not consider him as most to blame.

"The young Gamba joined a party of gossips that had collected round a spezeria, and joining in the conversation as if he had been unconcerned in the business, said it was a pity that a man was so dangerously wounded. 'Ah, the only pity is,' said a fellow, 'that in ten days the affair will be forgotten and the cursed English will go abroad as secure as ever.'

"Jane's music master comes and informs us that the report is the dragoon is better, but raves like a madman against the English.

"11 o'clock. Called on T. previous to going to Captain Hay's, met there Vacca who had just quitted his patient, the dragoon. V. thinks him better, but not out of danger. The man's story is that he was held by one of Lord B.'s servants, while the other stabbed him, and that he should not have drawn his sword had he not been horsewhipped by some one of the party. This was strongly denied by us to Vacca, who seemed to view the thing in a most unfavourable light, and declares that in any court of justice he could swear conscientiously that the wound was given with a stiletto having three sides like a bayonet.

"Called on Captain Hay with T. Found him doing well, but his face is much cut and bruised. On our mentioning to him what we considered a falsehood in the dragoon having said he was struck, Hay confirmed the fact by saying the young Count Gamba cut him with his whip as he passed. The affair consequently takes a serious turn in the man's favour.

"3 o'clock. Called on Lord B. The police had only proceeded so far as to require the evidence of his courier. Suspicion as to the person who really stabbed the dragoon much excited. Nothing else new. They ride as usual.

"7 o'clock. The wound neither better nor worse. Trelawny dined with us, and Mary passed the evening. It is a singular circumstance that an affair of a similar nature occurred to one of this man's brothers, and having been cured of a wound which he had received in a scuffle, he waited concealed for the person whom he suspected, stabbed him to the heart and flung him into the river!

"Wednesday, March 27th. Fine. The man better than yesterday, and hopes are entertained. It is T.'s opinion that on recovery this man will demand the *satisfaction of a gentleman,* and some of the *most respectable Italians* think that it ought not to be refused to him. T. breakfasted here, and we afterwards went to the post together. A letter from Roberts informs us that the boat will not be finished in less than 12 or 14 days.

"On our way met the young Count Gamba with a deposition from a gentleman of the name of Crawford, who from a balcony had seen Lord B. return. He says, that Lord B. did not dismount from his horse, but called to the servants from the door. They brought him a walking-stick with which he returned to meet the dragoon, who on seeing him put out his hand which Lord B. accepted, demanding his name. At this moment one of Lord B.'s servants interposed, and pushed the dragoon from his master's side, and on the dragoon putting his horse into a gallop, he observed a man rush at him with a pole, and nearly thrust him from his horse, from which he fell shortly afterwards. Lord B. seemed collected, and on requiring of the dragoon some explanation of his conduct, he replied, 'This is not the place,' and hurried onward, when he met the fatal blow from the pitchfork.

"12 o'clock. Walked with T. and S., and sailed up the river with them.

"4 o'clock. Went with T. to Lord B.'s.

"The man remains in the same state.

"Taaffe, who during the affair could not be found, and who has since talked so greatly of his valour upon the occasion, has been named by Jane *False Taaffe.*

"Walked with Mary and Jane, and met the Countess G., who accompanied us. At 9 p.m. Trelawny and S. called. Went to Lord B.'s together; found him engaged in a letter to the

Sunday, MAR. 3.—A note to, and a visit from Dr. Nott. Go to Church. Walk. The Williams' and Trelawney to dinner.

Monday, MAR. 4.—Greek lesson. Walk. Call on T. Guiccioli. See Albe. Write to Marianne.[10] Call on T. Medwin.

Tuesday, MAR. 5.—Copy. Walk. Jane and Edward in the evening.

Wednesday, MAR. 6.—Copy. A Greek lesson. Walk with Jane and ride with T. Guiccioli. Trelawney to breakfast. In the evening at the Williams'. Trelawney there.

British Ambassador. His servants Tita and Vincenzo had been examined, and Vincenzo acquitted, when the silly fellow accompanied Tita back to make his deposition, and who, though innocent, was mad enough to go into court armed with a stiletto and a brace of pistols. They were subsequently both imprisoned and remained confined in separate cells. Left Lord B. at 11. During our stay there his secretary was sent for by the police and examined, but nothing transpired.

"*Thursday, March 28th.* Fine. Vacca, who is prejudiced, says the man is neither better nor worse, and is further convinced of the wound having been given with a stiletto, as it passed through the dragoon's sword belt, and left a mark or hole that he could not mistake. Mr. Todd's opinion is that the man is better. Report in Pisa is that Lord B. and all his servants, with four English gentlemen, were taken in Lord B.'s house last night after a desperate resistance, that forty brace of pistols were discovered, stilettos, &c., and at Leghorn they have it, that the party returning home, Sunday evening, attacked a division of dragoons, and after being taken prisoners stabbed three of them in the neck, and that Lord B. and all the party had fled to Lucca.

"12 o'clock. Man as before.

"Nothing new.

"4 o'clock. Walked with Mary and Jane. All quiet.

"5 o'clock. Saw a party of dragoons on bridge watching Lord B. and party as it passed.

"7. [o'clock.] Mary dined. Antonio, the Countess G.'s servant, confined with the others. Went to the theatre.

"*Friday, March 29th.* Fine. The dragoon much better, and likely to do well. It is singular, Vacca, who has been so forward to instigate the police, should have pronounced the man out of danger three days ago.

"10. Walked with Jane to the Botanical Gardens, a place fitted for the improvement of the young students, but nothing to the advancement of the science. There is a museum and other curiosities here, but nothing worthy any particular notice, that I saw.

"1 o'clock. Called on Captain Hay. Found him doing well. He had heard that my name had been substituted for his in the affair, that my nose had been cut off, and that Lord B. and myself had left Pisa with as many horses as could be put to the carriage.

"2 o'clock. Vincenzo and another man liberated. Strong suspicions of Antonio, the Countess's man.

"Called on Lord B. He had received an answer from Mr. Dawkins, the Chargé d'affaires at Florence, offering every assistance, but speaking very lightly of the affair. Nothing new, excepting that a law officer from Florence arrived to take the several depositions.

"Taaffe's conduct highly blameable, but his very deposition damns him.

"7. Trelawny dined and passed the evening.

"*Saturday, March 30th.* Fine. Shelley breakfasted. The dragoon considerably recovered and doing well.

"Nothing new. At Florence the reports are favourable to us. Wrote a few lines. Walked with Mary and Jane. Called on the Countess.

"Wrote to Roberts, at Genoa, about a house. Passed the evening with the Shelleys."

[10] Mary to Mrs. Hunt, March 5, 1822 (*Letters,* I, 157–58).

Thursday, Mar. 7.—Write to Mrs. Gisborne.[11] Read Homer, Tacitus, and Dante. Ride with T. Guiccioli.

Friday, Mar. 8.—Greek lesson. Walk with Jane. Read Tacitus and Dante. A dinner at Albe's.[12] Jane and T. Guiccioli in the evening.

Saturday, Mar. 9.—Write to Papa. Walk with Jane. Read Homer, Tacitus, and Dante. Call on T. Guiccioli. The Theatre in the evening: "Ginevra di Scozia."

Sunday, Mar. 10.—Read Homer, Tacitus, and Dante. Walk with Jane. Ride with T. Guiccioli. The Williams' and Medwin to dinner.

Monday, Mar. 11.—Greek lesson. Tacitus. Read [Lady Morgan's] "Florence Macarthy."[13]

Tuesday, Mar. 12.—Finish "Florence Macarthy." Homer. Call on Mrs. Beauclerc. Ride with T. Guiccioli. Call on her in the evening with Jane. See Albe there.

Wednesday, Mar. 13.—Greek lesson. Read Homer. Walk with Jane. Spend the evening with the Williams'.

Thursday, Mar. 14.—Read Homer. Walk with Jane. They dine with us.

Friday, Mar. 15.—Greek lesson. Read Homer. Walk with Jane. Ride with T. Guiccioli. Go to the Theatre in the evening with the Williams' and Trelawney.

Saturday, Mar. 16.—Copy. Write. Walk. Trelawney to dinner and all the evening. Call at Casa Silva.

Sunday, Mar. 17.—Copy. Greek lesson. Mrs. Beauclerc calls. Walk with Jane, and ride with T. Guiccioli. Jane and Trelawney in the evening.[14]

Tuesday, Mar. 19.—Read Greek. Walk with Jane. Trelawney and the Williams' to dinner. Spend the evening at Mrs. Beauclerc's.

Wednesday, Mar. 20.—Write to Clare. Greek lesson. Walk with Jane. Ride with T. Guiccioli. Trelawney in the evening.

Thursday, Mar. 21.—Read Greek. Go in the boat. To the Theatre in the evening.

Friday, Mar. 22.—Italian and Greek lessons. Walk with Jane. Ride with T. Guiccioli. She calls in the evening.

Saturday, Mar. 23.—Translate Italian. Read Homer. Walk with Jane. Ride with T. Guiccioli. And the evening tutto sotto sopra.

[11] Mary to Mrs. Gisborne, March 7, 1822 (*Letters,* I, 158–61).

[12] Mary was not present; see Williams's journal (n. 9 above).

[13] 1818, 4 vols.

[14] The MS journal has a brief entry for March 18, according to the MS notes of Miss Grylls.

Monday, MAR. 25.—Go to the Hospital.[15] A day of bustle and nothings. Trelawney dines with us. Call in the evening on T. Guiccioli.

Tuesday, MAR. 26.—Vaccà calls. Call on Jane. Read Homer. Walk. Spend the evening with the Williams'.

Wednesday, MAR. 27.—Italian and Greek lesson. Walk. Trelawney dines with us. Call in the evening upon M. Mason.

Thursday, MAR. 28.—Translate. Make visits. Read Homer. Walk. The Theatre in the evening. Dine at Jane's.

Friday, MAR. 29.—Italian and Greek lesson. ἢ ταν, ἢ επι τας [With this, or on this.] Shelley. Walk with Jane. Edward and Jane in the evening.

Saturday, MAR. 30.—Read Lindsay's dramas[16] and "Telemaque."[17] Walk with Jane. Edward and Jane in the evening.

Sunday, MAR. 31.—Not well. Read Homer and "Telemaque." A hateful day. Trelawney and the Williams' to dinner.

Monday, APRIL 1.—Greek lesson. Write to M. Coster and to Clare. Walk. In the evening work, and finish "Telemaque."

Tuesday, APR. 2.—Translate Italian. Call on Mrs. Beauclerc and T. Guiccioli. Trelawney to dinner and the Williams' in the evening.

Wednesday, APR. 3.—Italian lesson. Write letters. Read Montaigne and Homer. Walk, and spend the day with the Williams'.[18]

15 For Mary's excellent account of the affair with the Italian dragoon, Sergeant-Major Stefano Masi, on March 24, see her *Letters,* I, 162–69. See also Dowden, II, 478–81; and White, II, 351–54.

16 David Lyndsay, *Dramas of the Ancient World* (Edinburgh, 1822).

17 François de S. de la Mothe Fénelon, *Télémaque* (1699).

18 Extracts from the *Journal of E. E. Williams* (pp. 50–55): "*Wednesday, April 3rd.* Fine. Walked with Jane. Called on Taaffe to learn further of the business—on Lord B. acquainting him with it. Lord B. willing to give his hand to Taaffe. As usual all right again. Mrs. B. wrote to Lord B., requesting his interference with Trelawny, and enclosing all the notes that had passed between them. Devil of an affair—all parties quarrelling and everybody defaming everybody.

"Walked with T. to see the boat that is to convey ourselves and furniture to Spezzia, about which I wrote last night. The S.'s dined and passed the evening here. Captain H[ay] departs for England.

"*Monday, April 8.* In the evening dined with S. and Mary, and went to see the play. A new troop of actors, tolerable in their way; but the piece they chose to make their *debût* in was not the most advantageous for such a purpose. It seemed, however, to have some interest for the Italians, who did not spare their plaudits. The scene was laid in England—the Secretary of State dying of a mysterious disorder, that baffled the skill of the physicians. A mysterious doctor at length offers to make a cure of the poor Secretary, provided he releases from prison one Jenkinson. The Secretary refuses, and the doctor declines to attend him, and so on. Jenkinson is at last released, and the Secretary finds himself better, to the great joy of the nation and his friends.

"*Wednesday, April 10.* S. receives his *Hellas.* Trelawny dined and passed the evening. We talked of a play of his singular life, and a plot to give it the air of a romance.

Thursday, April 4.—Finish δ of Homer. Translate Italian. Machiavelli's history ["Florentine History"].

Friday, April 5.—Not well. Greek lesson. Walk. Dine at the Williams', with Trelawney.

Saturday, April 6.—Read Greek. Italian. Walk. Trelawney to dinner.

Sunday, April 7.—Write to Mrs. Gisborne.[19] Read Italian and Machiavelli. The Williams' to dinner. T. Guiccioli in the evening.

"*Sunday, April 14th*. . . . Called on Lord B. He is commencing the fifth Canto of *Don Juan*. Trelawny and the S.'s dined here and passed the evening. . . .

"*Monday, April 15th*. Fine. Wrote a few lines. Heard from Spezzia that the persons to whom the houses belonged that we had calculated upon having this summer refuse to let them at all. This is a piece of spite uncommon in Italy, where all such feelings generally give place to a sense of interest. Called on Lord B., who imagines it is in consequence of the late disturbances that the Piedmontese Government object to S.'s residing there. Trelawny called in the evening. We intended to leave Pisa for Spezzia to-morrow, but Wednesday is now fixed. C[lair]e arrives from Florence.

"*Tuesday, April 16*. Fine. As equally unsettled as ever with regard to our trip to Spezzia. The Governor refuses to sign my passport, it being too old. Walked with Mary to see the Turkish prince Mahomet Effendi practise the djerrid; but an ill performer; a Mahratta would astonish him. Trelawny dines.

"*Friday, April 19*. . . . Mary and the Guiccioli underwent five hours' examination this morning. The Countess said to the judge that she could not swear, but that she thought Mr. Taaffe was the person who stabbed the dragoon.

"*Saturday, April 20*. Called on Lord B. Met Rogers the poet there, an old decrepid man, whose face bespeaks great imbecility of mind, but whose works prove the contrary.

"*Sunday, April 21*. Call on S. Talk over the subject of the play. He gave me a long lecture on the drama. Put me in bad spirits with myself. C[laire] passed the evening.

"*Monday, April 22*. My birthday. Forget whether born in 1793 or 1794—rather think the former [which is correct]. T. examined. I interpret.

"*Tuesday, April 23*. Left Pisa for Spezzia with C[laire] and Jane.

"*Thursday, April 25*. Return to Pisa. Meet S., his face bespoke his feelings. C[laire]'s child was dead, and he had the office to break it to her, or rather not to do so; but fearful of the news reaching her ears, to remove her instantly from this place.

"*Friday, April 26*. Mary, C[laire], and Trelawny depart for Spezzia. Poor C[laire] quite unconscious of the burden on her friends' minds.

"*Saturday, April 27*. Cloudy and heavy rain. Heard that the dragoon is quite recovered. At 12 weather clearer. The two boats arrived at the landing-place, and we commenced loading them: all completed by four o'clock. At half-past five, Jane, the two children, Shelley, and myself, with the nurse, left Pisa (the other servants having gone in the boat), and arrived at Pietra Santa at half-past eleven.

"*Sunday, April 28*. Fine. Arrive at Lerici at 1 o'clock. The harbour-master called. Not a house to be had. . . . S. wrote to Mary, whom we heard was at Spezzia.

"*Monday, April 29*. . . . Heard from Mary, at Sarzana, that she had concluded for Casa Magni—but for ourselves no hope.

"*Tuesday, April 30*. Fine. Jane and myself, having resolved to send our furniture back, took a boat to Spezzia to make some arrangements with the master of the inn. This fellow had the impertinence to ask us 32 francs a day. On our return to Lerici, found Mary there and the two boats entering the harbour. After some delay at the Douane, we towed them across the bay to Casa Magni, and there unloaded the two in less than an hour, and stowed the things within the house at the same time. Jane, myself, and children slept at the inn."

19 Mary to Mrs. Gisborne, April 6 [and 10], 1822 (*Letters,* I, 162–65).

Monday, APRIL 8.—Read Greek. Italian lesson. Read Macchiavelli. Walk. The Theatre in the evening.

Tuesday, APRIL 9.—Read Homer, Macchiavelli, Italian, and Tacitus.

Wednesday, APRIL 10.—Not well. Call on Miss Nott. Jane calls.

Thursday, APRIL 11.—Greek lesson. Translate Italian. Walk. Trelawney to dinner.

Friday, APRIL 12.—Italian lesson. Shelley goes with the Williams' and Trelawney to Leghorn. Walk. T. Guiccioli calls. Read Homer.

Saturday, APRIL 13.—Ride to the Baths. Read Macchiavelli and Homer. Write to Hunt.[20] Walk with Jane. Call on T. Guiccioli and the Williams'.

Sunday, APRIL 14.—Walk with Jane. Read Macchiavelli. Dine at the Williams' with Trelawney.

Monday, APRIL 15.—Clare arrives [from Florence]. Read Macchiavelli. Work. The Williams' in the evening.

Tuesday, APR. 16.—Read Macchiavelli. Spend the evening at Casa Silva.

Wednesday, APR. 17.—Italian and Greek lesson. Walk with Jane. Shelley at Leghorn. The Williams' in the evening.

Thursday, APR. 18.—Greek and Italian. Walk. Trelawney to dinner and during the evening.

Friday, APR. 19.—An examination at the house of T. Guiccioli. Walk. Read Tacitus.

Saturday, APR. 20.—Read Macchiavelli and Homer. Walk. Spend the evening at the Williams'.

Sunday, APR. 21.—Read Homer and Macchiavelli. Translate Italian. Trelawney to dinner.

Monday, APR. 22.—Greek and Italian lesson. Walk. The Williams' and Trelawney to dinner. Trelawney examined in the evening.

Tuesday, APR. 23.—Read [Shelley's] "Charles I." Letters. Trelawney here. Copy with him. Evil news.[21] Not well. [Claire and the Williamses had left for Spezzia.]

Wednesday, APR. 24.—Trelawney here. Walk. Read.

Thursday, APR. 25.—The Williams' and Clare return. Bustle and preparation.

Friday, APR. 26.—Leave Pisa, with Trelawney and Clare and Percy. Sleep at Massa.

Saturday, APR. 27.—At Spezzia.

Sunday, APR. 28.—Trelawney leaves us. Remain at Spezzia.

20 Mary to Hunt [April 10, 1822] (*Letters,* I, 165–66).

21 The death of Allegra of typhus fever on April 19 at the convent at Bagnacavallo.

Monday, APR. 29.—At Sarzana. Read [Anthony Hamilton's] "Memoirs of the Court of Charles the Second."[22] "Atala."[23]

Tuesday, APR. 30.—At Lerici. Get into our house at night.

Friday, MAY 4[–31].—The Williams' take up their abode with us. Begin "Ion Ludlow's Memoirs."[24]

22 The second part of the *Memoirs of Count Gramont.*

23 By François R. de Chateaubriand (Paris, 1805).

24 Extracts from the *Journal of E. E. Williams* (pp. 56–68); only a few of the extracts printed by Mary have been included: "*Thursday, May 2.* . . . S. broke the sad news to Claire. We were seated in Jane's room, talking over the best means to be pursued, when she guessed the purpose of our meeting.

"*Tuesday, May 7.* Fine. Surf continues as heavy as ever, and prevents our getting out. Wrote to my brother. In the afternoon I made an effort, with Jane in the boat, to put to sea, which appeared quiet and calm in the offing; but a sea struck her on the bow while launching, and a second on the broadside almost swamped her. I got out, however, and landed Jane, half drowned, on the rocks. In the evening a heavy thunder-storm passed over; one flash of lightning, over Lerici, was particularly vivid. The steeple of that place has already been struck, and the inhabitants say at a time when not a cloud was to be seen.

"*Wednesday, May 8.* Fine. Wrote to Medwin. Rowed in the little boat to Lerici. Heard from Trelawny that the *Don Juan* will be here to-morrow. At two, bathed. Fresh breeze, but water very warm. Every eye strains in hope of seeing the boat come in.

"*Thursday, May 9.* Fine. Recommenced writing. Found my mind most unsettled—a confusion, a flood of ideas that drowned each other. Our anxiety for the boat increases. Walked with Jane and planted for her.

"*Friday, May 10.* Fine. No boat arrives. Wrote a little. Heavy swell at sea and threatening weather. The things arrive from Genoa and news of the boat; she is afraid to put to sea.

"*Saturday, May 11.* Cloudy and threatening. Wrote during the morning. Went to Lerici with S. Heavy thunder and distant lightning, with rain. Wrote to Taaffe for my letters, having heard from the postmaster that he could not forward them without the postage being paid.

[*Sunday, May 12.* The boat arrives. Mary quotes this entry in her note on the "Poems of 1822."]

"*Friday, 17th May.* Fine. S. and Jane go to Carrara. Hove the boat down and smoothed her bottom. Unbent the mainsail, and took it to Magliana to see if the letters could be erased which Lord B., in his contemptible vanity, or for some other purpose, begged of Roberts to inscribe on the boat's mainsail. All efforts useless.

"*Sunday, May 19.* Fine. Wrote a little during the morning, but the bay and the boat have too many temptations, and I find I cannot collect my thoughts. Sailed in the evening.

"*Monday, May 20.* Fine. Sailed with Jane over to the Lazaretto, in order to see the sail-maker about the mainsail. Nothing to be done. A beautiful safe bay within.

"*Tuesday, May 21.* Cloudy and calm. Rose at half-past five and took Maglian down to Spezzia. I called on the Inspector of Customs, to request his interest in getting his (Shelley's) books on shore. They came from England, and were directed to Pisa, but having been forwarded to us here in the Piedmontese territories, it is necessary that they should be inspected at Genoa by certain persons appointed by the Governors of the Church in order to prevent any seditious or immoral publications from falling into the hands of this *free and pious people*—this is a tyranny that cannot last long. . . .

"T.'s application proves ineffective, and with the curses of all parties away went the books for Genoa. Sent to Genoa for some canvas. Claire departs for Florence—and Beta and Domenico leave Mary's service.

"*Thursday, May 23.* Fine. Worked all day at the boat, and find that I am a better hand with the pencil than the chisel; that is, that I can make plans better than make boats.

"In the afternoon lowering black clouds. Sailed for an hour, and before night much

The rest of May a blank, except that I read [Tasso's] "Gerusalemme Liberata." Clare at Florence [having left Spezzia on May 21].

Saturday, JUNE 1.—Read Homer, and one book of Virgil. Go out in the boat. Work.

Sunday, JUNE 2.—Read Homer and Virgil, and Bacon's "Natural History" and "Apothegms."

Monday, JUNE 3.—Read Bacon's "Apothegms." Work.

Tuesday, JUNE 4.—Read Homer (finish "Epsilon"), the second book of the "Georgics," and Kant's "Geographica Fisica."

Wednesday, JUNE 5.—Read "Geographica Fisica." Work. Go out in the boat.

Thursday, JUNE 6.—Shelley and Edward [Williams][25] go to Via Reggio.[26] Work. Read "Geographica Fisica."

alarmed for the safety of the boat: heavy sea running, but the wind is too strong from the S. E. to rise much during the night.

"*Monday, May 27.* Fine. Made further efforts to complete my boat of reeds, but in vain. . . .

"[*Friday*], *May 31.* Fine. At work on the boat. I find I have made it double the size I intended.

"*Saturday, June 1.* Fine. Out of patience with the boat. I take her to pieces and commence anew. Sailed with the whole party in the evening.

"*Sunday, June 9.* Fine. Hot and oppressive weather. Sailed during the forenoon to the outer island. On my return found Mary had been alarmingly unwell, and that she had [been threatened with a miscarriage] though I left her at breakfast perfectly well. Night, strangely better.

"*Thursday, June 20.* Fine. Shelley hears from Hunt that he is arrived at Genoa, having sailed from England on the 13th May.

"*Sunday, June 23.* S. sees spirits, and alarms the whole house.

"*Thursday, June 27.* The heat increases daily, and prayers are offering for rain. At Parma it is now so excessive, that the labourers are forbidden to work in the fields after ten and before five, fearful of an epidemic.

"*Saturday, June 29.* Shelley's books arrive from Genoa. This is a good fortune of which I had little hope.

"*Sunday, June 30.* Read some of Shelley's *Queen Mab*—an astonishing work. The enthusiasm of his spirit breaks out in some admirable passages in the poetry, and the notes are as subtle and elegant as he could now write.

"*Monday, July 1.* Calm and clear. Rose at four to get the top-sails altered. At twelve, a fine breeze from the westward tempted us to weigh for Leghorn. At two, stretched across to Lerici, to pick up Roberts; and at half-past found ourselves in the offing, with a side wind. At half-past nine arrived at Leghorn—a run of forty-five to fifty miles in seven hours and a-half. Anchored astern the *Bolivar,* from which we procured cushions, and made up for ourselves a bed on board, not being able to get on shore after sunset, on account of the health office being shut at that hour.

"*Tuesday, July 2.* . . . Met Lord Byron at Dunn's, and took leave of him. Was introduced to Mr. Leigh Hunt, and called on Mrs. Hunt. Shopped and strolled about all day. Met Lieutenant Marsham of the *Rochefort,* an old school-fellow and shipmate."

25 S&M, "Clare." See Williams's *Journal,* 64–65.

26 "To meet Claire on her way from Florence to Casa Magni," says Dowden (II, 513), who adds (p. 514) that Claire arrived at Villa Magni via land travel on June 7.

Friday, JUNE 7.—Read "Geographica Fisica." Shelley and Williams return to dinner (6) in the evening.

Saturday, JUNE 8.—Read Homer, third Georgic, "Geographica Fisica," and "Samson Agonistes." [Claire arrives.]

Sunday, JUNE 9.—Unwell. Read Madame de Stael's "Vie de Necker."

Monday, JUNE 10.—Read "Geographica Fisica" and "Samson Agonistes."

Tuesday, JUNE 11.—Finish first Volume of "Geographica Fisica." Work.

Sunday, [JUNE 12–] JULY 7.—I am ill most of this time.[27] Ill and then convalescent. Roberts[28] and Trelawney arrive with the "Bolivar," [Byron's boat]. On Monday, June 16 [17], Trelawney goes on to Leghorn with her. Roberts remains here until July 1, when the Hunts being arrived, Shelley goes in the boat with him and Edward to Leghorn. They are still there. Read "Jacopo Ortis,"[29] second volume of "Geographica Fisica," &c., &c.[30]

* * * * *

OCT. 2.[31]—On the 8th of July I finished my journal.[32] This is a curious coincidence. The date still remains—the fatal 8th—a monument to show that all ended then. And I begin again? Oh, never! But several motives induce me, when the day has gone down, and all is silent around me, steeped in sleep, to pen as occasion wills, my reflections and feelings. First, I have no friend. For eight years I communicated, with unlimited freedom, with one whose genius, far transcending mine, awakened and guided my thoughts. I conversed with him; rectified my errors of judgment; obtained new lights from him; and my mind was satisfied. Now I am alone—oh, how alone! The stars may behold my tears, and the winds drink my sighs; but my thoughts are a sealed treasure, which I can confide to none. But can I express all I feel? Can I give words to thoughts and feelings that, as a tempest, hurry me along? Is this the sand that the ever-flowing sea of thought would impress indelibly? Alas! I am alone. No eye answers mine; my voice can with none assume its natural

27 On Sunday, June 16, at 8 o'clock in the morning, Mary had a serious miscarriage (see the entry for Oct. 5, 1839).

28 Captain Daniel Roberts of the Royal Navy.

29 Ugo Foscolo, *Ultime Lettere di Jacopo Ortis* (Italy, 1802; published anonymously).

30 Shelley and Edward Williams were drowned on July 8 when their yacht, the *Don Juan,* sank off Via Reggio, having been run down by a larger vessel during a violent storm.

31 Mary returned to Pisa on July 20. On September 11 she went to Genoa, where at Albaro (near Genoa) she rented Casa Saluzzo for Byron and Casa Negroto for herself and the Hunts.

32 That is, the entry dated [June 12–]July 7 was actually written on July 8.

modulation. What a change! O my beloved Shelley! how often during those happy days—happy, though chequered—I thought how superiorly gifted I had been in being united to one to whom I could unveil myself, and who could understand me! Well, then, now I am reduced to these white pages, which I am to blot with dark imagery. As I write, let me think what he would have said if, speaking thus to him, he could have answered me. Yes, my own heart, I would fain know what to think of my desolate state; what you think I ought to do, what to think. I guess you would answer thus:—"Seek to know your own heart, and, learning what it best loves, try to enjoy that." Well, I cast my eyes around, and, look forward to the bounded prospect in view; I ask myself what pleases me there? My child;—so many feelings arise when I think of him, that I turn aside to think no more. Those I most loved are gone for ever; those who held the second rank are absent; and among those near me as yet, I trust to the disinterested kindness of one alone.[33] Beneath all this, my imagination never[34] flags. Literary labours, the improvement of my mind, and the enlargement of my ideas, are the only occupations that elevate me from my lethargy; all events seem to lead me to that one point, and the courses of destiny having dragged me to that single resting-place, have left me. Father, mother, friend, husband, children—all made, as it were, the team that conducted me here; and now all, except you, my poor boy (and you are necessary to the continuance of my life), all are gone, and I am left to fulfil my task. So be it.

Oct. 5.—Well, they are come;[35] and it is all as I said. I awoke as from sleep, and thought how I had vegetated these last days; for feeling leaves little trace on the memory if it be, like mine, unvaried. I have felt for, and with myself alone, and I awake now to take a part in life. As far as others are concerned, my sensations have been most painful. I must work hard amidst the vexations that I perceive are preparing for me—to preserve my peace and tranquillity of mind. I must preserve some, if I am to live; for, since I bear at the bottom of my heart a fathomless well of bitter waters, the workings of which my philosophy is ever at work to repress, what will be my fate if the petty vexations of life are added to this sense of eternal and infinite misery?

Oh, my child! what is your fate to be? You alone reach me; you are the only chain that links me to time; but for you, I should be free. And yet I cannot be destined to live long. Well, I shall commence my task, commemorate the virtues of the only creature worth loving or living for,

33 Trelawny.

34 *Shelley Memorials* (p. 231) reads "ever," which is probably correct.

35 Byron and the Gambas, who moved from Pisa to Genoa. The Hunts would also arrive in a day or two.

and then, maybe, I may join him. Moonshine may be united to her planet and wander no more, a sad reflection of all she loved on earth.[36]

Oct. 7.—I have received my desk to-day,[37] and have been reading my letters to mine own Shelley during his absences[38] at Marlow. What a scene to recur to! My William, Clara, Allegra, are all talked of. They lived then, they breathed this air, and their voices struck my sense; their feet trod the earth beside me, and their hands were warm with blood and life when they clasped in mine. Where are they all? This is too great an agony to be written about. I may express my despair, but my thoughts can find no words.

* * * * *

I would endeavour to consider myself a faint continuation of his being, and, as far as possible, the revelation to the earth of what he was. Yet, to become this, I must change much, and above all I must acquire that knowledge and drink at those fountains of wisdom and virtue, from which he quenched his thirst. Hitherto I have done nothing; yet I have not been discontented with myself. I speak of the period of my residence here. For, although unoccupied by those studies which I have marked out for myself, my mind has been so active, that its activity, and not its indolence, has made me neglectful. But now the society of others causes this perpetual working of my ideas somewhat to pause; and I must take

[36] Cf. *Epipsychidion,* 345–67, which symbolically identify Mary with the Moon.

[37] The desk had been left at Marlow in Peacock's care. In November, 1821, Mary requested Mrs. Gisborne to see that it was sent to Italy (*Letters,* I, 152). It is significant that when she received it on October 7, 1822, Mary mentioned reading only her own letters. Shelley's letters were missing, and these Mary wrote urgently to Peacock about, insisting that they must have been left at Marlow with other MSS. Peacock finally replied on April 15, 1823 (Peacock's *Works,* Halliford edition, VIII, 232–34), stating that no letters were found at Marlow after their departure in 1818. The method by which the Shelleys' possessions were packed and stored, as related by Peacock, makes it evident, however, that any number of letters could have been packed away by Madocks and never seen by Peacock. It is also a matter of fact that Mr. Madocks did have some Shelley papers about which Peacock knew nothing, for Charles S. Middleton saw them (see the preface to his *Shelley and His Writings* [London, T. C. Newby, 1858]).

In view of these facts it seems clear that the forger Major George Byron was doubtless telling the truth when he told William White that he got some Shelley letters from a "box" left by the Shelleys at Marlow. The originals of these letters he sold to Mary Shelley in 1845–46, and then proceeded to produce forgeries based on them, some of the forgeries being true copies of the originals.

Lady Shelley is certainly mistaken in stating (S&M, III, 713) that the letters in Mary's desk were copied before the desk was sent to Italy, and that the copies were used as the basis for the forgeries sold in 1852. Mary's journal proves that Shelley's letters were not in the desk, and Peacock's letter shows that the desk was locked and had never been opened.

[38] An unpublished letter from Mary to Jane Williams refers to the letters mentioned here and indicates clearly that they were written during only one of Shelley's absences from Marlow. The plural "absences" is therefore probably an error in transcription. The absence

advantage of this to turn my mind towards its immediate duties, and to determine with firmness to commence the life I have planned. You will be with me in all my studies, dearest love! Your voice will no longer applaud me, but in spirit you will visit and encourage me: I know you will. What were I, if I did not believe that you still exist? It is not with you as with another. I believe that we all live hereafter; but you, my only one, were a spirit caged, an elemental being, enshrined in a frail image, now shattered. Do they not all with one voice assert the same? Trelawney, Hunt, and many others. And so at last you quitted this painful prison, and you are free, my Shelley; while I, your poor chosen one, am left to live as I may.

What a strange life mine has been! Love, youth, fear, and fearlessness, led me early from the regular routine of life, and I united myself to this being, who, not one of *us,* though like to us, was pursued by numberless miseries and annoyances, in all of which I shared. And then I was the mother of beautiful children; but these stayed not by me. Still he was there: and though, in truth, after my William's death this world seemed only a quicksand, sinking beneath my feet, yet beside me was this bank of refuge—so tempest-worn and frail, that methought its very weakness was strength, and, since Nature had written destruction on its brow, so the Power that rules human affairs had determined, in spite of Nature, that it should endure. But that is gone. His voice can no longer be heard; the earth no longer receives the shadow of his form; annihilation has come over the earthly appearance of the most gentle creature that ever yet breathed this air; and I am still here—still thinking, existing, all but hoping. Well, I close my book. To-morrow I must begin this new life of mine.

Oct. 19.—How painful all change becomes to one who, entirely and despotically engrossed by their own feelings, leads as it were an *internal* life, quite different from the outward and apparent one! Whilst my life continues its monotonous course within sterile banks, an under-current disturbs the smooth face of the waters, distorts all objects reflected in it, and the mind is no longer a mirror in which outward events may reflect themselves, but becomes itself the painter and creator. If this perpetual activity has power to vary with endless change the everyday occurrences of a most monotonous life, it appears to be animated with the spirit of tempest and hurricane when any real occurrence diversifies the scene. Thus, to-night, a few bars of a known air seemed to be as a wind to rouse from its depths every deep-seated emotion of my mind. I would have

referred to is likely that of September 23 to the latter part of October, 1817, when Shelley was in London most of the time. Mary's letters of that period are printed in her *Letters* (I, 29–45).

given worlds to have sat, my eyes closed, and listened to them for years. The restraint I was under caused these feelings to vary with rapidity; but the words of the conversation, uninteresting as they might be, seemed all to convey two senses to me, and, touching a chord within me, to form a music of which the speaker was little aware. I do not think that any person's voice has the same power of awakening melancholy in me as Albè's. I have been accustomed, when hearing it, to listen and to speak little; another voice, not mine, ever replied—a voice whose strings are broken. When Albè ceases to speak, I expect to hear *that other* voice, and when I hear another instead, it jars strangely with every association. I have seen so little of Albè since our residence in Switzerland, and, having seen him there every day, his voice—a peculiar one—is engraved on my memory with other sounds and objects from which it can never disunite itself. I have heard Hunt in company and conversation with many, when my own one was not there. Trelawney, perhaps, is associated in my mind with Edward [Williams] more than with Shelley. Even our older friends, Peacock and Hogg, might talk together, or with others, and their voices would suggest no change to me. But, since incapacity and timidity always prevented my mingling in the nightly conversations of Diodati, they were, as it were, entirely tête-à-tête between my Shelley and Albè; and thus, as I have said, when Albè speaks and Shelley does not answer, it is as thunder without rain—the form of the sun without heat or light—as any familiar object might be, shorn of its best attributes; and I listen with an unspeakable melancholy that yet is not all pain.

The above explains that which would otherwise be an enigma—why Albè, by his mere presence and voice, has the power of exciting such deep and shifting emotions within me. For my feelings have no analogy either with my opinion of him, or the subject of his conversation. With another I might talk, and not for the moment think of Shelley—at least not think of him with the same vividness as if I were alone; but, when in company with Albè, I can never cease for a second to have Shelley in my heart and brain with a clearness that mocks reality—interfering even by its force with the functions of life—until, if tears do not relieve me, the hysterical feeling, analogous to that which the murmur of the sea gives me, presses painfully upon me.

Well, for the first time for about a month, I have been in company with Albè for two hours, and, coming home, I write this, so necessary is it for me to express in words the force of my feelings. Shelley, beloved! I look at the stars and at all nature, and it speaks to me of you in the clearest accents. Why cannot you answer me, my own one? Is the instrument so utterly destroyed? I would endure ages of pain to hear one tone of your voice strike on my ear!

Nov. 10.—I have made my first probation in writing and it has done me much good, and I get more calm; the stream begins to take to its new channel, inasmuch as to make me fear change. But people must know little of me who think that, abstractedly, I am content with my present mode of life. Activity of spirit is my sphere. But we cannot be active of mind without an object; and I have none. I am allowed to have some talent—that is sufficient, methinks, to cause my irreparable misery; for, if one has genius, what a delight it is to be associated with a superior! Mine own Shelley! the sun knows of none to be likened to you—brave, wise, gentle,[39] noble-hearted, full of learning, tolerance, and love. Love! what a word for me to write! Yet, my miserable heart, permit me yet to love—to see him in beauty, to feel him in beauty, to be interpenetrated by the sense of his excellence; and thus to love, singly, eternally, ardently, and not fruitlessly; for I am still his—still the chosen one of that blessed spirit—still vowed to him for ever and ever!

Nov. 11.—It is better to grieve than not to grieve. Grief at least tells me that I was not always what I am now. I was once selected for happiness; let the memory of that abide by me. You pass by an old ruined house in a desolate lane, and heed it not. But if you hear that that house is haunted by a wild and beautiful spirit, it acquires an interest and beauty of its own.

I shall be glad to be more alone again; one ought to see no one, or many; and, confined to one society, I shall lose all energy except that which I possess from my own resources; and I must be alone for those to be put in activity.

A cold heart! Have I a cold heart?[40] God knows! But none need envy the icy region this heart encircles; and at least the tears are hot which the emotions of this cold heart forces me to shed. A cold heart! yes, it would be cold enough if all were as I wished it—cold, or burning in the flame for whose sake I forgive this, and would forgive every other imputation—that flame in which your heart, beloved, lay unconsumed. My heart is very full to-night.

I shall write his life, and thus occupy myself in the only manner from which I can derive consolation. That will be a task that may convey some balm. What though I weep? All is better than inaction and—not forgetfulness—that never is—but an inactivity of remembrance.

And you, my own Boy! I am about to begin a task which, if you live, will be an invaluable treasure to you in after times. I must collect my materials, and then, in the commemoration of the divine virtues of your Father, I shall fulfil the only act of pleasure there remains for me, and be

39 S&M omits "gentle"; taken from *Shelley Memorials,* 237.

40 See Mary's *Letters,* II, 351.

ready to follow you, if you leave me, my task being fulfilled. I have lived; rapture, exultation, content—all the varied changes of enjoyment—have been mine. It is all gone; but still, the airy paintings of what it has gone through float by, and distance shall not dim them. If I were alone, I had already begun what I had determined to do; but I must have patience, and for those events my memory is brass, my thoughts a never-tired engraver. France—Poverty—A few days of solitude, and some uneasiness—A tranquil residence in a beautiful spot [Bishopsgate]—Switzerland—Bath—Marlow—Milan—The Baths of Lucca—Este—Venice—Rome—Naples—Rome and misery—Leghorn—Florence—Pisa—Solitude—The Williamses—The Baths—Pisa: these are the heads of chapters, and each containing a tale romantic beyond romance.

I no longer enjoy, but I love! Death cannot deprive me of that living spark which feeds on all given it, and which is now triumphant in sorrow. I love, and shall enjoy happiness again. I do not doubt that; but when?

Dec. 31.—So this year comes to an end. Shelley, beloved! the year has a new name from any thou knewest. When Spring arrives, leaves you never saw will shadow the ground, and flowers you never beheld will star it; the grass will be of another growth, and the birds sing a new song—the aged earth dates with a new number.

I trust in a hereafter—I have ever done so.[41] I know that that shall be mine—even with thee, glorious spirit! who surely lookest on, pitiest, and lovest thy Mary.

I love thee, my only one; I love nature; and I trust that I love all that is good in my fellow-creatures. But how changed I am! Last year, having you, I sought for the affection of others, and loved them even when unjust and cold; but now my heart is truly iced. If they treat me well, I am grateful. Yes, when that is, I call thee to witness in how warm a gush my blood flows to my heart, and tears to my eyes. But I am a lonely, unloved thing, serious and absorbed. None care to read my sorrow.

Sometimes I thought that fortune had relented towards us; that your health would have improved, and that fame and joy would have been yours, for when well you extracted from Nature alone an endless delight. The various threads of our existence seemed to be drawing to one point, and there to assume a cheerful hue.

Again, I think that your gentle spirit was too much wounded by the sharpnesses of this world, that your disease was incurable, and that in a happy time you became the partaker of cloudless days, ceaseless hours, and infinite love. Thy name is added to the list which makes the earth bold in her age and proud of what has been. Time, with unwearied but

41 S&M omits this and the next paragraph; text from *Shelley Memorials,* 240.

THE PROTESTANT CEMETERY AND ROME
From Monte Testaccio, 1819

slow feet, guides her to the goal that thou hast reached, and I, her unhappy child, am advanced still nearer the hour when my earthly dress shall repose near thine, beneath the tomb of Cestius.

1823

ITALY

FEB. 2.—On the 21st of January those rites were fulfilled.[1] Shelley! my own beloved! You rest beneath the blue sky of Rome; in that, at least, I am satisfied.

What matters it that they cannot find the grave of my William? That spot is sanctified by the presence of his pure earthly vesture, and that is sufficient—at least, it must be. I am too truly miserable to dwell on what at another time might have made me unhappy. He is beneath the tomb of Cestius. I see the spot.

FEB. 3.—A storm has come across me; a slight circumstance has disturbed the deceitful calm of which I boasted. I thought I heard my Shelley call me—not my Shelley in heaven—but my Shelley, my companion in my daily tasks. I was reading; I heard a voice say "Mary!" "It is Shelley," I thought; the revulsion was of agony. Never more——

But I have better hopes and other feelings. Your earthly shrine is shattered, but your spirit ever hovers over me, or awaits me when I shall be worthy to join it. To that spirit which, when imprisoned here, yet showed, by its exalted nature, its superior derivation——

FEB. 24.—Evils throng around me, my beloved, and I have indeed lost all in losing thee. Were it not for my Child, this would rather be a soothing reflection, and, if starvation were my fate,[2] I should fulfil that fate without a sigh. But our Child demands all my care now that you have left us. I must be all to him: the Father, Death has deprived him of; the relations, the bad world permits him not to have. What is yet in store for me? Am I to close the eyes of our Boy, and then join you?

The last weeks have been spent in quiet. Study could not give repose to, but somewhat regulated, my thoughts. I said: "I lead an innocent life,

[1] Shelley's ashes were buried in the Protestant Cemetery in Rome on January 21, 1823. The body of his son William could not be found. In March, 1823, Trelawny purchased a plot of ground in the cemetery and reburied the ashes in a more attractive grave. See Dowden, II, 536–37; White, II, 383; and Mary's *Letters,* I, 190 n.

[2] Mary's financial future was still very uncertain.

and it may become a useful one. I have talent, I will improve that talent; and if, while meditating on the wisdom of ages, and storing my mind with all that has been recorded of it, any new light bursts upon me, or any discovery occurs that may be useful to my fellows, then the balm of utility may be added to innocence."

What is it that moves up and down in my soul, and makes me feel as if my intellect could master all but my fate? I fear it is only youthful ardour—the yet untamed spirit which, wholly withdrawn from the hopes, and almost from the affections, of life, indulges itself in the only walk free to it, and, mental exertion being all my thought except regret, would make me place my hopes in that. I am indeed become a recluse in thought and act; and my mind, turned heavenward, would, but for my only tie, lose all commune with what is around me. If I be proud, yet it is with humility that I am so. I am not vain. My heart shakes with its suppressed emotions, and I flag beneath the thoughts that possess me.

Each day, as I have taken my solitary walk, I have felt myself exalted with the idea of occupation, improvement, knowledge, and peace. Looking back to my past life as a delicious dream, I steeled myself as well as I could against such severe regrets as should overthrow my calmness. Once or twice, pausing in my walk, I have exclaimed in despair——"Is it even so?" Yet, for the most part resigned, I was occupied by reflection—on those ideas you, my beloved, planted in my mind—and meditated on our nature, our source, and our destination.

To-day, melancholy would invade me, and I thought the peace I enjoyed was transient. Then that letter[3] came to place its seal on my prognostications. Yet it was not the refusal, or the insult heaped upon me, that stung me to tears. It was their bitter words about our Boy. Why, I live only to keep him from their hands. How dared they dream that I held him not far more precious than all, save the hope of again seeing you, my lost one? But for his smiles, where should I now be?

Stars that shine unclouded, ye cannot tell me what will be! Yet I can tell you a part. I may have misgivings, weaknesses, and momentary lapses into unworthy despondency, but—save in devotion towards my Boy—fortune had emptied her quiver, and to all her future shafts I oppose courage, hopelessness of ought on this side, with a firm trust in what is beyond the grave.

Visit me in my dreams to-night, my beloved Shelley! kind, loving, excellent as thou wert! and the event of this day shall be forgotten.

[3] Sir Timothy Shelley's letter of February 6, 1823 to Byron. Sir Timothy wrote that Mary's "conduct was the very reverse of what it ought to have been." "As to her child," he added, "I am inclined to afford the means of a suitable protection and care of him in this country, if he shall be placed with a person I shall approve." (See Mary's *Letters*, I, 216n.)

MAR. 17.[4]—Isabel [Booth], Friend of my youth, whom I have sometimes thought might now step upon the vacant scene and that we might both support each other, can you not hear and pity me?

MAR. 19.—As I have until now recurred to this book to discharge into it the overflowings of a mind too full of the bitterest waters of life, so will I to-night, now that I am calm, put down some of my milder reveries; that, when I turn it over, I may not only find a record of the most painful thoughts that ever filled a human heart even to distraction.

I am beginning seriously to educate myself; and in another place I have marked the scope of this somewhat tardy education, intellectually considered. In a moral point of view, this education is of some years' standing, and it only now takes the form of seeking its food in books. I have long accustomed myself to the study of my own heart, and have sought and found in its recesses that which cannot embody itself in words —hardly in feelings. I have found strength in the conception of its faculties; much native force in the understanding of them; and what appears to me not a contemptible penetration in the subtle divisions of good and evil. But I have found less strength of self-support, of resistance to what is vulgarly called temptation; yet I think also that I have found true humility (for surely no one can be less presumptuous than I), an ardent love for the immutable laws of right, much native goodness of emotion, and purity of thought.

Enough, if every day I gain a profounder knowledge of my defects, and a more certain method of turning them to a good direction.

Study has become to me more necessary than the air I breathe. In the questioning and searching turn it gives to my thoughts, I find some relief to wild reverie; in the self-satisfaction I feel in commanding myself, I find present solace; in the hope that thence arises, that I may become more worthy of my Shelley, I find a consolation that even makes me less wretched than in my most wretched moments.

MAR. 30.—I have now finished part of the "Odyssey." I mark this. I cannot write. Day after day I suffer the most tremendous agitation. I cannot write, or read, or think. Whether it be the anxiety for letters that shakes a frame not so strong as hitherto—whether it be my annoyances here—whether it be my regrets, my sorrows, and despair, or all these— I know not; but I am a wreck.

MAY 31.—The lanes are filled with fireflies; they dart between the trunks of the trees, and people the land with earth-stars. I walked among them to-night, and descended towards the sea. I passed by the ruined church, and stood on the platform that overlooks the beach. The black rocks were stretched out among the blue waters, which dashed with no

[4] Entry not in S&M; printed by Miss Grylls (p. 193 n.).

impetuous motion against them. The dark boats, with their white sails, glided gently over its surface, and the star-enlightened promontories closed in the bay: below, amid the crags, I heard the monotonous but harmonious, voices of the fishermen.

How beautiful these shores, and this sea! Such is the scene—such the waves within which my beloved vanished from mortality.

The time is drawing near when I must quit this country. It is true that, in the situation I now am, Italy is but the corpse of the enchantress that she was. Besides, if I had stayed here, the state of things would have been different. The idea of our Child's advantage alone enables me to keep fixed in my resolution to return to England. It is best for him—and I go.

Four years ago, we lost our darling William; four years ago, in excessive agony, I called for death to free me from all I felt that I should suffer here. I continue to live, and *thou* art gone. I leave Italy and the few that still remain to me. That, I regret less; for our intercourse is [so] much chequered with all of dross that this earth so delights to blend with kindness and sympathy, that I long for solitude, with the exercise of such affections as still remain to me. Away, I shall be conscious that these friends love me, and none can then gainsay the pure attachment which chiefly clings to them, because they knew and loved you—because I knew them when with you, and I cannot think of them without feeling your spirit beside me.

I cannot grieve for you, beloved Shelley; I grieve for thy friends—for the world—for thy Child—most for myself, enthroned in thy love, growing wiser and better beneath thy gentle influence, taught by you the highest philosophy—your pupil, friend, lover, wife, mother of your children! The glory of the dream is gone. I am a cloud from which the light of sunset has passed. Give me patience in the present struggle. *Meum cordium cor!* Good night!

> "I would give
> All that I am to be as thou now art;
> But I am chain'd to time, and cannot thence depart."[5]

[5] *Adonais,* XXVI.

1824[1]

ENGLAND

JAN. 18.—I have now been nearly four months in England and if I am to judge of the future by the past and the present, I have small delight in looking forward. I even regret those days and weeks of intense melancholy that composed my life at Genoa. Yes, solitary and unbeloved as I was there, I enjoyed a more pleasurable state of being than I do here. I was still in Italy, and my heart and imagination were both gratified by that circumstance. I awoke with the light and beheld the theatre of nature from my window; the trees spread their green beauty before me, the resplendent sky was above me, the mountains were invested with enchanting colours. I had even begun to contemplate painlessly the blue expanse of the tranquil sea, speckled by the snow-white sails, gazed upon by the unclouded stars. There was morning and its balmy air, noon and its exhilarating heat, evening and its wondrous sunset, night and its starry pageant. Then, my studies; my drawing, which soothed me; my Greek, which I studied with greater complacency as I stole every now and then a look on the scene near me; my metaphysics, that strengthened and elevated my mind. Then my solitary walks and my reveries; they were magnificent, deep, pathetic, wild, and exalted. I sounded the depths of my own nature; I appealed to the nature around me to corroborate the testimony that my own heart bore to its purity. I thought of *him* with hope; my grief was active, striving, expectant. I was worth something then in the catalogue of beings. I could have written something, been something. Now, I am exiled from these beloved scenes; its language is becoming a stranger to mine ears; my Child is forgetting it.[2] I am imprisoned in a dreary town; I see neither fields, nor hills, nor trees, nor sky; the exhilaration of enrapt contemplation is no more felt by me; aspirations agonising, yet grand, from which the soul reposed in peace, have ceased to ascend from the quenched altar of my mind. Writing has become a task; my studies irksome; my life dreary. In this prison it is only in human intercourse that I can pretend to find consolation; and woe, woe, and triple woe, to whoever seeks pleasure in human intercourse when that pleasure is not founded on deep and intense affection; as for the rest—

[1] Mary left Albaro for England on July 25, 1823. On January 14, 1824, she was living at 14 Speldhurst Street, Brunswick Square, London.

[2] When Percy Florence left Italy, he could speak only Italian.

"The bubble floats before,
The shadow stalks behind."

My Father's situation, his cares and debts, prevent my enjoying his society.

I love Jane [Williams] better than any other human being, but I am pressed upon by the knowledge that she but slightly returns this affection. I love her, and my purest pleasure is derived from that source—a capacious basin, and but a small rill flows into it. I love some one or two more, "with a degree of love," but I see them seldom. I am excited while with them, but the reaction of this feeling is dreadfully painful, but while in London I cannot forego this excitement. I know some clever men, in whose conversation I delight, but this is rare, like angels' visits. Alas! having lived day by day with one of the wisest, best, and most affectionate of spirits, how void, bare, and drear is the scene of life!

Oh, Shelley, dear, lamented, beloved! help me, raise me, support me; let me not feel ever thus fallen and degraded! My imagination is dead, my genius lost, my energies sleep. Why am I not beneath that weed-grown tower?[3] Seeing Coleridge last night reminded me forcibly of past times: his beautiful descriptions reminded me of Shelley's conversations. Such was the intercourse I once daily enjoyed, added to supreme and active goodness, sympathy, and affection, and a wild, picturesque mode of living that suited my active spirit and satisfied its craving for novelty of impression.

I will go into the country and philosophise; some gleams of past entrancement may visit me there.

MAY 14.—This, then, is my English life; and thus I am to drag on existence; confined in my small room, friendless. Each day I string me to the task. I endeavour to read and write; my ideas stagnate and my understanding refuses to follow the words I read; day after day passes while torrents fall from the dark clouds, and my mind is as gloomy as this odious day. Without human friends I must attach myself to natural objects; but though I talk of the country, what difference shall I find in this miserable climate. Italy, dear Italy, murderess of those I love and of all my happiness, one word of your soft language coming unawares upon me, has made me shed bitter tears. When shall I hear it again spoken, when see your skies, your trees, your streams? The imprisonment attendant on a succession of rainy days has quite overcome me. God knows I strive to be content, but in vain. Amidst all the depressing circumstances that weigh on me, none sinks deeper than the failure of my intellectual powers; nothing I write pleases me. Whether I am just in this, or whether

[3] Shelley's grave was at the foot of a tower of the old Roman wall which enclosed one side of the Protestant Cemetery.

the want of Shelley's (oh, my loved Shelley, it is some alleviation only to write your name!) encouragement, I can hardly tell, but it seems to me as if the lovely and sublime objects of nature had been my best inspirers, and wanting these I am lost. Although so utterly miserable at Genoa, yet what reveries were mine as I looked on the aspect of the ravine—the sunny deep and its boats—the promontories clothed in purple light—the starry heavens—the fireflies—the uprising of Spring![4] Then I could think, and my imagination could invent and combine, and self became absorbed in the grandeur of the universe I created. Now, my mind is a blank, a gulf filled with formless mist.

The last man![5] Yes, I may well describe that solitary being's feelings, feeling myself as the last relic of a beloved race, my companions extinct before me.

And thus has the accumulating sorrows of days and weeks been forced to find a voice, because the word *lucena* met my eyes, and the idea of lost Italy sprang in my mind. What graceful lamps those are, though of bare construction and vulgar use; I thought of bringing one with me; I am glad I did not. I will go back only to have a *lucena*. If I told people so they would think me mad, and yet not madder than they seem to be now, when I say that the blue skies and verdure-clad earth of that dear land are necessary to my existence.

If there be a kind spirit attendant on me, in compensation for these miserable days, let me only dream to-night that I am in Italy! Mine own Shelley, what a horror you had (fully sympathised in by me) of returning to this miserable country! To be here without you is to be doubly exiled, to be away from Italy is to lose you twice. Dearest, why is my spirit thus losing all energy? Indeed, indeed, I must go back, or your poor utterly lost Mary will never dare think herself worthy to visit you beyond the grave.

MAY 15.—This then was the coming event that cast its shadow on my last night's miserable thoughts. Byron had become one of the people of the grave[6]—that miserable conclave to which the beings I best loved belong. I knew him in the bright days of youth, when neither care nor fear had visited me—before death had made me feel my mortality, and the earth was the scene of my hopes. Can I forget our evening visits to Diodati? our excursions on the lake, when he sang the Tyrolese Hymn, and his voice was harmonized with winds and waves. Can I forget his attentions and consolations to me during my deepest misery? Never.

[4] S&M omits the part of this sentence beginning "as I looked"; text from *Shelley Memorials,* 223.

[5] Mary's novel, *The Last Man* (3 vols.), was published in February, 1826.

[6] Byron died on April 19, 1824, at Missolonghi, in Greece.

Beauty sat on his countenance and power beamed from his eye. His faults being, for the most part, weaknesses, induced one readily to pardon them.

Albè—the dear, capricious, fascinating Albè—has left this desert world! God grant I may die young! A new race is springing about me. At the age of twenty-six, I am in the condition of an aged person. All my old friends are gone. I have no wish to form new. I cling to the few remaining; but they slide away, and my heart fails when I think by how few ties I hold to the world. "Life is the desert and the solitude—how populous the grave,"—and that region—to the dearer and best beloved beings which it has torn from me, now adds that resplendent spirit whose departure leaves the dull earth dark as midnight.

JUNE 8.[7]—What a divine night it is! I have just returned from Kentish Town;[8] a calm twilight pervades the clear sky; the lamp-like moon is hung out in heaven, and the bright west retains the dye of sunset.

If such weather would continue, I should write again; the lamp of thought is again illumined in my heart, and the fire descends from heaven that kindles it. Such, my loved Shelley, now ten years ago, at this season, did we first meet, and there were the very scenes—that churchyard, with its sacred tomb, was the spot where first love shone in your dear eyes. The stars of heaven are now your country, and your spirit drinks beauty and wisdom in those spheres, and I, beloved, shall one day join you. Nature speaks to me of you. In towns and society I do not feel your presence; but there you are with me, my own, my unalienable!

I feel my powers again, and this is, of itself, happiness; the eclipse of winter is passing from my mind. I shall again feel the enthusiastic glow of composition; again, as I pour forth my soul upon paper, feel the winged ideas arise, and enjoy the delight of expressing them. Study and occupation will be a pleasure, and not a task, and this I shall owe to sight and companionship of trees and meadows, flowers and sunshine.

England, I charge thee, dress thyself in smiles for my sake! I will celebrate thee, O England! and cast a glory on thy name, if thou wilt for me remove thy veil of clouds, and let me contemplate the country of my Shelley and feel in communion with him!

I have been gay in company before, but the inspiriting sentiment of the heart's peace I have not felt before to-night; and yet, my own, never was I so entirely yours. In sorrow and grief I wish sometimes (how vainly) for earthly consolation. At a period of pleasing excitement I cling to your memory alone, and you alone receive the overflowing of my heart.

[7] Dated June 18 in S&M, and June 8 in *Shelley Memorials* (p. 224). Mary's letter of June 13, [1824] to Mrs. Hunt (*Letters,* I, 292–96) shows that June 8 is the correct date.

[8] Jane Williams had recently moved to 12 Mortimer Terrace, Kentish Town.

Beloved Shelley, good night! One pang will seize me when I think, but I will only think, that thou art where I shall be, and conclude with my usual prayer—from the depth of my soul I make it—May I die young!

Sept. 3.[9]—With what hopes did I come to England? I pictured little of what was pleasurable; the feeling I had, could not be called hope; it was expectation. Yet, at that time, now a year ago, what should I have said if a prophet had told me, that after the whole revolution of the year, I should be as poor in all estimable treasures as when I arrived.

I have only seen two persons from whom I have hoped or wished for friendly feeling. One, a Poet,[10] who sought me first, whose voice, laden with sentiment, passed as Shelley's, and who read with the same deep feeling as he; whose gentle manners were pleasing, and who seemed to a degree pleased; who once or twice listened to my sad plaints, and bent his dark blue eyes upon me. Association, gratitude, esteem, made me take interest in his long though rare visits.

The other[11] was kind; sought me; was pleased with me. I could talk to him, that was much. He was attached to another, so that I felt at my ease with him. They have disappeared from my horizon. Jane alone remains; if she loved me as well as I do her, it would be much; she is all gentleness, and she is my only consolation, yet she does not console me.

I have just completed my 27th year; at such a time hope and youth are still in their prime, and the pains I feel, therefore, are ever alive and vivid within me. What shall I do? Nothing! I study, that passes the time. I write, at times that pleases me; though double sorrow comes when I feel that Shelley no longer reads and approves of what I write; besides, I have no great faith in my success. Composition is delightful, but if you do not expect the sympathy of your fellow creatures in what you write, the pleasure of writing is of short duration.

I have my lovely Boy, without him I could not live. I have Jane, in her society I forget time, but the idea of it does not cheer me in my grieffull moods. It is strange that the religious feeling that exalted my emotions in happiness deserts me in my misery. I have little enjoyment, no hope. I have given myself ten years more of life. God grant that they may not be augmented. I should be glad that they were curtailed. Loveless beings

9 On June 21, 1824, Mary moved to 5 Bartholomew Place, Kentish Town.

10 Bryan Waller Procter (Barry Cornwall), who assisted with the publication of the *Posthumous Poems* (1824).

11 Possibly Vincent Novello, the musician, who was very much "attached," having a wife and several children. In her letter of October 20, [1823] to Hunt Mary wrote (*Letters,* I, 277): "Mr. Novello is my *prediletto.* I like him better and better each time I see him—his excessive good nature, enthusiastic friendship for you—his kindness towards me and his playing have quite won my heart."

surround me; they talk of my personal attractions, of my talents, my manners.

The wisest and best have loved me. The beautiful, and glorious, and noble have looked on me with the divine expression of love, till Death, the reaper, carried to his over-stocked barns my lamented harvest.

But now I am not loved! Never, oh, never more shall I love. Synonymous to such words are, never more shall I be happy, never more feel life sit triumphant in my frame. I am a wreck. By what do the fragments cling together? Why do they not part, to be borne away by the tide to the boundless ocean, where those are whom day and night I pray that I may rejoin?

I shall be happier, perhaps, in Italy; yet, when I sometimes think that she is the murderess, I tremble for my Boy. We shall see: if no change comes, I shall be unable to support the burthen of time, and no change, if it hurt not his dear head, can be for the worse.

Oct. 26.—Time rolls on, and what does it bring? What can I do? How change my destiny? Months change their names, years their cyphers. My brow is sadly trenched, the blossom of youth faded. My mind gathers wrinkles. What will become of me?

How long it is since an emotion of joy filled my once exulting heart, or beamed from my once bright eyes. I am young still, though age creeps on apace; but I may not love any but the dead. I think that an emotion of joy would destroy me, so new, so strange would it be to my widowed heart.

Shelley had said,

> "Lift not the painted veil which men call life."[12]

Mine is not painted; dark and enshadowed, it curtains out all happiness, all hope. Tears fill my eyes; well may I weep, solitary girl! The dead know you not; the living heed you not. You sit in your lone room, and the howling wind, gloomy prognostic of winter, gives not forth so despairing a tone as the unheard sighs your ill-fated heart breathes.

I was loved once! still let me cling to the memory; but to live for oneself alone; to read and communicate your reflections to none; to write and be cheered by none; to weep, and in no bosom; no more on thy bosom, my Shelley, to spend my tears—this is misery!

Such is the Alpha and Omega of my tale. I can speak to none. Writing this is useless; it does not even soothe me; on the contrary, it irritates me by showing the pitiful expedient to which I am reduced.

I have been a year in England, and, ungentle England, for what have I to thank you? For disappointment, melancholy, and tears; for unkind-

[12] The first line of one of Shelley's sonnets of 1818.

ness, a bleeding heart, and despairing thoughts. I wish, England, to associate but one idea with thee—immeasurable distance and insurmountable barriers, so that I never, never might breathe thine air more.

Beloved Italy! you are my country, my hope, my heaven!

DEC. 3.—I endeavour to rouse my fortitude and calm of mind by high and philosophic thoughts, and my studies aid this endeavour. I have pondered for hours on Cicero's description of that power of virtue in the human mind which renders man's frail being superior to fortune.

"Eadem ratio habet in re quiddam amplum atque magnificum ad imperandum magis quam ad parendum accommodatum; omnia humana non tolerabilia solum sed etiam levia ducens; altum quiddam et excelsum, nihil timens, nemini cedens, semper invictum."

What should I fear? To whom cede? By what be conquered?

Little, truly, have I to fear. One only misfortune can touch me. That must be the last, for I should sink under it. At the age of seven-and-twenty, in the busy metropolis of native England, I find myself alone. The struggle is hard that can give rise to misanthropy in one, like me, attached to my fellow-creatures. Yet now, did not the memory of those matchless lost ones redeem their race, I should learn to hate men, who are strong only to oppress, moral only to insult. Oh, ye winged hours that fly fast, that, having first destroyed my happiness, now bear my swift-departing youth with you, being patience, wisdom, and content! I will not stoop to the world, or become like those who compose it, and be actuated by mean pursuits and petty ends. I will endeavour to remain unconquered by hard and bitter fortune; yet the tears that start in my eyes show pangs she inflicts upon me.

So much for philosophising. Shall I ever be a philosopher?

1826

ENGLAND

SEPT. 5.—A month of peace—a whole month of happiness with my dearest friend [Jane Williams] at Brighton—and I have lived to hear her thank God that it is over . . . .[1]

SEPT. 17.—Thy picture[2] is come, my only one! Thine those speaking

[1] Entry not in S&M; printed by Miss Grylls (p. 191).

[2] The portrait of Shelley by Amelia Curran, which Mary had been trying since July, 1822, to get (see Mary's *Letters,* I, 175–76n.). Mrs. Julian Marshall (*Life and Letters of Mary W. Shelley* [London, Richard Bentley & Son, 1889, 2 vols.], II, 137) and I (*op. cit.*) are both wrong in dating the receipt of the picture 1825.

eyes, that mild yet animated look, unlike aught earthly wert thou ever, and art now!

If thou hadst still lived, how different had been my life and feelings!

Thou are near to guard and save me, angelic one! Thy divine glance will be my protection and defence. I was not worthy of thee, and thou hast left me; yet that dear look assures me that thou wert mine, and recalls and narrates to my backward-looking mind a long tale of love and happiness.

My head aches. My heart—my hapless heart—is deluged in bitterness. Great God! if there be any pity for human suffering, tell me what I am to do. I strive to study, I strive to write, but I cannot live without loving and being loved, without sympathy; if this is denied to me, I must die. Would that the hour were come!

The end of September.—Charles Shelley died during this month [September 16]. Percy is now Shelley's only son.

1827

ENGLAND

JUNE 26.—I have just made acquaintance with Tom Moore.[1] He reminds me delightfully of the past, and I like him much. There is something warm and genuine in his feelings and manner, which is very attractive, and redeems him from the sin of worldliness with which he has been charged.

JULY 2.—Moore breakfasted with me on Sunday [July 1]. We talked of past times—of Shelley and Lord Byron. He was very agreeable, and I never felt myself so perfectly at my ease with any one. I do not know why this is, he seems to understand and to like me. This is a new and unexpected pleasure. I have been so long exiled from the style of society in which I spent the better part of my life; it is an evanescent pleasure, but I will enjoy it while I can.

JULY 11.—Moore has left town; his singing is something new and strange and beautiful. I have enjoyed his visits, and spent several happy hours in his society. That is much.

JULY 13.—My friend has proved false and treacherous![2] Miserable

[1] Moore had sought Mary's assistance with his *Life of Byron*.

[2] Shortly before this date Jane Williams had "married" T. J. Hogg. She had told tales about Mary's deficiencies as Shelley's wife, and these had got back to Mary. See entries for February 12, 1828, November 23, 1833, and October 21, 1838. (See Mary's *Letters*, I, 368.)

discovery. For four years I was devoted to her, and I earned only ingratitude. Not for worlds would I attempt to transfer the deathly blackness of my meditations to these pages. Let no trace remain save the deep bleeding hidden wound of my lost heart, of such a tale of horror and despair. Writing, study, quiet, such remedies I must seek. What deadly cold flows through my veins; my head weighed down; my limbs sink under me. I start at every sound as the messenger of fresh misery, and despair invests my soul with trembling horror.

SEPT. 25.—Arundel.[3]— . . . But now my desire is so innocent. Why may I not hover a good genius round my lovely friend's[4] path? It is my destiny, it would seem to form rather the ties of friendship than love—the grand evil that results from this is—that while the power of mutual Love is in itself a mighty destiny—friendship though true, yields to the adverse gale—and the vessels are divided far which ought never to part company. . . .

How dark—how very dark the future seems—I shrink in fear from the mere imagination of coming time. Is any evil about to approach me? Have I not suffered enough?

OCTOBER 9.—Quanto bene mi rammento sette anni fa, in questa medesima stagione i pensieri, i sentimenti del mio cuore! Allora cominciai Valperga. Allora sola col mio Bene fui felice. Allora le nuvole furono spinte dal furioso vento davanti dalla luna, nuvole magnifiche, che in forme grandiose e bianche parevano stabili quanto le montagne e sotto la tirannia del vento si mostravano più fragili che un velo di seta minutissima, scendeva allor la pioggia, gli albori si spogliavano. Autunno bello fosti allora ed ora bello terribile, malinconico ci sei, ed io, dove sono?[5]

Friday, DEC. 5.—I am alone in London—and very unhappy. I have lost one friend and am divided from another. I weep much and cannot be consoled.[6]

3 Entry not in S&M; printed by Miss Grylls (pp. 193, 194–95).

4 Probably refers to Mary's close friend Isabel Robinson (Mrs. Sholto Douglas), whom Mary apparently was visiting on September 25, and with whom she was in a few days to make a trip to Dieppe.

5 [Translation:] "How well do I remember seven years ago, in this same season, the thoughts, the feelings of my heart. Then I began *Valperga.* Then alone with my Beloved I was happy. Then the clouds were driven by the furious wind before the moon,—magnificent clouds, which, grand and white, seemed as stable as the mountains, and under the tyranny of the wind appeared more fragile than a veil of finest silk. Came then the rain, despoiling the trees. Autumn, you were beautiful then, and now you are beautiful, terrible, and melancholy—and I, where am I?"

6 Entry not in S&M; from Grylls, 195.

1828

ENGLAND

FEB. 12.—Moore is in town.[1] By his advice I disclosed my discoveries to Jane.[2] How strangely are we made! She is horror-struck and miserable at losing my friendship; and yet how unpardonably she trifled with my feelings, and made me all falsely a fable to others.

The visit of Moore has been an agreeable variety to my monotonous life. I see few people—Lord Dillon, G. Paul, and the Robinsons,[3] *voilà tout.*

APRIL 11.—I depart for Paris, sick at heart, yet pining to see my friend (Julia Robinson).

JULY 8.—Hastings. There was a reason for my depression: I was sickening of the small-pox. I was confined to my bed the moment I arrived in Paris. The nature of my disorder was concealed from me till my convalescence, and I am so easily duped. Health, buoyant and bright, succeeded to my illness. The Parisians were very amiable, and a monster to look at, as I was, I tried to be agreeable to compensate to them.

NOVEMBER.—Trelawney has come back and Clare has arrived.

[1] Mary was now living at 51 George Street, Portman Square, London.

[2] See the entry for July 13, 1827.

[3] For the Robinson family, see Mary's *Letters,* I, 377–78 n.

1829

ENGLAND

OCT. 8.—I[1] was at Sir Thomas Lawrence's to-day whilst Moore was sitting [for his portrait], and passed a delightful morning. We then went to the Charter House, and I saw his son, a beautiful boy.

[1] Mary's residence was now 33 Somerset Street, Portman Square.

1830

ENGLAND

JAN. 9.—Poor Lawrence is dead. Having seen him so lately, the suddenness of this event affects me deeply. His death opens all wounds. I see all those I love die around me, while I lament.

JAN. 22.—I have begun a new kind of life somewhat, going a little into society and forming a variety of acquaintances. People like me, and flatter and follow me, and then I am left alone again, poverty being a barrier I cannot pass. Still I am often amused and sometimes interested.

MAR. 23.—I gave a *soirée,* which succeeded very well. Mrs. Hare is going, and I am very sorry. She likes me, and she is gentle and good. Her husband is clever and her set very agreeable, rendered so by the reunion of some of the best people about town.

JUNE 30.—I go to Southend for a month with Percy, coming once to town during that time to a ball at the Speaker's.[2]

AUG. 18.—Return to town. I see Mrs. Hare frequently, who is going to Italy, alas!

1831

ENGLAND

Tuesday, JAN. 11.[3]—I have been reading with much increased admiration "Paul Clifford." It is a wonderful and sublime book. What will Bulwer become? The first author of the age? I do not doubt it. He is a magnificent writer.

Monday, FEB. 14.—At the Opera again—heard David[4] who had so delighted me at Milan and Naples—his voice has lost some of its mellowness—but his style is perfect.

I went last Sunday with Paul and Gee to hear Mr. Benson[5] in the Temple Church—he is the only preacher I ever liked.

[2] Charles Manners-Sutton, speaker of the House of Commons.

[3] None of the entries for January 11, 1831—June 30, 1838, are in S&M. They were printed by Miss Grylls from the original MS journal. The 1831 entries are on pp. 209, 210–11.

[4] Giovanni Davide (1789–*c.*1851), Italian tenor (see Mary's *Letters,* I, 51, 128–29, 249).

[5] Christopher Benson (1789–1868), master of the Temple (see *D.N.B.*).

Thursday, JUNE 9.—Julia [Robinson] and I went to Ascot—we were a good deal amused—to a party tonight at the Speaker's.

Friday, SEPT. 9.—I was at the coronation of William 4 yesterday on the 2nd bench of the Earl Marshall's box—the best in the Abbey. It was a splendid spectacle yet not to be compared to the ceremonies at Rome—except for the beauty of some of the women, the Duchess of Richmond in particular,—and the gentlemanliness of the D. of Devonshire, Ld. Brougham was a very droll figure with his coronet over his wig. They were so stingy the poor King was obliged to poke with his pen—and the D. of D. to tilt the inkstand—to get out enough to write his name.

1832

ENGLAND

JUNE–SEPT., Sandgate.[6]—More than three months I spend at this place—Julia Trelawny[7] was with me most of the time and also her father who has returned from Italy. He is a strange yet wonderful being—endued with genius—great force of character and power of feeling—but destroyed by *being nothing*—destroyed by envy and internal dissatisfaction. At first he was so gloomy that he destroyed me—this wore off somewhat—yet I never feel comfortable with him—in soggezione as the Italians call it.

1833

ENGLAND

Saturday, Nov. 23.[8]—I am copying Shelley's letters. Great God, what a thing is life! In one of them he says, "the curse of this life is that what we have once known we cannot cease to know . . .". Life is not all ill till we wish to forget. Jane first inspired me with that miserable feeling, staining past years as she did—taking the sweetness from memory and giving it instead a serpent's tooth.[9]

6 Entry from Grylls, 216.

7 Trelawny's "first-born daughter" (see Mary's *Letters,* II, 63).

8 Entry from Grylls, 197.

9 See the entry for July 13, 1827.

1834

ENGLAND

Tuesday, DEC. 2.[10]— . . . Routine occupation is the medicine of my mind. I write the "Lives"[11] in the morning. I read novels and memoirs of an evening—such is the variety of my days and time flies so swift, that days form weeks and weeks form months, before I am aware . . . .

My heart and soul is bound up in Percy. My race is run. I hope absolutely nothing except that when he shall be older and I a little richer to leave a solitude, very unnatural to anyone and peculiarly disagreeable to me . . . .

It has struck me what a very imperfect picture (only *no one* will ever see it) these querulous pages afford of *me*. This arises from their being the record of my feelings, and not of my imagination . . . my imagination, my Kubla Khan, "my pleasure dome" occasionally pushed aside by misery but at the first opportunity her beaming face peeped in and the weight of deadly woe was lightened.

1838

ENGLAND

Saturday, JUNE 30.[1]—Rosa [Robinson] and I breakfasted at [Samuel] Rogers today. He told me several anecdotes. One he told me to write down as he had not time. It was told him by Talleyrand. Napoleon ordered and arranged his battles from a distance; when on the spot the battle was instantly fought. At the time that the encampment was formed at Boulogne, Napoleon reviewed his troops. News came that the Austrians were in the advance. Napoleon set off instantly for Paris—and after two days proceeded travelling day and night to ———. He was closeted with Talleyrand—he told him that there was to be a battle—he

10 Entry from Grylls, 230–31, 194. Mary was living at Harrow, where Percy Florence was attending school as a day student.

11 Volume I of Lardner's *The Cabinet Cyclopedia:* "Lives of the Most Eminent Literary and Scientific Men of Italy" (see *Letters*, II, 90 n.).

1 Entry from Grylls, 275.

was studying his arrangements—when suddenly he felt ill; he had but time to say, "Lock the door" and fell into a fit. Talleyrand did as he was desired. Berthier came to the door—no admittance—the Empress—the door was still unopened—for half an hour said Talleyrand I was there shut up with the Emperor before he recovered. Had he died, what would have been said or thought of me?

Sunday, OCT. 21.[2]—I have been so often abused by pretended friends for my lukewarmness in "the good cause," that, though I disdain to answer them, I shall put down here a few thoughts on this subject. I am much of a self-examiner. Vanity is not my fault, I think; if it is, it is uncomfortable vanity, for I have none that teaches me to be satisfied with myself; far otherwise,—and, if I use the word disdain, it is that I think my qualities (such as they are) not appreciated from unworthy causes.

In the first place, with regard to "the good cause"—the cause of the advancement of freedom and knowledge, of the rights of women, &c.—I am not a person of opinions. I have said elsewhere that human beings differ greatly in this. Some have a passion for reforming the world; others do not cling to particular opinions. That my parents and Shelley were of the former class, makes me respect it. I respect such when joined to real disinterestedness, toleration, and a clear understanding. My accusers, after such as these, appear to me mere drivellers. For myself, I earnestly desire the good and enlightenment of my fellow-creatures, and see all, in the present course, tending to the same, and rejoice; but I am not for violent extremes, which only bring on an injurious reaction. I have never written a word in disfavour of liberalism; that I have not supported it openly in writing, arises from the following causes, as far as I know:—

That I have not argumentative powers: I see things pretty clearly, but cannot demonstrate them. Besides, I feel the counter-arguments too strongly. I do not feel that I could say aught to support the cause efficiently; besides that, on some topics (especially with regard to my own sex), I am far from making up my mind. I believe we are sent here to educate ourselves, and that self-denial, and disappointment, and self-control, are a part of our education; that it is not by taking away all restraining law that our improvement is to be achieved; and, though many things need great amendment, I can by no means go so far as my friends would have me. When I feel that I can say what will benefit my fellow-creatures, I will speak: not before.

[2] Grylls (p. 207) dates this entry March 8, 1831, presumably from the MS journal, from which she restores some lines omitted in S&M. The contents of the entry would seem more appropriate to 1831 than to 1838, by which date it is unlikely that anyone was concerned about Mary's taking an active part in reform. In October, 1838, Mary was living at 41d Park Street, London.

Then, I recoil from the vulgar abuse of the inimical press. I do more than recoil: proud and sensitive, I act on the defensive—an inglorious position.

To hang back, as I do, brings a penalty. I was nursed and fed with a love of glory. To be something great and good was the precept given me by my Father: Shelley reiterated it. Alone and poor, I could only be something by joining a party; and there was much in me—the woman's love of looking up, and being guided, and being willing to do anything if any one supported and brought me forward—which would have made me a good partisan. But Shelley died, and I was alone. My Father, from age and domestic circumstances, could not "*me faire valoir.*" My total friendlessness, my horror of pushing, and inability to put myself forward unless led, cherished and supported,—all this has sunk me in a state of loneliness no other human being ever before, I believe, endured—except Robinson Crusoe. How many tears and spasms of anguish this solitude has cost me, lies buried in my memory.

If I had raved and ranted about what I did not understand; had I adopted a set of opinions, and propagated them with enthusiasm; had I been careless of attack, and eager for notoriety; then the party to which I belonged had gathered round me, and I had not been alone. But since I had lost Shelley I have no wish to ally myself to the Radicals—they are full of repulsion to me—violent without any sense of Justice—selfish in the extreme—talking without knowledge—rude, envious and insolent—I wish to have nothing to do with them.[3]

It has been the fashion with these same friends to accuse me of worldliness. There, indeed, in my own heart and conscience, I take a high ground. I may distrust my own judgment too much—be too indolent and too timid; but in conduct I am above merited blame.

I like society; I believe all persons who have any talent (who are in good health) do. The soil that gives forth nothing, may lie ever fallow; but that which produces—however humble its product—needs cultivation, change of harvest, refreshing dews, and ripening sun. Books do much; but the living intercourse is the vital heat. Debarred from that, how have I pined and died!

My early friends chose the position of enemies. When I first discovered that a trusted friend had acted falsely by me, I was nearly destroyed.[4] My health was shaken. I remembered thinking, with a burst of agonizing tears, that I should prefer a bed of torture to the unutterable anguish a friend's falsehood engendered. There is no resentment; but the

[3] This sentence is not in S&M; printed by Miss Grylls, 207.

[4] See the entry for July 13, 1827.

world can never be to me what it was before. Trust, and confidence, and the heart's sincere devotion, are gone.

I sought at that time to make acquaintances—to divert my mind from this anguish. I got entangled in various ways through my ready sympathy and too eager heart; but I never crouched to society—never sought it unworthily. If I have never written to vindicate the rights of women, I have ever befriended women when oppressed. At every risk I have befriended and supported victims to the social system; but I make no boast, for in truth it is simple justice I perform; and so I am still reviled for being worldly.

God grant a happier and a better day is near! Percy—my all-in-all—will, I trust, by his excellent understanding, his clear, bright, sincere spirit and affectionate heart, repay me for sad long years of desolation. His career may lead me into the thick of life or only gild a quiet home. I am content with either, and, as I grow older I grow more fearless for myself—I become firmer in my opinions. The experienced, the suffering, the thoughtful may at last speak unrebuked. If it be the will of God that I live, I may ally my name yet to "the good cause," though I do not expect to please my accusers.

Thus have I put down my thoughts. I may have deceived myself; I may be in the wrong; I try to examine myself; and such as I have written appears to me the exact truth.

Enough of this! The great work of life goes on. Death draws near. To be better after death than in life is one's hope and endeavour—to be so through self-schooling. If I write the above, it is that those who love me may hereafter know that I am not all to blame, nor merit the heavy accusations cast on me for not putting myself forward. *I cannot* do that; it is against my nature. As well cast me from a precipice and rail at me for not flying.

1839

ENGLAND

Feb. 12.—I almost think that my present occupation will end in a fit of illness. I am editing Shelley's Poems, and writing notes for them.[1] I desire to do Shelley honour in the notes to the best of my knowledge and

[1] *The Poetical Works of P. B. Shelley,* ed. by Mrs. Shelley (London, Edward Moxon, 1839, 4 vols.).

ability; for the rest, they are or are not well written; it little matters to me which. Would that I had more literary vanity, or vanity of any kind, I were happier. As it is, I am torn to pieces by memory. Would that all were mute in the grave!

I *much* disliked the leaving out any of "Queen Mab." I dislike it still more than I can express, and I even wish I had resisted to the last; but when I was told that certain portions would injure the copyright of all the volumes to the publisher, I yielded. I had consulted Hunt, Hogg, and Peacock; they all said I had a right to do as I liked, and offered no one objection. Trelawney sent back the volume[2] to Moxon in a rage at seeing parts left out. How very much he must enjoy the opportunity thus afforded him of doing a rude and insolent act! It was *almost* worth while to make the omission, if only to give him this pleasure.

Hogg has written me an insulting letter because I left out the dedication to Harriet. Poor Harriet, to whose sad fate I attribute so many of my own heavy sorrows, as the atonement claimed by fate for her death.[3]

Little does Jefferson, how little does any one, know me! When Clarke's edition of "Queen Mab"[4] came to us at the Baths of Pisa, Shelley expressed great pleasure that these verses were omitted. This recollection caused me to do the same. It was to do him honour. What could it be to me? There are other verses I should well like to obliterate for ever,[5] but they will be printed; and any to her could in no way tend to my discomfort or gratify one ungenerous feeling. They shall be restored, though I do not feel easy as to the good I do Shelley. I may have been mistaken. Jefferson might mistake me and been [sic] angry; that were nothing. He has done far more, and done his best to give another poke to the poisonous dagger which has long rankled in my heart. I cannot forgive any man that insults any woman. She cannot call him out, she disdains words of retort; she must endure, but it is never to be forgiven; not, indeed, cherished as matter of enmity—that I never feel—but of caution to shield oneself from the like again.

In so arduous a task others might hope for encouragement and kindness from their friends—I know mine better. I am unstable, sometimes melancholy, and have been called on some occasions imperious; but I never did an ungenerous act in my life. I sympathise warmly with others, and have wasted my heart in their love and service.

[2] Volume I was published late in January (before the twenty-sixth), 1839.

[3] In most copies of S&M this sentence has been cut out of the page (IV, 1222). It was not cut out of the Yale University copy, from which it has been taken.

[4] William Clark's pirated edition in the spring of 1821.

[5] *Epipsychidion,* for example, on which Mary furnishes no information in the 1839 *Poetical Works.*

All this together is making me feel very ill, and my holiday at Woodlay only did me good while it lasted.

MARCH.[6]—Illness did ensue. What an illness! driving me to the verge of insanity. Often I felt the cord would snap, and I should no longer be able to rule my thoughts; with fearful struggles, miserable relapses, after long repose, I became somewhat better.

OCT. 5.—Twice in my life I have believed myself to be dying, and my soul being alive, though the bodily functions were faint and perishing, I had opportunity to look at Death in the face, and did not fear it—far from it. My feeling, especially in the first and most perilous instance,[7] was, I go to no new creation, I enter under no new laws. The God that made this beautiful world (and I was then at Lerici, surrounded by the most beautiful manifestation of the visible creation) made that into which I go; as there is beauty and love here, such is there, and I felt as if my spirit would when it left my frame be received and sustained by a beneficent and gentle Power. I had no fear, rather, though, I had no active wish but a passive satisfaction in death. Whether the nature of my illness—debility from loss of blood, without pain—caused this tranquillity of soul, I cannot tell; but so it was, and it had this blessed effect, that I have never since anticipated death with terror, and even if a violent death (which is the most repugnant to human nature) menaced me, I think I could, after the first shock, turn to the memory of that hour, and renew its emotion of perfect resignation.

1840

ENGLAND

MARCH 5.—Ratcliffe taken ill.

JUNE 1.—(Brighton.) I must mark this evening, tired as I am, for it is one among few—soothing and balmy. Long oppressed by care, disappointment, and ill health, which all combined to depress and irritate me, I felt almost to have lost the spring of happy reverie. On such a night it returns—the calm sea, the soft breeze, the silver bow new bent in the western heaven—nature in her sweetest mood, raised one's thoughts to God and imparted peace.

Indeed, I have many, many blessings, and ought to be grateful, as I

[6] Mary moved to Layton House, Putney, during March, 1839.
[7] See the entry for July 7, 1822.

am, though the poison lurks among them; for it is my strange fate that all my friends are sufferers—ill health or adversity bears heavily on them, and I can do little good, and lately ill health and extreme depression have even marred the little I could do. If I could restore health, administer balm to the wounded heart, and banish care from those I love, I were in myself happy, while I am loved and Percy continues the blessing that he is. Still, who on such a night must not feel the weight of sorrow lessened? For myself, I repose in gentle and grateful reverie, and hope for others. I am content for myself. Years have—how much!—cooled the ardent and swift spirit that at such hours bore me freely along. Yet, though I no longer soar, I repose. Though I no longer deem all things attainable, I enjoy what is, and while I feel that whatever I have lost of youth and hope, I have acquired the enduring affection of a noble heart, and Percy shows such excellent dispositions that I feel that I am much the gainer in life.

Fate does indeed visit some too heavily—poor Ratcliffe, for instance, God restore him!

God and good angels guard us! surely this world, stored outwardly with shapes and influences of beauty and good, is peopled in its intellectual life by myriads of loving spirits that mould our thoughts to good, influence beneficially the course of events, and minister to the destiny of man. Whether the beloved dead make a portion of this company I dare not guess, but that such exist I feel—far off, when we are worldly, evil, selfish; drawing near and imparting joy and sympathy when we rise to noble thoughts and disinterested action. Such surely gather round one on such an evening, and make part of that atmosphere of love, so hushed, so soft, on which the soul reposes and is blest.

APPENDIX I

Other Textual Notes

Many notes on the text are in the footnotes. The following are not important enough to require immediate attention and are preserved here for the scholar who rightfully wishes to know just how the text has been handled. Textual readings below from the *Shelley and Mary* (S&M) text are obvious errors, which were made either by Mary in the original MS or by Lady Shelley in transcribing or proofreading. Correct readings as printed in the text of this edition follow the S&M readings.

Page,	*line* (fb = *from bottom of text*)	
5,	16	: S&M *throws;* Text *throw.*
11,	12	: S&M *Solure;* Text *Soleure.*
12,	9 *fb*	: S&M *Mumph;* Text *Mumpf.*
15,	6	: S&M *Strafford;* Text *Stratford.*
17,	10 *fb*	: S&M *Alix;* Text *Alexy.*
18,	11	: S&M *Kitchener;* Text *Hitchener.*
19,	19	: S&M *Baruel;* Text *Barruel.*
19,	8–9 *fb*	: S&M *Westminister;* Text *Westminster.*
20,	13	: S&M *informed;* Text *unformed.*
22,	15 *fb*	: S&M *Thursday;* Text *Tuesday.*
29,	8	: S&M *Shelley read;* Text *Shelley reads.*
32,	11 *fb*	: S&M *Thaliba;* Text *Thalaba.*
34,	3	: S&M *Westminister;* Text *Westminster.*
34,	8 *fb*	: S&M *Hamiatoff;* Text *Haimatoff.*
35,	2	: S&M *divinty;* Text *divinity.*
36,	20	: S&M *Shelley read "Paradise . . . ;* Text *Shelley reads "Paradise. . . .*
43,	17–18	: S&M *Shelley read Italian;* Text *Shelley reads Italian.*
52,	13	: S&M *Buisson;* Text *Boisson.*
53,	7	: S&M *Arveron;* Text *Arveiron.*
55,	15	: S&M *Quintius;* Text *Quintus.*
56,	10 *fb*	: S&M *comes from;* Text *comes for.*
64,	5	: S&M *"Valcenga";* Text *"Valcenza."*
68,	5 *fb*	: S&M *Shelley read 2nd book;* Text *Shelley reads 2nd book.*
75,	16	: S&M *chances;* Text *changes.*
78,	13	: S&M *"Alcestes";* Text *"Alcestis."*
82,	13	: S&M *from London;* Text *for London.*
85,	14	: S&M *translate;* Text *transcribe.*
86,	13 *fb*	: S&M *Colson;* Text *Coulson.*

Page,	*line* (fb = *from bottom of text*)	
95,	11 *fb*:	S&M *Jura;* Text *Susa.* (Shelley's letter of April 1818 to Peacock says *Susa.*—[Julian edition, IX, 294].)
97,	9 :	S&M *Mason;* Text *Manson.*
110,	11–12 :	S&M *Corregio;* Text *Correggio.*
113,	19 *fb*:	S&M *Senanges;* Text *Senange.*
123,	4 *fb*:	S&M *"Paradisio";* Text *"Paradiso."*
124,	14 :	S&M *Torloina;* Text *Torlonia.*
124,	17 :	S&M *Toide;* Text *Zoide.*
125,	15 :	S&M *Gusman;* Text *Guzman.*
126,	13 :	S&M *Carlisle;* Text *Carlile.*
129,	10 *fb*:	S&M *Fables;* Text *Fable.*
129,	1 *fb*:	S&M *Catalina;* Text *Catarina.*
134,	15 :	S&M *Perigano;* Text *Pugnano.*
137,	3 :	S&M *La Santini;* Text *La Tantini.*
145, 146,	5–6 *fb*: 3 :	S&M *Bernadini;* Text *Bernardini.*
150,	15 :	S&M *comments;* Text *"Comments."*
153,	7 *fb*:	S&M *Dancelli;* Text *Danielli.*
154,	8 :	S&M *Preguano;* Text *Pugnano.*
164,	3 :	S&M *Bartelini;* Text *Bartolini.*
186,	9 :	S&M *Lucerne;* Text *Lucca.*

APPENDIX II

Lost or Unprinted Letters by Shelley and Mary

These letters are unaccounted for by the Julian edition of Shelley's Correspondence (VII, VIII–X), F. L. Jones (ed.), *The Letters of Mary W. Shelley,* and other sources. (Letters which have been printed are identified, with references, in the notes.)

Date of Entry		*From To*
1814.	Aug. 2	Shelley (letters) to Mary
	Aug. 3	Shelley to Tavernier
	Aug. 13	Mary to Mrs. P.
	Sept. 14	Shelley (several letters) to ?
	Sept. 15	Shelley to Voisey
	Sept. 19	Shelley to Amory
	Sept. 20	Shelley to Hookham
	Sept. 20	Shelley to Tavernier
	Oct. 4	Mary to Isabel Baxter
	Oct. 4	Shelley to Mrs. Boinville
	Oct. 10	Shelley to Harriet
	Oct. 23	Shelley to Godwin
	Oct. 23	Mary to Isabel Baxter
	Oct. 26	Shelley to T. Hookham
	Oct. 27	Mary to Fanny Godwin
	Oct. 31	Mary to Claire
	Oct. 31	Shelley to Claire
	Oct. 31	Shelley to a Sussex man
	Nov. 2	Mary to Shelley
	Nov. 3	Mary to Shelley
	Nov. 6	Shelley ("A great heap of letters") to ?
	Nov. 8	Mary to Isabel Baxter
	Nov. 13	Mary to [? the Godwins]
	Dec. 6	Shelley ("a number of circular letters of this event" —his son Charles's birth) to ?
	Dec. 9	Shelley to Marianne de St. Croix
1815.	Jan. 2	Mary to [? Hogg]
	Jan. 3	Shelley to Peacock
	Jan. 4	Shelley (notes) to ?
	Jan. [12]	Mary to Peacock

Date of Entry				*From* *To*
	Feb.	5		Shelley to Longdill
	Feb.	5		Shelley to Charles Clairmont
	Feb.	6		Shelley (letters) to ?
	Feb.	9		Shelley (letters) to ?
	Feb.	23		Shelley to Fanny Godwin
	Mar.	7		Mary to Fanny Godwin
	May	8		Mary to James Marshall
1816.	Aug.	3		Mary to Fanny Godwin
	Aug.	3		Shelley (letters) to ?
	Aug.	10		Mary to Fanny Godwin
	Aug.	10		Shelley to Charles Clairmont
	Sept.	12	(rec'd)	Shelley to Mary
	Sept.	13	(rec'd)	Shelley to Mary
	Sept.	13		Mary to Shelley
	Sept.	15	(rec'd)	Shelley to Mary
	Sept.	17		Mary to Shelley
	Sept.	18	(rec'd)	Shelley to Mary
	Oct.	2		Mary to Fanny Godwin
	Oct.	30		Mary to Charles Clairmont
	Dec.	4		Shelley to Hayward
	Dec.	4		Shelley to Godwin
	Dec.	5		Mary to Everina Wollstonecraft
	Dec.	5		Mary to Shelley
	Dec.	6		Mary to Shelley
	Dec.	12	(rec'd)	Shelley to Mary
	Dec.	13	(rec'd)	Shelley to Mary
1817.	May	28		Mary to W. G.
	June	[7–]14		Mary to Isabel Baxter
	Nov.	4		Mary to William Baxter
	Nov.	5		Mary to Shelley
	Nov.	5		Mary to William Godwin [Jr.?]
	Nov.	6		Mary to Shelley
	Nov.	13		Mary to Isabel Baxter
	Dec.	3		Mary (letters) to ?
	Dec.	30		Mary to Isabel Baxter
1818.	Jan.	1		Mary to Isabel Baxter
	Mar.	22		Shelley to Byron
	Apr.	7		Mary (letters) to ?
	Apr.	8		Mary (letters) to ?
	Apr.	[12–]19		Mary to Charles Clairmont
	Apr.	[12–]19		Mary to Everina Wollstonecraft
	July	2		Shelley to Hunt
	Oct.	24		Mary to Mrs. Hunt
	Nov.	23		Mary to Godwin

Date of Entry			*From To*
1819.	Jan.	23	Shelley (letters) to ?
	Apr.	8	Mary to Mrs. Gisborne
	Sept.	15	Shelley to Torlonia
	Oct.	14	Mary to Mrs. Gisborne
	Oct.	14	Mary to Mrs. Mason
	Oct.	[15–]20	Shelley & Mary (letters sent to England on Oct. 16) to ?
	Oct.	28	Shelley to Peacock
	Oct.	28	Shelley to Longdill
	Oct.	28	Shelley to Horace Smith
	Nov.	6	Shelley to Peacock
	Nov.	9	Shelley to Godwin
1820.	Jan.	11	Mary to Mrs. Gisborne
	Jan.	11	Mary to Mrs. Mason
	Jan.	12	Mary to Sophia Stacey
	Jan.	12	Mary to Charles Clairmont
	Jan.	12	Shelley to Hunt
	Feb.	15	Mary to Hunt
	Mar.	2	Mary to Godwin
	Apr.	6	Mary to Godwin
	Apr.	[9–]23	Mary to Godwin
	May	26	Shelley to Horace Smith
	July	1	Shelley to Godwin
1821.	Jan.	3	Mary to Claire
	Jan.	29	Mary to Claire
	Mar.	4	Mary (letters) to ?
	Apr.	2	Mary to Prince Mavrocordato
	Apr.	4	Mary to Hunt
	May	9	Mary (letters) to ?
	May	31	Mary to Godwin
	May	31	Mary to Charles Clairmont
	Nov.	29	Mary to Claire
	Dec.	3	Mary (letters) to ?
	Dec.	8	Mary to Claire
1822.	Jan.	21	Mary to Claire
	Feb.	4	Mary to Claire
	Mar.	3	Mary to Dr. Nott
	Mar.	20	Mary to Claire
	Apr.	1	Mary to M. Costar
	Apr.	1	Mary to Claire
	Apr.	3	Mary (letters) to ?
			Total:
			Shelley 56+
			Mary 76+
			132+

APPENDIX III

References to Shelley's Works

Except for three or four small items, nothing is included in this table which does not relate to the works themselves as in the process of composition or as finished productions (i.e., to their writing, copying, reading, transmittal to a publisher, etc.). Shelley's reading, his activities, and current events, though they often have a direct bearing upon his literary efforts, are not noticed in the present summary of references.

Bracketed dates (such as July [15–]22) mean that the journal entry covers the days indicated. Mary's notation that "Shelley writes" or transcribes does not necessarily mean that he wrote or transcribed each day or on any particular day. Unbracketed dates (such as January 2–5) mean that there is a separate daily entry for each day.

Adonais. Mary reads, 1821, July 12.

Address to the People on the Death of the Princess Charlotte. Shelley begins, 1817, November 11; finishes, 1817, November 12; Mary reads, 1817, November 15.

Assassins, The. S. writes, 1814, August 25–27, September 10; reads to T. Hookham, 1814, September 15; writes, 1814, September 19; makes a note on Gibbon's discussion of the Assassins, 1815, April 8.

Alexy Haimatoff. See *Memoirs of* . . . .

Cenci, The. (Mary copies the Italian Cenci MS, 1818, May 18[–20], finishes on May 25; Mary (with Shelley ?) visits the Palazzo Colonna, and sees the picture of Beatrice Cenci, 1819, April 22; Mary (with Shelley ?) visits the Casa Cenci, 1819, May 11); Shelley writes, 1819, May 14, August 4, 7, 11; Mary copies, 1819, August [12–]20; S. sends to Peacock (on September 10), 1819, September [10–]12.

Coliseum, The. S. begins, 1818, November 25.

Defence of Poetry, A. Mary copies, 1821, March 12, 14–20.

Homer's *Hymns*. S. translates, 1818, January 20.

Homer's *Hymn to Mercury*. S. finishes translation of, 1820, July 14.

Letter Concerning Richard Carlile. S. writes, 1819, November 5; sends it to Hunt for the *Examiner*, 1819, November 6.

Masque of Anarchy, The. S. sends to Hunt, 1819, September 23.

Memoirs of Prince Alexy Haimatoff, by John Brown (T. J. Hogg), Shelley's Review of. S. writes, 1814, November 16–17.

Ode to Naples. S. writes, 1820, August [18–]25.

Peter Bell the Third. (S. reads Wordsworth's or Reynolds' *Peter Bell*, 1819, September 24); Mary copies, 1819, September [25–]28; S. writes, 1819,

September 30; Mary finishes copying, and it is sent to Hunt, 1819, November 2.

Plato's *Symposium*. S. translates, 1818, July 13–17 (finishes on July 17); finishes correcting translation, and Mary begins copying, 1818, July 20; Mary copies, 1818, July 21–22, 24–28, 30–31, August 1–3, finishes August 6; Mary reads to Mrs. Gisborne, 1818, August 27, finishes August 28.

Prometheus Unbound. S. writes, 1818, September 14, (?) [22–]24; Mary copies (?), 1818, December 18, finishes December 19; Mary reads, 1819, April 25; Mary copies, 1819, September [10–]12.

Queen Mab. S. reads one canto to Mary, 1814, October 6.

Revolt of Islam, The. [*Laon and Cythna*]. S. writes, 1817, May 9, 13, June 2, 20–21, July 8, [15–]22, August 5 [1–6], [10–]13, [14–]17, [25–]29, September 19, finishes September [20–]29; transcribes, 1817, October [10–]12; S. reads two cantos, 1817, November 29; S. finishes reading his poem aloud, 1817, November 30; alterations made with Mr. Ollier present, 1817, December 15, finished December 16; Mary reads, 1818, July 28, finishes August 3; S. reads aloud, 1819, August [12–]20.

Rhododaphne by T. L. Peacock, Shelley's Review of. Mary copies, 1818, February 18[–25] (copying done on February 20–21, finished on February 23).

Rosalind and Helen: A Modern Eclogue. Mary copies, 1818, February 18 [–25] (copying done on February 19), August 14–15, finishes August 16.

Shelley's Declaration in the Chancery Proceedings. Mary copies, 1817, February 2.

Spinoza's *Tractatus Theologico-Politicus*. S. translates, 1817 [October 24–] November 3; 1820, January 5, 8–9, 12, finishes first chapter on January 15, 16, 23, March 17, 21–22, 26–31, April 1–2, 4–8, [9–]23, June 2; 1821, November [11–]15.

Swellfoot the Tyrant. S. begins, 1820, August [18–]25.

Symposium, The. See Plato's *Symposium*.

Witch of Atlas, The. S. writes, 1820, August 14–16; Mary copies, 1820, December 12, 19, finishes, 1821, January 6.

Zastrozzi. Mary reads, 1814, October 10.

Unidentified Entries: S. repeats one of his own poems, 1814, October 7; S. writes, 1814, November 12; 1816, August 15–16, October 22–23, 26, November 2; 1817, January 2–5, December 3; Mary copies S.'s Poems, 1820, February [22–]25.

APPENDIX IV

Shelley's Reading

A. ALPHABETICALLY ARRANGED

The dates indicate journal entries. Bracketed dates introduced editorially into the text are ignored in this table. In many cases the reading was not done only, or even at all, on the date of the journal entry. For precautions concerning the use of dates in the journal, see the Preface, p. *xiii*. "L" means the Reading List for the year indicated (printed in the text at the end of the year specified).

Specific editions in the list below are not necessarily those read by Shelley. The editions noted are usually first editions, though there are instances in which this is not true, especially for early books and for books translated into English from French, German, and Italian.

Æschylus. 1815, February 13; 1817, July 22, 31, August 5, L; 1819, August 21, September 4; 1820, February 10;—*Agamemnon,* 1817, July 26;—*Fragments,* 1821, January 10;—*Persæ,* 1818, August 3;—*Prometheus,* 1816, L; 1817, July 13; 1818, March 26.

Æsop. *Fables,* 1815, February 16.

Adolphus, John. *Biographical Memoirs of the French Revolution* (1799, 4 vols.), 1814, November 15, L.

Aiken, Dr. See Mrs. A. L. Barbauld.

Alfieri, Vittorio. *Life of Alfieri. By Himself* (1804, 2 vols.), 1814, L;—Tragedies (probably *The Tragedies of Alfieri,* translated by C. Lloyd, 1815), 1815, L.

Anacharsis. See Barthélemy.

Anacreon. Odes, 1814, September 25. (Reading by Shelley or Mary?)

Apollonius Rhodius. [*Argonautica*], 1820, August 1, 25, L.

Apuleius. 1817, May 9, L;—"Cupid and Psyche," 1817, L.

Ariosto, Ludovico. *Orlando Furioso* (1532), 1815, April 15–23; L; 1818, May 30–31, November 8.

Aristophanes. 1818, June 22–29, July 2, 6;—*The Clouds,* 1818, June 16–19; —*Lysistrata,* 1818, June 21;—*Plutus,* 1818, June 20.

Arrian (Flavius Arrianus). *Historia Indica,* 1817, June 18, 20–24, L.

"Astronomy" in the *Encyclopedia* [? William Nicholson, *The British Encyclopedia,* 1807–1809, 6 vols.], 1820, L.

Athenæus. [*Deipnosophistae* (The Banquet of the Learned)], 1820, February 10.

Bacon, Francis. *Novum Organum,* 1815, L.

Baillie, Joanna. *Orra, A Tragedy* (1812), 1814, October 7.

Barbauld, Mrs. Anna Letitia, and Dr. Aiken. *Evenings at Home; or the juvenal budget opened. Consisting of a variety of miscellaneous pieces, for the instruction and amusement of young people* (1792–96, 6 vols.), 1820, April 2.

Barrow, Sir John. *Some Account of the Earl of Macartney . . . and a Journal of an Embassy to . . . China* (1807, 2 vols.), 1814, L.

Barruel, L'Abbé (Augustin). *Histoire du Jacobinisme* (1797), translated by R. Clifford as *Memoirs Illustrating the History of Jacobinism* (1797–98, 4 vols.),[1] 1814, August 23, 25, October 9, 11.

Barthélemy, Abbé J. J. *Voyage du jeune Anacharsis en Grèce vers le milieu du quatrième siècle avant l'ère vulgaire* (Paris, 1817, 7 vols., 5th ed.), 1818, June 22–30, July 2, 5–6.

Beaumont, Francis; and Fletcher, John; [and Massinger, Philip]. 1819, August 20, September 17, October 10;—*Bonduca,* 1820, May 6, 8;—*The Double Marriage,* 1820, August 25;—*The Faithful Shepherdess,* 1817, June 21, July 8;—*The Laws of Candy,* 1818, July 12;—*The Lovers' Progress,* 1820, September 10;—*The Maid's Tragedy,* 1818, July 9;—*Philaster,* 1818, July 10; 1819, August 11;—*Thierry and Theodoret,* 1820, May 9–10; —*A Wife for a Month,* 1818, July 15.

Beckford, William. *Vathek,* 1815, L.

Berkeley, George. 1817, December 12–14.

Bible. 1817, April 16; 1820, January 1, 9, 12–15, 21, 23, March 21;—New Testament, 1815, L; 1819, December 31; 1820, L;—St. Matthew, 1820, January 1, 5, 8–9;—St. Luke, 1819, December 31;—Old Testament, 1820, L;—Ezekiel, 1820, March 9, 22, L;—Isaiah, 1820, February 2, 10;—Jeremiah, 1820, February 10–11, 13, 16, 18;—Apocrypha, Tobit, 1820, March 10;—*The Wisdom of Solomon,* 1820, April 2.

Blackwell, Thomas. *Memoirs of the Court of Augustus* (Edinburgh, 1753–56, 3 vols.), 1814, December 19, L; 1816, L.

Boccaccio, Giovanni. 1819, August 21, September 4, 12–14; 1820, September 13, 16;—*Decameron,* 1820, L.

Boswell, James. *Life of Samuel Johnson* (1791), 1820, L.

Brown, Charles Brockden. *Edgar Huntley* (1801, 3 vols.), 1814, November 16–17, L.

Browne, Sir Thomas. *Religio Medici* (1642), 1815, March 14.

Burke, Edmund. *A Vindication of Civil Society* (1756), 1815, L.

Byron, Lord. 1814, August 3;—*Childe Harold,* Canto III (1816), 1816, L, 1817, May 28; Canto IV (1818), 1818, September 25;—*Don Juan,* Cantos I–II (1819), 1820, January 3, L;—*Heaven and Earth* (1823), 1821, December 14;—*Lara* (1814), 1815, February 15, L;—*Parisina* (1816), 1816, L;—*The Siege of Corinth* (1816), 1816, L.

Calderón de la Barca, Pedro. 1819, September 4, 12–17, 22; 1820, November 14, L.

[1] Shelley read this translation. His autograph copy of Vol. II is in the Berg Collection, the New York Public Library.

Casas, Bartolomé de las. *Brevissima Relacion de la Destruycion de las Indias* (Seville, 1552), 1820, February 10–11.

Cervantes, S. Miguel de. *Don Quixote,* 1816, October 7–8, 17, 19, 21, 23–25, 27–31, November 3, 5, 7, L.

Chaucer, Geoffrey. *Chaucer's Dream,* 1821, December 10;—*The Flower and the Leaf,* 1821, December 10 (both falsely attributed to Chaucer);—*Troilus and Creseyde,* 1821, June 21.

Cicero, M. Tullius. *Colectanea,* 1814, October 14, L;—*Paradoxa,* 1814, October 14.

Clarendon, Edward Hyde, Earl of. *The History of the Rebellion and Civil Wars in England* (1702–1704, 3 vols.), 1819, October 9, 11–13, 20, 24, 28, 30; November 2, 5–8.

Clarke, Dr. Edward Daniel. *Travels in Various Countries of Europe, Asia, and Africa* (1810–23, 6 vols.), 1818, January 7.

Coleridge, Samuel Taylor. Poems, 1815, L;—*Ancient Mariner* (1798), 1814, September 15, October 5; 1821, February 22;—*Christabel* (1816), 1816, August 26, L;—*France, An Ode* (1798), 1815, January 6;—*Ode to Tranquillity* (1801), 1815, January 6;—*Biographia Literaria* (1817, 2 vols.), 1817, December 8, L;—*The Statesman's Manual . . . A Lay Sermon* (1816), 1816, L;—*A Lay Sermon* (1817), 1817, L.

Le Criminel Secret, 1816, L.

Cromwell, Life of. See *Life of . . . .*

Curtius Rufus, Quintus. *Vita Alexandria,* 1816, August 4, November 22–25, L.

Dante. *Divina Commedia,* 1818, April 11, 19, 22, December 29; 1819, August 5, 7, 9–11, 20; September 14–17;—*Vita Nuova,* 1821, January 31.

Davis, John. *Travels of Four Years and a Half in the United States of America* (1803), 1817, L.

Davy, Sir Humphrey. *Elements of Chemical Philosophy* (1812) *(or Elements of Agricultural Chemistry,* 1813), 1816, October 29.

Defoe, Daniel. *A Journal of the Plague Year* (1722), 1817, L.

Diogenes Laertius. [*Lives of the Philosophers*],[2] 1814, December 4, L.

DuBois, Edward. *St. Godwin; a Tale of the Sixteenth, Seventeenth and Eighteenth Century.* By Count Reginald De St. Leon (1800) [a parody on William Godwin's *St. Leon*], 1814, L.

Dumont, Charles. *Mémoires d'un Détenu, suivis de divers fragmens de Littérature et d'Histoire naturelle* (Paris, 1795), 1816, August 25, L. (Reference may be to Riouffe, *q.v.*)

Edgeworth, Maria. *Castle Rackrent* (1800), 1816, November 8, L.

Edinburgh Review, No. LII [June 1816, Vol. 26], 1816, L; No. LIII [Sept. 1816, Vol. 27], 1816, L.

Edwards, Bryan. *The History of the British Colonies in the West Indies* (1793–94, 2 vols.), 1814, December 23, L; 1815, January 3.

Elphinstone, Mountstuart. *An Account of the Kingdom of Caubul, and its*

[2] Shelley's copy of this book passed to Leigh Hunt, then to James T. Fields. See Mrs. James T. Fields, *A Shelf of Old Books,* 35–40.

Dependencies in Persia, Tartary, and India (1815, 2 vols.), 1817, July 31, August 5, L.

Erasmus, Desiderius. 1815, February 13.

Erskine, Thomas, Baron. *Armata. A Fragment* (1817) [a political romance dealing with occurrences in the Indian countries of North America; published anonymously], 1820, L.

Euripides. 1815, February 13, L; 1818, May 10; 1819, January 8, 11, March 24, August 21, September 4; 1820, June 19–20, 23, L;—*Alcestis,* 1817, April 10;—*Hippolitus,* 1818, May 17; 1819, April 1;—*Medea,* 1819, March 26.

Eustace, John Chetwode. *A Classical Tour Through Italy* (1813), 1818, August 3, 5.

Fénelon, François S. de La Mothe. *Aventures de Télémaque* (1699), 1816, L.

Fergusson, Adam. *History of Margaret, Sister of John Bull* (1761) [a novel], 1814, September 15.

Fletcher, John. See Beaumont and Fletcher.

Fortiguerra, Niccolò. *Il Ricciardetto,* 1820, June 26, 29–30, July 1, 3–11, L.

Fox, Charles James. *A History of the Early Part of the Reign of James II* (1808), 1815, L.

Frederica Sophia Wilhelmina. *Mémoires de Fréderique Sophie Wilhelmine de Prusse, Margrave de Bareith; escrits de sa main* (Paris, 1811, 2 tom.); *Memoirs . . . Written by Herself,* translated from the original French (1812, 2 vols.), 1816, September 27, October 8.

Gibbon, Edward. *Memoirs (Miscellaneous Works of Edward Gibbon. With Memoirs of his Life and Writings composed by himself; illustrated from his Letters with occasional notes and narrative by John Lord Sheffield,* 1796, 2 vols.), 1815, January 31, February 2–3, 5, L;—*The Decline and Fall of the Roman Empire* (1783–90, 12 vols.), 1815, March 16, 18, April 8–10, L; 1816, November 25–26, 28–30, December 1, 3–4, L; 1817, August 5, 9, 13, 17, December 24–31, L; 1818, January 1–2, 7, June 18, 20–21.

Gillies, John. *History of Ancient Greece* (1786, 2 vols.), 1820, September 23, October 1, L.

Godwin, William. *Caleb Williams* (1794, 3 vols.), 1814, September 15; 1816, L;—"Godwin's Miscellanies" (? *The Enquirer: Reflections on Education, Manners, and Literature, in a series of Essays,* 1797), 1817, L;—*Essay on Sepulchres* (1809), 1814, L;—*The Life of Chaucer* (1803, 2 vols.), 1815, March 5, 15, L;—*The Lives of Edward and John Philips, Nephews and Pupils of Milton* (1809), 1815, L;—*Mandeville* (1817, 3 vols.), 1817, December 2, L;—*Political Justice* (1793, 2 vols.), 1814, October 7, L; 1816, November 29–30, December 1, L; 1817, November 29, L; 1820, March 22, 26, April 1, 4, L;—*St. Leon* (1799, 3 vols.), 1815, L.

"Greek Romances," 1820, June 27–29, July 2, 5–6, 9, 13, L.

Guarini, Giovanni B. *Pastor Fido* (1590), 1815, April 8–10, 15, L.

Hamilton, Elizabeth. *Memoirs of Modern Philosophers* (Bath, 1800, 3 vols.), 1816, L.

Hamilton, Life of Lady. See *Life of . . . .*

Hazlitt, William. See Thomas Holcroft.

Herodotus. 1815, L; 1818, July 16–18, 20–22, 24–31, August 1–2; 1820, October 1; 1821, December 2–4, 11.

Hesiod. 1815, L.

Histoire de la Philosophie Moderne, 1817, June 14.

Hobbes, Thomas. (Mainly *The Leviathan,* 1651), 1820, March 9–10, 13, 15–17, 21, L;—"Hobbes on Man" (*De Homine,* 1658), 1820, March 11.

Hogg, Thomas Jefferson. *Memoirs of Prince Alexy Haimatoff,* by John Brown (1813), 1814, October 7, November 16, L; (1815, January 3).

Holcroft, Thomas. *Memoirs of Thomas Holcroft, by himself* (completed by William Hazlitt, 1816, 3 vols.), 1816, October 1, L.

Homer. 1815, L;—*Hymns,* 1817, July 11–13, L; 1818, January 20;—*Hymn to Mercury,* 1820, July 14;—*Iliad,* 1817, June 2–3, 30, July 1–4, 8–9, L.

Horace. 1821, March 3;—*Epistles,* 1820, September 9;—*Odes,* 1816, December 3, 5; 1818, August 8.

Hume, David. 1817, December 11; 1818, January 7;—*History of England* (1763, 8 vols.), 1818, June 19–22, 25, 29, July 9–10, 13–15, 20–22, 25, 29–31, August 1, 3–5, 12–13, 15.

Hunt, Leigh. *The Story of Rimini* (1816), 1816, L.

Jonson, Ben. *The Alchemist,* 1817, August 24, L; 1819, August 6–10;—*The Case Is Altered,* 1821, March 8;—*Catiline's Conspiracy,* 1817, L, 1820, March 13, 15;—*Cynthia's Revels,* 1817, August 17, L;—*Every Man in His Humour,* 1821, May 14, 20;—*The Fall of Sejanus,* 1817, L; 1820, March 11;—*The Sad Shepherd,* 1819, September 15–16;—*A Tale of a Tub,* 1821, March 12;—*Volpone,* 1817, August 24, L.

Kant, Immanuel. 1821, September 1.

Keats, John. *Hyperion* (1820), 1820, October 18;—Poems (*Lamia, Isabella, The Eve of St. Agnes, and Other Poems,* 1820), 1820, L.

Kotzebue, August F. F. von. *The Most Remarkable Year in the Life of Kotzebue, Containing his Exile into Siberia. By Himself,* translated by B. Beresford (1806, 3 vols.), 1815, L.

Labaume, Eugène. "History of the Russian War" (*A Narrative of the Campaign in Russia,* translated from the French [by E. Boyce], London, 1815), 1815, L.

Lacretelle Jeune, Jean Charles D. de. [Shelley read both Lacretelle's *History* and its continuation (published separately) by Rabaut St.-Étienne. Apparently he read the former in 1816 and the latter in 1817, but since it is impossible to be sure of this, the entries (with one exception) are repeated for both writers.] *Histoire de la Révolution Française* (Paris, 1801–1806, 5 vols.), 1816, September 29, L; 1817, April 17, 22–23, May 3, 13–15, 19, June 5, L.

Laignelot, Joseph François. *Conspiration de Rienzi,* 1815, L, 1816, L.

Lamb, Lady Caroline. *Glenarvon* (1816), 1816, L.

Lamb, Charles. *Specimens of English Dramatic Poets* (1808), 1817, L.

Lawrence, James Henry. *The Empire of the Nairs* (1811), 1814, L.

Le Sage, Alain René. *Le Diable Boiteux,* 1815, March 23.

Lewis, Matthew Gregory. *The Monk* (1796), 1814, L.

"Life of Cromwell" [probably *Memoirs of Oliver Cromwell and His Children, Supposed to be Written by Himself* (1816, 3 vols.)], 1816, October 13–14, L.

"Life of Lady Hamilton" [*Memoirs of Lady Hamilton, With Anecdotes of Her Friends,* &c. (1815, 2nd ed.; anonymous)], 1815, L.

Livy (Titus Livius). [*The History of Rome (Annales)*], 1815, January 24, 30, February 1, 4, 6–7, 13–14, 16, 24, March 15, 20–27, L; 1818, December 3, 5, 9–10, 12, 17–18, 22–23, 28–29; 1819, January 1, 3–5.

Locke, John. 1820, March 31, April 1, 2, 4, 23, L;—*An Essay Concerning Human Understanding* (1690), 1815, L; 1816, November 15–23, December 5, L.

Louvet de Couvray, Jean B. "Louvet's Memoirs" [*Quelques Notices pour l'Histoire; or a Narrative of the Dangers to which I was Exposed since the 31st of May, 1793* (London, 1795)], 1814, L.

Lucan (Marcus Annæus Lucanus). [*Pharsalia*], 1819, September 15.

Lucian. Works, 1816, September 29, October 21–22, November 10–14, December 5, L; 1818, August 16.

Lucretius Caro, Titus. *De Rerum Natura,* 1815, April 18; 1816, July 28–29, L; 1819, March 15–16, 22; 1820, June 28–30, July 3–6, 8, L.

Lullin de Chateauvieux, J. Fréderic. *Manuscrit venu de St. Hélène, d'une manière inconnue* (London, 1817; anonymous), 1817, June 4, L.

Macaulay, Catherine. *The History of England from the Accession of James I to that of the Brunswick Line* (1763–83, 8 vols.), 1820, July 18, August 25, September 4, L.

Macpherson, James. *Ossian,* 1815, L.

Malthus, Thomas R. *An Essay on the Principle of Population* (1798), 1818, October [1–4], 5, 6.

Manso, Giovanni B. *La Vita di Torquato Tasso* (Venice, 1619), 1818, April 6, 11, May 11.

Maimbourg, Louis. *The History of Arianism,* translated by William Webster, (1728–29, 2 vols.), 1814, December 22.

Massinger, Philip. 1819, October 9. (See Beaumont and Fletcher.)

Maturin, Rev. Charles R. *Bertram* (1816) [a tragedy], 1816, L.

Medwin, Thomas. Medwin's "Journal in India" (apparently in MS), 1820, November 4, 6.

Milman, Henry Hart. *Fazio* (1815) [a tragedy], 1816, L.

Milton, John. 1816, August 21–23;—*Areopagitica,* 1815, L;—*Comus,* 1814, October 19; 1815, January 13;—*Lycidas,* 1815, L;—*Paradise Lost,* 1815, L; 1816, November 15–22, L; 1817, December 22, 30; 1819, April 16–17, August 4, 21;—*Paradise Regained,* 1815, January 30, L; 1820, May 30, June 5–6.

Monboddo, James Burnett, Lord. *Antient Metaphysics: or, the Science of*

Universals (Edinburgh, 1779–99, 6 vols.), 1820, September 21–23, October 1, L.

Montaigne, Michel E. de. *Essais,* 1816, September 24, October 18–27, 29–30, November 2–5, 7–10, L.

Montesquieu, Charles de Secondat, Baron de. *Lettres Persanes* (1721), 1816, L.

Moore, Dr. John. *A Journal During a Residence in France* (1793–94, 2 vols.), 1814, December 3, 6, L.

Moore, Thomas. *Epistles, Odes, and Other Poems* (1806), 1817, L;—*Lalla Rookh* (1817), 1817, August 24, L.

Morgan, Sydney, Lady. *France* (1817, 2 vols.), 1817, December 16–20, L.

Moritz, Carl Philipp. *Travels, Chiefly on Foot, through Several Parts of England,* translated [from the German] into English (1795), 1816, L.

Moschus. Works, 1816, L.

Müller, Johannes von. *Universal History* (1811, 3 vols.), translated by J. C. Prichard (1818, 3 vols.), 1820, January 23, L.

Ockley, Simon. *The History of the Saracens* (1708–18, 2 vols.), 1815, March 15, L.

Ovid (Publius Ovidius Naso). *Metamorphoses,* 1815, April 9, 18; 1817, L.

Paine, Thomas. *Rights of Man* (1791–92), 1817, December 5, L.

Paltock, Robert. *Life and Adventures of Peter Wilkins* (1751, 2 vols.) [a novel], 1815, L.

Park, Mungo. *Journal of a Mission to the Interior of Africa in 1805* (1815), 1816, L;—*Travels in Africa* (1799), 1814, December 10, 12, L.

"Persian," 1814, November 25.

Petrarch (Francesco Petrarca). *Trionfe della Morte,* 1819, September 17.

Petronius, Gaius. [*Satyricon*], 1814, L.

Philosophie Moderne, Histoire de la. See *Histoire . . . .*

Plato. 1817, February 23; 1820, February 14, 16–17, 19; 1821, April 19;—*Phædon,* 1820, May 9, L;—*Phædrus,* 1818, August 4–5; 1820, May 2, L;—*Republic,* 1818, October 20, November 7, 9; 1819, October 9–10, 24, 28, November 2, 6–8; 1820, September 4, 9, L;—*Symposium,* 1817, August 13, L; 1818, July 9–10, 12–17, 20.

Pliny the Younger (Gaius Plinius Caecilius Secundus). *Letters,* 1816, July 29–30, August 1–4, L;—*Panegyricus* ("Panegyric of Trajan"), 1816, August 4, 6.

Plutarch. 1814, October 19; 1815, L; 1817, July 9;—*Parallel Lives,* 1816, August 18–20, November 17–19, 25–27, L; 1819, January 6, August 4–5;—"Life of Alexander," 1816, November 28;—"Life of Marius," 1819, March 30–31.

Pope, Alexander. 1814, August 28;—*Essay on Criticism,* 1821, May 26;—*The Rape of the Lock,* 1821, May 23.

Procter, Bryan W. (Barry Cornwall). *Dramatic Scenes* (1819), 1820, November 4.

Prud'homme. 1814, December 2.

Quarterly Review, 1816, December 3.

Rabaut Saint-Étienne, Jean Paul. (See Lacretelle.) *Précis d'Histoire de la Révolution Française* [after 1790], 1816, August 28, L; 1817, April 17, 22–23, May 3, 13–15, 19, June 5, L.

Radcliffe, Ann. *The Italian* (1797, 3 vols.), 1814, L.

Reynolds, John Hamilton. See *Peter Bell* under Wordsworth.

Richardson, Samuel. *Pamela* (1741), 1816, November 21–23, L.

Riouffe. *Mémoires d'un Détenu, pour servir à l'Histoire de la Tyrannie de Robespierre,* 1816, August 25, L. (Reference may be to Dumont, *q.v.*)

Robertson, William. *The History of America* (1777, 2 vols.), 1820, September 13, L;—*The History of the Reign of the Emperor Charles V* (1769, 3 vols.), 1820, September 19, L.

Roscoe, William. *The Life of Lorenzo de'Medici* (1795, 2 vols.), 1816, December 2–4, L.

Rousseau, Jean Jacques. 1820, March 26;—*Émile* (1762), 1816, September 22, L;—*La Nouvelle Héloïse* (1761), 1816, L;—*Rêveries d'un Promeneur Solitaire* (1776–78), 1815, L.

Sacchetti, Franco. *Novelle* (1724), 1821, May 11.

Sallust (Gaius Sallustius Crispus). 1815, L.

Schlegel, August W. von. Probably *Über dramatische Kunst und Literatur* (1809–11), translated by J. Black as *Lectures on Dramatic Art and Literature* (1815), 1818, March 16, 20–21.

Scott, Sir Walter. *Guy Mannering* (1815), 1818, January 7;—*Rob Roy* (1818), 1818, April 24;—*Tales of My Landlord* (1st Series, 1816), 1817, February 23, L;—*Waverley* (1814), 1817, February 23, L.

Seneca, L. Annæus. 1815, February 13, April 18, May 4–5, 10–11;—Tragedies, 1815, L;—Works, 1815, L.

Shakespeare, William. 1814, August 27, September 4; 1815, L; 1816, December 1; 1819, April 21;—*Antony and Cleopatra,* 1817, August 29, L;—*Cymbeline,* 1818, October 5–7;—*Hamlet,* 1818, April 20;—*Henry IV,* Pt. I, 1820, January 21–22;—*Henry IV* [Pt. II?], 1820, February 19, 21, 25;—*Henry V,* 1820, March 2;—*Henry VI,* 1820, March 7;—*Henry VIII,* 1818, August 10–11;—*King John,* 1820, January 21;—*King Lear,* 1821, February 20; *Macbeth,* 1817, April 21;—*The Merchant of Venice,* 1817, February 11;—*Much Ado About Nothing,* 1817, December 13;—*Othello,* 1817, August 29, L;—*Richard III,* 1818, August 6–8;—*The Tempest,* 1820, January 12–14;—*The Winter's Tale,* 1818, October 8–10.

Shelley, P. B. 1814, October 7;—*Queen Mab* (1813), 1814, October 6, L;—*The Revolt of Islam* (1818), 1817, November 29–30, L; 1819, August 20.

The Shipwreck of the "Wager," 1821, December 7.

Sismondi, Simonde de (Giovanni C. Leonardo). *Histoire des Républiques Italiennes* (Paris edition, 1808–18), 1819, January 20.

Solis y Ribadeneira, Antonio de. *Historia de la Conquista de Méjico* (1864, 5 vols.), translated by Townshend (1724) as *History of the Conquest of Mexico,* 1820, February 21, 25, L.

Sophocles. 1815, February 13; 1817, August 29, L; 1819, August 21, September 4; 1820, January 1, 5, 9, 12–15, 21, L;—*Ajax,* 1818, June 3–4;—*Electra,* 1818, June 3;—*Trachiniæ* ("Hercules"), 1820, January 15;—*Œdipus Tyrannus,* 1817, August 17; 1818, September 24;—*Philoctetes,* 1818, June 2.

Southey, Robert. *The Curse of Kehama* (1810), 1814, September 17, L; 1815, L;—*Madoc* (1805), 1814, L; 1815, L;—*Thalaba* (1801), 1814, September 20–21, 23–24, L.

Spenser, Edmund. 1819, October 20; 1820, May 20;—*The Faerie Queene,* 1814, November 29, December 2; 1815, L; 1817, April 12–14, 23–25, 29, May 9, 13, 15, 19–21, June 5–6, 14, July 8, 10–11, 22, L;—*The Shepheardes Calendar,* 1818, June 14–17.

Spinoza, Baruch de. (Shelley's translation of) *Tractatus Theologico-Politicus,* 1817, November 3; 1820, January 5, 8–9, 12, 15–16, 23, March 17, 21–22, 26–31, April 1–2, 4–8, 23, June 3; 1821, November 15.

Staël, Madame de. ("Account of the Revolution") *Considérations sur la Révolution Française* (1818), 1819, November 5;—*Corinne* (1807), 1818, December 13–15;—*De la Littérature considérée dans ses Rapports avec les Institutions Sociales* (1800), 1815, March 15, L.

Stewarton, ———. *The Female Revolutionary Plutarch* (1806, 3 vols.; anonymous), 1814, November 20.

Suetonius Tranquillus, Gaius. [*Lives of the Caesars*], 1814, December 14, 15, 19, L.

Swift, Jonathan. *Gulliver's Travels* (1726), 1816, November 9, 11, 13–15, L;—*A Tale of a Tub* (1704), 1815, L.

Tacitus, Cornelius. 1818, January 7;—*Annales,* 1816, August 6, 8–11, 13–17, L;—*Germania,* 1816, August 24–26, L;—*Historiæ,* 1814, August 24.

Tasso, Torquato. 1816, October 5–6, L; 1820, December 27;—*Aminta* (1573), 1815, L; 1818, April 6;—*Gerusalemme Liberata*[3] (1581), 1815, L. (See Manso's *Vita di Tasso.*)

Terence (Publius Terentius Afer). 1818, January 7.

Theocritus. [*Idyls*], 1815, L, 1816, L; 1818, August 7–13; 1820, May 26.

Thomson, James. *The Castle of Indolence* (1748), 1815, L.

Thucydides. [*The History of the Peloponnesian War*], 1815, L.

Travels Before the Flood (1796, 2 vols.), 1820, L.

Virgil (Publius Maro Virgilius). 1815, L;—*Æneid,* 1816, August 4; 1818, January 6, 24; 1820, March 26, 29–31, April 1, 25–27, May 2, 4, 20, June 25, L;—*Georgics,* 1818, August 12, 15; 1820, September 16, L.

Voltaire, François M. A. de. 1818, March 26;—*Candide* (1759), 1814, December 26; L; —*Histoire de Charles XII* (1731), 1815, L;—*Essai sur les Mœurs et l'Esprit des Nations* (1753–56), 1815, April 20;—*Memoirs of the Life of Voltaire* (By Himself, London, 1784), 1820, March 27, April 2, L;—*Zadig* (1747), 1814, L.

"Wager," The Shipwreck of the. See *The Shipwreck of . . . .*

[3] Shelley's autograph copy of this poem (seconde editione, London, R. Zotti, 1812, 2 vols.) is in the Berg Collection, the New York Public Library.

Weber, Veit. *The Sorcerer, a Tale from the German* (translated by Robert Huish, 1795), 1814, L.

White, Henry Kirke. Probably *The Remains of Henry Kirke White, With an Account of his Life by Robert Southey* (1807, 2 vols.), 1814, L.

Wieland, Christoph Martin. *The History of Agathon* (1766), translated by John Richardson (1773, 4 vols.), 1814, L;—*Aristipp* (1800–1802, 4 vols.), 1818, May 2;—*Peregrine Proteus, the Philosopher* (1791), translated by W. Tooke (1796), 1814, November 24–26, L.

Wilson, John (Christopher North). *The City of the Plague, and Other Poems* (1816), 1817, L.

Winckelmann, Johann Joachim. *Geschichte der Kunst des Altherthums* (Dresden, 1764), translated into French by Jansen as *Histoire de l'Art chez les Anciens* (1798–1803), 1818, December 24, 27–29, 31; 1819, January 2–3, March 14.

Wolcot, John (Peter Pindar). "Peter Pindar's book," possibly *Works* (1816, 4 vols.), 1816, September 28.

Wollstonecraft, Mary. *An Historical and Moral View of the Origin and Progress of the French Revolution* (1794), 1814, December 23, L;—*Letters Written during a Short Residence in Sweden, Norway, and Denmark* (1796), 1814, August 31, L;—*Mary. A Fiction* (1788), 1814, August 17, 31, L;—*The Wrongs of Woman* (1798), 1814, L.

Wordsworth, William. 1817, April 11;—*The Excursion* (1814), 1814, September 14, L; 1815, L;—"Poems" (probably collected edition of 1815), 1815, L;—*Peter Bell* (1819) [by Wordsworth or by John Hamilton Reynolds], 1819, October 24.

Xenophon. *Memorabilia,* 1818, June 13–14, 16–17.

B. CHRONOLOGICALLY ARRANGED

The column on the left indicates only generally where Shelley was during each month. Names and titles under "List Only" signify reading which is noted by Mary in the "List of Books Read" during the year, but which is either apparently or definitely not accounted for by the daily journal entries.

1814

[France, &c.]	AUGUST:—Barruel, Byron, Pope, Shakespeare, Tacitus, Mary Wollstonecraft.
[London]	SEPTEMBER:—Anacreon (?), Coleridge, Adam Fergusson, Godwin, Shakespeare, Southey, Wordsworth.
[London]	OCTOBER:—Joanna Baillie, Barruel, Cicero, Coleridge, Godwin, T. J. Hogg, Milton, Plutarch, P. B. Shelley.
[London]	NOVEMBER:—Adolphus, Charles B. Brown, T. J. Hogg, "Persian," Spenser, Stewarton, Wieland.
[London]	DECEMBER:—Blackwell, Diogenes Laertius, Bryan Edwards, L. Maimbourg, Dr. John Moore, Mungo Park, Prud'homme, Spenser, Suetonius, Voltaire, Mary Wollstonecraft.

LIST ONLY:—*Life of Alfieri, by Himself;* Sir John Barrow, Diogenes Laertius, E. Du Bois, Godwin, J. H. Lawrence, M. G. Lewis, Louvet de Couvray, Petronius, Ann Radcliffe, Southey, Voltaire, Veit Weber, Henry Kirke White, Wieland, Mary Wollstonecraft.

1815

[London] JANUARY:—Coleridge, Bryan Edwards, Gibbon, (T. J. Hogg), Livy, Milton.

[London] FEBRUARY:—Æschylus, Æsop, Byron, Erasmus, Euripides, Gibbon, Livy, Seneca, Sophocles.

[London] MARCH:—Sir Thomas Browne, Gibbon, Godwin, Le Sage, Livy, S. Ockley, Madame de Staël.

[London] APRIL:—Ariosto, Gibbon, Guarini, Lucretius, Ovid, Seneca, Voltaire.

[London] MAY [to 13]:—Seneca.

[Bishopsgate] JUNE–DECEMBER:—*(Journal is lost.)*

LIST ONLY:—Alfieri, Francis Bacon, Beckford, Bible, Burke, Coleridge, Charles J. Fox, Godwin, Herodotus, Hesiod, Homer, Kotzebue, Labaume, Laignelot, *Life of Lady Hamilton,* Locke, James Macpherson, Milton, R. Paltock, Plutarch, Rousseau, Sallust, Seneca, Shakespeare, Southey, Spenser, Swift, Tasso, Theocritus, James Thomson, Thucydides, Virgil, Voltaire, Wordsworth.

1816

[Bishopsgate] JANUARY–JULY 20:—*(Journal is lost.)*

[Geneva] JULY [21–31]:—Lucretius, Pliny the Younger.

[Geneva] AUGUST:—Coleridge, Curtius, Dumont (or Riouffe), Milton, Pliny the Younger, Plutarch, Rabaut St.-Étienne, Tacitus, Virgil.

[Bath] SEPTEMBER:—Frederica S. Wilhelmina, Lacretelle, Lucian, Montaigne, Rousseau, John Wolcot.

[Bath] OCTOBER:—Cervantes, Frederica S. Wilhelmina, Sir H. Davy, Thomas Holcroft, *Life of Cromwell,* Lucian, Montaigne, Tasso.

[Bath] NOVEMBER:—Cervantes, Curtius, M. Edgeworth, Gibbon, Godwin, Locke, Lucian, Milton, Montaigne, Plutarch, S. Richardson, Swift.

[Bath] DECEMBER:—Gibbon, Godwin, Horace, Locke, Lucian, *Quarterly Review,* William Roscoe, Shakespeare.

LIST ONLY:—Æschylus, Blackwell, Byron, Coleridge, *Le Criminel Secret, Edinburgh Review* (Nos. LII and LIII), Fénelon, Godwin, Elizabeth Hamilton, Leigh Hunt, Laignelot, Lady C. Lamb, Maturin, Milman, Montesquieu, C. P. Moritz, Moschus, Mungo Park, Rousseau, Theocritus.

1817

[Bath] JANUARY:—

[London] FEBRUARY:—Plato, Walter Scott, Shakespeare.

[Marlow]	March:—
[Marlow]	April:—Bible, Euripides, Lacretelle (or Rabaut St.-Étienne), Shakespeare, Spenser, Wordsworth.
[Marlow]	May:—Apuleius, Byron, Lacretelle (or Rabaut St.-Étienne), Spenser.
[Marlow]	June:—Arrian, Beaumont & Fletcher, *Histoire de la Philosophie Moderne,* Homer, Lacretelle (or Rabaut St.-Étienne), J. F. Lullin de Chateauvieux, Spenser.
[Marlow]	July:—Æschylus, Beaumont & Fletcher, Elphinstone, Homer, Plutarch, Spenser.
[Marlow]	August:—Æschylus, Elphinstone, Gibbon, Ben Jonson, Thomas Moore, Plato, Shakespeare, Sophocles.
[Marlow]	September–October:—
[Marlow]	November:—Godwin, P. B. Shelley, Spinoza.
[Marlow]	December:—Berkeley, Coleridge, Gibbon, Godwin, Hume, Milton, Lady Morgan, T. Paine, Shakespeare.

List only:—Apuleius, Coleridge, John Davis, Defoe, Godwin, Ben Jonson, Charles Lamb, Thomas Moore, Ovid, Plato, John Wilson.

1818

[Marlow]	January:—E. D. Clarke, Gibbon, Homer, Hume, Walter Scott, Tacitus, Terence, Virgil.
[London]	February:—
[France]	March:—Æschylus, Schlegel, Voltaire.
[Milan]	April:—Dante, Manso (Tasso), Walter Scott, Shakespeare, Tasso.
[Leghorn]	May:—Ariosto, Euripides, Manso (Tasso), Wieland.
[Baths of Lucca]	June:—Aristophanes, Barthélemy, Gibbon, Hume, Sophocles, Spenser, Xenophon.
[Baths of Lucca]	July:—Aristophanes, Barthélemy, Beaumont & Fletcher, Herodotus, Hume, Plato.
[Baths of Lucca]	August:—Æschylus, Eustace, Herodotus, Homer, Horace, Hume, Lucian, Plato, Shakespeare, Theocritus, Virgil.
[Este & Venice]	September:—Byron, Sophocles.
[Este & Venice]	October:—Malthus, Plato, Shakespeare.
[Este to Rome]	November:—Ariosto, Plato.
[Naples]	December:—Dante, Livy, Madame de Staël, Winckelmann.

1819

[Naples]	January:—Euripides, Livy, Plutarch, Sismondi, Winckelmann.
[Naples]	February:—
[Rome]	March:—Euripides, Lucretius, Plutarch, Winckelmann.
[Rome]	April:—Euripides, Milton, Shakespeare.
[Rome–Leghorn]	May–July:—

[Leghorn] AUGUST:—Æschylus, Beaumont & Fletcher, Boccaccio, Dante, Euripides, Ben Jonson, Milton, Plutarch, P. B. Shelley, Sophocles.

[Leghorn] SEPTEMBER:—Æschylus, Beaumont & Fletcher, Boccaccio, Calderón, Dante, Euripides, Ben Jonson, Lucan, Petrarch, Sophocles.

[Florence] OCTOBER:—Beaumont & Fletcher, Clarendon, Massinger, Plato, Spenser, Wordsworth (or J. H. Reynolds).

[Florence] NOVEMBER:—Clarendon, Plato, Madame de Staël.

[Florence] DECEMBER:—Bible.

1820

[Florence] JANUARY:—Bible, Byron, J. von Müller, Shakespeare, Sophocles, Spinoza.

[Pisa] FEBRUARY:—Æschylus, Athenæus, Bible, Las Casas, Plato, Shakespeare, Solis y Ribadeneira.

[Pisa] MARCH:—Bible, Godwin, Hobbes, Ben Jonson, Locke, Rousseau, Shakespeare, Spinoza, Virgil, Voltaire.

[Pisa] APRIL:—Bible, Mrs. Barbauld, Godwin, Locke, Spinoza, Virgil, Voltaire.

[Pisa] MAY:—Beaumont & Fletcher, Milton, Plato, Spenser, Theocritus, Virgil.

[Pisa–Leghorn] JUNE:—Euripides, Fortiguerra, "Greek Romances," Lucretius, Milton, Spinoza, Virgil.

[Leghorn] JULY:—Fortiguerra, "Greek Romances," Homer, Lucretius, Catharine Macaulay.

[Baths of Pisa] AUGUST:—Apollonius Rhodius, Beaumont & Fletcher, C. Macaulay.

[Baths of Pisa] SEPTEMBER:—Beaumont & Fletcher, Boccaccio, Gillies, Horace, Catharine Macaulay, Monboddo, Plato, Wm. Robertson, Virgil.

[Baths of Pisa] OCTOBER:—Gillies, Herodotus, Keats, Monboddo.

[Pisa] NOVEMBER:—Calderón, Medwin, B. W. Procter.

[Pisa] DECEMBER:—Tasso.

LIST ONLY:—"Astronomy" in the *Encyclopedia,* Bible, Boccaccio, Boswell's *Johnson,* Thomas Erskine, Keats, *Travels Before the Flood.*

1821

[Pisa] JANUARY:—Æschylus, Dante.

[Pisa] FEBRUARY:—Coleridge, Shakespeare.

[Pisa] MARCH:—Horace, Ben Jonson.

[Pisa] APRIL:—Plato.

[Baths of Pisa] MAY:—Ben Jonson, Pope, Sacchetti.

[Baths of Pisa] JUNE:—Chaucer.

[Baths of Pisa] JULY–AUGUST:—

[Baths of Pisa] SEPTEMBER:—Kant.
[Baths of Pisa] OCTOBER:—
[Pisa] NOVEMBER:—Spinoza.
[Pisa] DECEMBER:—Byron, Chaucer, Herodotus, *The Shipwreck of the "Wager."*

1822

[Pisa–Lerici] JANUARY–JULY:—*(No reading recorded.)*

Index

In this index such references as 36–41 do not mean that a topic is treated continuously through those pages, but that it appears once or oftener on each page. The peculiar nature of the journal, which is a tissue of names and actions frequently repeated on the same page, makes this kind of condensed reference both desirable and necessary.

As for Appendix IV on Shelley's reading, the index denotes (by the phrase "Shelley's reading of") each author listed in the Appendix, which gives references to all the journal notations of the reading of that author by Shelley. The page numbers in parentheses following the reference to Appendix IV indicate the appearances of the author's name in the chronological arrangement of Shelley's reading in that Appendix; for example: Æschylus: Shelley's reading of, 218 (228–30). Page references to literary titles appearing in Appendix IV are not given in the index, except as these titles appear in the journal itself. The notation "Shelley's reading of" is always given first under any author to whom it is appropriate; and the titles of an author's works are arranged alphabetically.

A

C

D

E

F

G

H

I

M

N

O

P

Q

R

T

U

V

W

Mary Shelley's Journal

EDITED BY FREDERICK L. JONES

HAS BEEN SET

IN ELEVEN-POINT LINOTYPE GRANJON

WITH ONE POINT OF LEADING

AND HAS BEEN PRINTED ON

WOVE ANTIQUE PAPER

UNIVERSITY OF OKLAHOMA PRESS

NORMAN

F